THE MOORSTONE

Also by Michael Knaggs

Catalyst
Heaven's Door
Lost Souls
The Blue Men

For Mary

THE MOORSTONE

With very best wishes

Mitch Knaggs

MICHAEL KNAGGS

Copyright © 2025 Michael Knaggs

The moral right of the author has been asserted.

Apart from any fair dealing for the purposes of research or private study, or criticism or review, as permitted under the Copyright, Designs and Patents Act 1988, this publication may only be reproduced, stored or transmitted, in any form or by any means, with the prior permission in writing of the publishers, or in the case of reprographic reproduction in accordance with the terms of licences issued by the Copyright Licensing Agency. Enquiries concerning reproduction outside those terms should be sent to the publishers.

The manufacturer's authorised representative in the EU for product safety is Authorised Rep Compliance Ltd, 71 Lower Baggot Street, Dublin D02 P593 Ireland
(www.arccompliance.com)

This is a work of fiction. Names, characters, businesses, places, events and incidents are either the products of the author's imagination or used in a fictitious manner. Any resemblance to actual persons, living or dead, or actual events is purely coincidental.

Troubador Publishing Ltd
Unit E2 Airfield Business Park,
Harrison Road, Market Harborough,
Leicestershire LE16 7UL
Tel: 0116 279 2299
Email: books@troubador.co.uk
Web: www.troubador.co.uk

ISBN 978 183628 151 1

British Library Cataloguing in Publication Data.
A catalogue record for this book is available from the British Library.

Printed and bound in Great Britain by 4edge Limited

Typeset in 11pt Aldine by Troubador Publishing Ltd, Leicester, UK

For Carol

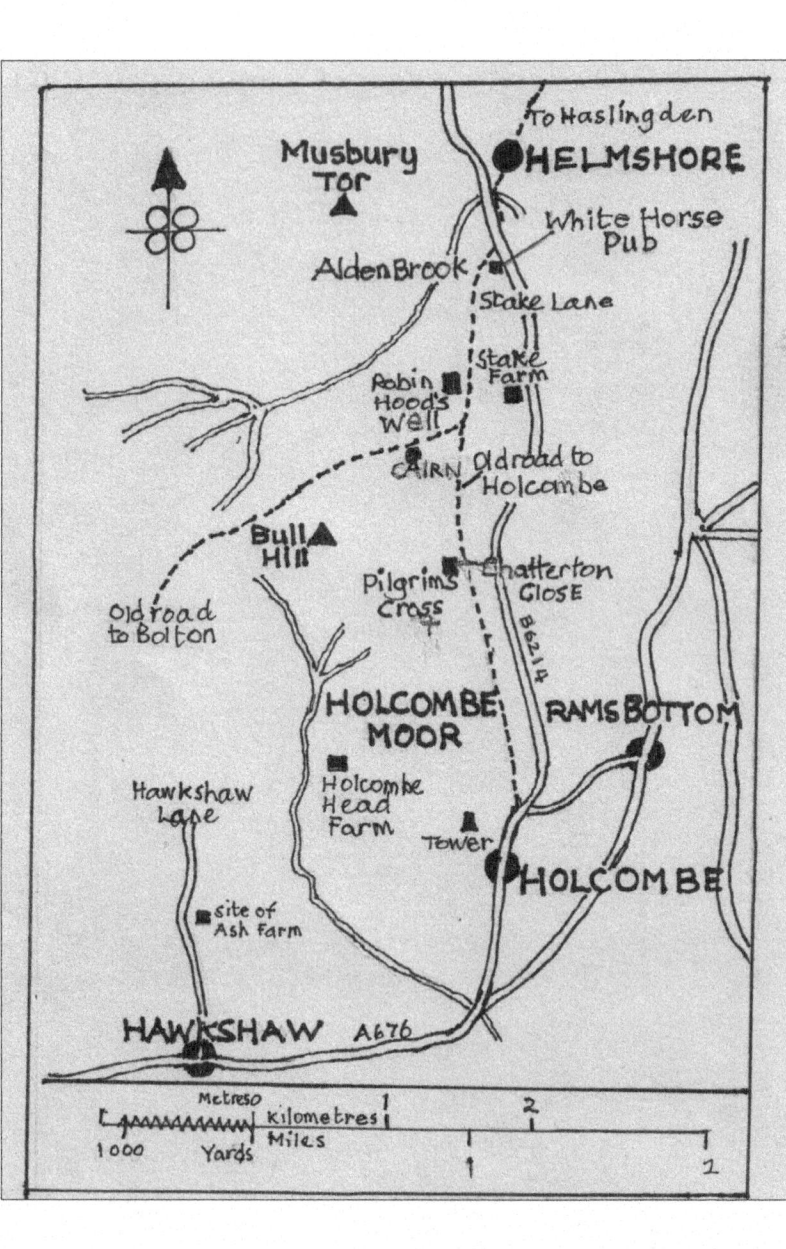

A heap of stones still marks the fatal spot,
To tempt aside the curious stranger's foot;
Not pick'd and carted there in careless loads
From off the heather and the mountain-roads
But one by one by trembling fingers laid
Down to the memory of the hapless maid;
And to this present, wandering lovers, dear,
Still drop a stony tribute, and a tear.

John Fawcett Skelton
from *Hawkshaw Lane and Other Poems (1872)*

PART ONE

PROLOGUE

The young woman is running for her life up the steep, rough track towards the heavy wooden field gate. She leans against it; this is where she would normally stop to regain her breath after such a climb. Not this time. She heaves it open, lurching through it onto the desolate moorland. Mist swirls around her. She lifts her heavy skirts, which are dragging in the coarse vegetation, slowing her progress as she ascends the short climb away from the gate.

Suddenly, like a curtain rising, the mist lifts to reveal a bright full moon, lighting up her way but making her visible to the one who is chasing her. Above the swishing sound of the grasses against her clothing she can hear the dull thud of heavy boots behind her.

She stops and turns, the crest of the rise temporarily blocking her view of her pursuer. The top of a head appears, bobbing up and down with the rhythm of the man's steady running. She turns again and fear spurs her forward, always knowing that there can be no escape. The mist had been her only friend, her one chance of salvation, and it had deserted her. She presses on, now feeling the vibration of those heavy footsteps through her own delicate shoes.

She can hear his laboured breathing; he is close enough to reach out and touch her. She stops and turns to confront him.

CHAPTER ONE

Friday 21 December

Detective Inspector Jo Carter's first day at the headquarters of the Bury Division of Greater Manchester Police was going well. Her introduction to staff – police and civilians – in all departments was relaxed and friendly, the people generally welcoming. The one exception was, unfortunately, a key person in her own department. This was not a surprise, nor a particular concern. She had been warned about the individual – perhaps 'made aware' was a more gentle way of putting it – by her immediate boss, Detective Superintendent Mallory Jones, and Jo was prepared to meet the challenge head-on.

As a member of the police's Flexible Response Team network, Jo was used to handling local resistance as a routine part of her role. She thought back to her move to Guildford after her promotion to the FRT and the opening speech of her new boss at the time, Detective Superintendent John Mackay, as he described the differences between her new role and her previous experience as a local area detective inspector. The biggest challenge, John had pointed out, was integrating with the area force without a visible show of elitism, even though in reality it was that quality that was the main requirement for selection to the FRT. He had warned that she might find herself piggy-in-the-middle between the law and the lawless for a while.

He had been exactly right, this was Jo's third such assignment and she didn't have to wait long for the head-on clash to manifest itself. The knock on her office door was followed by her second-in-command entering the room, uninvited, and dropping onto one of the two chairs opposite her across the desk. Detective Sergeant Andy Mills was in his mid-thirties, tall, athletic, with dark, intense eyes, and undeniably attractive. He was dressed casually but smartly in designer jeans, white button-through shirt and a black soft-leather, funnel-neck jacket. His smile was wide, showing a set of perfectly white teeth, but was more mocking than friendly.

'Do come in, DS Mills, and, please, take a seat,' she said.

'Why thank you, ma'am, or do I call you Jo?' He spoke with just the hint of an American accent.

'No, ma'am is fine, thank you.'

'I've just got a few questions on behalf of the team. Some personal stuff so we can know you better.' The smile became more of a sneer. 'Okay?' Jo said nothing. 'So, do you have a boyfriend?'

'No, that wouldn't be appropriate.'

'You mean you're gay?'

'Married.' Jo held up her ring finger. 'I would expect a detective to notice this.'

'In my experience a lot of single women wear them to deter predators.'

'I wonder why.'

'So, where's your husband?'

'At home, in Leicester.'

'He's not much good there, is he?'

'Oh, he's good *anywhere*, believe me.'

'Good at what?'

'Everything he turns his hand to, and not just his hand – to answer your next question.' Jo sucked in a breath, wishing she could delete part of her reply.

'Okay, name one thing he's good at?'

'Mmm... rugby.'

'Gosh, very impressive. What position does he play, dummy half?'

Jo leaned across the desk so their faces were very close together. She held his eyes until the smirk faded and he looked away. 'I can't remember the name of the position, but it rhymes with *wanker!*' The last word came as a shout.

Heads turned in the operations room, Andy coloured and got to his feet, his eyes turning almost black with anger. He left the office and hurried through the open plan area towards the stairs beyond.

CHAPTER TWO

Saturday 22 December

The man and woman were walking hand in hand through a bustling Mill Gate Shopping Centre in Bury, Greater Manchester. The shop windows were bright and welcoming with seasonal decorations, and the line of stalls along the concourses between the shops added their own diverse displays to the festive atmosphere. A brass band played a selection of carols and children dressed as elves and Santas jingled their collection tins at the smiling shoppers. The couple themselves were attracting a fair amount of attention, most of it directed towards the male member of the twosome. Sebastian Carter, at a centimetre under two metres tall, was broad-shouldered, slim-waisted and boyishly handsome, and towered over the pretty woman at his side. Jo Carter was of Caribbean ancestry – she described herself as 'three-quarters West Indian' – around five-and-a-half feet tall with a slim rounded figure. Her naturally dark and curly hair hung down to her shoulders and shone with auburn highlights.

'I don't know why I bother to take time to look my best,' Jo said. 'Nobody ever notices me.'

'I don't know why you bother either…'

'Well, that's nice, thank you. Perhaps I *won't* bother in future.'

'What I mean is, you can't improve on perfection, so it's a waste of time trying.'

'Nice escape, Seb,' Jo said, smiling.

They walked on a little, Jo noticing that people were now looking at them and laughing.

'Now what?' She turned to look up at Seb, only to find his head was missing; it was now level with her own. She stepped to one side; Seb's knees were bent and he was walking duck-style. 'What on earth...?'

'I'm trying to look inconspicuous so people will look at you instead.'

Jo laughed. 'Come on, in here.' She pulled him through the sliding doors of WHSmith. 'I need two more cards for work and another diary. Then we'd best get back to your mum's if we're heading out tonight.'

Fifteen minutes later, they were driving back to Seb's parents' house in Summerseat, where they would be spending the Christmas holiday together. Jo's latest assignment had landed her in the town where her husband had been born thirty years ago and where he had lived up to his leaving to attend Nottingham Trent University at the age of eighteen. They had met on one of Jo's previous postings at Leicestershire constabulary headquarters where Seb was a detective sergeant.

'It's really good of your parents to offer to have me for the whole of my time here,' Jo said as they turned onto Newcombe Road towards Summerseat village where Seb's parents lived in a new development on Kay Street near the River Irwell. 'I don't want to offend them, but I really don't think it would work. You know what the hours are like and...'

Seb laughed. 'I agree. If you knew what they were like when Sal and I were teenagers. Always wanting to know exactly what we were doing, where we were going, what time we'd be back. Par for the course, I suppose. And they'd be the same with you, wondering why you're not back yet, worrying you weren't eating properly and the rest. I'll mention it to them.' He chuckled. 'And anyway, they probably only offered in the hope you'd say no.'

'Well, that makes me feel so much better. But don't say anything yet. Don't want to raise their hopes before Christmas only to dash them afterwards by deciding to stay.'

★

The Racconto Lounge in Bury town centre was vibrant with excited diners, exactly what one would expect on the last Saturday evening before Christmas Day. The restaurant was impressive, with a cathedral-high ceiling and walls covered in framed paintings of all styles and eras, providing a blaze of colour illuminated by clusters of globe lanterns. The table for six was tucked at the side with a padded bench seat along the wall, two chairs facing it and one at each end. Seb and Jo, Seb's parents, Roy and Bella, his sister Sally and her husband, Jonno, settled themselves into their seats. Jonno went to order drinks and returned with six copies of the menu. The single A3 sheet was packed with choice and they took so long to choose their mains that Seb and Jonno were onto their second drinks before they were ready to place their order at the bar.

'So,' Jonno said, addressing Jo. 'Seb tells me you're a fart.'

Bella and Sally spluttered into their drinks.

'For God's sake, Jonno, what sort of a question…?' Sally said.

Jo laughed. 'I've been called a lot worse, Jonno. An F-R-T, actually. Or, more accurately, I'm *part* of the FRT, the national Flexible Response Team. We get posted to assist local forces by bringing specialist knowledge and expertise where it's in short supply due to the absence of key people or simply the size of the police presence.'

'And members of the FRT are handpicked from forces all over the country,' Seb added, smiling across at his wife. 'They are to the police what the SAS is to the army and the SBS to the navy. Special people.'

'A special, hand-picked fart,' Jonno said. 'Well I never.'

'Jonno, will you please…' Bella said.

'Hey, I'll share a secret with you.' Jonno leaned across and whispered to Jo, loud enough for them all to hear. 'I'm an oil-lamp, Jo – an obviously incompetent, lazy, laterally moving person.'

They all laughed, after taking a couple of seconds to work it out.

'First time I've felt thankful for being a fart,' Jo said.

'So do you enjoy working in different places?' Bella asked. 'It can't be easy, just getting to know people and then having to move on.'

Jo reached out and took Seb's hand. 'Well, sometimes I take them with me,' she said, to more laughter. 'That's how I met this big guy here, of course. Transferred to Leicester from my home base in Guildford. He was my number two and helped me through a bad patch. I knew he fancied me when he followed me into the Ladies...'

There followed some knowing whoops from around the table. Seb held up his hands for silence. 'I can explain. Jo was looking unwell and had left in a hurry for the Ladies. She was in there a long time and I was worried so I went in to check if she was okay and...'

'I've heard some excuses,' Jonno interrupted. 'In there a long time, you say. How long would that be, Jo?'

'About four minutes.'

More whooping.

'More like twenty-four minutes,' Seb said.

'Why didn't you just drill a hole through from the Gents?' Jonno asked.

'Because the Gents is on a different floor,' Seb replied.

Two smiling waiters appeared with their starters bringing a temporary halt to the laughter.

'Enjoy,' they said in unison.

'It's lovely that you decided to change your name when you and Seb married,' Bella said, when they finished the first course. 'So many women now decide to keep their maiden name, especially professional women who have made it to a senior level. Like they'll suddenly become somebody different and have to start again at the bottom.'

'It's to save money on business cards,' Jonno said. 'When you've just had three thousand printed, it makes no sense to have the wrong name on them.'

'Cottrell isn't my maiden name, anyway,' Jo said. 'It was my first husband's and I'm happy to get rid of it and, of course, more than happy to be a Carter.'

'So what was your family name?' Sally asked.

'Payen, spelt P-a-y-e-n.'

'Hold on,' Jonno said. 'I'm sure I've just seen that on the menu.' He grabbed a copy and scanned the sheet, his forehead wrinkled in concentration.

'It's French Caribbean,' Jo laughed, 'if that helps you find it.'

'Well I think it's a nice name,' Bella said.

'But not as nice as Carter.' Jo took Seb's hand again.

'Will you two behave yourselves,' Jonno said. 'You're married now, you shouldn't be doing that; touching each other. Isn't that right, Sal?'

'Really, darling? So where did this come from?' She patted her stomach. 'The angel of the Lord?'

'Sally,' Bella chastised. 'Don't be so irreverent.'

'Sorry, Mum. But at least it's topical.'

The waiters arrived again. Four this time, two to remove the starter plates and two to deliver the mains. Silence, except for the sound of chomping jaws, returned to the table.

★

The temperature had fallen to below zero when they left the restaurant and boarded the pre-booked taxi awaiting them on The Rock for the short drive back to Summerseat. The VW Sharan was designed to seat up to seven people 'comfortably', according to the brochure, and it lived up to its promise even when one of the seven was a two-metre-high rugby player. They threaded their way through the throng of festive revellers moving around the town centre from bar to bar for a few hundred metres before picking up speed and heading north on Crostons Road.

'So what have you two got planned for tomorrow?' Sally asked.

'Seb's going to treat me to a tour of Holcombe Moor.'

'Oh, I'm so jealous,' Sally said, with some enthusiasm. 'Now I wish we weren't going home so early tomorrow. When we were kids, it was our regular walk just about every Saturday, all four of us, ending up at the top of the Peel Tower. It will be a bit chilly out there but I'm sure you'll love it.'

'It's one of the things we were deprived of when my brother and I were kids,' Jonno said, 'wandering about on hills in the freezing cold. We had to make do with toys and games. It was torture, I can tell you.'

They all laughed.

'How did I end up with him?' Sally said.

Jonno put an arm round her shoulder and pulled her towards him. 'Just lucky, I guess.'

CHAPTER THREE

Sunday 23 December

The group set out from the house on Kay Street close to the River Irwell in Lower Summerseat at just after ten o'clock on a bright, sunny, but chilly December day. Sporting a variety of outdoor clothing, they picked their way along Pollards Lane, which was unpavemented and slippery in places. Roy Carter was dressed formally in a charcoal-grey overcoat, dark blue suit, white shirt and deep-pink tie. Bella's trouser suit was the same colour as her husband's tie and toned beautifully with her purple suede jacket. They wore matching woollen scarves pulled high to protect their mouths from the bitter air. The couple following them, just a few paces behind, each wore lined black walking trousers, a grey fleece mid-layer and a puffer jacket, Jo's a mid-grey and Seb's orange. They carried rucksacks on their backs and walking poles in their gloved hands.

Branching right into Queen's Place, they passed the row of tall terraced houses, three stories high and looking even higher with their front entrances several steps up from the road. The generations parted at the T-junction with Rowlands Road; Roy and Bella turning left for the Methodist church, and Jo and Seb right down the narrow, winding approach to the railway bridge.

'Another treat in store for you,' Seb said, as they passed under the bridge onto Railway Street. 'A ride on the East Lancs Railway. Regular timetable from Bury to Rawtenstall, *and* they do special events. I fancy the Day Out with Thomas the Tank Engine, but you might prefer the Vintage 1940s Weekend. They're both really…'

'You're skating on very thin ice, Sebastian Carter,' Jo said through gritted teeth.

'*And* they do dining events, including – listen to this – *including* Valentine's Night. So what do you think of that? Seriously, it's a great experience; Sal and I absolutely loved it.'

'What, Valentine's Night? I'm not sure you should be telling me this.'

'No, riding on the train. If you're really good, they let you pull the whistle. And I'm very good at pulling, as you know, so I got to do it a lot.'

Jo laughed. They walked on past the garden centre up to the sharp bend to the left, and crossed over into Robin's Road. The car park of *al Bosco*, the attractive stone-built Italian *ristorante*, was already filling up, well in advance of its midday opening time. They continued down the lane, past large detached houses set back on their right and the leafless trees to the left, their tangled branches sparkling with frost in the sunshine. Eventually, they reached a row of idyllic sandstone terraced cottages before the tarmac ended to be replaced by a stony track reaching the last few.

'This is fabulous,' Jo said, 'what a lovely place to live.'

'It's where Sal always said she wanted to live when she was younger. But I think there's far too much green for Jonno.'

'Well, if she's not moving here, then I'll have her house,' Jo said.

'What do you mean "I"? Don't forget me.'

'Well, of course, you'd always be welcome,' Jo said. 'Seriously, though, it would be a lovely place to live.'

The track ended at some double gates to a large detached property and they headed left along a narrow, muddy path with a stream on the left and trees rising up a slope to their right, the sun sparkling through the network of branches with a flashing-light effect as they walked along. The path emerged near a farm at the end of Woodhey Road, which took them on past a row of expensive detached properties towards its junction with Bolton Road.

'Bet you'd prefer one of these,' Seb said.

'Not at all,' Jo said. 'I'm perfectly satisfied with my terraced cottage, thank you.'

'You're right,' Seb said. 'Easily big enough for two.'

They reached the junction and crossed over to the Hare and Hounds pub on the corner of Holcombe Old Road. In spite of its being closed at this early hour, the light stone building, with its array of window boxes adorned with Christmas greenery and red berries, and windows bright with twinkling lights, sent out a clear invitation to the two walkers.

'This is our planned stop-off point on the way back,' Seb said. 'Our incentive to complete the walk.'

'How far did you say this walk is?' Jo asked.

'There and back, around eight miles, give or take.'

'And how far have we come so far, do you reckon?'

'About one-and-a-half. Why?'

Jo frowned. 'So that's... five more miles to get back to here.'

'Yep. Eight minus three. Very good.' He paused. 'Unless that's too far for you, of course.'

'Which way?' Jo asked, refusing to be drawn into another exchange about her age.

Seb waved his arm in the direction of the narrow road which climbed alongside the pub.

'Holcombe Old Road,' he said.

They set off along the tarmac road to where it forked after about eighty metres, taking the cobbled lane to the right, and climbing steadily past fields and trees to the driveway of Darul Loom, the Islamic college, which was almost completely hidden by the densely packed belt of mature trees. Just a glimpse of its sandstone walls was visible through the metal gates as they turned left, a few metres past it, and ascended further through a small settlement of houses, of different designs and sizes, finally climbing a flight of large slabs and an awkward stone stile to join Moorbottom Road.

'This is where the walk *really* begins,' Seb said.

'Well, I can't say I'm sorry we've reached the end of the warm-up,' Jo said. 'Just remember, I'm a city girl. When do we get to stop for coffee and biscuits?'

'At the Pilgrims Cross.' Seb pointed to the left, where the rough stone track curved round to the right.

'And how far...?'

'Less than two miles, and that'll be about halfway.'

Jo sighed. 'Okay. Race you – *not*.'

Within a few metres, Jo had stopped worrying about distance, time or hunger as she embraced the vista in front of them. A steep, grass and gorse-covered hillside rose to a ridge on their right and the view opened up spectacularly to their left, the high ground sweeping round ahead of them enclosing a deep valley, criss-crossed by streams and paths. Two kestrels hovered above the ridge, their wings working hard but their heads stock-still as they surveyed their hunting ground. The sound of jackdaws was all around them. In the distance, the contrasting skyline of Manchester city centre was clearly visible but far enough away not to impose on the wildness of the scenery.

'So, what do you think?' Seb asked.

'Fabulous,' Jo said. 'Hard to believe this is just a few miles away from the middle of Bury. I can understand why you and Sally love it so much.'

Seb beamed. 'Right, let's keep going. There's more to come.'

They circled the bottom of Holcombe Hill, then climbed a minor path off to the right. The day had warmed a little and the earlier frost had melted, leaving the path and surrounding area boggy and slippery in places. They picked their way carefully northwards as the panorama extended to the right giving clear views for miles all round. Eventually they reached a large monument, shaped like an elongated cube, standing on a stone base to a height of about two metres. The top of each vertical surface was curved into the shape of an arch and writing etched into all four sides explained the purpose and history of the monument.

'And this is?' Jo asked.

'The Pilgrims Cross.'

Jo paused for a moment, clutching her chin as if in deep thought.

'Well, excuse me for asking, but aren't crosses usually cross-shaped?'

'Usually, yes. You'd normally have to read the writing to find out why not in this case, but let me summarise. This is the *site* of an ancient Pilgrims Cross, erected here in 1176, or earlier. No-one knows why and when the cross was removed but its foundation was here until 1901...'

'So this is the base of the cross?'

'No, I haven't finished yet.'

'Sorry, please go on.'

'The base of the cross or "socketed foundation" as it's called on here...' he pointed to the words on the stone '... was vandalised in

1901, and replaced by this memorial stone in 1902. There, now I've finished. Any questions?'

'No, that's very clear *and* very interesting. But when you said we'd have something to eat at the Pilgrims Cross, I assumed it was a pub.'

'Well, I'm sorry to disappoint...' Seb began, with a hangdog look.

Jo laughed. 'I am *anything* but disappointed, my love. This is perfect. The best picnic spot I've ever seen.'

They sat pressed together on the base of the monument at the side that gave most shelter from the chill breeze, and dug into the rucksacks for their lunch. Ham and pickle sandwiches, Pringles, tomatoes, a substantial wedge of Bella's homemade fruit cake and a chunky KitKat; along with half a flask of coffee each.

'That should more than compensate for all the good the exercise will have done us,' Jo said.

'And we haven't even got to the pub yet.'

They leaned against each other when they'd finished their lunch, Seb extricating his arm from his side and wrapping it round his wife. They kissed, only pulling back at the sound of voices and a dog barking nearby. A middle-aged couple with an excited border collie were passing. They waved and smiled, Jo and Seb returning the greeting.

'People,' Jo said. 'Who the hell do they think they are, spoiling things like that?' She kissed him briefly again. 'So what next, Sir Ralph?'

'The Peel Tower, and it's not a pub, by the way. But before that, the best view on the moor. Up there.' He pointed to a path rising away from the memorial. 'Bull Hill.'

They repacked their bags and heaved them onto their backs, picked up the poles and set off. Jo had to admit, it was worth the steep pull to the trig point at the top to experience the all-round spectacle of this part of the West Pennine Moors. Even the motorway to the east and the evidence of industry to the north could not detract from the feeling of remoteness and freedom.

'Wonderful,' Jo said. 'Really wonderful.'

'And over there,' Seb said, pointing to a brown-coloured monolith in the mid-distance, 'is our next stop. The Peel Tower. A couple of miles and then we're in striking distance of the Hare and Hounds. Then home before dark – well, perhaps just after.'

They retraced their steps down to the Pilgrims Cross and continued in the same direction on the indistinct and sodden path towards their objective. Halfway there, they dropped down to a short but tricky crossing of a stream, then climbed again to reach their destination. The structure's base was a huge cube, topped by battlements, from the centre of which rose, slightly tapering, the square-section tower itself, to a height of forty metres.

'Well, here it is,' Seb said. 'A monument to our founder, Sir Robert Peel. Well, not exactly *our* founder – the Met's founder.'

'But a lot of the principles and practices he introduced still apply across all forces,' Jo said, 'So I guess we owe Sir Robert a debt of gratitude. We might not even have jobs if it wasn't for him. I bet it's a good view from the top.'

'Probably equally as good as from Bull Hill when you can get up there. It's only opened a few days a year by volunteers. And it's a long dark climb.'

'That's okay, I'll stick with Bull Hill,' Jo said.

They left the tower and descended along the winding path to the narrow, cobbled road that was part of Holcombe Old Road, passing the Islamic College where they had turned off it before and retracing their earlier steps to the Hare and Hounds. It was exactly 3.15 p.m. when they entered the pub.

★

When they left an hour later, darkness had fallen. They walked in contented silence, hand in hand, their poles collapsed and stowed in their rucksacks, down the narrow cul-de-sac of Pot Green and through the pedestrian walkway at the end on to Summerseat Lane. Reaching Waterside Road, the final leg of their journey, Jo turned to Seb.

'When we were walking past those big houses on the way out, you said you bet I'd like one of those and I said I'd prefer a cottage. Remember?'

'Yes, of course.'

'And you said you agreed because it was enough for two. What did you mean by that?'

Seb frowned. 'I meant there are just the two of us, so the cottage would be big enough. I don't understand…'

'It's okay. I guess I'm a bit sensitive, what with Sal expecting a baby and knowing how much you're looking forward to being an uncle. I just thought…'

'Hey, look, we've had this conversation before. The way things are right now with you on assignments wherever they decide to send you, we can revisit that in the future – *possibly*. You are enough for me; I've said that all along and I mean it. And spending as much time as I can with my wife is a big enough challenge. Okay?'

'Okay.' They walked on a few steps. 'I love you, big guy.'

'And I love you… old girl.'

They laughed.

'Just this once I'm prepared to overlook that. Just this once.'

CHAPTER FOUR

Monday 24 December

Jo wasn't sure what to expect on her first official working day at the Bury Divisional headquarters on Dunster Road near the town centre. What she didn't expect was an anonymous text with a very unusual message – a single digit '1'. There was no indication of the source of the message, no iPhone number for her to reply with a request for clarification. But, if it was some kind of practical joke, Jo was determined not to give the perpetrator any satisfaction by raising it with her new colleagues.

She spent the first part of the morning observing the team at work in the operations room, moving between workstations, asking questions and making entries in her battered notebook. The team were working on a series of targeted break-ins, which had featured some brutal attacks on residents in the Ringley Road area of the six-town borough, and the aftermath of a failed drug-raid that had been triggered by an apparently phoney tip-off. The team had been forthcoming and friendly with the exception of DS Mills, whose responses had been clipped and impatient. Jo decided not to press the point, Christmas Eve seeming to be the wrong time to encourage the start of a vendetta. She would deal with it after the festivities and found herself quite looking forward to it.

From 10.30 onwards, she met individually with her team for brief one-to-one interviews. They covered mainly personal circumstances Jo felt necessary to be aware of in order to effectively manage their time and, particularly, their ability to respond quickly to the need for extra days and longer hours. She was relieved that when it came to her sergeant's turn, he had been called away on an urgent mission. Relieved, and ever so slightly disappointed in herself for *being* relieved.

At just before noon, she was called into her boss's office. The detective superintendent got to his feet behind the old-fashioned desk as she entered and extended his hand. They shook hands and took their seats across from each other. Mal's office was large but sparsely furnished with filing cabinets along one wall and a couple of tall bookcases against another. Jo noticed there were very few books on the shelves, which contained mostly ring-binders of every imaginable colour, and piles of wallet files. The only item of furniture with any character was a leather-seated tilt-and-swivel on castors.

'Well, Jo, this is just a social chat, really. Starting a new assignment two working days before Christmas Day isn't ideal, I know, but I just wondered about first impressions – the team, the town. I imagine it's a bit different to Guildford and Leicester and Brighton. So…?' he spread his arms to invite a reply.

'First impressions really great, sir. People are friendly and welcoming… so far, although they've not got to know me yet. And the town, well, I had a great meal out with my husband and his family on Saturday, and a fabulous walk on Holcombe Moor yesterday. So couldn't be better.'

'So, as far as the team is concerned, *full* cooperation and acceptance? That's what you expect based on first impressions?'

Jo hesitated and smiled. 'Why the emphasis on "full", sir?'

'Oh, it's just that I heard on the station telegraph that a derogatory word passed between you and your detective sergeant. I think "wanker" was the expression, unless I'm wrong.'

'The word was used, sir, but it was not directed at DS Mills. More like a clue in charades. You know…' she took hold of her ear '…sounds like.'

Mal frowned. 'I think DS Mills will be your biggest challenge in terms of winning people's support and respect. And you shouldn't take it personally; he does have a history of rubbing people up the wrong way.' His features relaxed into a smile. 'When he was working Merseyside some joker suggested the DS stood for Dark Satanic.'

Jo laughed. 'Well, I guess that puts him in good company.'

'Certainly unlikely company. Anyway, what I really wanted to say is that I'm sure you've got things to sort out and it seems pointless you starting anything here, so unless you're planning to join the gang for a drink or two later this afternoon, I suggest you make an early dash for it.' He checked his watch. 'Nearly twelve-thirty, so right now. Up to you, of course, but my guess is they'll be wanting to discuss their new boss, which would be difficult if the only item on the agenda was right there listening to them.'

'Those were my thoughts as well, sir. And even if they're not discussing me, a complete stranger in their midst is not exactly going to contribute to a relaxed atmosphere. I've just got a few things to check, sir, then I'll take you up on your offer. And I haven't wished DS Mills a Happy Christmas yet.'

'I shouldn't let that delay you, DI Carter. He may well have a happier one if you don't.'

*

Benny Morrison looked round the neat little kitchen diner and decided it was time to address the build-up of mugs and dishes on the worktop next to the sink. Neat, it might be, tidy it was not. His mind had been elsewhere for the last couple of days, that was his excuse. He removed the washing-up bowl from the Belfast sink, inserted the plug and placed the offending pots into it before spraying them with a generous amount of Fairy liquid and running the hot water. His iPhone trilled on the dining table and he picked it up, checking the screen while he turned off the tap.

'Now what?' he muttered to himself before answering. 'Morning, Helen,' he said with exaggerated bonhomie. 'To what do I owe…?'

'Look, Benny, it's Christmas, the wrong time for family drama. We've not always seen eye to eye with you I know, but we would like you both to come to dinner on Christmas Day.'

'She's forgiven me, then?'

'What do you mean?'

'Well, we didn't exactly part on the best of terms when she left the pub on Saturday night.'

There was silence for a few moments before Helen Wright spoke again. 'I don't understand, Benny, isn't Phoebe with you?'

'No. I thought when she left me, she would be going home – to *our* home, I mean. But when I got back, she wasn't there, so I assumed she'd gone over to you.'

Benny could hear an exchange in hushed voices.

'She didn't come back here.' There was anxiety in the voice now. 'Didn't you think to check she was alright? Why didn't you phone? Where could she be? What...'

'Hold on. I didn't phone because she's done this before, several times. If she's not with you, she'll probably be hiding at one of her friends.'

'Are you sure she's not with you? You're not in this together – teaching us a lesson.'

'She's *definitely* not with me. Look, I'm a parent as well, don't forget. I know what worrying about your kids is all about. We need to start making a few phone calls. But I'm sure she'll be staying with one of her friends, to teach us *all* a lesson.'

'We only have contact numbers for a few of her friends from before she went to Sheffield. Could you...?'

'Yes, I'll ring round and put it out on our WhatsApp group. I'll get back to you as soon as I find out where she is.'

*

By 2.30 p.m., Benny had contacted the whole of the social group that he and his girlfriend, Phoebe, belonged to. None had seen her since Saturday evening at around 6.30 except one person. A dog-walker had met her, one hour after that, on Holcombe Moor. Benny contacted Helen again, hoping that she had turned up at her parents' house in the meantime. The anxiety in her mother's voice as she answered the phone told him before he had chance to ask. Benny tried to reassure her before they ended the call but his own growing unease made it hard to be convincing.

Helen Wright reported her daughter missing to the police at 3.30 p.m. PC Lindsey Davenport took down the details, assuring her that they would circulate Phoebe's description and last known whereabouts immediately, and suggesting that she may be planning a dramatic reappearance later on Christmas Eve or on Christmas Day.

'And please contact us tomorrow if your daughter hasn't turned up,' she added.

Lindsey passed on the information to DS Andy Mills, who was still at the station in the operations room with DC Eva Johnston.

'Right, let's get this circulated to all hub stations,' he said. 'Sounds like a lovers' tiff and a job for uniform. Bad timing for the family… and us, for that matter.'

CHAPTER FIVE

Tuesday 25 December

'He's been!' The voice came from downstairs.

Jo disentangled herself from her husband's gentle embrace and rolled over to grab the phone from the bedside table.

'Seven-twenty,' she said. 'Did somebody just shout "he's been," or did I dream it?'

'That was dad from down below, checking that Santa has remembered to call. Apparently, he has.'

He stretched, yawned and pulled Jo back into the same embrace. He let his hand wander down into her pyjama bottoms.

'Would you like your present now or later?'

'What about now *and* later. And I wonder if it's the same one I've got for you.'

They giggled like naughty children.

'I assume the "he's been!" is another Carter-child tradition, like freezing on hillsides. Is there a traditional reply?'

'I think "yippee" was a popular response when we were younger.'

'Shall we try one of those then?'

'Why not?' Seb said. 'After three… one, two three.'

'*Yippee!*'

They shouted in unison, then fell to giggling again, cut short by the sound from the next bedroom of Sally and Jonno adding to the celebration of Santa's visit.

'*Yippee!*'

'You're all mad,' Roy called up the stairs through his laughter.

'Well, you started it,' Seb called back.

They showered together in the en-suite – Seb's bulk making the task very nearly impossible – and dressed. By the time they entered the lounge to inspect the delivery, the Christmas tree was twinkling with lights and carols were playing on the mini hi-fi system in the dining room. Sally and Jonno arrived, the latter rubbing his hands and giving a whoop at the presents around the base of the tree, carefully arranged for maximum effect the previous evening by the people currently gazing upon them in mock surprise but genuine delight.

'I wonder which twelve of those are mine,' he said.

'I won't put all the other lights on now,' Roy said. 'It takes about ten minutes to switch them all on and the same to switch them off.'

'We've got twenty-one sets this year,' Bella tutted from the kitchen. 'Every year he says he'll do less and every year he adds more.'

'Have you seen the Chevy Chase movie *National Lampoon's Christmas Holiday?*' Seb asked. 'He plays a guy called Clark Griswold, who is so passionate about Christmas he always goes way over the top with the lights and decorations. Sal and I used to say that on the first of December every year, Dad turned into Clark Griswold.'

'And he still does,' Sal said. 'It's a wonder the power surge doesn't black out half of Summerseat.'

Bella appeared in the doorway. 'Breakfast first, children. Then presents, then church.'

'Aaaw, do we have to?' Jonno stamped his foot. 'I'm not hungry, and it's too cold outside.'

'Yes you do,' Sally scolded. 'Now don't be a naughty boy.'

They chatted and laughed over a delicious cooked breakfast, after which all hands pitched in to wash up and clear away. Seb and Sally assisted Bella with the preparation of the turkey and vegetables, while Jo and Jonno set the table for Christmas dinner. Roy had changed his mind and set about activating the rest of his festive lightshow. After an excited opening of presents, Jonno falling just eight short of his anticipated dozen, they left the house at just after ten for the Christmas Day service at the Methodist church on Rowlands Road. Seb, at Bella's insistence, had exchanged his sparkling festive sweater, which featured a portrait of Rudolph, whose famous red nose could be illuminated by pressing a concealed switch, for a smart blazer from his old collection of clothes still at the house, along with a cream shirt and blue tie.

'This blazer's a bit tight now, Mum,' he complained. 'It's the one I had in year eleven .'

'It is *not*,' Bella insisted.

'At least you took the badge off.'

Jonno, by association, had also adopted the imposed dress code, although the Lancashire Cricket Club tie he borrowed from Roy did not look quite right with the soft collar of his white polo shirt.

After the service, and the ritual hand-shaking, hugging and air kissing, they returned to the delicious smell of roasting turkey with a feeling of total contentment.

★

At a few minutes before 2.00 p.m., as they took their seats for dinner, the call came through to Jo from on-duty PC Lindsey Davenport. Jo excused herself and went into the kitchen to take it. Lindsey told her of the report of the missing girl phoned in yesterday by her parents. which had been passed on to DS Mills who had circulated the details to other local stations.

'They called again half an hour ago,' she said, 'to say their daughter had not turned up at either boyfriend's or parents' on Christmas Eve or today. I've checked with the other stations, but they've had nothing reported. Sorry to dump on you, ma'am, but you are the most senior officer available.'

'That's okay,' Jo said, 'but can you rustle up a couple more of the team with suitable apologies, including DS Mills, as he was party to the original call.'

She returned to a circle of anxious faces turned towards her.

'I'm so sorry, Bella, but I'm going to have to pass on this wonderful feast. I would be really grateful if you would plate it up for me. I'll be back as soon as possible.'

'But, what…?' Seb began.

'A nineteen-year-old woman. Reported missing yesterday and has not turned up today.'

'Do you really have to go in?' Seb asked. 'If she was only reported missing yesterday, then…'

'She was *reported* missing yesterday, but no-one has seen her since seven-thirty on Saturday evening.'

'Even so, surely someone else…Uniforms should be on to this.'

'I guess so, and I'm sure they will be, but I'm the new girl and it will look bad if I fail to respond to the first call on my services.' She turned to the others. 'I really am sorry.'

'That's okay, love,' Roy Carter said. 'Off you go and we'll see you later. And don't worry about the meal, I'll make sure to keep it safe.'

'Thanks, Roy.' Jo smiled.

Seb followed her out of the room and up the stairs, and sat on the bed while she changed into trousers, shirt and jacket.

'Tell you what, I'll come with you,' he said.

'You will *not*. This is way off your patch and anyway, think of how your mum would feel if you *chose* to waste your dinner. And don't you go eating mine as well. Sooner I go, the sooner I'm back.'

She leaned in to kiss him and he grabbed her and pulled her to him, kissing her back. She leaned away from him with a gasp and a smile.

'Especially if you're planning to do that again later.'

'Oh, I've got much more than that planned for later,' he said with a lecherous arching of his eyebrow.

*

When Jo arrived at the station, the only other member of the CID team already in attendance was Andy Mills. Jo looked round the office. In spite of attempts to recognise the season with a small, table-standing Christmas tree, greetings cards pinned to a wall-mounted board, and sprigs of holly and coloured lights – currently extinguished – draped around desks and cabinets, the effect fell well short of the idyllic setting she had just left.

Her sergeant offered a surly response to Jo's rather forced 'Merry Christmas'.

'I was certainly hoping it would be.'

'Yes, a shame it's been interrupted but as you were here for the original call. And we need someone with local knowledge.'

Andy shook his head. 'Can't understand why they would appoint someone *without* local knowledge.'

Jo met the remark with a wide smile. 'I guess they must have had their reasons.'

Two more of the team arrived before Andy could reply. DCs Mohammed Malik and Eva Johnson. Mo was in his late twenties, tall and slim with a handsome face and well-groomed hair and beard. He discarded his waterproof coat to reveal a smartly-cut mid-blue suit with an open-necked pink shirt. Jo noticed his brown leather shoes shone with a high polish. His colleague was about the same height and age as Jo, with a pretty face and shoulder-length chestnut hair pulled back into a ponytail. She wore a faux-suede jacket over close-fitting jeans and tee shirt which showed off a curvaceous figure.

'Merry Christmas, you two,' Jo said. 'Really sorry to drag you in on Christmas Day.'

Mo looked at Andy. 'Christmas Day? What's that? Sorry, you've lost me.'

Jo smiled and Eva laughed. Andy's expression didn't change. The door opened and a young woman in uniform poked her head into the room.

'Now, ma'am?'

'Yes, come in, Lindsey,' Jo said. 'Mo, could you grab another chair.'

PC Lindsey Davenport was of average height, slim and with auburn hair cut very short. She was holding a notebook with her index finger tucked in the pages to mark a place.

'I've asked PC Davenport to take us through the two calls before we decide how we go forward with this. I know two of you were here for the first call, but please bear with us for mine and Mo's benefit. Lindsey, please go ahead.'

Lindsey took the seat Mo had brought and referred to her notes.

'It was exactly three-thirty yesterday when I took the call from Mrs Helen Wright. Her daughter, Phoebe, who is nineteen years old, doesn't live with them but with a Mr Benny Morrison in Helmshore. However, neither her parents nor Mr Morrison had seen Phoebe since the afternoon of Saturday, the twenty-second of December. Each had assumed that Phoebe was at the other's house.'

'Why would they think that?' Jo frowned. 'Did Mrs Wright say?'

'Apparently there has always been some tension between the parents and Mr Morrison, who is twenty years older than their daughter. Mrs Wright said Phoebe had had an argument with both sides on that day. So each party assumed she'd stormed off to the other.'

Andy sighed. 'God, what are you women like?'

Eva glared at him. Jo ignored the comment. 'Go on, Lindsey.'

'I took down the details. The Wrights had last seen Phoebe at around one o'clock and Mr Morrison at six-thirty when she had left the White Horse pub in Helmshore. She was seen by a dog walker an hour or so later heading across Holcombe Moor.'

'At seven-thirty?' Jo asked.

Lindsey checked her notes. 'Around that time. The dogwalker said between then and seven-forty.' She turned a page. 'I told Mrs Wright we would circulate the information right away and the usual stuff about the vast majority of people who go missing turn up within a couple of days.' She looked up from her notebook. 'But given that it's Christmas, and where she was last seen, I don't suppose that sounded very reassuring. I said if she didn't turn up or get in touch later yesterday or early today, to get back to us. Then I passed the details to DS Mills, who said to circulate it to the other hub stations, which I did.' She closed the notebook. 'And she didn't turn up and Mrs Wright called again at one-thirty-five today.'

'Okay, thanks, Lindsey. Just stay for now so we all know what's going to happen. Might help if the Wrights call again for an update.' She turned to the others. 'Do any of you need to be somewhere else? Silly question today of all days. But DC Davenport is right; at any other time we could be a bit more relaxed and optimistic, but Christmas Day? I'd like to move this forward right now, so, I repeat, if any of you need to be at home or somewhere else, that's fine. I'm sure, with a little *local* help, I can get a foursome together. Two to follow up Mr Morrison's story, and two to the speak with the Wrights.'

'I'm in,' Mo said.

'Me, too,' Eva added.

They all looked at Andy.

'How could I refuse such a unique opportunity to celebrate the birth of the Son of God,' he said with a wide, mirthless smile.

★

The first port of call for Jo and DC Malik was the White Horse in Helmshore, where the argument between Morrison and Phoebe had taken place on Saturday. The pub, at just after 4.00 p.m. was full of noise with the laughter of families enjoying Christmas fare in the restaurant and dining areas in the bar. The place had been decked out so that every corner, nook, and cranny displayed a reminder of the season. Christmas pop songs were playing at just the right volume so they could be heard by everyone without intruding on the babble of joyful conversation filling the place. The waiters wore Santa hats and red tops with fur trim, the girls with matching skirts which, Jo observed, must have been distractingly short for many of the male diners present.

Jo introduced herself and Mo to the landlord, Jonny Fisher.

'I'm sorry to spoil the atmosphere on this day of days, but I need to speak to people who were here on Saturday evening. We're trying to establish the whereabouts of one of your customers, who was in here that evening.' She turned away from the bar to scan the pub. 'Were any of the people in today here on Saturday?'

'Very few. Different crowd altogether.' He nodded towards a group of three males and one female standing a couple of metres away at the bar. 'That lot were in, but I'm sure none of the others were. Whose whereabouts are we talking about?'

'A girl called Phoebe Wright. We believe she may be staying with a friend and we're trying to establish which one. Okay?'

The landlord smiled. 'Phoebe, eh, and that's the official line, is it? So a senior detective is required to track down this friend. You're talking to an ex-copper here, you know, but I will tow the *official* line.'

'Thank you, Mr Fisher. But we do actually believe that is where she is. Can *you* tell us what happened here on Saturday? I believe someone didn't enjoy their dinner.'

Jonny snorted a laugh. 'That's right. We welcome constructive criticism, but that went a bit far. You heard what happened?'

'Mr Morrison told us briefly over the phone. We're on our way to see him now.'

'Well, Benny – Mr Morrison – and Phoebe had an argument. Nothing unusual about that. Phoebe's like a magnet for all the guys in here and the arguments are usually linked to all the attention she gets. But this time it was something really trivial. They sat down over there...' he pointed to a table near the window '... to order a meal. Phoebe wanted a starter; Benny didn't because he wanted to finish the meal quickly so he could get a good seat to watch the football. Bloody stupid, Benny had had a bit to drink, mind. She refused to give in so Benny ordered for her...'

'A starter?'

'Main course. When it arrived, she just tipped the plate over and left the pub.'

'What did Benny do? Go after her?'

'No, he helped clear up the mess. You could see he regretted what had happened. He really dotes on her, but, you know, after a few drinks...'

'Boys will be boys. Yes, I know. Thank you, Mr Fisher.'

'Please, call me Jonny.'

'Thank you, Jonny, and if you don't mind, we'll have a word with this lot about Saturday. We'll be very discreet, I promise.'

The discussion with the group yielded nothing new. Two of them had seen the exchange which had led to the flying main course, but could only corroborate what they already knew. However, as they were about to get back into the car, one of the men from the group called after them. He seemed slightly uneasy and kept a wary eye on the pub entrance as he spoke.

'Look, I didn't like to say this in there, but when Phoebe left, one of the guys went after her. He was gone for quite a long time.'

'When you say went after her, do you mean he left at the same time?'

'Well, yes, he did leave at the same time, but this guy is really keen on Phoebe. He sort of looked round to check nobody was watching him, then he slipped out after her. I'm not saying he did anything; he's a nice guy, but you might want to have a chat with him.'

'Did he come back to the pub?'

'Yes, but he was gone a long time.'

'How long?'

'Couldn't be sure because I didn't see him actually come into the pub later, just noticed he was back, but must have been an hour or more.'

'And how did he seem?' Jo asked.

'Okay, I guess. No different. Look, please don't tell him or Benny I told you this.'

'Thank you, Mr...?'

'Simpson. Joey Simpson.'

'And you haven't yet told us who this follower is and where we can have that chat with him.'

'His name's Marlon Finch. He lives on Spinner Street in Helmshore – end terrace with a pull-on space for a car. But I think he's round at his parents' today. They live in Helmshore as well, but I don't know the address.'

'I'm sure we'll find him. Thank you, Mr Simpson. You've been very helpful.'

'And you won't tell Marlon...'

'I see no reason at all why we would need to do that.'

★

'How sad for them on this of all days,' Eva said, as she and DS Mills left the Wrights' house in Hawkshaw and got back into the car. 'When they should be enjoying themselves with their family.'

'You mean like we should?' Andy said, buckling himself into the passenger seat.

'Oh, come one, Andy, you know what I mean. They are absolutely sick with worry. Like Helen Wright said, they could have accepted their daughter not being there on Christmas Day if she just preferred to be somewhere else, but not knowing *where* she is must be unbearable.'

'Yes, well you know how these things always end. We swing into action and mobilise half the force and they just turn up as if nothing has happened.'

'They don't *always* end up like that, and you know it. Don't you get a feel something's wrong, because I do.'

Andy was silent for a moment. 'Can't say I do, but... we'll see.' He checked his iPhone. 6.20 p.m. 'Fancy a drink at the Hare and Hounds on the way back? Old times' sake, and all that, and seeing as you're driving.'

Eva laughed. 'Didn't I always? Best not, on duty don't forget.

Should get back to base. And anyway, I need to get back to my sister's as soon as possible'.

'Okay, your loss,' Andy said, and slumped down in his seat.

★

Benny Morrison answered the door with a look of hope and expectancy, which disappeared in a second when confronted by the two police officers. He was pleasant-looking with longish, fair hair and a neatly trimmed goatee beard; tall but with a slightly stooping posture, which might have been a consequence of his current anxiety. He wore a pair of old faded jeans and a baggy sweater, giving him an overall retro-bohemian look.

The living room he led them into had a sad Christmas look about it. The artificial tree, a metre tall, lacked any sort of attention to detail with one set of lights hanging off it at one side. It looked as though someone – Benny, Jo assumed – had started to decorate it and simply lost the will to complete it. The half-dozen presents under it were poorly wrapped and unopened. A number of greeting cards had been randomly placed around the room on flat surfaces and a few more were stacked in an untidy pile on a low table under the window.

'So when you dropped her off at her parents' at twelve-thirty, how did she seem?'

'She was fine with me but clearly not looking forward to seeing her folks.'

'Because you say they don't approve of you?'

'They don't approve of Phoebe *living* with me, if that's the same thing. My eldest daughter is sixteen, only three years younger than Phoebe, and I think her mum keeps ramming that fact down her throat as if Phoebe is breaking some natural law or something. So, it didn't surprise me the visit ended badly. She always seems really tense whenever she's been there. I think it's as much Phoebe's fault as it is theirs, because she goes round every time ready for a fight and that's what usually happens.'

'How did you and Phoebe meet in the first place?'

'What's that got to do with anything?'

'When there's a significant difference in ages...' She shrugged.

Benny appeared slightly uncomfortable. 'I teach Art and Design at Bury Church of England High School That's when we *first* met. She was an excellent pupil and we shared a lot of the same taste, got talking. Nothing untoward, if that's what you're thinking. In fact, by the time she left she'd moved on to drama, though she retained an interest in art, watercolours mainly. Then we met again a year or so after she left at an exhibition in Manchester. Went for a drink, and so on…'

'Okay, fine. And how long have you been cohabiting?'

'We've been together for around eight months and she moved in with me in August. But she's backwards and forwards to her parents a lot; sometimes stays over for a couple of nights, and while she's there I'm under strict instructions not to phone her. She says it would annoy them and undo any good her staying there would do. Sometimes it feels like she hasn't really moved at all. I guess it's not easy to break ties when they live so close.'

'What was the purpose of her going on Saturday?'

'Christmas Day. She wanted us to get together with her parents for at least part of today. Not necessarily for a meal but just to spend some time being civilised with one another. And she would have got what she wanted – more than, in fact, because her mum phoned me on Christmas Eve to invite us both round for a meal. That's when we realised she'd gone missing. We both assumed Phoebe was at the other's house.'

'Right, let's go back to Saturday. When did you next speak to Phoebe after dropping her off?'

'I phoned her mobile around four o'clock. I thought she'd be at the Horse by then. I figured she'd get a lift there from her dad.'

'So that was three and a half hours after you'd dropped her off at their house?'

'That's right.'

'And how long would that car journey take – from her parents' house to the pub?'

'Hardly a journey, about ten minutes, certainly less than fifteen.'

'When you phoned her, where was she?'

'She was here – at least, that's what she told me.'

'How did she seem?'

'Just like she always seems after visiting her mum and dad.

Pissed off and angry. I asked her was she coming to the pub. She wasn't all that keen but I said she should come and we'd eat there.'

'So, if she wasn't all that keen, what did she want to do?'

Benny looked uncomfortable again. 'She wanted me to go home and we'd get a pizza and watch a couple of movies. She loves Christmas movies. I wish I'd done that now.'

'Tell us what happened at the pub.'

'My fault I suppose. I wanted to eat early so we could get a good seat to watch the evening match.'

'Who's "we", Mr Morrison?'

'Me and Phoebe. She's just as keen as I am – usually. That's what we'd planned to do.'

'Okay, go on.'

'Phoebe didn't turn up until around six, two hours after I'd phoned her. We sat down straight away to eat, but we'd missed all the fast food from the pre-dinner menu and it was looking like a long time for the meal. Phoebe insisted she wanted a starter. I said it would take too long, so just have a main course. She insisted. I insisted.' Benny waved his arms around. 'Really stupid. Like a couple of spoilt kids. I went to the bar to place the order. She said had I ordered a starter for her. I said to wait and see. Toby, the waiter, arrived with two mains. Phoebe took one look at hers then stood up and tipped it over the table and just about ran out of the pub. I'm not sure she wasn't aiming for me.'

'What time was that?'

'Around six-thirty, six-forty.'

'So you didn't have to wait long after all?'

Benny shook his head his head. 'That's another thing. I ordered something that I knew would be quick. It wasn't my first choice by a long way and I knew it was just about the last thing Phoebe would want. That's me teaching her a lesson for not getting there earlier. What a fucking prat. God knows what I was thinking.'

'So, you went after her?'

'No. I just sat there, dying of embarrassment. Poor Toby. He's a lovely lad. I thought he was going to burst into tears, like it was somehow his fault. So, I helped him clear up the mess.'

'Then you went after her?'

'No again. I finished off my meal, had another drink. I'd had too many already, and decided she could stew for a while.' Shakes his head again. 'I'm really not as big a bastard as I sound. I think the world of Phoebe. I really…'

His voice broke. There were a few moments of silence.

'Where are your children, Mr Morrison? Daughters, did you say?'

'That's right, two girls, sixteen and fourteen. Lovely kids, live with their mum down in Leicester.'

'How long have you been separated?'

'Separated about three years, divorced nine months. March this year.'

'Will you be seeing them over the holiday?'

'My daughters always come up for New Year; stay three or four days. We have a great time, and there's no animosity between me and Jill – that's my wife, ex-wife.'

'And you're expecting them this year?'

'Yes, they're due here on Friday. I'll need to get this place in order.'

'When did you last see them?'

'In the flesh, we went on holiday together in July to Cornwall. The four of us – I mean Jill as well. Like I said, Jill and I are still very close as friends. People think it's a bit weird, but it feels very natural. Separate rooms, of course; no sex or anything. But it works for both of us, well, all of us.'

'You said "in the flesh".'

'The girls and I Skype every week, usually on a Sunday, and sometimes in between when they have something they want to tell me.'

'How does Phoebe feel about that? You still having a good relationship with your ex-wife? Has she met any of your family yet?'

Benny looked a little sheepish. 'Well, she wasn't all that happy about me going on holiday even though it had been arranged before we got together and it was before she moved in with me. But since she moved in, she's been fine, as far as I can tell. Although she doesn't join in on the Skypes.'

'So she hasn't met your daughters yet? In the flesh or virtually?'

'Not yet.' He frowned. 'Surely you can't think that's why she's disappeared? Because she can't face meeting them?'

'*Something* has made her disappear, Mr Morrison. We shouldn't rule out anything yet, should we?'

'I'd take that as a reason right now, rather than something... bad happening to her.' Benny sighed. 'If I'm honest, I can't see this relationship lasting very long. I'd like to believe otherwise but, I mean, look at me. You've seen what Phee's like, and don't tell me looks aren't everything. I know that. But when you consider the age difference as well... Anyway, that's not important right now. Just feeling sorry for myself.'

'I believe you and Mr and Mrs Wright rang round her friends to check if any of them had seen her after she left the pub?'

'That's right. Nobody had, but one old guy out walking his dog saw her on the moor about an hour after she left the pub. I told Helen and she passed it on to your colleague when she reported her missing.'

'Who was he, this old guy, and how did he come to tell you? I assume he wasn't one of the friends you contacted.'

'He's somebody who knows Phoebe's family from when they lived in Helmshore before moving to Hawkshaw. He mentioned he'd seen her to one of Phoebe's friends; one of the ones I contacted.'

'And his name – this man?' Jo asked.

'I don't know, but I'll give you Shana's number. She's the girl he spoke to.'

He took out his phone and scrolled through his contacts, showing Jo the screen so she could add the number to her own list.

'We'd like a list of everyone in your group who was there on Saturday, just in case Phoebe mentioned something about going away. Tomorrow will do, as early as possible.'

'Okay, but I don't think she spoke to anyone except me. We just sat down straight away at the table and we waited to be served.'

'She didn't go to the Ladies, up to the bar...?'

'Possibly... in fact, yes, she did, the Ladies. But she was only gone a few minutes.'

'But long enough to tell someone if they were in there with her?'

'I guess so.'

'Right. The list then, tomorrow, Mr Morrison.'

Jo checked her watch and handed her phone to Mo. 'Can you

get the dog walker's address from this Shana, and we'll need a phone number, we could do with speaking to him later today.'

Mo took the phone and left the room.

'Do you know whereabouts on the moor this man saw Phoebe?'

'Well, I don't think it was actually *on* the moor as such, but on a track at the edge of it. It's the old road between Ramsbottom and Helmshore. I don't know exactly where on the track.'

'What time did you get back from the pub, Mr Morrison?'

'Not late. Around ten-thirty. I thought she was in at first. There was a light on in the back room.'

'So that was four hours after Phoebe had left the pub. Did you try to contact her during that time?'

Benny sighed. 'No. As I said, I'd decided to let her stew.'

Jo shook her head. 'I see, so…'

Benny leaned forward. 'Look, she didn't try to contact me either. I'm not sure I wasn't the more injured party. She was late getting to the pub, which was why I was in a hurry, and I don't think I deserved having a dinner thrown over me – *nearly* over me. I've said it was my fault, but I don't think Phoebe was blameless.'

Jo waited in silence for a few moments before speaking; 'I assume you've checked around to see if there's anything of hers missing. Anything she's taken.'

'Yes, I've checked, but it's not easy to be sure because, as I said, she's backwards and forwards to her folks' house. She brings stuff then takes it back and brings different stuff. I don't know what she keeps where. But some of her make-up and toiletries are missing from the bathroom'

'But if she is staying with a friend then she'd take a bag with her, wouldn't she? Are there any bags missing?'

'Her small shoulder bag's gone, with her purse, her phone and stuff, but she takes that everywhere, along with her pink woolly hat – never seen without it.' He gave a little laugh.

'Her purse and her phone?'

'Yes. Well, I say purse, more like a wallet, with cards and the like.'

'Does she have a laptop or computer?'

'No she uses my PC – separate email accounts but we use the same computer. I know she has Facebook, X and Instagram on her iPhone.'

'What about coats, jackets?'

'No, all the ones she keeps here are still here, except the fleece she was wearing when I dropped her off in Hawkshaw and when she came to the pub.'

Mo re-entered the room nodding to Jo and handing her the phone.

'Okay, Mr Morrison,' Jo said, getting to her feet. 'We'll leave it there for now. Sorry to have disturbed you on Christmas Day.'

'I should be thanking you,' Benny said, with a break in his voice. 'You're the only people I've spent Christmas with. And I didn't even offer you any mulled wine.'

Jo smiled. 'That's okay. And you will let us know when you hear from her.'

'Of course, and thank you for saying "when" and not "if".'

★

Mo's phone pinged with an incoming text as they got in the car. He checked the message.

'Numbers for the dog walker, Mr Jack Grimshaw. Landline and mobile. Actually, that name sounds familiar, like it's been mentioned before somewhere.'

'Can you remember in what context?'

Mo screwed up his face in thought. 'No. I might be wrong anyway. It's a classic Lancashire lad's name. Probably heard it on *Coronation Street*.'

'Let's phone him. I'd like to speak to this Marlon Finch tonight if possible. That's if we can find him. I feel like the Grinch who stole Christmas. That story used to make me cry when I was little.' She nodded to Mo's phone. 'Try the mobile first, and put him on speaker if we get him.'

The call was answered immediately. 'Yes?'

'Mr Grimshaw?'

'That's me.'

'This is the police, Mr Grimshaw. Nothing to worry about. I'm putting you on speaker.'

'Hello, Mr Grimshaw,' Jo said. 'We're sorry to disturb you on Christmas Day. I'm Detective Inspector Carter with Bury CID and my colleague is Detective Constable Malik. We are trying to locate someone who we believe is staying with friends nearby, but who has not been seen by her family for a few days. The person in question is Phoebe Wright. I believe you know her.'

'Phoebe? Yes, certainly I do. Her family lived just a couple of doors from us until they moved away. Well, I guess Hawkshaw isn't exactly away. In fact, I saw Phoebe on Saturday evening on the moor around half seven, I think.'

'So we believe, which is why we're calling you. We'd like to talk to you about when and where you saw her, but given that it was three days ago, I don't think we need to take up your time tonight. Would you be able to attend a meeting tomorrow morning at the main station in Bury? Shall we say ten o'clock if that's not too early.'

'Yes, that's fine. It will be good to see the old place again.'

'You're familiar with the police station? For all the right reasons, I hope.'

Jack laughed. 'Used to be a copper. Not CID, too thick for that, uniform then admin. Absolutely loved the place.'

'We look forward to seeing you tomorrow, then. You can tell us if standards have slipped since you left. Goodnight, Mr Grimshaw, and Merry Christmas.'

Jo nodded to Mo who ended the call.

'Is there anyone around here who *isn't* an ex-copper?'

'That's why he sounded familiar. Jack Grimshaw left before I started, but he was a well-liked copper – bit of a legend. That's saved me lying awake tonight trying to work out where I'd heard the name. I seem to remember there was something else, though. I think he was accused of something, then cleared. As I said, it was before my time.'

'Right. Be interesting to know what he was accused of. In the meantime, let's go find Mr Finch.'

★

'Looking for Marlon, are you?' The woman had poked her head out of the front door of the adjoining terraced cottage. 'He'll be at his mum and dad's down Lune Street – next street but one. He always goes there for Christmas Day. What's he done?'

'What do you mean?' Jo asked.

'Well, I assume you must be police, knocking on doors at this time on Christmas Day. Either that or carol singers, but I don't hear any singing.'

Jo laughed. 'Very well observed, Mrs...?'

'Davenport. *Miss* Davenport.'

'We *are* police, Miss Davenport,' Jo said, 'and *not* carol singers, and Mr Finch has done nothing wrong. We just need some information from him as part of a routine enquiry. Nothing that will spoil his day. Do you know the number of his parents' house?'

'No, but you can't miss it. It's the one with Christmas lights round the front door and along the top of the hedge.'

'Thank you,' Jo said, 'and a Merry Christmas.'

'Merry Christmas.' She closed the door.

Miss Davenport was right, they couldn't miss it. It stood out like a beacon in the otherwise darkened street. They were welcomed into Number 23 as if they were expected guests, with smiles and offers of refreshment, which they had accepted in the form of coffee. Jo, Mo and Marlon were soon seated comfortably in the back room of the cottage around a large rectangular dining table in front of an open fire. Mrs Finch followed them with a tray containing two cups of coffee, a large malt whisky and three generous portions of Christmas cake.

Marlon Finch was in his mid-twenties, slim, with a pleasant, blue-eyed face and short dark hair. He wore jeans and a multicoloured festive sweater adorned with Santas and reindeer. It looked new and Jo guessed it was a Christmas present. She also noted that he looked a much more likely suitor to a nineteen-year-old than an art teacher twice her age, then chastised herself for the stereotyped observation.

'So, you think I could have been the last one to see her?' Marlon said.

'I wouldn't put it like that, Mr Finch, but possibly the last of the group of people who were with her in Helmshore on Saturday evening.'

'I felt really sorry for Phoebe. I know she's having a rough time with her parents and I guess the last thing she needed was to be treated like shit by Benny. He's crazy about her, actually, but when you're with your mates and you've had a few to drink, you get all laddish, like it's a sign of weakness to show how much you like someone. So, when she ran out of the pub…'

'What time would that be?'

'Shortly after six-thirty, I guess. I went after her to check she was okay. She wasn't really. She told me to piss off, said she knew what I wanted. Well, I don't deny I've always fancied her. I mean how could you *not*, she's a beautiful girl, but she was wrong on that occasion. That's not what I wanted.'

'Just to be absolutely clear, Mr Finch, so we're not worried about niceties, what was it that she thought you wanted and that you *didn't* want, on that occasion?'

'Well, you know. To have sex with her. Like I said, I've always fancied her… and I'm sure she knew this.'

'*Knew*, Mr Finch?'

'I mean *knows* this. Slip of the tongue. Look, I'm also pretty sure that she *doesn't* fancy me, so there's nothing going on behind Benny's back, if that's what you're digging for.'

'Never crossed my mind. Go on, Mr Finch.'

'Anyway, in the end she calmed down and actually thanked me for caring about what happened to her. I walked with her for a few minutes then she said she was okay and wanted to be on her own. She wished me Merry Christmas and gave me a kiss on the cheek.'

'So where do you think she was going, Mr Finch, when you left her?'

'Back to Benny's cottage on Crest Lane. That's where she lives. It's only about a ten-minute walk from the pub. We were almost there when I left her.'

'So let's say maximum fifteen there and fifteen back. You should have been away from the pub for less than half an hour. It's been suggested you were gone for a lot longer than that.'

'I didn't go straight back. I walked around a bit, thinking. Thinking about Phoebe actually.' He sighed and shook his head. 'I might as well tell you this. You're bound to find out when you start checking with people down Crest Lane. I went back to the cottage and knocked on the door. No reply, so I shouted through the letterbox. "Hi, Phoebe, just checking you're okay." It was something like that. Still no reply. She probably thought she'd been right in assuming what I wanted her for. I'm not sure she wasn't right, to be honest. As I said, I've always liked and I'm much closer to her age than Benny, for God's sake…' His voice rose a little. 'Anyway, there was a light on inside but no sound at all, so I left, went back to the pub.'

'What time would that be?' Jo asked.

'Don't know. Hang on though, the late game had just kicked off, so, just after eight, I guess.'

'And you left the pub with Phoebe at around six-thirty. So, let's say you were gone for an hour and a half. Minus half an hour for getting there and back, that's still quite a lot of walking around.'

'You could do two complete circuits of Helmshore in that time,' Mo said.

'Actually, I went onto the moor. Through the gate near Robin Hood's Well and along the old road towards Holcombe Village. I was thinking I might have a pint in the Shoulder of Mutton but decided it was too far and doubled back.'

'And decided to check on Phoebe before going back to the pub. That would be ten to fifteen minutes before eight o'clock?'

'That's right.'

'Okay, Mr Finch. One more question, did Phoebe explain why she was in such a mood with Benny?'

'I don't think it was just about Benny, to be honest. She'd had a bit of a set-to with her folks earlier and I got the impression the argument over the meal was the last straw.'

'And she didn't say, or hint, at what she might be planning to do or where she was planning to go.'

'No, otherwise I'd have mentioned it already, wouldn't I?'

'Quite. Well, I think we've done as much as possible today, but I'd like you to come to the main police station in Bury, near the retail park, tomorrow and show us on a map where this all played out. Shall we say ten o'clock in the morning. And we're sorry we interrupted your Christmas Day; thank you for your understanding and please pass on our thanks to your mum for that wonderful cake.'

'I will, and I'll be there at ten tomorrow. I want to help. Christ, I hope she's okay.'

★

'So the timing checks out against what Morrison said and what he said Phoebe told him.'

Andy sighed and shook his head. 'Why do we use last names for men and first names for women?' he muttered, half to himself.

It was ten minutes after eight o'clock and the four detectives were seated round a table in the otherwise empty operations room. Andy was half turned away from the table with his feet up on another chair whilst Eva had been feeding back details of their meeting with Phoebe's parents. Andy had contributed nothing and seemed totally detached from the meeting.

'Sorry, not sure I got that, sergeant,' Jo said. 'Something about first and last names?'

'It doesn't matter. What I said was…'

'That's okay,' Jo interrupted. 'If it doesn't matter, no point in repeating it.' She turned back to Eva. 'So, Phoebe arrived at twelve-thirty, left at one-thirty. Her dad didn't give her a lift and we don't know how she got back to Helmshore. That's if she *did* go back. We don't know for certain that, when the boyfriend spoke to her on the phone at four o'clock, she was where she said she was, at the house in Crest Lane. Though there's no reason to believe otherwise at this stage. Did she take anything with her from her parents' house when she left?'

Andy turned towards the table. 'What's that got to do with anything?'

'Morrison reckons there are no bags missing from their house in Helmshore, except a small shoulder bag. If she has gone to stay with a friend, then you'd expect her to take a bag with her, for clothes and stuff. If she did, it has to be one she took from Hawkshaw on Saturday.'

'That makes no sense,' Andy said. 'Surely, she only decided to run off after the incident in the pub, so why would she take a bag from her folks' house hours before that happened?'

'I'm not suggesting that would be *why* she took the bag at the time…'

'So, she took it on the *off chance* that she might decide to run away later. Brilliant.'

'It could have contained Christmas presents,' Jo said, 'or more of her stuff she'd decided to take to the love nest. We'll check tomorrow with the dog walker if she had a bag with her when he saw her.'

'Christmas presents,' Andy said, rolling his eyes. 'Oh, yes, I'd forgotten it was Christmas Day. Can I go now, miss?'

Jo glared at him. 'I'd be interested to know how she got back from Hawkshaw to Crest Lane, *if* she went back there, and whether she saw or met anyone between half-one and six o'clock.'

'And how do you propose to find that out?' Andy asked.

'No idea right now. We've asked the dog walker, a Mr Jack Grimshaw, and Marlon Finch to come in at ten o'clock tomorrow morning to show us on the map exactly where they saw Phoebe after she left the pub.'

Andy snorted. 'Jack Grimshaw. Well, I never. Up to his old tricks again, perhaps.'

'Meaning?' Jo asked

'Nothing. Doesn't matter.'

'No, I think it *does* matter if you know something about a possible key witness that we don't.'

Andy sighed. 'There was talk at one time about him having sex with someone who was a prosecution witness in a murder trial. Result was the witness was discredited and her testimony was excluded. Crown got a guilty verdict anyway and Jackie-boy was investigated and cleared.'

'So, what happened to him?'

'Nothing. Very popular guy so he easily rode it out. But you know how mud sticks and there were always comments flying around; all in fun, but it meant Jack could never completely put it behind him. Asked for a transfer into Admin and took early retirement soon after. That would have been around five years ago, Well, I say early. I think he'd done his thirty years, but feeling was he'd have carried on but for that.'

'You said, "up to his old tricks again". Does that mean there's still some lingering concern about his innocence?'

'No, just my little joke.'

'No doubt the sort of *little joke* that prevented him putting the experience behind him.'

Andy gave a wide smile. 'No doubt.'

Jo and Andy locked eyes, with the latter looking away first.

Jo turned to Eva. 'Could you speak to Mr and Mrs Wright in the morning before ten o'clock and ask if Phoebe took anything with her when she left. Particularly some sort of bag. Thank you. Let's leave it for today. Tomorrow, which I know is Boxing Day, before someone reminds me, we check cash cards, phone, social media, and get her picture out on local TV as early as possible. And if we get an early start, perhaps we can get away in time for what's left of Christmas. Let's assume in the meantime she's around somewhere just playing with us. I hope that's true and if she is, we don't need to do any of that tonight. And if she isn't, and something bad has happened to her, we're too late anyway.'

Jo stood up. 'Thank you for your time today. Sorry to spoil your Christmas Day. Enjoy what little is left of it.'

Andy was heading out of the room before Jo had finished speaking. The others followed. Jo went into her office and spent a few minutes bringing her file notes up to date on her PC and adding bullet points to her notebook. As she was putting on her coat to leave, Eva appeared in the doorway.

'Hi, Eva, forgotten something?'

Eva hesitated, seeming uncomfortable. 'Just forgot to say Merry Christmas, ma'am.'

'Thank you. Merry Christmas to you, too. And what else?'

'Sorry?'

Jo, smiled. 'You don't have to be a detective to work out that was *not* the reason for you coming back, welcome though it was. So, what's on your mind, Eva?'

'Nothing, really.' Jo remained silent, eyes wide open, inviting Eva to continue. 'Well, I feel a bit bad really, but... about DS Mills. I mean, he's my boss and I don't like going behind his back, but I'm afraid you haven't exactly made a friend there. He's been going on about you to me all afternoon. I don't think he appreciated you calling him a wanker. Not that you're wrong, by the way.'

Jo smiled. 'I didn't actually call him a wanker. I just used the word, loudly, in a different context.'

'Okay, but that's what everyone in the room thought had happened. Which has made you popular with everybody else, but Mills can be a real bastard. He has a thing about women "on the front line," as he calls it. Thinks we should be typing reports and making tea, in between having sex with him and people like him. And he has a reputation for being a racist.'

'Which means I'm a sort of double-whammy in his eyes.'

'I'm afraid so. He's a good detective, tipped for inspector some years ago when he was working on Merseyside, then had a disciplinary issue and a short suspension for using excessive force detaining a suspect. It was a black woman who turned out to be pregnant and almost lost her baby. He was, supposedly, overcome with remorse for his actions, which saved his job, but not his promotion. He was transferred to Bury after his suspension ended. That was around six years ago before it became a regional hub under the New Justice Regime. And I say, *supposedly* overcome by remorse, because he told us the woman got exactly what she deserved. I've always felt that there's an undercurrent of menace about him; like he could be a dangerous person to cross. In fact, you're more of a *triple* whammy, because there'd been some talk of him being considered for promotion again, then you were drafted in.' She shook her head. 'Now I feel bad about telling you all that. I've always said people should be left to form their own opinions…'

'If it makes you feel any better, Eva, I know all about DS Mills's record and the incident you described. I make a point of checking the background and employment history of *all* the people I work with on assignment. So, you haven't disclosed anything I didn't already know or haven't worked out, but I do appreciate you're letting me know.'

Eva smiled. 'So, what have you found out about me?'

Jo laughed. 'Only that you're a real goody-two-shoes. Not even an overdue library book on record. Really boring. Anyway, off you go.' She checked her watch. 'Nearly nine o'clock. Not much of a Christmas Day. What will you do now?'

'Well, it's back to my sister, Kerys, in the hope that her family won't have eaten and drunk everything. What about you, ma'am?'

Jo rubbed her stomach. 'Just realised how hungry I am and hoping they've plated up my dinner as promised. I'm not sure this is a good time to eat a full meal, but I'm going to do it anyway.'

Eva laughed. 'Well, *bon appetit*. I'll see you in the morning.'

'Bye, Eva, and thank you again.'

Jo sat back in her chair for a moment, her mind going back

to Benny's doubts about the prospect of a long term relationship with Phoebe. It reflected her thoughts to some extent about her own circumstances. The age difference with Seb, six years, had been a source of merry banter since their relationship began over two years ago, but the fact that it was frequently raised, albeit in fun, was an indication that both parties were only too conscious of it. It seemed that it had yet to be just accepted as irrelevant. At least, that was Jo's feeling. She was also aware of Seb's wanting to have a family, in spite of his constantly assuring her that it was not as important as their being happy together. Jo was thirty-six, well within the child-bearing age range for women whose early priority was to establish a successful career before going on to raise a family. But her current role in the police, which she loved, meant separation from Seb for several months at a time. This latest assignment had underlined the major changes raising a family would bring to both their lives.

She put those thoughts to one side, because right now the love of her life was waiting for her in front of a roaring fire and a Christmas tree. As she picked up her laptop and shoulder bag to leave, her mobile pinged with an incoming text. She checked the screen. It showed a single digit – '9'.

*

It was exactly 9.15 p.m. when Jo arrived back at Seb's parents' house. Instead of using her key to go straight in, she remembered Miss Davenport's earlier comment and knocked on the door. As someone appeared behind the frosted glass panel, she began to sing.

'Good King Wenceslas looked out…'

Seb's voice from inside joined in, 'on the feast of Stephen…' followed by the rest of the household in raucous disharmony… 'Where the snow lay round about…' dissolving into equally raucous laughter. The door flew open and Seb stepped outside, sweeping his wife up into his arms and carrying her over the threshold. He shouted through to the kitchen.

'Quick, quick. Engage the microwave.'

Seb carried Jo through to the dining room and plonked her down on the chair she had vacated seven hours ago, the cutlery, wine glass and Christmas cracker still in place just as she had left them.

'And after you've eaten,' Jonathan said, 'you've got four hours of charades to catch up on.'

It was after midnight before the joyous party ended, Jo mindful of her early start the following morning and limiting herself to a couple of glasses of wine and a small malt whisky-and-water. Inevitably, as they lay together wrapped in each other's arms, talk turned to Jo's day at the office.

'On balance,' Seb said, just before they drifted off to sleep, 'I can't really see anything sinister happening to your missing girl. People don't get attacked on desolate moorland in the middle of the night except by the Hound of the Baskervilles.'

CHAPTER SIX

Wednesday 26 December

Jo was out of bed by seven o'clock, showered, then took her clothes downstairs to dress so as not to wake her sleeping, and almost certainly hung-over, spouse. The rest of the house remained in a state of somnolence, to an accompaniment of gentle snoring. Just prior to her leaving, she changed her mind about disturbing Seb, heaving him onto his back and planting a long kiss on his lips. His arms swung round her, as if by some conditioned reflex, pulling her close to him.

'Not now, big boy. See you later,' she whispered, easing herself away.

She entered the station building just before eight o'clock, expecting to be the first one there except for the unlucky skeleton crew covering the early shift of the bank holiday. She was surprised to see Detective Superintendent Mallory Jones seated at one of the workstations in the operations room.

'Morning, sir. I didn't expect you to be in today.'

'Morning, Jo. I like to keep you all on your toes. Don't want any slacking, you know.' He sighed. 'But the real reason is that I couldn't wait to get out of the house. We had the whole family round yesterday, both kids plus spouses and a total of five grandchildren. At least I think there were only five… Place looks like a bomb's hit it. Stuff everywhere. I said to Mary, shall we bother to tidy it up or just enter it for the Turner Prize.' Jo laughed. 'Anyway, while I'm here, and so I haven't told my dear wife a complete lie, I'd like to hear all about *your* Christmas Day. Bit of a bugger, getting that dropped on you, and I'm not even sure it's ours to deal with. Holcombe Moor is half Greater Manchester's and half Lancashire's. It came to us because it was *reported* within the Bury area, but… Anyway, perhaps you could give me the main bullet points.'

'Certainly, sir. Can I get you a coffee first?'

'Not for me, thanks, but get yourself one and bring it up to my office.'

As she was standing by the coffee machine, her phone pinged. She checked the incoming text on the screen. Another digit, this time followed by a semi colon – '5;'.

★

When Jo entered Mal's office, the senior officer was leaning back in his chair looking relaxed. In front of him on the desk was a half bottle of Famous Grouse whisky and a shot glass containing what Jo assumed must be a sample from it.

'I don't encourage my detectives to drink on duty, but a few drops in your coffee might give it a more festive taste and remind you what day it is and what else you might be doing. And take it as a token of my gratitude for grasping the nettle yesterday.'

'Oh, thank you, sir,' Jo said, holding out her coffee cup and wondering, too late, whether this was some sort of test and she was meant to refuse. The trickle of amber liquid into her coffee told her that it wasn't, and she took a long sip followed by a contented 'Mmm' as she put it down.

'Just the main points, then,' Mal said.

'Okay…' Jo opened her notebook '…Phoebe Wright, aged nineteen, of Crest Lane, Helmshore, was dropped off by her partner, Benny Morrison, at her parents' house in Hawkshaw at twelve-thirty p.m. on Saturday the twenty-second of December. There seems to be a lot of animosity between Phoebe and her parents about her boyfriend and she apparently stormed out of their house at around one-thirty. She was next reported seen at the White Horse pub in Helmshore at around six p.m., where she had prearranged to meet Morrison, along with other friends, to watch a football match on TV. She and Morrison had an argument and she stormed out of the pub at between six-thirty and six-forty.'

'She did a lot of storming that day, didn't she? Do we know what the argument was about?'

'Yes, apparently Morrison wouldn't order her a starter when they sat down for a meal.'

'I see, nothing trivial, then. Go on.'

'A couple of hours *before* she turned up at the pub, Morrison had spoken to her on the phone, at which time she was at their house in Crest Lane. Or she said that's where she was. We can check that, but we've no reason to believe it wasn't true because Phoebe did go back to Crest Lane when she left the White Horse after the argument. One of the crowd she was with, a Marlon Finch, escorted her part of the way home. He went back later to the house, he said to check that she was okay. That was about a quarter to eight, but by that time she had already left because she was seen by a dog walker around seven-thirty setting out across the moor in the direction of Hawkshaw.'

'Really? At that time of night. Have you spoken to the dog walker yet?'

'Yes, and he's coming into the station today to show us on a map exactly where he saw her. His name's Jack Grimshaw, by the way. You probably know him.'

Mal smiled. 'I certainly do know him. He was an excellent copper and an even better friend. Bring him up to my office when you've finished with him.' He shook his head, still smiling. 'Good heavens, Laughing Jack.'

'He'll be in around ten, sir, so it will be after that.'

'Good. So what next?'

'We start with checking cash card activity, phone, social media. Door to door in and around Crest Lane, probably from tomorrow because she was seen leaving the area, anyway. And with your permission I'd like to get her face on local TV midday news today if possible. I guess that's your call, sir.'

'Do it, Jo. You've got the reins.'

'Thank you, sir. Oh, and with one scenario being that she's bunked off to a friend's, we'll be checking whether she's taken a bag – rucksack, say, or holdall – from Crest Lane or her parents. Mr Grimshaw should be able to tell us whether she had one with her. And we hope, of course, that she'll turn up before we do all this.'

'Okay, DI Carter. I'll wait here for a visit from Laughing Jack, then I'll get off home to the bomb site. Don't forget to bring him up, unless you decide to arrest him for something, of course, then I'll pop down and see him in the cells.' He smiled up at Jo as she got to her feet. 'No rush, by the way. I'm happy to wait as long as possible.'

*

The operations room was looking more business-like when Jo returned although most of the workstations remained unoccupied. Mo and Eva were each at their desks and looked up from their screens with a bright 'good morning.' Andy was reclining in his chair holding a cup of coffee in one hand and his iPhone in the other. He ignored Jo and continued thumbing the screen. As always on a Boxing Day, Jo thought, the Christmas decorations already looked a little redundant.

'Morning, gang,' Jo said.

'So we're a gang now, are we?' Andy said. 'That's new. Must be a regional thing.'

Jo walked across to the briefing room at the far side from her office.

'Let's get a board going,' she said. 'Not that we've got much for it yet.'

The briefing room was designed for group meetings with a long rectangular table down the centre and twelve chairs around it – five each side and one at the ends. The wall separating it from the operations room was of frosted glass, including the panelled door, primarily for security reasons, so nothing could be accidentally revealed to visitors to the open plan working area. On the opposite long wall was a whiteboard stretching the length of the room, one metre off the floor and one metre high. This served as a write-on board, magnetic board and projection screen for multiple active cases. At the moment only one case was featured – a local drug-running investigation, concurrently floundering on misinformation received from various conflicting sources. The associated information occupied a small section at one end of the board. The four detectives took their seats around the opposite end of the table.

'Okay, who's the best writer?' Jo asked.

'Mo, definitely,' Eva said, pointing to her colleague.

'Right, grab the marker, DC Malik. And quickly, because we have Messrs Finch and Grimshaw arriving at ten.'

'Can I start us off?' Eva asked. She held up an A5-size picture of a beautiful young blonde woman posing for what looked like a publicity shot. 'Our runaway, taken from a poster advertising a play by a local dramatic society, and donated by Mr and Mrs Wright.' She attached it with a small magnet to the board.

'Thanks, Eva. What an absolute beauty. Let's hope we can find her soon. Marker at the ready, Mo, let's run through the facts, characters, times and places.'

Fifteen minutes later, the unfolding story had been neatly added to the incident board next to Phoebe's picture.

'I guess the two most likely scenarios are, one, she sets off for parents' home and gets abducted, or worse, on the way. Two, is hiding at a friend's house somewhere to teach Benny and her parents a lesson.'

'Pretty fucking spiteful if it's the second one,' Andy said.

'True, but let's hope it is. Eva, don't forget to speak to the Wrights this morning about her taking anything from their house when she left on Saturday? I'm wondering about a bag.'

'Already spoken to them. Helen Wright phoned before eight o'clock for an update and I asked her then. She didn't collect anything; apparently, it wasn't that kind of leaving. She just got up from where she was sitting and rushed out of the house.'

'She seems to be pretty good at that sort of exit. So, two scenarios. Anyone think of a third?'

'She's at Benny's just teaching her parents a lesson?' Andy said.

'Except she was seen heading away from there. But, okay, just possible. If so, she was very quiet when Mo and I spoke to Benny at his home yesterday. And Benny knows he will be in *real* trouble if he's hiding her and wasting our time. We're expecting Jack Grimshaw, the dog walker, at ten o'clock, and Marlon Finch who, he claims, escorted her home after her bust-up with Benny on Saturday. I've asked them to show us on a map of the area where their part of the action took place.' She checked her watch. 'Nine-fifteen. If they arrive as planned that gives us forty-five minutes. I think we should see them separately so there's no cross-fertilisation of accounts.

They're not suspects, but if what they tell us is true, they are the last two people we know who saw her before she disappeared. Anyway, we can play it by ear at the time. I'd like all four of us to be present when we interview them, but in the meantime, can we try to locate her phone and check any card transactions over the past four days, including Saturday night. DS Mills, can you get people lined up for a search of the moor if we need one after we've spoken to Messrs Grimshaw and Finch.'

Andy opened his eyes wide in mock surprise. 'You want me to pull people in on Boxing Day on the off chance they might have something to do?'

'Exactly, got it in one. It's a missing girl, tell them. I'm sure you can charm them into acting selflessly under the circumstances. And Mo, can you arrange to get Phoebe's face on local television today. I'll speak to the TV people before it goes out to get the right context. We'll need to let the Wrights and Benny know beforehand. And can one of you set up an OS map or similar for the area in one of the meeting rooms downstairs.'

Jo stood up. 'Okay, let's go.'

'And what will you be doing, *ma'am*? Andy asked.

Jo smiled. 'Oh, I'm sure I'll think of something, sergeant. There's a wordsearch in the Sunday supplement I haven't had time to look at yet. And if I've no luck with that I'll draft something to go out with Phoebe's face and circumstances on today's lunchtime news. Any more questions? Okay? Back here at five to ten.'

★

Marlon Finch and Jack Grimshaw arrived together at 10.00 a.m., the former a little the worse for wear after a very late and liquid Christmas Day. Jo met them in Reception, accompanied by a male uniformed officer.

'Thank you for coming in, gentlemen,' Jo said, 'I'm sorry to bother you again, but we need to get as much information as we can as soon as possible. Mr Finch, you come with me, and PC Winfield here will take you, Mr Grimshaw, up to the cafeteria until we're ready for you. You can check out the menu and see if it stacks up against what it was when you were here.'

She led Marlon to a small meeting room picking up two drinks from a vending machine on the way. Andy, Mo and Eva were seated at a rectangular table with three vacant chairs. She introduced Marlon to Andy and Eva and waved him to sit down. In the corner of the room, an OS Explorer map of the West Pennine Moors, folded to display the relevant area of Holcombe Moor and Helmshore, was attached with bulldog clips to a board which rested on an easel.

'The purpose of our asking you here, Mr Finch, as we explained yesterday is to track Phoebe's movements, as much as we can, on the afternoon and evening of the twenty-second…'

'And to give you the opportunity to account for your own movements,' Andy added.

Marlon shifted on his chair. Jo paused, tight-lipped, as if she were struggling to stop words coming out of her mouth.

'As we will be asking everyone involved, Mr Finch, as a matter of routine,' she continued. 'So, from the time you arrived at the White Horse take us through what happened.' She turned to the map. 'Start by showing us where the pub is.'

Marlon stepped across to the map, screwing up his eyes to focus, as if fighting against something inside his head. Jo picked up a marker pen from the easel.

'This is the White Horse pub in Helmshore, here.' He pointed to the location and Jo circled it on the map.

'Which is where all the guys were. From what time?'

'Well, they all arrived at different times to watch the football so most of them were there for the first match at two o'clock. I arrived shortly after twelve-thirty; I was one of the first. And when you say "guys" there were nearly as many women in the crowd as well. It wasn't just a lads' thing.'

'But not Phoebe, not yet.'

'No.'

'Would she usually be around for that sort of gathering?'

'Yes, usually she'd be one of the crowd with Benny.'

'Was anything said about her not being with the crowd on that day?' Mo asked.

'Such as?'

'Any comments, theories as to why she wasn't there?'

'No, we knew why. Benny said she'd gone to see her parents to try to sort out what was happening on Christmas Day.'

'Show us where her parents live,' Jo said.

'Here, in Hawkshaw.' He pointed to the map and Jo drew a circle round the spot. 'Posh new build with a huge garden,' Marlon added.

'So you've been to her parents' house?'

'No, Benny has told us about it. A bit different to his mid-terrace.'

'Which is where – Benny's terrace?'

'I thought you went there yesterday?' Andy asked.

'I did,' Jo said, 'but we didn't use a map, because Mo drove us there.'

'And, of *course*, he has local knowledge.' Andy nodded knowingly at the two DCs.

'Benny's cottage, Mr Finch. Show me, please.' Jo circled the location. 'That's quite a distance between the two houses.' Jo checked her notes. 'Benny said he called her at around four p.m. I assume that was just after the match finished, got to get your priorities right. And she was at home? The mid-terrace.'

'If you say so. I wasn't party to the call, was I?'

Jo studied the map. 'She left her parents at one-thirty p.m., they said. How would she get home from there, do you think?'

'I know Benny dropped her off there before he went to the Horse, but no idea how she got back. She might have walked down to the Hare and Hounds.' He pointed it out on the map. 'About three quarters of a mile from Hawkshaw. Got lots of friends round there; sure to be someone who'd give her a lift.'

'Okay, but...'

'Or she could have walked across the moor, past the Pilgrims Cross.' He traced the route along footpaths and farm tracks. 'But it's a fair way, about five, five-and-a-half miles. Couple of hours – a bit less if you're in a hurry. If I remember, the weather was okay, so if she left at one-thirty, then two hours means it wouldn't have got dark before she got home.'

Jo nodded. 'So when did she arrive at the pub? Can you remember?'

'I didn't see her arrive. We were kind of spread out between the two bars. First I knew was hearing her and Benny arguing in the other bar.'

'What were they arguing about?'

'I think Benny was pissed off that it had taken her so long to get there. He'd kept going on about being hungry and wanting to eat earlier. But I don't know how long she'd been there at that point.'

'What time was that?'

'That would be soon after six, because that's when the evening menu kicks in. He'd missed his chance of just getting something cheaper from the lunch menu, which includes the afternoon up to six.'

'And soon after that Phoebe left? Some cock-up with the meal order, I believe.'

'Yes, she wanted a starter and Benny said no, because he wanted to finish his meal well before the late kick-off so he could get a good seat to watch it. She wouldn't order a main until she'd had a starter, so Benny ordered something for her. When it came, she tipped the plate over onto the table and ran out.'

'And that would be when?'

'Half six, twenty to seven.'

'And you followed and walked home with her. Directly, this way?' Jo turned back to the map and traced with her finger the short distance between the pub and Benny's cottage.

'That's right.'

'So, show us now where you went walkabout afterwards.'

Marlon showed the route on the map.

'I went down through the farm gate, here, and along the old road as far as the empty house at Chatterton Close. Then I doubled back.'

Jo studied the board for a few seconds then turned to Marlon.

'Thank you, Mr Finch, that's been very helpful. We're now going to speak to Mr Grimshaw, who you met earlier. I think it would be useful if you could stay.'

'That's fine. Anything to help find Phoebe.'

'Thank you. Mo, could you get him, please.'

Mo returned a few minutes later with Jack Grimshaw. Jo smiled and waved him to an empty chair.

'Thanks for waiting, Mr Grimshaw. You've already met DC

Malik and this is DC Johnson. I believe you know Detective Sergeant Mills from when you were still with the police.'

Jack up screwed his eyes to look at Andy.

'Oh yes. Doc Holliday!' he said.

'I'm your Huckleberry,' Andy replied, in a strong American accent. The two men shared the private joke with a laugh.

'What…?' Jo looked from one to the other.

'I'll explain later, ma'am,' Eva said.

'I'll look forward to it,' Jo said. 'Can we move on. We're piecing together Phoebe's movements on the night of the twenty-second, Mr Grimshaw, and you seem to be the last person to have seen her before she disappeared. The last person we *know* who saw her, that is. So will you show us exactly where you saw Phoebe on Saturday night. If not exactly, then approximately.'

'I can tell you exactly, because I was heading back to Helmshore with Rory, my dog, and I saw her coming the other way. We met at the gate near Robin Hood's Well, close to Pleasant View Farm. I held it open for her.'

'Show me on the map.' Jack pointed to the place and Jo circled it with the marker pen. 'And your house is where, Mr Grimshaw?' Jack indicated again, and Jo made the circle. 'Did Phoebe say anything?'

'Just "hello" and "thank you" as she passed through the gate. We know each other quite well. We were neighbours until her parents moved to Hawkshaw.'

'Then where did she go?'

'Well, she set off up the path towards Bull Hill. That surprised me – I mean it's not difficult to follow with a nearly full moon, but I'd have thought it was a bit creepy. I asked her where she was going and would she be okay. She just said "I'll be fine" or something. Sort of waved her arm in the air without looking back.'

'How did she seem? Stressed, angry?'

'Nothing like that. She seemed okay. Like she said, just… fine.'

'Show me the path to Bull Hill.'

Jack pointed it out. 'If she was heading for Hawkshaw, she wouldn't actually go over Bull Hill, she'd be coming along this path…' he traced it with his finger on the map '… and past the Pilgrims Cross.'

Jo nodded. 'The Pilgrims Cross? That's the path where I went walking with my husband on Sunday, and I know what you mean about walking it after dark. What was she wearing, can you remember?'

'A woolly hat, light-coloured, and a sort of light fleece jacket. Jeans and high boots, nearly up to her knee.'

'That's a remarkably precise description, Mr Grimshaw, for a brief meeting at seven-thirty p.m. in December. I take it there aren't any street lights close to that gate.'

'No, but it was a clear sky and a bright moon and I noticed what she was wearing because it didn't look suitable for walking around on the moor at that time of night.' Jack smiled. 'And, don't forget, I used to be a copper myself. Long time ago, but I still notice things that don't look right.'

Jo turned to Marlon. 'What was she wearing in the pub?'

'Sounds like the same: jeans, boots, light fleece. And she always wears that pink woolly hat – inside and out. It's a sort of chosen image, I suppose. Never takes it off for anything.'

Andy sneered. 'Oh, I'm sure she must take it off for *some* things. You've just never been lucky enough to be there at the time.'

Jo turned back to Jack. 'Can you remember if she had a bag with her?'

'Yes, she did. A rucksack.'

Jo's eyes opened with surprise and interest. 'And how big was the rucksack?'

Jack shrugged. 'How long is a piece of string? I don't know, just a rucksack.'

'Does it matter?' Andy asked Jo.

'Yes, it does,' Jo said. 'Tell you what, let's take a break. Mo, Eva, can you get these gentlemen some more coffee or tea? I've just got to get something from my car.'

When Jo returned no more than three minutes later, the refreshments were in place, including a cup of coffee for herself. She held up a rucksack.

'Right, this is mine. Twenty-five-litre. I use it for day walks – just right for spare or additional clothing, towel, food, water, maps, first aid stuff.' She slipped it onto her back, tightening the straps to ease it into place. 'There's not much in it now so it hangs a bit flat, but could you say whether Phoebe's was smaller, bigger, about the same size?'

'I'd say bigger, unless it just looked that way because it was full.'

'It was full?'

'Yes, in fact, it was bulging, as though she'd had a job getting everything in it and fastened up.'

'Interesting… And you say that was around seven-thirty?'

'Or a few minutes after. Certainly no later than quarter to eight.'

Jo turned to Marlon, then back to the map. 'So that's about the time you would be heading back towards Helmshore after your walk along the main track. Did you see or hear anything at all of Phoebe or Mr Grimshaw?'

Marlon bristled a little. 'If I had then I'd have told you by now, wouldn't I? *No,* I did *not* see anyone or hear anything.'

Jo turned to Andy. 'Any questions, DS Mills?'

Andy shook his head without speaking.

★

Sergeant Geoff Brazendale along with eleven other uniformed officers, including members of the local search-trained tactical aid unit, were gathered, standing and sitting, around the long table in the briefing room when Jo and her team entered. Eva and Andy took the two available chairs and Mo went to stand by the map from the interview room which had now been attached to the incident board. Jo addressed the group.

'Good afternoon, everybody. For those of you, most of you, who I didn't meet last week, I'm Detective Inspector Jo Carter. I'm sorry I'm meeting you again or for the first time on Boxing Day under these circumstances. We have a missing person, a young woman living in Helmshore, who was last seen on Saturday at around seven-thirty p.m. on Holcombe Moor. DC Malik will take you through the details in a moment. We've arranged for a mobile command vehicle close to her last sighting for the search HQ. It's not designed for comfort but I am assured it has a heater and a kettle.' There was a ripple of laughter. 'We don't know yet what we are looking for. Hopefully not a body at this stage and not on the moor. The chances of someone being subjected to an attack on

Holcombe Moor at that time in mid-winter are remote to zero. So just any evidence of someone who has passed that way who is not your standard hill walker. I passed that way myself, or close by, on Sunday, and there were a number of other walkers about. So, there's bound to be a lot of evidence of footfall. We collect anything that might remotely point to Phoebe passing that way and we'll sort out the likely from the unlikely later.' She nodded to Mo. 'All yours, DC Malik.'

Mo turned to the map. 'This is where ex-Sergeant Jack Grimshaw saw Phoebe at between seven-thirty and seven-forty-five on Saturday evening, whilst out walking his dog.' There were a few brief asides at the mention of Jack's name. 'At the time she was wearing a pink woolly hat, light fleece top, jeans, and long boots. She was carrying a full rucksack, about this size.' He held up Jo's bag, which had been stuffed full of towels to its maximum load. 'That was the last time she was seen by neighbours, friends, or family. Jack says she was heading in this direction along the path towards the Pilgrims Cross. Prior to that, earlier the same evening, she had been in the White Horse in Helmshore – here – wearing the same clothes, but without the rucksack. At around six-thirty, one hour before she was seen on the moor, she left the pub after an argument with her boyfriend. We assume she went to their house, here, in Crest Lane, which is around fifteen minutes' walk from the pub. She was escorted there by one of the guys in the pub, a Marlon Finch, who had seen her leave after the argument. He left her, he says, close to Crest Lane. For her then to get to where she was seen by Jack at that time, she would have spent no more than twenty minutes in the house before leaving again.'

Mo turned to Jo, who nodded for him to continue.

'Under normal circumstances, the most likely reason for her to be heading across the moor in that direction would be to visit her parents in Hawkshaw. It's a fair distance, more than five miles, but apparently, she has made the trek before on many occasions. However, this time she did not arrive at *chez* Mum and Dad.'

'And whereas that is very worrying,' Jo said, 'we know she had with her a full rucksack, which suggests she may have planned to go somewhere else to stay, with friends, perhaps. Because we also know she has clothes and toiletries at both houses, so there would be no need to be carrying what appears to be a fair amount of stuff from one to the other.'

She turned back to Mo, who continued.

'At around the time Jack was holding the gate open for Phoebe and watching her set off across the moor, Marlon Finch was walking along this track, here, the old road from Ramsbottom to Helmshore. However, he says he didn't see her and that would probably be true given the lie of the land.'

'So,' Jo went on, 'we start the search from the MCV, and continue along the path towards Hawkshaw. I am not familiar with the area, but DS Mills is and will be there to oversee. This is the fourth day since Phoebe disappeared, and we're all aware that the chances of finding a missing person reduce dramatically with time after the first forty-eight hours. So, whereas I'm not suggesting that every second counts, it goes without saying that the urgency to find her still applies.' Jo looked round the room. 'Are there any questions?' One young woman raised her hand. 'Yes? And please say your name. I need to get to know you.'

'PC Debbie Pitman, ma'am. Do you yet have a theory as to what *has* happened to Phoebe? It might help us in what we're looking for.'

'Either she is hiding somewhere to deliberately cause her parents and partner to worry after, it seems, she fell out with both of them on that day. Or she has come to harm whilst crossing the moor. The fact that there will have been so many people all over the moor since Saturday, and nothing reported, gives me hope that it is not the latter.'

Another hand went up. Jo nodded towards him.

'PC Danny Wainwright, ma'am. With the exception of Good Friday, Boxing Day is one of the most popular days of the year for walkers on that part of the moor. It could be very busy up there. What should we say about why we're there, because we will certainly be asked what's going on?'

'That's a very good point, Danny.' She checked her watch. 'It's twelve forty-eight. There's an appeal going out on the local news this lunchtime after the main news at one o'clock, in about half an hour. So, we'll have gone public by the time we get the search underway, although it's unlikely anyone up there will pick up that news item. We'll get you each a copy of the appeal so you can paraphrase that into your own words if you get asked, but please don't give any more information than is in the statement itself. We are playing down that second scenario, of Phoebe coming to harm, and suggesting we believe she is staying with friends but need to make contact with her. That's the truth, but not quite the whole truth.'

*

The search team left along with Andy immediately after the whole group had watched the appeal on *Look North* and verbatim copies of it had been handed out. Jo called DC Malik into the briefing room, where she was still studying the incident board.

'Let's find somewhere we can set up an incident room closer to the action if necessary, preferably in Helmshore,' she said. 'It seems that's where it's all happening. From what the boss says, the investigation is more Lancashire's than Greater Manchester's, so they might know somewhere. Just in case that works out better for us than travelling back and forth. Anything from the phone or cards?'

'Not yet, ma'am, but…'

The door opened and Eva poked a smiling face into the room.

'Excuse me for butting in, ma'am, but we've got a location for the phone. We can pinpoint to a radius of five metres through triangulation, but I think we can get a lot closer than that; an exact position, in fact. It's not necessarily the phone's *current* position, but its last *known* position. What's interesting, though, is that it's where it was on Sunday the twenty-third, the day *after* Phoebe went missing.' She walked over to the map and traced with her finger round one of the circles Jo had drawn on the map. 'This circle is approximately what triangulation tells us and…' she placed her finger in the centre of the circle '…this is Benny's house in Crest Lane.'

Jo paused to think, before speaking. 'And Mr Morrison told us he'd checked, and she'd taken her phone with her, didn't he?'

'I guess he could have missed it.'

Jo frowned and pursed her lips. 'I wonder. In the first place, I find it amazing that he chose not to try to contact Phoebe, who, allegedly, he's crazy about, for nearly two days before discovering she was missing. At which point, you would expect the first thing he would do was to phone her and should have heard the phone ringing, unless it needed charging or was on silent. I can't quite get my head round this. Mo, let's go right now to pay him another visit. Eva, there's no chance we could be mistaken about the phone's location?'

'None at all, ma'am.'

'Right, Let's get going, Mo,' Jo said.

★

They headed out of Bury town centre, Mo driving north along Croston Road and through Brandlesholme, to where the houses gave way to open countryside. Here the green changed to a paler tone where a thin layer of snow covered the ground. Ahead, around the tall tower on Holcombe Hill in the distance, the covering was white with deeper snow.

'They must have had quite a downfall up there,' Jo said, pointing towards the hill.

'It's because it's so much higher than the town. They get it up there when we don't get anything in Bury. Helmshore might be snowbound.'

'Really?'

Mo smiled. 'No, not really. Anyway, we'll soon see.'

They drove in silence for a few minutes.

'Okay, Detective, worst-case scenario – something bad has happened to Phoebe. Remember this is worst case, not most likely. What are the chances of a random attack by an opportunist lying in wait on Holcombe Moor on a Saturday night in December?'

'Zero, ma'am.'

'Zero. So not random but consistent with the statistical norm of victim knowing the attacker, and knowing them well. So, who have we got?'

No reply.

'DC Malik, you're the only other person in the car, so, who have we got?'

'Sorry, ma'am, I thought the question was rhetorical and just a lead-in to *you* telling *me*.'

Jo sighed. 'Go on. Who?'

'*Statistical* favourite would be her partner, Benny. Effectively stood up by Phoebe, then humiliated by her attacking him using her own main course as a deadly weapon...' Jo giggled '...and probably pissed off by all the attention she gets from the other guys. Had a lot to drink already up to the time she left. Plus, the fact that he doesn't seem to know whether she's moved in with him or not. Then there's the possible ex-wife complication of a good relationship turning back into more than just friendship and Phoebe showing no apparent interest in his daughters who clearly mean a lot to him.'

'That's very good, Mo. But a motive for some sort of violent action?'

'None of those things on its own, but all together...'

'Except, of course, she was seen on the moor at around seven-thirty and Benny didn't leave the pub until ten o'clock.'

'So he says. But with everyone in the White Horse focused on the match, it wouldn't be that difficult to sneak out and back again. Perhaps he did phone her, arranged to meet her, and... whatever. He'd take her phone so we couldn't check it and find out about his call to her.'

'But wouldn't he ditch the phone – rather than take it home with him? Who else is in the frame?'

'Marlon Finch. We know he was with her after she left the pub. We know he was hanging around for an hour or so, which would have included the time she left her house and started off across the moor. We also know he fancies her and had been drinking. He could have followed her from Crest Lane. He'd have to stay hidden when Jack Grimshaw came on the scene, but that would be easy around there, especially at that time.'

'There was a full moon, but go on, this is good.'

'He followed her onto the moor, offering to walk with her wherever she was going. She'd tell him to piss off, feeling pretty vulnerable, I'd guess. He tries it on, she resists, and things get out of control. Once he's committed the act, he feels he has no choice. He finishes her off.'

'Okay, so we have two in the frame...'

'Three, ma'am. Jack Grimshaw. Long odds outsider, but with the palest of shadows hanging over his past.'

'Do you really think he's a possibility?'

'No, but he was the last person we know who saw Phoebe entering an area where she would be an easy target for anyone seeking to harm her. I don't think we can ignore him, with or without that previous incident on his record.'

'Agreed. That's good, Mo; you've made it all sound credible enough to depress me. How much further to Benny's?'

'Nearly there.'

★

Jo knocked on the door of 17 Crest Lane, a neat, stone-built, mid-terraced cottage with white-framed sash windows and an eggshell-blue door. It was part of an attractive row of ten similar properties, and carved into a large stone set in the wall above the door of number seventeen was the road name and, underneath, the date of construction, 1871. They had a long wait before the door opened.

Benny was wearing a creased white button-through shirt outside a pair of baggy jogging pants. His feet were bare, his beard skewed to one side as if he had been lying on it, and his hair was even more untidy than usual. He blinked his bloodshot eyes, which he seemed to be struggling to focus. Jo guessed he had just got out of bed, having spent all night in the clothes he was wearing, and with very little sleep.

'What?' his voice was hoarse and soft.

'Just a few more questions, Mr Morrison,' Jo said. 'We won't keep you long. You don't look too well, if you don't mind me saying.'

'So, given the circumstances, I should be a picture of health and feeling on top of the world, should I?'

'Of course not, and it's those circumstances you refer to that we'd like to talk to you about. Can we come in?'

Mo reached for his phone. 'Excuse me, I need to get this.'

He stepped back from the door as Jo moved inside, gently pushing Benny ahead of her.

'Look…' Benny began to speak, but Jo raised her hand for quiet and waited a few moments until Mo followed them into the house and closed the door behind him. He raised his eyebrows with an unspoken question. Jo shook her head.

Benny glanced from one to the other. 'What's going on?'

'May we sit down?' Jo asked.

Benny sighed and led them through to the small living room where they had met previously. They took the same seats as before in three armchairs round a circular coffee table.

'When we spoke last time – here, in this room – you told us what Phoebe had taken with her. Right?'

'I said I *couldn't* tell you, not for certain, because…'

'You said she'd taken a small shoulder bag.'

'Oh, that. Yes, I thought you meant coats and bags. Yes, she rarely goes anywhere without it. That and her woolly hat.'

'And tell us again what was in the bag or what you believe was in the bag.'

'I assume it would be what she always uses it for. Wallet, iPhone, driving licence, tissues, diary, small notepad, pen, nasal spray – I think. And lipstick. Well, not lipstick, as such; one of those lip-moistening sticks. And probably some paracetamol.'

'You're very familiar with the contents of Phoebe's bag.'

Benny snorted a laugh. 'It's a bit of an in-joke between us. The bag opening is really small for the size of the bag and the zip sort of sticks halfway, anyway. So, whenever she needs to get something out, she has to take most of the stuff out to get what she wants. And if it's a phone call, she usually just tips it up and empties it so she can answer in time. So, yes, I'm very familiar with the contents of the bag.'

'About the phone, Mr Morrison. You are sure she took it with her?'

'Absolutely. She keeps it in her bag all the time, except at night when it's next to the bed.' His voice broke a little.

'You see, we've done a trace on the phone and it tells us it's here. In this house or very close to this house. What do you say about that?'

'That you're mistaken. Have you any idea how many times I've called her over the past three days? Probably about a hundred. I think I would have heard it, don't you?'

Jo turned to Mo. 'DC Malik?'

'I've just called Phoebe's number,' Mo said. 'It rang out seven times then went to voicemail.'

Jo shook her head. 'We didn't hear it.'

'What's going on? Is that what you were doing out there? I'm telling you, the phone isn't here.'

'Oh, the phone's here alright, or it *was* here, on the twenty-third of December, the day after Phoebe went missing. Or out in the street, or next door in your neighbour's, or in your garden at the back. So, can you tell us where it is, please?'

'Do you seriously believe Phoebe would set out on this… jaunt, and not take her phone with her.'

'No, I don't. Which is why I wonder how it got back here. That's why we need to understand the "circumstances" you mentioned before.'

'Oh, I see. Phoebe came back here. I did her in and buried her under the floorboards with her phone. Damn. I thought I'd got away with it.'

'I think, Mr Morrison, you should…'

Benny sprang to his feet, eyes wide. 'Wait. I wonder… Follow me.'

He led them upstairs to the bedroom, going to Phoebe's side of the bed and opening the drawer in the bedside cabinet. He lifted out a mobile phone case and removed the phone, screwing up his eyes to inspect it. He held it up so they could see.

'*Shit.*'

The two detectives exchanged glances. 'That looks suspiciously like a mobile phone, Mr Morrison,' Jo said.

Benny stared at it. 'Yes, but it's the wrong one.'

★

Jo, Mo and Eva were seated at the table in the briefing room close to the map on the incident board. Right now their focus was on the screen of Jo's iPad and the faces of Andy Mills and Geoff Brazendale in the mobile command vehicle on the moor. The search was barely under way and the light was already fading, so there was nothing to report so far except that a nightshift of two officers would take over from the search party to occupy the MCV between the hours of 6.00 a.m. and 6.00 p.m.

Jo shared the details of their meeting with Benny.

'Apparently, Phoebe has two phones. Her own personal one, which she carries all the time – except right now, it appears – and one provided by her employer. She must have her work phone with her because her personal one is at home. We can't access it yet because Morrison doesn't know the passcode, so it's with the techies. She's an ambulance driver, not for the emergency service but for transporting care patients, delivering them to hospital and GP appointments and taking groups from care homes out for the day.'

'She works for the NHS?' Eva asked.

'For a company *contracted* by the NHS. They quite often have to change her schedule at very short notice, so when she's working, she has to carry the phone at all times, but only uses it for work purposes. Mo?'

'Company's called Easy Rider. I tried to contact them, but no-one's answering; office closed until tomorrow. I left a message but we're trying to find someone to speak to today so we can get her work's phone number. Benny Morrison doesn't know the number, but he said it's a very basic phone, got no apps or anything. He believes it's so it's always ready to receive a call. I get the impression he doesn't know a lot about mobile phones. Sounds like a pay-as-you-go.'

'Anyway, when she's not working,' Jo continued, 'she keeps it in the drawer of her bedside cabinet. So, Benny says, when he was trying to work out what she had taken with her, he assumed the phone in the drawer was her work phone when, in fact, it was her regular phone. When we checked it today, it was switched on, and on silent, but the battery had run down, presumably sometime on Sunday, which is why they couldn't track its location after that. Mo phoned it while we were there and… well, nothing.'

'So, if the phone she took is a pay-as-you-go,' Eva said, 'there is no way we can get its location. And no way for anyone to contact her, other than through work. Which must have been the reason she switched the phones. Which makes it likely that she *has* done a runner and deliberately covered her tracks.'

'Eva Johnson,' Andy put in, 'specialist subject, the bleeding obvious.'

Jo ignored the comment. 'Got it in one, Eva. She set off to stay with someone. Have we got the addresses for all her close friends?'

'You're not seriously suggesting we get warrants to search all their houses?' Andy asked.

'You got it in one, as well, DS Mills. I'm *not* suggesting that. But if she's setting off across the moor towards... Hawkshaw, is it? – then we could eliminate anyone living in Helmshore or Haslingden or Ramsbottom.'

There was a minor interruption in the command vehicle as someone entered. Geoff moved off-screen then back again, holding up a blue rucksack.

'DC Brown has just brought this in, ma'am. Found close to where the Rosendale Way crosses the path to the Pilgrims Cross. It was on top of a dry-stone wall.'

Mo got up and pointed out the location on the map.

Jo nodded a thank you. 'A wall. Why would someone abandon a rucksack in full view like that? Is it damaged? Strap broken?'

'No, well used but in good working order. Good quality, too. DC Brown thinks someone may have spotted it some way off the track and put it there assuming the owner had left it by accident and would retrace their steps. Like you do if you find a kid's glove or toy on the pavement. You pick it up and put it close by where it's easy to see.'

'What's in the bag?'

Geoff spoke to someone off-screen. 'Nothing at all, ma'am.'

Jo remained silent for a few moments. 'I take your point, Sergeant, about someone placing it where it could easily be seen. Not sure I can understand how someone could forget to pick up a rucksack. It seems rather a large article to leave behind by accident.'

'I agree, ma'am, but if it was a group of walkers, sometimes they share rucksacks and take turns to carry one. Possibly someone missed their turn. Unlikely, though, in this case when the rucksack fits with the story of the missing girl.'

'What's your team doing now?'

'Maxi here – DC Brown – says they'll be concentrating the search in the area around the wall, but, of course, that might be some distance from where the bag was picked up. And we're running out of light for today. We'll carry on for another hour or so with torches, but after that we'd have to go over the same ground tomorrow, anyway. As we're putting out appeals for sightings of the girl, it might be an idea to ask for information about the rucksack. Like, would the person who placed it on the wall contact the police to let them know exactly where they found it. If that *is* how it got there.'

'That's a good idea,' Jo said, nodding towards Eva. 'Can you sort that?'

'Yes, ma'am.' She checked the time. 'Four forty-five. I guess I should do it now, if we want to get it on the six-thirty local slots.'

'Yes please.' She turned back to screen. 'Sergeant, could you send me some pictures of the rucksack. I'll show them to Morrison and Grimshaw. See if they recognise the bag. Thank you, Geoff, please carry on around that area for now and we'll get an appeal for information out as soon as we can. In the meantime, can you bag the rucksack and put it back at first light where you found it, with one of your team watching over it so we don't lose it. Just in case we're barking up the wrong tree and someone does come looking for it. Then send me a picture of it on the wall.'

There was a pause as Maxi left.

'Until we get the rucksack properly identified as the one Phoebe was carrying,' Jo said, 'it doesn't move us on at all. But if we assume it is, then this could be bad news. It seems unlikely someone would set off across the moor with a full backpack, only to discard it within a few hundred yards. And how did it come to be empty?'

'Unless she had a change of clothes in the bag, or additional clothes,' Andy suggested. 'Like a down jacket, for example. That would virtually fill the rucksack on its own. She puts on the jacket, transfers stuff she needs into a smaller bag, also in the rucksack, then ditches it and carries on, looking a lot different.'

'Makes sense, but why? Why not put the jacket on before she set off?'

'Perhaps to make sure that if someone saw her before she got clear away, they would give a wrong description. And somebody did, our Jack. Girl in a light fleece carrying a rucksack. Not anymore, possibly.'

'I really hope that's right, because the alternative scenario is grim. Intercepted or followed on the moor then robbed and very much worse.' She checked her watch. 'Okay, it's nearly five. Let's call it a day and save the guys' torch batteries. By the morning we may have the co-ordinates of where the rucksack was originally found if we get a response from the TV appeal. That's assuming we're right that it was moved. Thanks, guys, and thank your team from me, sergeant.'

Jo ended the chat and turned to Mo. 'Who needs Christmas anyway?'

Mo smiled. 'Certainly not me, ma'am.'

Jo laughed as her phone pinged with the arrival of the first photos of the rucksack. Eva entered the room.

'All set up, ma'am. They need to speak to you before quarter to six to check if you want to add anything to the earlier appeal.' She stuck a Post-it note to the table in front of Jo with a name and phone number on it.

'Okay, thanks Eva. You've not missed anything, and we're wrapping up for the day while there's still a bit of Christmas left.'

Jo's phone rang out with an incoming call. She checked the name on the screen and pressed the speaker key for them all to hear.

'Mr Morrison, what a coincidence, we are just about to send you some pictures.'

'Not Phoebe. Oh, God, no.'

'No, no, my apologies, that was a bit insensitive of me. We have no news yet as to where she is.'

'Oh, thank God. I mean, thank God it's not…'

'I know what you mean. Why were you calling me?'

'Look, after the confusion with the phones I decided to go right through the house again to check if anything else wasn't right and, guess what, there's a rucksack missing. It's mine, not Phoebe's. It's a really old one and it hangs on a hook in the back porch. But it's always covered completely by three or four coats hanging on the same hook. Anyway, it's gone. She must have taken it. I'm amazed she knew it was there. The coats haven't been worn or moved for months, certainly not since she moved in.'

'What colour was the rucksack?'

'Blue. Why?'

'I'm going to send you a couple of photos of a rucksack. I want you to tell me if it's yours.'

'So you have found something?'

'I'm sending them now. Take a look. I'll wait until you've seen them.'

Less than two minutes of complete silence later, Benny spoke in an excited voice.

'That's it, definitely. Is that good news or bad news? Where was it found?'

'Found on the moor close to where she was last seen. Good or bad news? We don't know yet, but it's good that you've ID-ed it. We have something more to work with. One question, Mr Morrison, that I meant to ask you before. Did you and or Phoebe keep a lot of cash in the house?'

There was a pause before Benny answered, as if he was working out the relevance of the question. 'I certainly don't. Not sure about Phoebe. I know she gets occasional tips from her customers, but I don't think it comes to much. Why do you want to know?'

'She hasn't used her cash card in the last few days – not that she would necessarily have done, anyway, over the holiday. It's just something we need to keep an eye on. Thank you for your help with the phone and the rucksack.'

Jo ended the call and Mo left the room to chase up contact details for Easy Rider.

'You know, DS Mills might be correct in his theory of her changed appearance,' Jo said to Eva. 'And if he is, I guess Phoebe must have intended going much further than one of her pals living locally. We need to widen the net tomorrow.' She looked at the map on the display board. 'If she wasn't heading for Hawkshaw, there'd be no reason to stay on the path over the moor. More likely she'd drop down to the main road. Tomorrow, we check buses along the route and local taxi firms. And depending on what we find, trams and trains as well. Also, we need a full sweep of CCTV around Bury later on Saturday. My ex-boss used to say he'd never met anyone as good as me at getting a feel for a case. Well, he'd be disappointed right now, because one minute I'm convinced Phoebe is lying dead somewhere and next minute that she's perfectly well and enjoying running us ragged.'

Eva smiled. 'Try to focus on that second possibility, ma'am, at least until tomorrow. And if we are thinking of trains, ma'am, perhaps we should get her face out on national news.'

'Not yet, unless, of course, we do spot her at a train station. But let's see what the search and the door-to-door reveals, if anything. And get the addresses of Phoebe's closest friends so we can start whittling down her possible hiding places around here.'

'Okay, ma'am. Well, then I'll bid you good night and...'

'Just before you go, would you take a look at this.' Jo led her across to her office and pointed to a whiteboard on an easel in the corner. 'What do you think of these? Three texts, from what I assume is a burner or burners, arriving on successive days. Any ideas?'

On the board were written the three messages, one beneath the other alongside the dates they arrived:

24/12 – 1
25/12 – 9
26/12 – 5;

Eva considered the digits for a long time. 'Do you think they're part of a series? The first three digits of a longer message?'

Jo picked up the marker and wrote them out in a line. *195;*

'I guess the semi-colon suggests it is, and that there will be more to come.'

'Can it be something to do with Phoebe's disappearance?'

Jo screwed up her face in concentration. 'I got the first clue just after I arrived here on Monday morning. Around nine o'clock, which was six and a half hours before Phoebe was reported missing. So, if it is related to her, whoever sent the text must have had something to do with her disappearance, or at least the plan to make her disappear.'

CHAPTER SEVEN

Thursday 27 December

Jo arrived at the station at 7.50 a.m. after sneaking out of the house for the second successive morning. Sally and Jonno were returning home today to Altrincham and she had been tempted to wake them to say goodbye, but they had looked so contented, asleep in each other's arms, that she decided against it. And anyway, they'd said their goodbyes the previous evening before they all retired to bed early, after a much more relaxed evening.

Mo and Eva were already there, checking through CCTV with the map from the briefing room on its easel close to the screens.

'You guys must really love this place,' Jo said. 'What have we got?'

Mo leaned back in his chair. 'Managed to get Mr Easy Rider's iPhone number yesterday. Josh Reeves was not impressed at being disturbed on Boxing Day; he hadn't seen the news and knew nothing about Phoebe Wright's disappearance. I asked him for the iPhone number he used to contact her and he gave me her private number. He said he doesn't know anything about a second phone, he always uses that same number.'

'So what's the second phone used for? Perhaps our Phoebe has hidden depths.'

Mo shrugged. 'Maybe.'

'Anything from the TV appeal?'

'Not yet,' Eva said. 'It's going out again this morning.' She nodded to her screen. 'This is from the security camera at the Shoulder of Mutton last Saturday. It covers the car park but it takes in the bus stop as well. Jack Grimshaw saw her at around seven-thirty heading up onto the moor. If she'd dropped down to the lower track straight away once she was out of his sight, a fast walk or a jog would get her to the Shoulder around eight o'clock earliest. So, we've started looking from ten to eight – *just* started, in fact.'

'And have you seen anyone arriving at the pub?' Jo asked.

'No, but the cameras don't cover the main entrance.'

'Inside the pub?'

'No cameras.'

'I thought they had to have cameras now to get a licence'

'New pubs applying for a licence, yes,' Eva said. 'Older, established pubs don't have to have CCTV unless they have a lot of trouble with fights and stuff, then we can suspend licences until they instal them. The cameras covering the car park are there because the manager chose to have them. Cameras inside can be really bad for business if punters know they're being watched. Especially if you're supposed to be somewhere else.'

Jo smiled. 'So, what exactly are we looking for?'

'Phoebe getting into a car or onto a bus,' Mo said. 'That time of the evening, buses were every thirty minutes at ten past and twenty to the hour. So, if it's on time…' he nodded at the screen '… we're twelve minutes away.'

'It's a real long shot but if she was planning to go further afield, there are three bus stops along that stretch of Lumb Carr Road, close to places where there are paths down from the track.' Eva turned to the map. 'Here at Chatterton Close, here at Higher Tops near Harcles Hill Farm, and where the track meets the road at the Shoulder. There's no surveillance at the other two stops, as you'd expect on a remote stretch of country road, so this is the only one we can check.'

'Right.'

'Anyway,' Eva continued, 'she'd most likely be the only person boarding at that time at either of the other two stops, so she'd be easy to remember by anyone on the bus. So, we reckon it's unlikely she'd take that risk when she could mix with passengers getting on at the pub. The bus always fills up at this stop around that time with people heading into Bury and further into Manchester. She'd be one of a large, inebriated crowd who mostly wouldn't pay her any attention or remember anything about her.'

'All makes sense but assumes an awful lot,' Jo said. 'Not the least being that she got safely off the moor.'

'As we said, ma'am. It's a long shot.'

The door to the room opened and Andy entered.

'Morning. Any brownie points left or have you got them all with the early start?'

'Morning, sarge,' Eva replied. No-one else spoke.

'Watching tele, are we?'

'CCTV at the Shoulder of Mutton last Saturday,' Jo said.

'Why?' No-one answered. 'That's miles from where she was last seen.'

'One-point-six miles,' Mo said. 'Thirty-minute brisk walk.'

They all looked up as DC Kirsty Milner entered the room. 'Excuse me, ma'am, but we've already had a response about the rucksack.'

Jo checked her watch. 'God, that was quick. When did the second appeal go out?'

'Seven-fifty, ma'am, so, yes, that's really quick. A guy with a party of walkers on Sunday. He'd left the party briefly for a pee and found the rucksack stuffed behind a clump of grass. He said it looked like it was hidden rather than just left behind by accident, but didn't see any point in leaving it there. He's being picked up by one of Geoff's guys and taken to the MCV to show them on the map.'

'Thanks Kirsty. Is it far from where he placed the bag?'

'A few hundred metres, I think. The man said there was nowhere close to where he found it to display the bag.'

'So we've been wasting people's Christmas holidays looking in the wrong place,' Andy said.

'Keep us posted with any updates, Kirsty.' She turned to Andy as Kirsty left. 'Best get back to the MCV, sergeant. This new development needs local knowledge from the leadership.'

Andy glared and snorted. 'Sorry, not had my morning cuppa yet.'

'Tell you what, I'll check that the kettle in the command vehicle is still working while you're on your way there. We'll patch through to you anything we get from the cameras. Thank you.'

She turned back to the map, then the screen.

'Bus arriving, right on time,' Mo said.

The door slammed as Andy left.

'Right,' Jo said, 'check the exact time and the bus reg number if we can. Now, we watch and hope. Even if she is one of the passengers, I don't hold out too much hope of a pink woolly hat.'

The screen showed a few people who had been standing in the car park, mostly smokers, moving across to board. From the bottom of the screen, a crowd of fifteen to twenty people came into view heading for the bus.

'Slow now, Mo; edge it forward. We're looking for a nineteen-year-old woman wearing... whatever. Should be a cinch!'

The door opened and Kirsty popped her head in.

'Feed's come through from Interchange. I've added the link to the case file.'

'Thanks, Kirsty,' Eva said.

All eyes stayed focused on the screen. There were seven females who boarded the bus. Five were clearly part of larger groups, the other two appeared to be on their own. Mo paused the stream with the two single women clearly visible.

'Let's get stills of those two right away,' Jo said, 'and the others as well for completeness. None of them fit Phoebe's description as she was last seen. No long blonde hair.'

'No, but *some* hair,' Eva said.

'Meaning?'

'If you had distinctive long blonde hair, you'd hide it by tucking it out of sight into a cap or hood or, in this case, a *non*-pink woolly hat. Both the women who are on their own have their hair very visible.' She pointed to the screen. 'This one with short fair hair and no head covering, and this one with long dark curls hanging down from a baseball cap.'

Jo nodded. 'So, probably neither of them. What time is the next bus, Mo?'

'In real time, half an hour after this one, but right now whenever we want it. We can jump forward to eight-forty but we'd miss anything happening in the car park in between.'

'Like what?' Jo asked.

'Like Phoebe getting a lift somewhere from someone.'

Jo sighed. 'I know most police work isn't all that exciting, but this all seems a bit tenuous to be spending time on. Fast forward, anyway. We'll catch any vehicles arriving or leaving or both. And what was that about the Interchange that Kirsty mentioned?'

'Saturday evening's stream from the cameras at the Bury terminus. It should show us who got off at the end of the route and whether they went on from there.'

'On the Metro, you mean?'

'Or another bus ride but the tram will take you furthest and fastest if you're looking to put distance behind you.'

'Except we now know she didn't even get on the bus or that particular bus. What about taxis. Are we onto that?'

'Damon's checking local firms for anyone picking up along the road or at the Shoulder. Nothing so far or he would have been bursting in here, keen to impress.'

'Damon?'

'Detective Constable Damon D'Arcy,' Mo said, 'a.k.a. Deecy-D'Arcy. Back from holiday today. Part of the team.'

'Right, I'll go and make his acquaintance. I'll leave you to carry on, Mo. Get some help from the team if necessary. We've come this far so let's check the Interchange footage and see if we can ID anyone from the bus. And you might as well do the same with the next bus from the Shoulder, just for completeness. Eva, after I've seen Damon, you and I will drop in on the Wrights again to check if they can tell us anything more than they told you and DS Mills. Something they might have remembered in the last twenty-four hours. We'll be straight back here, Mo. Let's see if you can surprise us when we return.'

★

Phoebe's parents' house could not have been more different to where she cohabited with Benny Morrison. Jo estimated that the spacious through-lounge into which they were shown was quite a bit larger than the whole footprint of Benny's cottage. At one end of the room patio doors overlooked a long garden which dropped down in a series of lawned terraces to a large pond surrounded by a variety of mature trees. Jo and Eva settled into the two luxurious armchairs whilst Helen and Philip Wright sat close together holding hands in the centre of the matching four-seater sofa.

'Let me say right away there has been no more news about Phoebe's whereabouts,' Jo said, 'but we are following up a number of leads, one of which is the possibility of her leaving the area. Which is why we are keen to establish if she took anything with her when she visited you last Saturday. I know you told my colleague that she didn't take a bag when she left, but…'

'That's right,' Philip said. 'It wasn't that sort of departure. Whatever it was that triggered it, Phee just got up – she was sitting there where you are now – and charged out of the room.'

'I went after her,' Helen said, 'but she was already at the front door. Just grabbed her coat off the hall stand and left. Not a word.' She gave a little sob. 'I really don't know what we've done to deserve this.'

Philip squeezed her hand.

Jo and Eva exchange glances. 'You said she grabbed her coat from the hall stand?' Jo said. 'Our understanding is that she wasn't wearing a coat when she was dropped off at your house. Can you remember what she was wearing when she arrived?'

The couple hesitated. 'I remember we were out the back in the conservatory' Helen said. 'Phee let herself in with her key and came through. Now what was she wearing? Can you remember, Philip?'

'A light-coloured fleece, I think, jeans, boots, and, of course, the pink woolly hat – wouldn't recognise her without it, I don't think.' He gave a little laugh which quickly ended.

'But no coat?'

Helen shook her head. 'She wasn't wearing a coat when she came through to the conservatory. She must have taken it off in the hall and hung it up. Well, that's what we assumed, but you're saying she didn't have one when she arrived.'

'Not according to Mr Morrison who dropped her off.'

'Oh, him…' Helen rolled her eyes and looked away.

Philip squeezed her hand again. 'Come on, Helen, why on earth wouldn't he be telling the truth?'

'Your husband's right, Helen,' Jo said. 'There's no reason at all for Mr Morrison to lie about that. The coat must have been on the hall stand before Phoebe arrived. I assume that's a possibility, with Phoebe coming and going between the houses and moving her stuff from one to the other all the time. Wouldn't you agree?'

The Wrights appeared confused and exchanged searching looks before Philip replied.

'What do you mean by coming and going, and moving her stuff? She *never* comes to the house. We hadn't seen her for weeks – no, *months* – before Saturday. In fact, since she moved in with Benny, she only came back a couple of times in the days just afterwards to collect some of her stuff.'

Jo frowned. 'So the coat. Could that have been there on the hall stand before last Saturday? Would you necessarily have noticed if a coat had been taken? Could you check now for us, please?'

Helen and Philip got up and went through to the hall, before resuming their seats.

'There are about six coats hanging there,' Helen said, 'all bunched together.' She looked at her husband. 'I really don't know.'

'Anyway,' he said, 'what's this got to do with anything? It sounds a bit like clutching at straws to me.'

'Building a picture, Mr Wright, so we have a true description of Phoebe's appearance at the time she disappeared. Can you think what kind of coat it *could* be?'

'I have no idea,' Helen said. 'She has quite a lot of coats and jackets but I thought they were all at the other house. If she did leave one behind in the hall, I don't remember noticing it.'

'Okay, thank you, Mrs Wright – both of you. If you do remember anything, could you get in touch, please? I think you've got a contact number for Detective Sergeant Mills.'

Philip nodded towards Eva. 'Actually, it was this lady who gave us her card with a phone number.'

'I see. Then please contact DC Johnson if anything comes to mind about the coat Phoebe took from the hall. And before we go, can we just clarify one thing? You're saying that since Phoebe left home to live with Mr Morrison, you have only seen her a couple of times to collect the last of the stuff she needed, and that was just after she moved out. Is that right?'

'That's right,' Philip said, 'the last of the stuff except, it seems, for the coat she took on Saturday. And before you leave, can you please tell us anything you know about what has happened to our daughter?'

'As I said, Mr Wright, we are still building a picture. There is no evidence of anything bad happening to her, although it would be wrong of me to rule that out. But for now, we are assuming Phoebe is alive and well and may just feel she needs some space.'

Helen took a tissue from the pocket of her cardigan and dabbed her eyes. Philip struggled to speak. 'If that is the case, then it's a pretty cruel thing to do, if you ask me.'

Jo nodded. 'I would have to agree with you, Mr Wright, but right now, we must hope that is the case.'

It was just after midday when they left the Wrights and headed back to the station, Eva driving.

'Curiouser and curiouser...' Jo said.

'What's that?'

'Alice in Wonderland. *Phoebe* in Wonderland. If Morrison is telling the truth about Phoebe going AWOL on a regular basis, and she isn't going to her parents', then where the hell *is* she going? And wherever that is, is that where she is now?'

'I guess he could be lying, just to cover up what's happened now. You know, to take the urgency out of her disappearance by claiming it happens regularly. But why would he do that?'

'Unless he's got something to hide.'

'But he seemed genuinely upset...'

'Well he would be, wouldn't he? Let's say he confronted her somewhere on the moor and overreacted in a blazing row, accidentally going too far and doing her in... You'd expect him to be devastated, no acting required. He just invents the fact that she regularly takes off somewhere.'

'But he would know we'd find out she wasn't staying at her parents'. Right?'

'But that works in his favour. He claims Phoebe *tells* him that's where she goes, so the focus shifts onto her and what the hell she's playing at.'

'So do you think he *is* lying?'

'Well, he's not telling the truth, is he, but if he's saying what he genuinely *believes* is true, then he's not technically lying.'

'Just thought,' Eva said. 'If she's not visiting her parents, where are all these clothes and stuff going to and coming from?'

Jo shook her head. 'As I said, curiouser and curiouser.'

'Gut feel?'

'Nothing right now, except we need to speak to the boyfriend again.'

*

'This is interesting – well, a *bit* interesting.'

Mo was in the same place he was when they left and still scanning the CCTV capture. Only now he had two PCs on his desktop. He pointed to a bus pulling in at the terminus in Bury town centre on one of the screens.

'This is the same bus that picked up the crowd at the Shoulder, here arriving at Bury Interchange. We don't know how many people got on and off on the way. Most buses now have CCTV on board, but not this one. What we *can* see is that almost everyone who boarded at the Shoulder went all the way. And most of them entered the Metro station.' Further images on the other screen showed a noisy crowd boarding a tram. Mo went back to the screen showing the entrance to the station. 'This is the interesting bit. I said *almost* everyone from the Shoulder went through to the Interchange. This is just under five minutes after the bus pulled in and everyone got off. Watch this…' The stream showed a number of people arriving from different directions and entering the station. 'That woman there…' Mo paused the image '…is the one with the long dark curls and the glasses and the baseball cap who boarded the bus at the Shoulder. She goes on to get the next tram after the one her co-passengers boarded.'

Jo and Eva exchanged puzzled glances.

'You said something about it being interesting. I assumed by interesting you meant significant or relevant, in which case I'm missing something.'

'Me, too,' Eva added.

Mo shrugged. 'Well, she got off the bus before it reached the terminus, but was planning to take the tram from there anyway. So why not go all the way unless she was trying to throw someone off the scent? And I did say only a *bit* interesting.'

No-one spoke for a few moments.

'I think you might need a break, detective,' Jo said. 'She might have just needed a cashpoint or…'

'Well, no, ma'am. We can track her on CCTV from where she

got off the bus, on Bolton Street, to the Metro Link. She walked straight there and didn't stop anywhere. And anyway, we know she hasn't used her cash card.'

'Okay. Did she make a call on the way or send a text? Perhaps just a bit of privacy...'

'No, nothing like that. Just a fast walk from where she got off, straight to the station. Would you like to see the footage, ma'am?'

'No, thank you.' Jo smiled. 'That's very Hercule Poirot of you, Mo, but I'm still a bit unsure why you're interested in this woman. I thought we had eliminated her as a possible sighting.'

Mo sighed. 'I guess in the absence of anything exciting, something a bit interesting can grab you.'

'What about the next bus stopping at the Shoulder. Anything?'

'Nearly all lads piling on. Just two girls, one who could be related to you, ma'am, and the other to me. So certainly not our errant, pure white, blonde-haired Phoebe. We did check for taxis and a couple did pick up from the car park. All lads again. If they picked up at the front entrance, the camera wouldn't catch them but Damon still hasn't come up with anything through the taxi firms. Anyway, I doubt if she'd take a taxi if she was keeping a low profile.'

'Agreed. Well, we've got a bit of news, or at least a discrepancy between what the parents and Mr Morrison tell us. Benny claims Phoebe spends time, a couple of days at a time, with her parents in an effort to keep them sweet. He also says that while she is there, he is under strict instructions – his words, I recall – not to phone her because that would annoy them and undo any bridge-building she's done. Those *weren't* his words, but that's the gist. Mr and Mrs Wright, however, say Phoebe *never* goes there, and they told Eva at the previous meeting that the reason she went on Saturday was because it was Christmas and she felt she ought to make her peace with them for the sake of the season.'

'So, somebody's lying, and it's unlikely to be the parents,' Mo said.

'Agreed. So, two possibilities. One, Phoebe has lied to Benny about where she goes when she leaves him for a couple of days. That would fit with her telling him not to contact her while she's away. Or, two, Benny is just saying she spends time away to make her current disappearance seem like part of a pattern. If he is doing that, it must mean he's responsible, in part at least, for her disappearance.' Jo sighed, shaking her head. 'It's five days since she was last seen and, as we know, the chances of finding a missing person reduce dramatically with time. I think you're right, Eva, we have to get her on national TV.' She checked her watch. 'Twelve-fifty-five. Eva, you and I will drop in on Benny. See if you can track him down and arrange to meet him at, say, two o'clock. I'll set up the appeal on national TV and let the Wrights know before it goes out.

*

'All I can tell you is what she tells me.'

It was 2.20 p.m. and Benny was sitting in the back of the unmarked police car in the car park of the White Horse pub in Helmshore. Jo was next to him with Eva in the driver's seat twisting round to face them.

'So, how often does this happen, this being away for a couple of days?'

'Every three or four weeks, pretty regular. Usually a couple of nights.' He shook his head. 'But why move in with me, that's what I don't understand.'

'Meaning what, exactly?'

'It's obvious, isn't it? It's got to be another guy, or more than one guy. I can see it now. The way she is with the guys in the pub.' He was getting angry. 'They're *all* over her, *all* the time. And she doesn't exactly discourage them. She laps it up...'

'Hold on a minute, Mr Morrison – Benny. This is a missing person we're talking about. Missing for five days now, and over Christmas. How likely is it that she's spent that time at someone else's place?'

'So what are you saying? She's dead somewhere? Because that seems to me the only alternative to her spending that time at someone else's place. Or am I missing something obvious?'

'I meant at another lover's place. Whatever the reasons for her *regular* absences, it's unlikely that this is the same. For starters, she didn't tell you this time she would be away. Plus, it's been five nights not two, *and* her story about staying with her parents would hardly work over Christmas, would it? They would certainly try to contact her sometime during the holiday.'

Benny took this on board and was quiet for a while, then shook his head. 'Actually, I really *can't* believe she's spending that time with other guys. She does flirt a lot, but if I'm honest, it's all in fun. I get a bit riled at times, probably because I'm older than most of them – all of them, in fact. And, you've seen her picture, she's *really* beautiful. It would be weird if no-one paid her that sort of attention.'

'Tell us about her job, Benny. Is it possible that has anything to do with these absences?'

Benny frowned in concentration before answering. 'As I told you before, she picks up people from their homes to take them for treatment at hospitals and health centres. Also, from care homes and sheltered accommodation, and occasionally from hospitals, to take them to shopping centres, concerts – usually daytime concerts – and parks and stately homes and such. And to the coast as well, Blackpool and Cleveleys, I think. Giving vulnerable or sick people a safe day out. She seems to love it, but it never involves her being away overnight. It couldn't, because of the need for her passengers to get back.'

'How far does she go with these people? Is it just around Greater Manchester and Lancashire?'

'Mainly, but she's been as far as Buxton and North Wales. Chester a couple of times, and regularly over to Meadowhall in Sheffield. That's probably the furthest they go. But only day trips.'

'Does she have use of the minibus between trips?'

Benny laughed. 'It's actually a non-emergency ambulance and it's got that written on its sides, so it's not a vehicle you'd use privately, although sometimes she drives home in it so she's ready to use it the next day.'

'So, where is it now?'

'She's got time off over Christmas and New Year so it will be back at the depot. She only brings it home if she's using it the next day.'

Jo paused. 'You say this flirting is all in fun, but is there anyone in your crowd who you feel might be a bit more serious about her? Anyone you see as, shall we say, competing for her affection.'

'Out to screw her, you mean?'

'Not necessarily, it could be a case of true love, but if that makes the question easier to answer, then yes, anyone you feel who is out to screw her?'

Benny shook his head. 'I can't imagine *any* of them turning down the opportunity if it presented itself. That's the way we're made, isn't it? But we're a close-knit bunch of friends and I can't see it happening.' Benny smiled. 'Now if we were to end the relationship, you might very quickly see a queue forming.'

Jo smiled. 'But nobody special right now?'

Benny screwed up his face in thought. 'Perhaps Marlon. He seems to hang around her a lot. But he doesn't tend to flirt with her like most of the others. I guess he does seem more serious with her, but as far as I'm aware, he's never tried it on with her. As I say, as far as I'm aware.'

'That's Marlon Finch?'

Benny looked up with a start. 'That's right. What do you know about him?'

'Nothing, other than he was here last Saturday. He's just one of the names on a long list of people who we've spoken to. Do you have a problem with him?'

'*I* don't have a problem with him. I'm not sure if Phoebe has, when I think about it.'

'Well, he didn't come over as any different to any of the others we questioned. Thank you, Benny. We'll leave you to get back inside.'

Benny opened his door, hesitated. 'You will let me know if… when…'

'Of course. You'll be the first, *joint* first, with Mr and Mrs Wright.'

★

It was 3.15 when they left Benny's and the light was already starting to fade.

'Tell you what,' Jo said, 'let's walk from here to the MCV along the way Phoebe would have taken, just to get a feel for her escape route. What do you think?'

Eva looked down at Jo's feet. 'I see you have your sensible shoes on, so you might just make it. It will take us twenty minutes or more and it's a bit of a climb.'

'Not a path, then?'

'A path, but a steep one. And, to be honest, with the drop in temperature and slippery under foot, it might be a bit dodgy coming back down. But I'm game if you are, ma'am.'

'Okay, let's do it. We can cadge a lift back to the car. I'll pull rank if we don't get any volunteers.'

They set off along the road out of Helmshore, turning right at the White Horse pub onto Alden Road, the start of their climb. After about half a kilometre they turned up a tarmac drive on the left, turning right onto the path just before some wooden gates to a large private house. It was a long steady climb with some icy sections where the pathway was made up of large stone slabs. They passed the running water feature on the right known as Robin Hood's Well, pointed out by Eva, and finally reached the gateway where Jack Grimshaw had been the last known person to have seen Phoebe. They leaned on the wide metal gate to get their breath back. Just beyond stood the mobile command vehicle and generator that was the temporary headquarters for the search of the moor.

'Christ, how did they get that thing up here?' Jo asked.

'Well, not this way, that's a fact. They'd have come along the vehicle track from the south, but I believe they had to reverse quite a lot of the way.'

'I bet there was a whole lotta cursing going on. Are we anywhere closer to establishing an incident room in Helmshore? Just in case we decide to move the nerve centre a bit closer to the action.'

'Kirsty's on it, so it should be very soon.'

'She's pretty good, isn't she? Has she been with the team for long?'

'She was a uniform with us for quite a while... I'm going to have to tell tales again, I'm afraid.'

'Up to you, detective, I don't want you to say anything you can't live with. I assume we are talking DS Mills again? Remember, I've had sight of his record. It mentions an unnamed female uniformed colleague who put in for a transfer. Was that our Kirsty?'

'Yes, it would be. She moved to Salford, then applied for a transfer into CID and found her first posting would be back with us. They told her if she wanted, they'd offer her the *next* posting that came up but she accepted the position here. That was about five months ago. She told me there was no way she was going to run away from him a second time.'

'That took some balls. At least the first time she had some protection through a different chain of command. She seems relaxed and settled, though. Has it worked out okay?'

'Just about okay. There's always a bit of tension when they're working together, especially in a small group. And they've never been paired in an investigation. That's worked so far, but it restricts the flexibility within the wider team. It might not always be possible to keep them apart.'

Jo sucked in her breath through gritted teeth. 'Right, Eva. I'm going to fix that before I leave. That will be my legacy – at least, *part* of my legacy – when I move on from here. I'm not having my team disrupted and limited by a chauvinist, racist prick like that. Our secret, DC Johnson. Okay?'

Eva smiled. 'Okay, ma'am. I'll look forward to it.' There was silence for a few moments. 'By the way, any more cryptic clues?'

'None today. Not yet, anyway. Right, let's visit the nerve centre.'

They pushed their way through the gate and took the six steps up to the rear access door of the vehicle's incident room that sat, like a huge metal box, behind the cab.

A female uniformed officer was standing in front of largescale map of the area leaning against the wall. Andy was standing beside her, his hand resting on her shoulder. He stepped back quickly and turned towards them and the woman moved away from the map. She picked up her coat from a chair back and headed for the door.

Jo stepped in front of her. 'You alright, constable?'

'Yes, ma'am,' she said, flushing a little. 'Just need to get back to the search team.'

Jo stepped aside. 'Okay. Off you go.'

Andy shrugged and smiled. 'Would you like me to show you round our new police station? Won't take long.'

The inside of the MCV was set out like a small open plan office; a worktop along one side with half a dozen chairs facing laptops connected to power sockets, and a long narrow table occupying the other side, on which, leaning against the wall, was a whiteboard and a map. At the end furthest from the door was a collection of mugs, a kettle, and jars containing coffee and tea bags on top of a metal cabinet, in front of which was a surgical-type trolley displaying several items.

Jo nodded towards the map. 'You can show us what we've got so far.'

On the map there were a number of small round stickers, some red, but mostly green. On each one was a handwritten number. Starting with one, the highest numbered sticker was twenty-three. On the whiteboard, each number one to twenty-three had been listed, with a six-figure numerical reference beside it along with a brief note.

Andy smiled. 'This is really complex, so I'll speak very slowly. The stickers on the map show approximately where items have been found and bagged. Red for those which might relate to the misper, green for those that almost certainly don't. With me so far? Not going too fast?' Neither replied. Andy laughed and continued. 'On the board, here are the twenty-three listed items showing the grid reference point where each was found and a brief description. Now I know what you're thinking.'

Jo waited, raising her eyebrows with the unspoken question.

'You're thinking why red for go and green for no go? Surely it should be the other way round, but, hey…'

'Where are the items?'

'Perhaps I could show you where as part of the tour.'

Jo read from the board. 'The buff, the make-up pouch, the gloves…'

'Just one glove.'

'The head-torch, the tissues. Show me.'

Andy sighed, rolling his eyes. 'You don't want the tour, then?' He pointed the trolley at the end of the room. 'On there.'

'Let's get it over here near the map.'

Andy looked at Eva and swept his arm towards the trolley, inviting her to go and get it.

'Sergeant. Over here, now,' Jo snapped.

Andy hesitated a few seconds, as if considering how to react. He walked over to the trolley, sending it towards where Jo and Eva were standing with a hard shove. The trolley rolled across the floor,

Eva stepping in front of Jo to stop it before it reached her. Jo had not moved an inch, still considering the list of items. She reached into her coat pocket, removing a plastic bag containing a pair of surgical gloves which she slipped onto her hands.

'So these are *all* the red items?'

'Yes, just the five items,' Andy replied, seemingly deflated at his failure to antagonise his boss.

'Have forensics made an appearance yet?'

'No, they said they'll wait until we've got more for them to see. There are markers on the ground at the location of each find, so they can follow up anything they feel needs further sampling.'

Jo studied the map. The five red stickers were clustered together near an elevated piece of land called Beetle Hill. Jo pointed to it.

'That's close to where the rucksack was found by the walker, right?' She traced a line with her finger on the map. 'This is the path she was on where Grimshaw saw her. What is this one here?' She indicated a more prominently marked path.

'That's the Rosendale Way,' Eva said.

'And that goes down to the main track above the road to Helmshore, and then continues to the road itself. So, if these are her things, she might have set off across the moor to fool her dog-walker friend into thinking that's the direction she was headed, then made some sort of switch, put on a jacket she had in the rucksack, perhaps, then dropped down to the main track and… away.'

'Or she was attacked, robbed and killed and what we're finding is the aftermath of the robbery,' Andy put in. 'Or history repeating itself. Husband follows spouse onto moor and does her in. Hides the body under a pile of stones. Spooky.'

'You're not suggesting we might have a copy cat murder?' Jo asked.

'Er, no, ma'am,' Eva replied, 'that was a long time ago.'

'How long?'

Eva frowned in concentration as she calculated. 'About two hundred and sixty years.'

★

The incident room was buzzing with activity when they arrived back at just after 4.30 p.m. The late shift had arrived and the early crew were finishing their work for the day or passing it on to the incoming group. Several workstations were occupied by more than one person and the level of noise from the multiple conversations created a vibrant atmosphere in the room. Jo called Kirsty into her office.

'Any progress on a local incident room?'

'There are no police buildings in Helmshore or Haslingden, so the best we could do is Haslingden library. It's about two miles away from the White Horse and Phoebe's home and has off-street parking. They said we could have up to six reserved spaces. It's about ten miles, say, twenty-five minutes, from here.'

'That's good, the library it is if we need it. True crime section might be useful.'

Jo went over to where Mo was sitting glued to his screen, exactly where they had left him. She motioned for Eva to join them.

'I assume you have moved since we went, DC Malik.'

'Yes, ma'am. The gents, twice. I've tracked one of the two non-Phoebes who got the eight-ten bus from the Shoulder, as far as Piccadilly Train station.'

'Is that good, do you think? I mean in the context of this case, rather than as a successful exercise in CCTV usage.'

'Probably more the latter, ma'am. It's the curly one and she repeated the same trick as she did in Bury.'

'Remind me.'

'The tram she boarded in Bury went direct to Piccadilly train station. She didn't get off there, so I started backing up to each stop. She got off at Market Street. That's in the centre of Manchester. Loads of cameras around, but loads of people as well, so we lost her in the crowds. But, seven minutes later, she turns up at the train station. She buys a ticket, with cash, and boards the nine-fifty to London Euston, right on the minute as it was leaving.'

'Excellent, detective, and how exactly does that move us forward, case-wise?'

'I don't know – I mean, I guess it doesn't. It's just strange that she would get off the bus, then the tram, before they had each got to where she wanted to go. Like she was expecting someone might be waiting for her at the final stop.'

Jo sighed and sat down, silent with her thoughts for a long time. 'Let's go through to my office. But let's get a coffee first.'

When the three were seated round Jo's desk, she leaned back in her chair, hands clasped behind her head.

'There might be something in what you say, Mo, about getting off the bus and the tram before her destination. We know now, which we didn't know before, that our Phoebe disappears regularly for a couple of days at a time, so she must be pretty devious to keep that from Benny. We need to check out her friends again, but it doesn't seem likely that these absences are sleepovers with her mates. I think she's a bit old for that.'

Mo leaned forward. 'Jodi checked her friends' addresses like you asked, the ones in the White Horse crowd. Eleven in all – popular girl, not just with the lads. Most are local to Helmshore and Haslingden. Plus one in Tottington and a couple in Bury, but none of these last three are within walking distance of where she was last seen.'

'Okay, but we'll speak to them all anyway. This time about her other disappearances; if she's ever stayed with them in the past. Just a phone call to each, because I think we know the answer. And if we're right about the answer, and she isn't having sleepovers every few weeks, then our missing person becomes more of a mystery person. What could she possibly be doing which involves her being away from home, both homes, without letting those closest to her know where she is? Even if we find out, I'm not sure that will take us any closer to knowing where she is now. Or *what* she is – dead or alive.'

'Shall I get onto her friends now ma'am?'

Jo checked her watch. 'Five-twenty. Eleven phone calls, five minutes each; one hour, give or take. That would be good, DC Johnson, and by my calculation will complete a twelve-hour day. So, get off home after that and aim for a civilised start time in the morning. Nine o'clock, *earliest*. Right?'

'Oh, thank you, ma'am,' Eva said, wide-eyed with mock gratitude. 'Might even have time for some cornflakes.'

'Well, make the most of it, I'm stepping out of character for you just this once. And you, DC Malik. If there's nothing for you to do right now...'

'I was planning to check where curly-girl got off the train, just for completion. It makes five stops along the way – Stockport, Macclesfield, Stoke, Milton Keynes and Watford junction. I've requested the capture from each, plus Euston, so I'd better stay back and wait in case someone is working late at one of those places to get it to me.'

'Okay, but let that be where your tracking her ends today. The CCTV record will still be there tomorrow. I'm going home, my *temporary* home. Can I access the coverage online? Can you set that up so I can watch on my laptop?'

'No problem, ma'am. I'll email you a link.'

'Then I'll bid you both goodnight with thanks for a marathon day's work.'

*

The call was taken at the police station in Blackburn town centre at 10.23 p.m. and three patrol cars were diverted to the scene of the disturbance. When they arrived, the mayhem had ceased, to leave a simmering stand-off between two groups of males. Some young women were being comforted just outside the main door of the pub, but they seemed more distressed than injured. The arrival of an ambulance had proved to be the calming influence on the earlier event.

The uniformed sergeant in charge established that only one person was inside the ambulance being treated for cuts and bruises to his face and head, and a few others were sitting on the ground at the back of the vehicle, holding bloody swabs against their foreheads, noses and ears. One paramedic was securing a sling around the arm of another man. The police began to round up the rest of the crowd and organise them into small groups for interviewing. The girls moved back into the pub. The sergeant followed them in.

The place had been wrecked. Bar staff and customers were in the process of standing tables up again and putting seats back in place. Some of the chairs were damaged with broken legs and backs. Bottles, some not yet emptied, and broken glasses were scattered around the floor and splinters of glass were strewn over a wide area.

There were traces of blood on the floor near the door and on one of the table tops.

'So, what's the story, Jonny?' the sergeant asked.

'Argument over a girl, two at it like cage fighters then everybody else pitches in on one side or the other. Completely out of the blue. I mean, these are my regulars. This is their local; never been any trouble before. I don't know why it happened; I was changing a barrel downstairs and heard shouting and glass breaking and came charging back up. There were chairs and bottles flying and guys on the ground.'

'We've started taking statements so we'll get to know what sparked it. Who were the first two? We'll take them in and they can cool down overnight in a nice little police bedsit. Where are they?'

'Outside with the paramedics. One of them got a good beating; the one who started it. Come with me, I'll introduce you.'

The two men went outside where an unmarked police car had arrived . One of the occupants, in civilian clothes, was talking to the injured man in the ambulance and one of the others who was now standing but still nursing a wound to his forehead.

'Those are the two,' the landlord said. 'The ones who kicked it all off.'

The new arrival spotted the sergeant and waved him across. Detective Inspector Alistair Crossley was a large man. A little under six feet tall, broad and muscular, he had the appearance of a rugby union front row forward. His rugged features and rather flattened left ear added to the image.

'One will need a visit to A&E for some stitches, sergeant, then they're both for the cells,' he said. 'But we need to decide *whose* cells.'

CHAPTER EIGHT

Friday 28 December

The incident room was a picture of calm at 7.30 a.m. compared with the energy of the previous afternoon during the shift changeover. Jo picked up a coffee on her way through to her office, noting only Kirsty of the early crew was at her workstation, concentrating so hard on her screen that Jo's hearty 'good morning' made her jump.

'Oh, morning, ma'am. Sorry, miles away.'

Jo settled into her chair and placed the coffee on the desk in front of her, determined to have a gentle start to the day. Less than fifteen minutes later Eva knocked and poked her head round the office door.

'Morning, ma'am.'

Jo looked at her watch, frowning and holding it close to her eyes in mock confusion. She tapped it with her finger.

'I don't know what's wrong with this thing. It's showing seven fifty-five and I know it must be at least nine o'clock...'

'Actually, ma'am...'

'Don't tell me. The clocks have gone forward, or is it back?' She frowned. 'I did mean it, you know, DC Johnson. Nine o'clock earliest.'

'I know. Sorry, ma'am. Didn't sleep too well, so... you know how it is.'

Jo sighed. 'I do know. I didn't either. I had this bizarre dream where I was surrounded by hundreds of TV monitors and DC Malik's head was in every one wearing an old-fashioned railway porter's hat and blowing a whistle.'

Eva laughed. Mo put his head round the open door.

'Am I missing something?'

'After yesterday, DC Malik, I can't imagine you missing *anything*.'

Andy arrived at his work station then walked across. 'Lots of merriment in here. What's the joke? Has a body turned up or something?'

'DC Malik,' Jo said, 'take DS Mills through the footage of the two girls from the Shoulder. See what he thinks. Don't keep him too long though, I'm sure he'll be wanting to get back to the MCV as soon as possible.'

'Actually,' Andy said, 'forensic are on site and I've terminated the search, sent the guys home pending their report, so...'

'You mean that's what you're *recommending*?' Jo interrupted, barely containing her anger. She turned to the two DCs and nodded towards the door. 'I'll see you in a few minutes.'

The two officers seemed more than willing to leave at that point. They closed the door behind them. Andy sat down and smiled across the desk at Jo.

'What the fuck is going on here, Mills?' Her voice was soft and matter-of-fact. 'Is this personal or just another chapter in your bigotry against anyone who isn't male or white. In which case, I would agree that I'm a sort of bonus target.'

Andy held his smile in place. 'I'm sure I don't know what you mean. I'm struggling to understand what I've done to bring on such a libellous attack. And you're suggesting that *I'm* somehow out of line. Accusations like that are not exactly going to establish a good working relationship.' The smile had disappeared and there was anger in his dark eyes. He got to his feet. 'It might be best if I leave now before we say things we regret.'

'*Sit down, sergeant.*' Jo realised her voice must have carried because several faces in the operations room turned towards her office. 'We need to sort this out now,' she continued, in a low voice. 'And you know exactly what I mean – your hostility towards me ever since I arrived. We are looking for a missing person. That has to take priority over your discontent at having to report in to a black, female boss. And one with no local *fucking* knowledge.'

Andy lowered himself slowly onto his chair. 'Hostility? I really don't know what...'

'Indifference, then, mocking indifference.' She leaned across the desk and held his eyes, finding it hard to control her anger and keep herself from shouting the words. 'This is the second time a black women has got in the way of a promotion, isn't it? The first one had the temerity to get herself beaten up by you and then complain about it. Selfish bitch. And the second one... well, here I am, guilty as charged. But who's really to blame in both of those two cases? A certain Dark Satanic Mills, a good detective with a bad record when it comes to tolerating diversity. I didn't request a transfer here, sergeant, but I believe we have an excellent team out there and I'm very much looking forward to working with them. And no individual is going to spoil it for me. I want you on my side, but if you're *not* on my side, then you're just in the fucking way, and I won't have that. It's up to you.'

Jo leaned back in her chair and spread her arms, inviting him to speak. Andy sat in silence for a full half-minute, his expression blank and giving no indication as to how he had received Jo's message. When he spoke it was in the same quiet tones of his superior.

'Full marks for your homework. You've certainly done a lot of digging and perhaps I should feel flattered that you've taken the trouble.' He held up a hand as Jo leaned forward again. 'But you're not the only one who's been digging up the past. Detective Sergeant Jo Cottrell, half of the dynamic duo of Gerrard and Cottrell, who famously arrested John Deverall, the killer of the Brady brothers in East London five years ago. Quite the celebrities for a while; so that bit didn't take much research. What was less famous, in fact, not reported at all and hardly mentioned on your record, was your part in the death of the Enderby family. A father, mother and small child in your charge who drowned off the coast of Essex because you let them slip away in the night past police surveillance. In fact, it seems there was no surveillance at all. Tell me if I'm wrong.'

Jo felt herself go cold. She struggled to retain her expression and posture when her whole body wanted to sag into as small a space as possible. It took her a long time to respond, but when she did her composure had returned.

'Full marks for your homework as well. You are *not* wrong. An error of judgement I have had to live with, which I am sure will follow me around for the rest of my career – the rest of my life, in fact.' She paused, detecting the faintest expression of regret in her sergeant's eyes. He looked briefly away before speaking.

'Look,' he said. 'We are where we are. These things are in the past and we have both moved on. You'll get the support you need from me, but I am not good at hiding my feelings and I'm no yes-man. So don't expect smiling compliance all the time. We *will* work together, but I don't have to like it. Now, can I leave.'

Jo paused. 'Only if you go straight to DC Malik and check the CCTV capture.'

Jo continued sitting completely still at her desk after Andy had left, reliving that terrible day. She had never forgotten, or stopped thinking about, the incident he had referred to. An eight-year-old boy, who had gone missing after a fatal shooting on the Cullen Field Estate in East London, had turned up back at his parents' house as if nothing had happened. Jo, who was a local detective sergeant at the time, had visited them that same evening with a family liaison officer and had informed the parents that they would need to question the boy about his involvement in the shooting. As the child had been asleep at the time of their visit, Jo had decided to leave them until the following day. During the night, the family had left their house and driven to a caravan site on the coast near Southend. The following day, all three had been cut off and drowned by the treacherous in-rushing tide.

Although it was by no means certain that they had taken their own lives rather than have their son taken from them again, eye-witnesses to the drowning reported seeing them standing calmly together as the sea rose around them. Whatever the circumstances, what Jo knew for certain was that if she had arranged for surveillance on the house overnight, the family would almost certainly be alive today. Her boss and mentor, DCI David Gerrard, had pointed out that if they were determined enough to drive to Southend to end their lives, they would have found another way if that avenue had been closed to them. In spite of that, the pain and the guilt had never left her.

She remembered with pride and affection her close relationship with David and how that had been so important for their success. As the new girl here, she would have appreciated such support from an existing and experienced number two. On the other hand, she felt the battle had to be fought and was pleased that both parties knew where they stood with the other. Only time, and a very short amount of time, would tell whether the situation had been retrieved, or even improved. She wasn't planning on holding her breath.

Eva peered in through the open office door. 'Just been swept aside by a departing detective sergeant, ma'am. Will I be safe in here?'

Jo's face was devoid of humour. 'I hope he was departing in the direction of the television lounge to watch the DC Malik Show.' Her mobile beeped with an incoming text. 'Well, would you believe it?' She held the phone up so Eva could see the screen. Eva screwed up her eyes to read the single digit.

'Seven.'

Jo got to her feet and walked over to the whiteboard resting on the easel, adding the digit to the three earlier ones.

195;7

'Any ideas?' Eva shook her head. 'No? Okay, let's come back to that later. What's new?'

'Not sure you'll like this, ma'am. We have Benny Morrison and Marlon Finch in the holding cells.'

'*What?*' Jo said, wide-eyed.

'Big fight last night at the White Horse in Helmshore. Benny found out about Marlon following Phoebe when she left the pub. Accused him of attacking her and, well, killing her and dumping her body.'

'That's a giant leap for mankind, following her to killing her.'

'I believe large quantities of alcohol had been consumed by both parties and almost everyone else present. The fight started with pushing and shoving and developed into bottles and furniture. And it appears their confrontation quickly polarised the allegedly close-knit set of friends that Benny described into two warring factions. The place was badly smashed up, as was Benny – he spent four hours in A&E at Fairfield before being brought here. Actually, it was Blackburn that got the call and attended the scene, but when they realised who the main combatants were and that they were fighting over Phoebe, they figured we should question them as part of our enquiry.'

Jo leaned back. 'That was good of them, wasn't it?' She was on her feet and pacing. '*Shit*. This is going to look like we told Benny about Marlon.' She turned to Eva. 'Which we didn't, did we? He mentioned Marlon first, the last time we spoke to him, and we said very specifically that he was just one of the crowd we talked to; nobody special. Right?'

'Absolutely right. It was Benny who said he felt Marlon behaved differently towards Phoebe than the others. Probably preyed on his mind and – well, you know how things get distorted when you've had a lot to drink. And, by the way, the pro-Marlon faction were keen to point out to Benny that no-one could vouch that *he* hadn't left the pub during the evening. And, after all, he was the one who had a problem with Phoebe at the time when everyone else was being nice to her.'

'I assume the uniforms took statements last night. I guess we should talk to them both seeing how they've taken the trouble to come and see us.'

'Just a thought, ma'am. What about getting DS Mills to see them with another one of the team. Different faces might get different information. I remember it from a course I was on a while back. They won't be *quite* as careful about remembering what they've said in the past if they're not faced with the same people.'

'I think I've been on the same course. Makes sense, or *would* make sense except for what has just passed between me and the sergeant. But, worth a try, I guess. No point in spending a tight police budget on training courses if we don't apply the lessons we learn from them. Would you send DS Mills through, please, Eva? Second thoughts, *I'll* get him. You get me copies of the statements the uniforms took last night?'

Jo and Andy went through the statements in near silence along with DC Jodi Lawson, passing each one round and back to Andy. Jodi was Indian, and attractive in the classical way of the sub-continent; slim, graceful, with sharp features and large, beautiful eyes.

'Might I suggest,' Andy said, 'that we see them together.'

'Why?' Jo asked.

'Right now, I reckon they'll still be really pissed off with each other. We might be able to capitalise on that if we can play one off against the other, get a few accusations flying around. Something might get said in anger that they've kept quiet about so far. It's worked before – for me, anyway.'

'Not for me,' Jo said, 'but that's because I've never tried it. Makes sense, good idea. Two in with two – you okay with that?' Andy turned to Jodi. 'Okay, DC Lawson?'

'Sure.'

'Good,' Andy said. 'I think we're ready.'

★

Marlon and Benny were seated side by side across the rectangular table from Andy and Jodi. They had decided on one of the more informal rooms off the reception area with vertical blinds on the glass panelled wall and a plain solid wall opposite, so there was no hint of one-way glass and hidden observers. Marlon looked dishevelled and pale, with slight bruising around one of this eyes. Benny had been the clear loser in the encounter with a cut above his one open eye, bruising to his cheek and chin, and a bandaged left hand.

Since the two men had entered the room, already occupied by the detectives, there had been complete silence for over eight minutes while Andy went through the sheets of paper on the table in front of him. From time to time he looked up at one or the other of them with an impassive expression and an occasional shake of the head. After finishing with each page, he passed it to DC Lawson, who mimicked his focus and intensity. Finally, Andy gathered the papers together again and looked up, moving his attention from one to the other several times before speaking.

'Okay, guys, let's stop pissing around. Which one of you killed Phoebe Wright?'

'*What?* That's fucking ridiculous.' Benny half rose from his chair.

'Sit down, Mr Morrison, and please do not use language like that in front of DC Lawson.'

Benny slumped back onto his chair and looked across to Jodi.

'Sorry.'

Jodi remained stone-faced, showing no acceptance of the apology. Andy turned to Marlon.

'So, it must be you, then.'

Marlon smiled, without humour. 'Six days since Phoebe went missing and you've got nothing, have you? Not a thing. So, it's desperation time – wild accusations…'

'Got nothing, you think,' Andy said. 'Let me tell you what we've got. We've got one guy…' he pointed at Benny '… who had a blazing argument with her, who was attacked with a bar meal, humiliated in front of all his mates and who seems to have slipped away during the evening when everyone was watching the tele.'

'Hey, just a…'

'Shame, you missed a good match in spite of a shit referee. Some of those decisions in the second half. Christ.'

'Look, I watched the match, all the way through.'

'So, what did you think of the referee?' Andy said, matter-of-factly.

Benny relaxed a little with the change of subject and tone. 'Crock of shit, like you said. Don't know where they get some of them from. And you're right, even with VAR, some of those decisions…'

'Such as?'

'What?'

'Give us an example of one of the decisions that helped you reach the conclusion that the ref was a crock of shit.'

'Well… there were so many.'

'Should be easy to remember just one, then. The disallowed goal, for example?'

'Yes, there was that…'

Andy screwed up his eyes in a frown, turning to Jodi.

'Did you see the match, DC Lawson?'

'Twice, sir.'

'*Twice?*'

'I was on duty as a volunteer steward inside the ground *at* the match, then watched it with my brother on iPlayer the next day.'

Andy smiled. 'Aren't the stewards supposed to be facing the *crowd* all the time when the game is in play?'

'Yes, sir, but sometimes you get sort of turned around.'

'I *see*. So, tell me, what did you think of the disallowed goal?'

'There was no disallowed goal, sir.'

'Really? Could you have missed it, do you think?'

'Look, alright, alright.' Benny did stand up this time. 'I did slip out of the pub. I went to the gents and didn't go back into the bar. I went outside and walked around. I was thinking about what a mess I'd made with Phoebe. Okay?'

Andy made a very deliberate study of the papers in front of him. The silence lasted over a minute before he looked up again.

'You've had three previous meetings with our colleagues and not once did you mention that you left the pub. Why is that?'

'Because it's irrelevant. I was just mooching round outside. I might as well have been inside the pub for all the difference it makes.'

Marlon snorted a laugh. 'Well, *well*...'

'And as for you, Mr Finch,' Andy turned to the other man, 'we all *know* you followed her home, that you fancy the young lady, and that you were lurking out on the moor at the time she set out across it on her own. Stop me if any of this is wrong, by the way.'

'Quite a lot of it, actually. I did not *follow* her home; I walked part of the way with her. Are you suggesting I then went to wait for her on the moor? How could I possibly know she would be heading out that way? At that time of night, it's just about the last thing you'd expect anybody to do.'

'She might have told you what she planned to do.'

'Well, she didn't and...'

'Okay, here's a scenario. You *did* walk her home and she told you to piss off and stop bothering her – that's what *you* said she said, wasn't it?'

'She didn't tell me to piss off, she said she was okay to walk home the last bit on her own.'

'That's pretty much the same thing in my experience.'

'It was nothing like...'

'So you hang around wondering what to do next and, guess what, it's your lucky night, because out she comes and heads off out of Helmshore, up Stakes Lane towards Holcombe Moor. You follow her again, managing to dodge the friendly dog walker – easy to stay out of sight at that time, even with a full moon – and catch up with her near where the Rossendale Way crosses the path. She tells you to piss off again, but you're not taking "no" for an answer this time. Do you want to finish the story?'

Marlon sprang to his feet and banged his fist down hard on the table, wincing a little from the impact. 'That's a load of fucking bollocks...' he turned to Jodi '... and that comes *without* an apology. And who was it who knocked on Benny's door later that night and shouted through the letter box, while I was out on the moor strangling his girlfriend?'

'Was that how you did it?'

'*No*, I'm just saying...'

'Knocking on the door was a master stroke, I must admit. After you've done the deed, you hurry back to the house, knock and shout, loud enough so the neighbours will hear. They'd automatically assume that Phoebe must be inside but just not answering the door. And from there it's just a few minutes and you're back in the pub.'

'That's absolute *shite*!'

Andy looked at Jodi and shrugged. '"Absolute shite," he says, DC Lawson. What do you think?'

'A few minutes ago Mr Finch suggested we had nothing. I think we've got quite a lot. *Two* suspects with the means, the motive and, now we find, *both* with the opportunity.'

★

'So, what do you think?'

Andy and Jodi had joined Jo and Eva in the DI's office.

'Neither of them did it,' Andy said. 'If, indeed, there is an "it" that has been done.'

Jo sighed. 'Okay. So, you favour the run-away-and-hide scenario?'

Andy shrugged. 'Rucksack says that's what she *planned*, so, yes, I favour the hide-and-seek theory. Question is, did she set out to do that but never made it? But, whatever; those guys didn't do anything.'

'In your *opinion*.'

Andy looked away. 'That's all any of us have to offer right now.'

'Okay. Did you get to see DC Malik's pictures?'

'Just started when you pulled me in.'

'Okay, can you get back to them and see if anything hits you that we missed.'

Andy stood up and saluted. 'Aye, aye, ma'am. Permission to call for a pee on the way.'

'If you must,' Jo said, unsmiling, 'and let me know when you hear from forensics.'

Andy turned and marched from the room.

Jo turned to Jodi. 'Anything to add, detective? How do *you* think it went in there?'

'I agree with the sarge, ma'am, I don't believe either are involved directly with Phoebe's disappearance. He gave then a pretty hard time in there. They were very uncomfortable, but I don't believe they had anything to hide.'

'What do you mean by "involved directly"? What would constitute indirectly?'

'Well, if Phoebe had just got fed up with the whole set-up. Benny taking her for granted as "one of the gang", I think he said in one of his interviews , and the rest of the gang, including Marlon, sucking up to her all the time with their tongues hanging out. I'm *assuming* only their tongues.'

Jo and Eva laughed. 'So where are they, our battling knights? I guess we should let them go.'

'Not yet, ma'am,' Jodi said. 'They're facing charges of violent behaviour in a public place and criminal damage to the pub. That will probably feel like a lottery win so soon after being accused of murder.'

'Okay, but could you make whoever is dealing with them aware that Benny Morrison's two teenage daughters are travelling up from Leicester today to stay with him over New Year. Let's ensure he can be there to receive them. He's going to have enough trouble explaining how he got his new face.'

Jodi left the room. Jo and Eva were silent for a few moments.

'I've been wondering, Eva, has our friendly sergeant ever tried it on with you? Not that you need to tell me. It's none of my business, as long as it doesn't impact on the team.'

'A bit more than tried it on, ma'am. We were an item for a while. Only a short while, six months or so, soon after he arrived. I mean, whatever he's like *inside*, his *outside* is pretty attractive, don't you think?'

'Definitely. A very attractive guy, physically. He must have to work very hard to overcome that and be so *un*attractive overall.'

Eva snorted a laugh. 'When he arrived, the girls thought it was Christmas come early. Actually, come to think of it, it was mid-December, so not all that early. I guess we all wondered which of us he might go for, like a bunch of schoolgirls. Pathetic, really, but we'd just given up on our previous fantasy target, Jamie Taylor, the new forensic scientist, a.k.a. Dr Dish. He's just *perfect*, by the way, there's no other way to describe him. I must introduce you to him soon. Anyway, when Andy arrived he looked like a half-decent second prize, so the hunt was on again. I *seemed* to be the lucky one until I realised he was chasing just about every female officer at Bury station, CID *and* uniform.'

'So you threw him out?'

'Well, he wasn't really *in*. He stayed most nights at my place, but had his own pad, very close to where you are now, at The Spinnings in Summerseat. He's still there, as far as I know. I confronted him and said I thought we should finish it and he just sort of shrugged and said "okay", and that was it. He never mentioned it again, ever. The relationship meant absolute zero to him.'

'I'm really sorry, I shouldn't have…'

'Don't be sorry, ma'am. I've never before got over somebody so quickly and completely. But I guess that's probably why I felt bad about betraying him, telling you about his history. Incidentally, I only found out about him, like you did, checking his record after we'd finished. Felt like a lucky escape. I have to say, though, he can be a lot of fun as well. At our parties at Christmas or for birthdays or whatever, he puts on his cowboy accent and dresses the part. His favourite party piece is his Doc Holiday impression. You know the scene from *Tombstone* where he juggles with the little whisky cup in the saloon in front of Johnny Ringo. He's really good, although I think he looks more like Johhny Ringo than Doc Holiday. You know the film?'

'Do I? My ex-boss is a western fanatic and pretty much ordered me to watch a whole list of his favourite movies ostensibly so we had something other than work to talk about. And, yes, Andy does remind me of Johnny Ringo, who I have to admit I really fancied, baddie though he was.'

They were silent for a moment, smiling with their own thoughts of another time.

'And he's a bit slippery, as well.' Eva laughed at the memory. 'I told him the date of my birthday, twelfth of June, and not to forget it. I wrote it down for him in his notebook. *Eva's birthday, 12/6*. Anyway, he missed it and when I challenged him about it he said when he checked he assumed it was the sixth of December, because Americans always put the month first. Like 9/11 – eleventh of September.'

'So, what about my big speech, about sorting him out before I leave. What do you *really* think about that?'

'One hundred per cent behind you, ma'am. Although part of me would like to see him survive.'

★

Jo spent the late morning and early afternoon checking the case notes on file, and discovered that the forensic report was in, although not flagged by Andy as she had requested. She read his entry, summarising the main points.

Early forensic report confirms, through finger-printing, that rucksack had been used by Phoebe. Other less distinct prints found – up to three sets. Two sets would presumably be Benny and the person who found it on the moor. These can be eliminated by taking prints from the two people concerned. DNA results will take a couple of days but may not be necessary for progressing the case.

Trace prints on individual items suggested no-one except Phoebe had handled more than one item. Phoebe's prints were on all items. Two possibilities:

1. Phoebe herself had removed them from the rucksack – hide-and-seek scenario.

2. Someone wearing gloves had removed them, searching for something worth stealing – worst-case scenario.

Jo sighed. Which does nothing to point the way forward, she thought. Six days since Phoebe disappeared and this latest piece of information firmly put them right back at the start of the investigation with '*Possibilities 1. and 2.*' Even so, she was becoming more and more persuaded that Phoebe had done a runner and was using skills and experience to cover her tracks gained from her regular disappearances.

She checked her watch – 2.20 p.m. She was planning an early finish to meet up with Seb and view a property in Bury for her to rent during her assignment period. She left the office, where Mo was still checking the CCTV capture in the operations room. There was no sign of Andy.

'So, detective, anything else that's a bit interesting?' she asked Mo.

'Nothing except what the sarge pointed out.'

'Which was?'

'He said the face didn't seem to go with the hair.'

'Whose face and whose hair?'

Mo turned to a screen, which showed an enlarged still of the girl with the curls just outside the entrance to the Metro station in Bury.

'The one I followed from the Shoulder through to Piccadilly Station. The sarge said the hair didn't go with the girl's features. Said the hair looked sort of Caribbean. Wrong texture for a delicate face. And I really don't think he was being racist, ma'am. Not on this occasion.'

Jo thought the "not on this occasion" spoke volumes. 'So, a wig, is that what he thinks?'

'I guess.'

'Where is he, by the way?'

'Left, ma'am. I thought he would be checking in with you about what he'd seen.'

'Left for where? Did he say?'

'No, ma'am. Shall I contact him and find out?'

'No thank you, detective. I think that's my job.' She sighed. 'But for another day.'

★

Jo and Seb met the estate agent to view the property later that afternoon. A neat, terraced cottage on the very edge of Burr's Country Park, it was just about close enough to be able to walk to the police station, although she felt it was unlikely she would ever do that, and at the start of a lovely country trail which would take her through the park to Summerseat and beyond to Holcombe. A walk which she might often enjoy in linking up with her in-laws.

The owners of the property had recently retired and were taking what the estate agent called a 'gap year' to visit their children and families in New Zealand and Canada and take the opportunity of exploring the world in between. The downside, however, was that they required whoever rented the property to commit themselves for the full twelve months. Leaving within that period would require the tenant to pay the balance in full. Jo had no idea how long she would be on her current assignment and, although the estate agent assured her it was unlikely that the owners could enforce that condition, Jo felt it would be inappropriate for a senior police officer to be seen wriggling out an agreement, legal or not. They told the agent they would discuss it that same day and let her know within twenty-four hours.

'No rush,' the agent said. 'The office will be closed from six o'clock today until after New Year. Open again on Wednesday the second of January.'

★

'What about this for an idea?' Roy Carter cut across the discussion which had been circulating, without any promise of a meaningful conclusion, for over half an hour since they had finished their evening meal. 'Why don't Bella and I rent the property for the full year. You can occupy it, of course, Jo, for as long as you need to, and pay the rent, or put it on your assignment expenses, but when you leave, if it's before the end of the year, we can use it as a sort of guest house for friends coming to visit us up to the end of the tenancy. That's assuming, of course, that the owners will allow that.' He smiled. 'But, don't forget, Jo, you are welcome to stay here with us for as long as you like. So, this isn't just a way of getting you out of our house.'

'That's very generous, Roy,' Jo said, 'but all that does is leave you with an empty house to pay for instead of me. I'm sure you have lots of friends visiting but surely not enough to fill the place continuously for what might be several months.'

'I guess we could use it when we come up here to visit,' Seb suggested.

'You most certainly *will not*,' Bella said, with some feeling. 'You come to visit; you stay *here*.'

'Yes, Mum. Sorry, Mum. Silly me.' Seb, suitably cowed, smiled his apology.

'Yes, silly you,' Jo said. 'Look, why don't I look for somewhere else. Somewhere without any conditions?'

'But you said it was perfect,' Roy said.

'As a property, but clearly not as a deal. You do know, don't you, that I'm not desperate to leave here. But I do think...'

'We've been through this,' Seb interrupted. 'We all agree it's important for you *and* for Mum and Dad that you have a place of your own. You'll be working all hours and they'd be staying awake until you came in every night and phoning you at work to check that you're okay. They can't help it; it was like that for Sally and me and...'

'Of course, we wouldn't be doing that,' Bella said. 'Jo's the *police*, for goodness' sake, so...'

'Yes, we would,' Roy put in with a smile. 'It goes with the territory, parenthood, she's one of our kids now, whether she likes it or not. If she's not where we think she should be, we'd be ringing round to find her, just like this missing girl's parents.'

There was silence for a few moments before Jo spoke again. 'We've got until Tuesday to decide. But I do think it's perfect, and I think I'll take it. And, just for the record, Roy, I *do* like being one of your kids.'

CHAPTER NINE

Saturday 29 December

The delicious smell of bacon wafted around the dining room as Jo and Seb sat facing each other across the table and silently studied their iPhone screens in the usual ritual accompaniment to breakfast. The room was still adorned with sprigs of holly, a small tree on a corner table and cotton wool snow along the sill of the large window overlooking the side garden. However, as always in the aftermath of Christmas Day, the decorations seemed to have lost their festive magic.

'What time are you going in today?' Seb finished his last piece of toast and picked up his empty plate to take through to the kitchen.

'I'm not going in, at least that's the plan. I guess we'll see.'

'Good idea. It's probably best to take a break. Not much you can do if the investigation stalls except go back to it with a fresh pair of eyes.'

'I didn't say I wasn't working – just not going in to the station. And who said it's stalled, anyway?'

'You did. Not in those words, but in what you told me last night.'

'We are following a number of leads and...'

'Yes, I know. Possibilities one and two, just like on day one, you said.'

Jo sighed and leaned back, tilting the dining chair on to its two back legs. Seb wrapped his arms around her from behind, hugging her and kissing her gently on the side of her neck.

'Look, Mum and Dad are going shopping into Bury. Why not let me take your mind off everything except just one thing?'

Jo turned her head to the side so his kissing reached her lips.

'That's a brilliant plan, DS Carter, but it comes at a price.'

Seb stood up, his hands resting gently on her shoulders. He sighed. 'Go on.'

'I'd like you to watch a movie. Well, not exactly a movie, just moving pictures.'

Seb sighed. 'CCTV. Well, if that's the price I have to pay...'

'I promise you'll think it was worth it.'

Seb smiled. 'I don't doubt that. I assume that's payment in arrears?'

'Payment for what?' Roy appeared in the doorway.

'Just police stuff,' Seb said. 'I thought you were going out.'

'Your mum's got a headache. Just taken some paracetamol and we're heading out later. I'm just going to grab another coffee.'

He disappeared into the kitchen. Jo and Seb looked at each other and shrugged.

'Payment in advance, then, I guess,' Seb said. 'Lead me to the screen.'

★

'I only ask for your help because of your aptitude for interpreting CCTV images. I still remember the time you clocked that the guy we *thought* we were following in Kennington was three inches shorter than he should have been.'

Seb studied his fingernails on both hands. 'I suppose it was rather clever,' he said. 'Pointless denying it.'

'Right, so now's your chance to convince me it wasn't a fluke.'

They were sitting side by side on their bed, on top of the duvet, backs to the bedhead and legs stretch out in front of them. Jo had powered up her laptop and opened the link to the CCTV capture Mo had sent her a couple of days ago.

'Okay, this is the Shoulder of Mutton car park. I'll just skip to the relevant bits.' She opened her notebook to a page of numbers, indicating different times. Watching the time display on the stream, she held the cursor on the fast-forward icon, stopping the action at the time of the arrival of the bus at 20.10.

'Okay, this is the first bus that Phoebe could have got on if she had been heading into Bury.'

Seb leaned forward. 'And you said there were just two unaccompanied females getting on.' He pointed to the screen. 'That would be these two.'

'That's right. And we reckon neither is Phoebe. She has very distinctive long blonde hair and you can clearly see the hair on both of these girls. Nothing like.'

'Right, so why am I watching this? Unless of course, this is some weird form of foreplay. Is that why we're doing it on the bed? Easy to move on from this position, just cast aside the laptop, and we're at it.'

Jo sighed. 'No, it isn't. That's not to say that couldn't happen after Roy and Bella leave, but right now, I'd just like you to look closely at these girls and see if anything jumps out at you. You being the expert and all.'

Seb reached across and moved his finger over the pad. He clicked on the enlarge icon then moved the image around to study the face of each girl.

'And you've no idea what Phoebe was wearing?' Seb asked.

'When she set off across the moor, she was wearing a light fleece, jeans and long boots – up to her knee. Plus, a pink woolly hat. But we believe she may have changed her clothes, or *added* some clothes. She set out with a full rucksack which, as you know, was found empty. We did find other items scattered around but they wouldn't have filled the rucksack.'

'Did you find the boots?'

'No, but she was wearing them when she set off. So, they weren't in the rucksack.'

'I know, but if she discarded them to change her appearance, you'd think they would have been found with the other stuff. They are a pretty big item.'

'Perhaps she didn't discard her boots.'

'In which case, that completely rules out these two women. I mean, this one…' he pointed to the screen '… has a decent size bag with her, but not one large enough to conceal a pair of knee boots.'

'That's the girl DC Malik seems to be obsessed with. He's tracked her on camera as far as Piccadilly train station and clocked her getting on the London train.'

Seb frowned and looked hard at the enlarged image of the girl. After a long silence, Jo turned to him.

'What?'

'There's just something...' Jo waited out the silence. 'The hair,' Seb went on. 'It's, like... coarse... thick ... stiff, even. Apart from the colour, almost ... how can I put this?'

'Caribbean?'

'Yes. But the features of the face are really delicate, like... Scandinavian. They just don't go together somehow.'

'You don't have to tiptoe around, Seb. If you think my features only go with coarse hair, just say so.'

'No, what I mean...'

Jo laughed. 'I *do* know what you mean. And I also know you think I'm the most attractive woman in the world.' She put her arm through his and squeezed him closer. '*And*, that is exactly what DS Mills said.'

'What, that you're the most attractive woman in the world?'

'No, not that – well, not in so many words. About the girl's hair not going with the face. So, we could be looking at Phoebe, in disguise, and DC Malik might just have stumbled on to something.'

'Or he knows it's her.'

'*Thinks* it's her, don't you mean? He can't *know* it's her, can he?'

'I suppose not.'

They remained silent for a few moments, both listening for any movement downstairs.

'Do you think they've gone yet?' Jo asked, in an unnecessary whisper.

Seb swung his legs off the bed and looked out of the window.

'Car's still there. Let's crack on with this. It means I have longer to look forward to you reimbursing me.'

'Is that's what they call it up north? Okay, next episode of this exciting drama.' Jo moved the stream forward to show the girl entering Bury Metro station. 'DC Malik pointed out that all the passengers getting on the bus at the Shoulder got off it at the terminus. All, that is, except this girl, who got off a couple of stops before and walked straight to the Metro station.' Jo pointed at the screen. 'That's why she's going in alone. All the other passengers are already in there. Or I should say *were* in there. By now, they've boarded a tram heading into Manchester. This girl gets on the next tram leaving.'

'The significance being what, exactly?'

'Not sure, but she does the same thing arriving in Manchester. The tram goes direct to Piccadilly station, but she gets off a couple of stops before, and walks to the station. Malik thinks she might be trying to avoid being tracked, either by camera or by person or persons unknown.'

'If that *is* the missing girl, she's gone to a lot of trouble with a disguise and an escape plan, and a lot *more* trouble to avoid being followed. It's a lot of work just to take a break from nagging parents and an inattentive boyfriend.'

'Unless it's a plan that's already in place, which she uses to disappear every few weeks. A process that is just second nature. And if it is, I'd say there's a lot going on in this young lady's life that we don't know about.'

They sat in silence again with their own thoughts before Seb spoke.

'Is there any more?'

'Not much, just her in Piccadilly Station catching the late train to Euston. I'll show you.'

Jo moved the recording forward again to where it showed the girl getting her ticket from a machine.

'See, she uses cash to buy the ticket. I thought all the machines took cards only these days. Must be another northern thing.'

The girl started walking along the concourse in front of the gates to the platforms. The image jumped to a train in a different station with people embarking and disembarking.

Jo screwed up her face in puzzlement. 'Where the hell is this?'

'Stockport, there's the name on the wall. That would be right, first stop on the way to London.'

'Yes, but there's some coverage missing. It showed her boarding the train in Manchester; walking through the gate and along the platform, then getting on. Someone's erased it.'

'Maybe it was sent as two files and a bit fell between the two, got missed out.'

'But I thought the Transport Police had provided us with a direct link. Anyway, it's not there.'

'Can you remember exactly what the missing bit showed?'

'She walked along the concourse, showed her ticket and went

through the gate, along the platform and got into one of the front carriages. In fact, she ran, because the guy was closing the doors ready for the train to leave.'

'And that was what time? Can you remember?'

'Yes, it was the nine-fifty train.'

Seb frowned. 'Nine-fifty. I don't suppose you recall which platform.'

'Yes again, platform five.'

Seb leaned to the side so he could turn to look directly at Jo.

'You're sure? Nine-fifty, platform five.'

'I'm sure. I remember the platform number because it was the same as the one for the train we used to get when we were kids going on holiday to Margate. Why?'

'That was *not* the London train. It was the train to Sheffield, and I'm sure of that because it's the one I'll need to take if I can't get home by car on Tuesday. You change at Sheffield for Leicester.'

They sat in silence again, each considering the implications of the missing CCTV coverage and the wrong destination. They turned to the window at the sound of a car pulling out of the drive. Seb took the laptop from Jo and placed it very deliberately on the bedside table. He turned back to her with a devilish smile and a raised eyebrow.

'At last,' he said. 'Tickets, please.'

*

The sound of an incoming message punctured the mood of soporific perfection.

'Oh, no. Please not.' Jo extricated herself from her husband's arms with a little difficulty and absolute reluctance. 'Eleven thirty-five,' she said, turning back into Seb's embrace, still clutching the phone. 'You did all that in just half an hour. I'm impressed.'

'I thought you were pretty good yourself. What's the message?'

Jo freed her arms and snuggled closer to Seb while she opened the text.

'Fuck!'

'Is that a direct order, Inspector?'

'It's the boss.' She read aloud. '"Sorry to bother you. Could you make review meeting at 12.30?" He's actually put a question mark after that, as if it's a request. "Will contact DS Mills and have him also attend. Can then leave you in peace over holiday." Great, that creep will, I have no doubt, manage to get there before I can.'

She swung her legs off the bad and sat up, hitting the key pad a lot harder than necessary in sending her reply. She turned round to Seb, still looking at the phone.

'How does this sound? "Really sorry, sir, but I'm just in the middle of the best shagging session of my life so far. So, you can stick your fucking meeting up Mills's southern orifice." What do you think?'

'I think you should stop pussy-footing around and tell him straight.'

Jo laughed. Seb leaned forward and grabbed the phone, reading the message on the screen. '"No problem, sir. Will see you at 12.30." What a creep.'

Jo took back the phone, checked the time on the screen and placed it on the bedside table. She lay back on the bed, spreading her arms and legs. 'Right, eleven forty-two. I need to leave here at twelve fifteen, latest. Ten minutes to get ready – that's twelve o-five. So, the answer to your question, "Is that a direct order, Inspector?" is "yes", and you've got twenty minutes.'

★

As Jo had predicted, Andy Mills had already arrived and, judging by the two near-empty cartons of coffee on the Super's desk, had been there for some time. She wondered for a moment if the boss had given Andy an earlier time for the meeting in order to see him first without Jo in attendance, before dismissing it as new-girl paranoia.

One encouraging sign was that the senior officer was wearing jeans, trainers, a tee shirt and leather bomber jacket. Jo hoped this was an indication of his intention not to stay for very long.

'Thanks for coming in, Jo.' As if reading her thoughts, he spread his arms and looked down at his jacket and jeans. 'As you will discern, being a detective, I am not here to stay. But I have a dinner this evening with senior council leaders, including the Mayor of Bury, and they are bound to ask for an update on the missing girl case.'

'Why would they be interested in the detail, sir? It's hardly part of their remit.'

Jo detected a sigh from Andy and a shaking of his head.

'There's a lot of points-scoring on these occasions, Jo. They press us on any adverse crime figures or lack of progress on particular cases; we push back with complaints about unfinished work on roads, parks, etc. Then we'll all turn on GMT and grill them about reduced timetables and slow service. It's all done in a light-hearted way, but there are real barbs flying around all the same.'

Jo frowned. 'GMT?' Prompting another sigh from Andy.

'Greater Manchester Transport,' Mal said. 'Anyway, from what I've heard from DS Mills, it looks as though I'll be the whipping boy on this occasion. On the back foot from the start.'

Jo turned to glare at Andy. 'Oh, and what *have* you heard from DS Mills, sir?' The words were out before she could stop them.

'Only the truth, ma'am.' Andy smirked back at her.

Mal leaned forward, elbows on the desk. 'That you have made no progress at all and have failed even to establish whether this is an abscondment or an abduction. Or a murder.'

Jo fought hard to remain calm. She turned her back on her sergeant as much as the arrangement of the chairs would allow. 'You are correct, sir, in that we still have not established whether we are looking for a missing girl or a body. That bit is true. But as for progress, bearing in mind we are just four days into the investigation, I think perhaps my definition differs from DS Mills's and, seemingly, yours as well, sir.'

'My definition of progress,' Mal put in, 'is the achievement of results and…'

'Then we *definitely* disagree on the definition… sir.'

'I think you should be careful, DI Carter, in how forcefully you state your case. Whatever the correct definition, you are not speaking from a position of strength.'

Jo did not flinch. Her expression remained unchanged.

'Perhaps we could discuss performance parameters privately at some other time, sir, without spectators.' She nodded towards Andy. 'But right now, I think I can give you something to push back with when the port is circulating later this evening.'

She smiled at Mal who, after a few moments of silence, returned her smile with a shaking of the head. Jo sensed Andy stiffen in his chair.

'Very well, detective, but we *will* have that conversation, and soon. Go ahead. Arm me for the fight.'

★

The atmosphere in the Detective Superintendent's office was noticeably warmer and more relaxed. That was down to one thing – DS Mills's departure following Jo's summation of the case, presenting the same facts with a more optimistic focus. Certainly, the senior officer appreciated the positivity. His abrupt dismissal of the sergeant with a clipped 'I don't think we need detain you further, enjoy the rest of the day' had been greeted with a confused, then angry expression and a slamming of doors on his leaving. The performance was not lost on the senior officer.

'I don't think your number two is very happy right now.'

'He seemed at one with the world when I arrived,' Jo pointed out. 'I suspect his mood swings are dependent on me. That is, whether I am present or absent.'

'DS Mills has had his problems…'

'I am aware of his record, sir. I did a full check on his past history before I arrived, so nothing has surprised me so far.'

'He is basically a good detective, and I have mentored him carefully since his transfer here to a point where we have established… well… a good personal relationship based, I believe, on mutual respect and trust. But I wonder sometimes whether he has just too much baggage to reach his potential.'

'I've seen enough to agree that he is, or could be, a good detective, which makes the situation all the more frustrating.'

'And the rest of the team?'

'Excellent. Really enjoying working with them.'

'Well, I'm here to help if you need me to take any action.'

'Thank you, sir, but I'll sort out the issue with DS Mills. That's part of my job.'

Mal leaned back in his chair and was silent for a while as if gathering his thoughts and choosing his words.

'Look, Jo, this has nothing to do with the situation between you and Andy, but part of the problem, I believe, is your picking up this very *local* case almost by accident.' He held up his hand as Jo looked to interrupt. 'I know why you picked it up. You were the most senior officer on point when the call came, went straight into the station on Christmas Day, and worked the full day. And we agreed, you and I, that you should be given time to resolve the case for the sake of your credibility with the wider team. It was the right decision, and you've shown yourself to be diligent, hardworking and effective. But we have a number of detectives who are equally qualified, with the local knowledge... what?'

Jo had leaned back in her chair with a sigh and a roll of the eyes.

'I'm sorry, sir, but this local knowledge thing gets thrown at me by you-know-who several times *every* day, as if a degree in geography, which includes a thesis on the West Pennine fucking Moors is essential to the case. I am surrounded by excellent people with local knowledge. It could be argued that I bring an added dimension being new to the area. And sorry for the language, sir.'

'Apology accepted, but nevertheless, the issue behind your assignment is a bigger fish to fry than the disappearance of one girl in circumstances that are looking increasingly like there is not even any foul play involved.' He paused. Jo remained silent, looking down at her hands folded on her lap. 'In spite of any disappointment, Jo, I do expect you to understand.'

Jo nodded, still looking down.

'So how will you break the news to the team, sir? Not that I have any right to ask.'

'This isn't a disciplinary, Jo. You make it sound as if we're talking about a performance issue. It's the very fact that you're the best chance we have to help bring down a criminal practice that's affecting the whole region.'

'Thank you for the vote of confidence, sir. I really do appreciate that, but it *feels* like a failure all the same. And I *do* understand. But we are only a few days...'

'It was one week ago today when she went missing.'

'That's right,' Jo said, 'but we were only alerted on Christmas Day.'

'Christmas Eve, actually; we only started *looking* on Christmas

Day. However, I'll give you that, we're just four days in to the search. But, as I'm sure you know, the first few days are critical in a situation like this. In fact, we're probably already past that optimum period, and the chances of finding a missing person reduce dramatically after that.'

'I do feel we are really moving forward, as I said. It's not quite as straightforward as being just another misper, either. We've established the fact that Phoebe Wright regularly goes missing, or at least she's frequently not where the people closest to her believe she is, if that's not the same thing. Let me have one week at least, sir.'

'Well I certainly wasn't planning to change anything before New Year.'

'And will the next person in charge be DS Mills?'

'I don't know yet who will take over. It doesn't necessarily warrant an officer of your seniority unless we can be sure that foul play is involved. And if I do hand it to Mills, I'll make sure he knows the reason he's taking over, to free you up for more critical issues.'

He paused, as if wondering whether to continue.

'Look, let me share this with you. The only reason we, Bury, have got the case at all is that it was *reported* on our patch. Lancs were quick to agree we run with it, especially as it required resources over the Christmas period, but Phoebe's home is in their area, as is the place where she was last seen on the moor. Only *just* in their area, but theirs all the same. So she's really Lancashire's missing person. Having said that, we've run with it and have all the info and contacts, so it's a bit late to try and fully offload it now. But what I've been thinking is that we assign it officially to a DI in Blackburn and have him work with Mills, essentially *through* Mills. That will put the accountability in the right place but let our angry sergeant lead the chase. It also means that your relinquishing the reins will be clearly seen as the result of a geographical realignment of responsibilities and nothing to do with the status of the investigation itself.'

Jo raised her eyebrows in appreciation. 'That seems to tick all the boxes, sir. But won't DS Mills be a bit pissed off having to report in to the same level person but in a different jurisdiction?'

'Not if we get the right person – a certain Alistair Crossley, someone we've ridden tandem with many times. Andy and Alistair have a good relationship. I'm sure our boy will be fine.'

Jo shrugged. 'So it really is just me that pisses him off.'

'We'll see, won't we? Could be working apart will help form some sort of bond.'

Jo spluttered. 'Don't hold your breath, sir. From his initial comments to me, and his previous record, I think he's more interested in bondage than bonding. But, as you say, sir, we'll see,' she added, as Mal's expression hardened a little.

'You made a very good point before, Jo, about you possibly laughing off his initial approach if you hadn't met him with preconceived opinions. I've always believed that we should form our own opinions of people rather than adopting others' views. So, when we do separate you, cut him some slack and… well, we'll see. Okay?'

'Yes, sir,' Jo nodded.

'*But*, let me stress,' Mal went on, 'nothing has been finally decided yet.'

They sat in silence for a few moments, then Mal leaned forward, putting both palms on the desk, elbows wide, signalling he was about to stand up.

'Well, I must be going. Thank you again for coming in and for providing the weapons for what might just be a pre-emptive strike tonight. I think I'll offer to bring them up to date before they ask.'

'Now, are you sure, sir? Won't that spoil it for the enemy?'

'I sincerely hope so. And if I don't see you again beforehand, a Happy New Year to you and Seb.'

As Jo stepped out of the building a few minutes later into the cold air, her phone pinged with an incoming text. She checked the screen. One digit. '7'.

★

Back in their room, Jo and Seb were studying the sequence of digits before making themselves scarce in time for the bridge night that Roy and Bella hosted every last Saturday in the month. The numbers were on the screen of the laptop resting, as before, on Jo's knees as they sat on the bed.

195;77

'It could be a date, I suppose,' Seb offered, 'Nineteenth of May, nineteen seventy-seven.'

'We're a semicolon short for that. There'd be one between the nine and the five.'

'Even so, it might be worth checking what happened on that day. Just google it. Unless you can remember, of course.'

Jo turned to him, wild-eyed, and punched his arm, very hard. 'I'm not rising to these barbed references about our age difference anymore.'

Seb winced and rubbed his arm. 'So that punch was your way of not rising. I hope I never get to find out what *is* rising. Seriously, though, let's check that date and see if there's some clue in there.'

Jo googled 'What happened on 19 May 1977'. Fifteen minutes later Seb summarised their attempt to identify anything that could be connected to the missing girl.

'David Berkowitz,' he said, 'so-called "Son of Sam". Murdered six people in New York between August 1976 and July 1977. Closest incident to our date of nineteenth of May 1977 was on the eighth of March when he intercepted and killed a nineteen-year-old female student walking home from college. The only link is the sex and age of the victim, so I think we can dispense with the date theory.'

'Anyway,' Jo said, 'we don't know yet whether we've received the full message. That's if it is a message and not some random numbers generated by spinning a wheel or throwing dice.'

'I'm more interested in why you're receiving them at all. I mean, why you in particular. Is there no way to trace the phones? The techies can do almost anything these days. If something exists, they can usually find it.'

'My guess is it's just a bit of mischief. If someone is playing silly buggers, I don't want to give them the satisfaction of seeing me treat it as some sort of threat. And I'm told the reason we can't get a handle on the source is because it's being done by a burner or burners. No link to the user or the location.'

'Most likely culprit must be Mills, surely.'

'I've thought of that, of course, but I can't see a motive, and he certainly hasn't given any hints in any of our exchanges. I don't see what he can be getting out of it. Having said that, and if there is more to come, we might find out when the message is complete.'

Seb checked his watch.

'Six-thirty. Better decide what we're doing tonight. I said we'd be out by seven-thirty before all the card-sharps arrive. If we're going to eat somewhere we might have to book a table.'

'What about the Shoulder of Mutton? That's nice and handy. We could walk there and back. Or get a taxi there and walk back. How far is it?'

'Both ways, about two-and-a-half miles, but...'

'That's okay, isn't it? We can do that. Half an hour each way.'

'Yes, but it's too close to the job. You'll be checking out cameras and showing the bar staff pictures. So, we are *not* going there.'

'Hare and Hounds? Even closer.'

'No, too close. I know. Owd Betts. Up on Scout Moor through Edenfield on the Rochdale Road. Great little place, out on its own.'

'Owd Betts? That's a tea room isn't?'

'A tea room? What...? You're thinking of Betty's Tea Shop.'

'So, Betty's branching out? Diversifying. Then I agree, we must help her succeed. Let's go.'

CHAPTER TEN

Sunday 30 December

Jo and Seb had the luxury of a natural awakening with no alarms to prompt their rising. It was past 9.30 a.m. when they finally descended to the dining room. The table was set for just two people with Roy and Bella, it seemed, having long since finished breakfast. They could hear Roy humming 'White Christmas' in the hall and the sound of catering activity in the kitchen. The multifuel burner crackled and sparked behind its glass door as the newly lit fire gained purchase on the pine logs.

'Good afternoon,' Roy called through from the hall where he was donning his coat and outdoor shoes.

Seb popped his head out of the dining room.

'Going out?'

'Just as far as the log pile,' Roy said.

'I'll do that,' Seb said.

'Next time perhaps. Right now, you and your lovely wife need to get your breakfast. Sally and Jonno should be here soon. Did you have a good time last night? You were back late, weren't you?'

'Just after midnight. Delicious meal at Betts and it was such a fabulous night – full moon, light as day – so we went for a bit of a walk up Knowl Hill.'

'What, at that time? You must be daft.'

'I won't tell my aforementioned lovely wife you said that, because it was her idea. Since that walk on the moor, she'd been straining at the leash, so…'

'Yes, but surely you pointed out…'

'That we would need to be careful – yes, of course. But once she's made up her mind… Anyway, we had our boots and puffers in the car. The wind farm looked amazing with the moonlight on the turbines. Spooky, in fact. Turning very slowly; no sound. Anyway, the answer to your question is, yes, we did have a good time.'

'Good. We'll make a Manc out of her yet, or a Lanc.'

'Oh, I think she's well on her way.'

Bella called from the kitchen as Roy popped out to top up the log basket.

'Full breakfast? You'll have to be quick, I'm going to church in a few minutes.'

'We'll do that, Mum, thanks. Big meal last night, anyway, so we'll probably pass.'

'Okay. Anything planned for today?'

'You'd best ask the planner, here she comes now.'

'Morning, Bella.' Jo joined them in the kitchen. 'Sorry we're so late.'

'You deserve a bit of a lie-in. Seb says you'll not want a cooked breakfast.'

'No thank you. Big meal last night, and a romantic, moonlit walk. He's such a big softie, your son.'

Bella laughed. 'So what's on the agenda for today?'

'We thought we'd show Sal and Jonno the cottage when they arrive and, as it's a nice day, perhaps walk there through Burr's Park. What do you think?'

'I think it's a great idea, and I'm sure Sal will, too. Jonno might be less enthusiastic, but if the three of you gang up on him…'

'That's the plan,' Jo said. 'And if he refuses, I'll arrest him for loitering.'

★

It took all of fifteen minutes after setting off before Jonno pointed out that his strong preference today would have been to watch the rugby match on Sky Sports.

'I was really looking forward to it after that long drive from Altrincham,' he said, winking at Jo. 'Fighting our way through all that traffic.'

'I must have been asleep for that bit,' Sally said. 'Honestly,

Jonno, what are you going to be like as a dad if driving a few miles is going to tire you out.'

Jo slipped her arm through Sally's. 'He'll be a fantastic dad, Sal.' She laughed. 'He's just winding you up.'

This time they took a different route down to the railway bridge, along Miller Street with its traditional terraced cottages on one side and a modern complex of apartments on the other. A short rise to the right brought them onto the long platform of Summerseat station, one of the stops on the East Lancashire Railway line between Bury and Rawtenstall. They passed a chalk board titled 'Train Departures'. The only message displayed, in a hand written scrawl, announced the first train ever to leave the station for Manchester Victoria at 12.35 p.m. on the 25th September 1846, with eighteen carriages and two locomotives.

'Not mad busy, then?' Jonno observed.

At the end of the platform they dropped down to rejoin Miller Street and passed under the railway bridge. This time they followed Wood Road Lane up to where it turned over the river onto a small settlement of cottages and commercial buildings. Instead of following the road, they ascended some steps on the left, crossing the railway line and climbing up more steps to a grassy path.

'That was a bit more exciting,' Jonno said, 'having to step over the railway line. Really dangerous. I mean anything could have happened.'

'Have you ever visited the Planet Earth, Jonno?' Seb asked.

'I know where you got that from,' Jonno replied. 'Captain Blackadder asking General Melchett.'

'That doesn't mean it's not a relevant question.'

'You can talk, Seb Carter,' Sally said. 'When we did this walk as kids, he always threatened to tie me to the tracks.'

Seb looked at Jonno and shrugged. 'Always forgot the rope. Mind like a sieve back then.'

They soon came to a large pond on the right, which they could just about see through the densely tangled branches of trees and bushes separating it from the path.

'This used to be the high point of the walk,' Sally said, 'before all this stuff grew up and blotted it out. There were always scores of birds around the lake: waders, ducks, geese, gulls. I assume they're still there but we just don't get to see them anymore. No idea why they've let it get like this.'

'Probably some birds' rights group insisting we should respect their privacy,' Jonno suggested.

They continued along the path to a tarmac road where they turned right past another pond, this one with no obstacles to spoil the view. It was devoid of wildlife but on two small islands, stone sculptures of small children and a cluster of ducks offered eye-pleasing decoration. A little further on they crossed the railway line again, this time under a bridge, and, right on cue, a steam engine passed noisily overhead, prompting Jonno to claim a 'lucky escape', to Jo and Seb's laughter and Sally's rolling eyes. From there, the path followed a fence separating them from fields on the left whilst on the right the land fell away down a tree-covered slope to the River Irwell. Eventually, they reached the spectacular Irwell Weir, where a group of hardy young canoeists were being trained on how to negotiate the seemingly perilous drop over the falls into the swirling pool below. Most of them were aligning themselves, eager to try, with just a couple hanging back away from the edge.

'I'm with those two guys,' Jonno said.

'Me, too,' Jo added.

They stayed to watch for a while, applauding each canoeist who made the descent, to the delight of both trainer and trainees. Eventually, Seb suggested they move on.

'Which way, Sal? Follow the river or across the field.'

'If we stick by the river we can show them the mousetrap.'

'A mousetrap?' Jonno said. 'Not sure I can deal with that level of excitement. I mean, there won't be a mouse *in it*, will there?'

'Unlikely,' Sally said. 'I can't believe you haven't seen this before.'

'Oh, I'm sure I'd remember seeing a *mousetrap*.'

Jo looked at Seb and frowned.

'Wait and see,' Seb said.

The steel trap, located close to the main car park next to a huge chimney, was over five metres long and two metres wide, with all the attachments of a real trap, but assembled with none of the deadly tension.

'Christ, Jo, if the mice are this big around here I wouldn't be shacking up anywhere close,' Jonno advised. 'Think how much it's going to cost you in cheese to bait one of these things.' He shook his head and smiled. 'It's great. I can't wait to show the baby this.'

'Always assuming there's no rugby on the tele,' Sally said.

They continued along Woodhill Road to the lower car park and Stock Street, the site of Jo's new intended residence. The rough-surfaced road was host to a delightful row of sandstone terraced cottages, with a variety of coloured doors and frontages adorned with seasonal decorations in tubs, troughs, pots and hanging baskets. Jo pointed out their new residence to Sally's delight.

'Oh, it's lovely, Jo. What a find. I'm sure I could be happy here.'

'Apart from the mice,' Jonno pointed out.

They headed through the car park and along a well-made path past some old industrial remains on the right and a picturesque little lake on the left with small metal piers jutting out a couple of metres over the water to accommodate local anglers.

'You'll be able to come and feed the ducks before you go to work,' Sally said.

'Joking apart,' Jo replied, 'wouldn't that be wonderful? This is such a great place.'

Crossing a bridge further along, they came to the visitors' area of the park which included a café, toilet, an information centre and storage for canoes and other outdoor equipment. A number of picnic tables were placed along the full length of the building, none occupied today in the chill air and stiffening breeze.

'It's twenty minutes past one,' Seb consulted his watch. 'About an hour's walk back and we want to make it before it gets too dark. So say we leave here no later than two o'clock. We have two choices for refreshment. The café here, or the Brown Cow pub, just over there.' He pointed through the trees.

'Oh, the café definitely,' Sally said.

'Why?' her brother asked.

'Because they have Sky Sports in the Brown Cow.'

★

They left the café and crossed the field back to the weir, passing the Brown Cow and the caravan park on the right. From there they retraced their steps home, arriving whilst it was still light, as planned, but after the low sun had disappeared.

'Do you know what I fancy?' Jonno said, after they had taken off their outdoor gear and were seated comfortably around Roy's newly loaded multifuel burner in the lounge.

'Nicole Kidman?' Seb said. 'At least that's what you told me the last time we watched *Paddington*.'

Sally looked at her husband with wide questioning eyes.

'No, no, no,' Jonno said. He paused. 'That's *who* I fancy. *What* I fancy is a sherry.'

'I'm not sure we have...' Bella began.

'And it just so happens,' Jonno continued, reaching behind his armchair and retrieving a bottle of Harveys Amontillado. 'Here's one I made earlier. Anyone else?'

They all raised their hands. 'I'll get the glasses,' Seb said, heading for the dining room.

'Nicole Kidman,' Sally said, glaring at her husband in playful anger. 'What has she got that I haven't?'

'It's more about what you've got that she hasn't,' Jonno said. He leaned across and patted her stomach. 'Our little one.'

They all laughed as Seb returned with the glassware. At that same moment, Jo's phone sounded. She checked the screen.

'Sorry, I need to take this.'

She returned a few minutes later and took her drink from Seb.

'Problem?' he asked.

'Not a new one, and certainly not one that's going to spoil the evening.' She raised her glass. 'Cheers.'

In spite of her dismissal of the phone conversation, she couldn't suppress a feeling of guilt at how perfect everything was for her compared to the party on the other end of the call.

CHAPTER ELEVEN

Monday 31 December

When Jo arrived at the station the following morning it took her a few moments to identify what was different about it before she realised that all evidence of the festive season had gone. In spite of the relative paucity of the Christmas decorations in the operations room compared to those at the Carters' residence, the place did look rather sad now that the display had been removed.

Eva was already at her workstation. Jo checked her watch. 7.45 a.m.

'For God's sake, DC Johnson, can't you let me get here first just once?'

Eva laughed. 'Morning, ma'am. Only just arrived myself.'

Jo picked up the empty coffee carton from Eva's desk and peered into it.

'You brought the empty cup into work with you, then? And are you responsible for the removal of all glad tidings of comfort and joy from our workplace?'

'It's a CID team tradition, ma'am. All decorations taken down before New Year's Day, and the first one in on New Year's Eve does the dirty deed. So, how was your weekend, ma'am?'

'Pretty good, to be honest, but ended with a rather awkward call yesterday evening from Philip Wright. Had me on speaker so his wife could hear and berated me for not being out on the moor with a torch and a magnifying glass looking for his daughter.' She shook her head and sighed. 'That's such a mean thing to say, isn't it? They must be beside themselves with worry. Any new thoughts over the weekend?'

'Not really new, and stating the bleeding obvious, I think there's more to Phoebe than meets the eye. These mysterious absences, the switched phones, the discarded rucksack. Mo seems obsessed with this girl on CCTV, almost as if he knows her.'

'Really? I want him to check again which train she got on at Piccadilly. He said it was the London train, but Seb, my pet sergeant, is sure it's the one to Sheffield. I had the footage on my laptop, but it's been deleted. Don't know how.'

'Well, unfortunately, Mo won't be in today. Called in ill. Tummy trouble. He said he'd try to get in later, but I told him not to bother. If he's got a bug, I'd rather he kept it to himself.'

'Absolutely agree.'

'But he said he'd work from home. He's been checking through the door-to-door stuff again. He said several people in Crest Lane confirm that they heard someone knocking on Benny's door and shouting Phoebe's name between a quarter to and eight o'clock. The same time Marlon said.'

'Right, I think we'll leave him to it. I suppose if I were a really caring boss, I'd phone him and tell him to take it easy and forget about work until he feels better. What do you think?'

'You could, I suppose, but it won't make any difference.'

'Good, so I'll just let him get on with it.'

'So, what about you, ma'am? Have you come up with anything?'

'Well, I agree with you about the secret life of Ms Wright, although that doesn't tell us whether she's alive or dead. Nine days now since she disappeared and frankly, I'm wondering where the hell to look next. I think another chat with her boss might be useful, and this time we'll do it face to face. He might have seen a different side to her. It's a pity Benny can't remember the dates when she's been away, not that I'd expect him to. It might be worth pressing him again. We could check them against her driving schedule. Even if he can remember, say, just a couple, it might give us something to go on.'

Eva reached for the phone. 'So, Benny first, then Easy Rider?'

'Right, if they're awake at this time. And while you set that up, I suppose I should walk the last few paces to my office and check my email and voicemail.' She opened the door of her office, turning back. 'I wonder when DS Mills will turn up. Hopefully in time for the eight o'clock meeting.'

Andy stepped into her office a couple of seconds later.

'Good morning. Did I hear my name mentioned? Hopefully not in anger.' He smiled. 'I trust you had a pleasant weekend.'

'I did, thank you, eventually. And you?'

'Let's say "promising" and leave it at that.' He continued smiling for a few more seconds, then turned and went back into the operations room.

★

'So, what's happened to DC Malik?' Andy asked. He and Eva had followed Jo into her office after the meeting.

'Tummy problems, apparently.'

Andy chortled. 'Ah, Delhi belly.'

'Well, I didn't think I'd ever hear that expression again,' Jo said. 'You never disappoint, DS Mills, except for getting the wrong country.'

'We're a bit behind the times here up north, you know. I'm sure we'll catch up eventually.'

'I've spoken to Benny and he's given me a couple of dates.' Eva interrupted the verbal tryst like a referee separating two boxers. 'He remembered on one occasion he'd gone to watch Man City away at Newcastle. It was a midweek match, Wednesday, fourteenth of September. He seems to think she was away on the Thursday night as well. Another time, her absence coincided with a stag do. Friday, fourth of November. Doesn't remember how long she was away that time.'

'*Quelle surprise*. Right, thanks, Eva. I wonder why he couldn't have told us that before when we asked him. And Easy Rider?'

'Office closed until Wednesday. I left messages, landline and mobile numbers. You know – police – get in touch – urgent.'

'Tell you what,' Andy took out his iPhone, 'let's gang up on him. What's his mobile number, Eva?'

She held up her phone and Andy punched in the digits. He held it to his ear for a few seconds, then pressed the speaker symbol. The phone rang out for a long time until the familiar female voice informed them the person they were phoning was unable to take the call right now, inviting them to leave a message after the tone. Andy introduced a suitably angry edge to his voice.

'This is Bury CID, Mr Reeves. Please phone Detective Sergeant Mills on this number as soon as you pick up this message. It is very important that you act *immediately*.'

'I'll text him as well,' Andy said. 'People let their phones ring for ever but they always check their texts.' He left the same message and put the phone back in his pocket. It rang out almost immediately. Andy answered, pressing the speaker button again.

'Detective Sergeant Mills, Bury CID.'

'Hello, this is Josh Reeves,' in a voice somewhere between anxious and angry. 'You asked me to...'

'Yes, Mr Reeves, I'm sure you know what I'm calling in connection with. We need to check your records for when and where Phoebe Wright was working on two particular dates. Do you have those records with you?'

'No, they're at the office and we're closed until...'

'Wednesday. Yes, we know that, but we need to see them right away. Where are you right now?'

'At home.'

'You're not trying to be funny, are you, Mr Reeves? Where is home?'

'Turks Road in Radcliffe.'

'And your depot is... just remind me?'

'On the Bury–Bolton Road near the turn-off to Ainsworth.'

'So, about a mile away from your house?'

After a brief pause, in a resigned voice. 'Bit more than that.'

'How soon can you get there, Mr Reeves?'

'Look this isn't on, you know, I told...'

'Ten minutes?'

'Well, I...'

'It's just coming up to nine-fifteen. Shall we say nine-thirty?'

'I'm still in bed.'

'Okay, ten o'clock then. We'll see you there.'

★

Josh Reeves's windowless office was through a door off the reception area. It was not much more than two metres square, the majority of the floorspace taken up by an ancient wooden desk. A line of old metal filing cabinets lined one wall, the only other items of furniture being three plastic stacking chairs, currently unstacked, one behind the desk and the other two in front of it.

'We have eight drivers in total. Phoebe is the best, and the most useful. She's an excellent self-taught mechanic. Great under the bonnet, saves me a shit-load of cash with minor repairs and adjustments. Certainly the most popular with customers, and the other drivers as well.' Josh Reeves allowed himself a chortle. He was short and squat, with broad shoulders and large belly, which tested the buttons on his jacket. Aside from the chortle, his face was set in a permanent scowl behind several days' stubble.

'I think I can guess why,' Andy said with a knowing lift of the eyebrows. 'Great under the bonnet – what about under the blanket?'

Jo sighed. This was the first time she and Andy had worked part of the case together with no-one else in attendance. She had left Eva to investigate the missing CCTV footage, suggesting she contact Mo, reversing, or forgetting, her decision not to bother him. With Andy driving, they had spent the five-minute journey from the station to the depot in complete silence before parking alongside an elderly black Ford Fiesta in front of the office.

'We have two dates we'd like you to check, please, Mr Reeves,' she said. 'We assume you do keep records of where each driver is on any particular day.'

'Of course. We have to provide full details when we submit invoices to the NHS. They're very careful when it comes to parting with money.'

'Understandably,' Jo said.

'I agree, but it means a hell of a lot of paperwork.' He opened one of the drawers of his desk and lifted out a huge ledger.

Andy gave a lopsided, mocking smile. 'So when you said paperwork you meant it literally?'

'Just for now. We're getting everything put on the computer as soon as possible. I've got a second-year Computing Science student coming in on Wednesday to spend a few days sorting it for me before he goes back to uni. So, which dates are we looking at?'

'Let's start with Wednesday the fourteenth of September and the following day, Thursday the fifteenth. Okay?'

Josh heaved open the ledger, with its heavy faux-leather cover and landscape A3 pages, turning them until he reached the one for week commencing twelfth of September. The seven days of the week were across the top of the page; the eight drivers' names listed at the side. Phoebe's name was first on the list. Josh pointed with a stubby index finger sporting a broken nail.

'Wednesday, she took a group from Magnolia House residential care home in Tottington to Bury Market. Always a bit of a challenge that one. They have carers with them, of course, but keeping them all in sight in the crowds is a bloody nightmare.'

'They just wander around?'

'More or less, under watchful eyes. Hey, don't look at me; my job's just to get them there and get them back. And to be fair we haven't lost anyone yet.'

Andy smiled, with the same expression as before. 'Except a driver, it seems.'

'So, next day, Thursday?' Jo said.

'Thursday, she picked up a group from Highfields in Whitefield...'

'What's that exactly?'

'Retirement scheme. Six Towns sheltered housing. They went to Tatton Park for the day. Lunch then a tour of the grounds and house. Or perhaps the other way round, tour first, then a meal.'

'Did she have the vehicle overnight Wednesday to Thursday?'

'Can't remember, but I guess she would. Certainly, overnight Thursday. I do remember that. They got back to Whitefield quite late from Tatton Park. Hold-up on the M60. So, she phoned to ask if she could go straight home and bring it in Friday.'

'She wasn't working Friday?' Andy asked.

'No. Back in the following Tuesday.'

'So why would she do that, do you think?' Andy asked. 'I mean, she almost passes this place on her way from Whitefield to Helmshore. Seems strange she would waste part of a day off when it would only take a few minutes to drop it here the day before.'

'Don't know. She has to then get from here to Helmshore, don't forget. Boyfriend sometimes picks her up or one of the other drivers gives her a lift. I didn't care, to be honest. If she was going to bring it back late, I'd have to stay until she got here. So, it suited me to let her keep it overnight.'

'What time did she bring the vehicle in on Friday?' Jo asked.

'I don't know the exact time but I remember it was after ten o'clock because that was when I had to stand in for one of the drivers who called in sick.' He pointed to an entry on the page. 'I was hoping Phee would get back in time for a bit of extra work. But she hadn't appeared.'

'Was anyone here when she did arrive who would have that information?' Jo asked. He shook his head. 'So, you've no way of knowing when she got here?'

'Not for certain. I asked her when she came in the following Tuesday and she said it was around eleven. Apologised for being late. Headache or something.'

'Time of the month, perhaps,' Andy offered, smiling at Jo.

'Were those the two dates, then?' Josh asked.

'No, that counts as one. Second date was Friday the fourth of November.'

Josh turned the pages again to the week in question and drew his finger across the top row entries.

'Wednesday to Friday she was on the hospitals run, along with three other drivers. Picking up people at home or from care homes to attend hospital appointments. Not Phoebe's favourite part of the job, just short trips of a few miles each. I think she finds it a bit harrowing at times.'

'It doesn't give any details here of where she made the pick-ups,' Jo said.

'What we're doing on those days is backing up the NHS non-emergency ambulances, filling in for when they don't run to schedule. For example, when patients aren't ready at the pick-up time or when they're taken after referral to another facility, it throws the schedule out. Plans are changing all the time through the day, and sometimes we're called at only a few minutes' notice to head out somewhere to pick somebody up. So, we don't record every visit on here, although the drivers are required to keep a record.'

'And do they?'

'Doubt it. Nobody ever checks.'

'So, they could be anywhere?' Andy put in.

'No, of course not.' Josh bristled. 'They go where they're told, otherwise we'd have a load of people phoning up asking where the fuck they'd got to, wouldn't we? And that has never happened. Not once.' He sighed. 'Well, perhaps a couple of times; but not with Phoebe.'

'So, how many calls would the drivers get to do on a typical one of these days?' Jo asked.

'It varies a lot based on waiting times, the state of the patients, whether they need help getting ready, and the distances travelled. With some jobs it's just one patient to one hospital. Other times, they'll do a round trip picking up half a dozen and dropping them off at different places. But what I can tell you, if this is what you're getting at, the days are mad-busy. The drivers are lucky to get any time to eat their lunch, even just sitting in the ambulance.'

'And I assume all the calls for assistance come through you, Mr Reeves? That would be necessary so you could coordinate the pick-ups. Like the hub of a taxi company.'

'That's exactly right and exactly what it feels like.'

'And what about the planned outings. Are they organised through you or directly by the drivers?'

'Bit of both really. Each driver has a number of care homes and housing schemes that they service. That way they build up a relationship with the customers. So, they work out their own schedule with a two-week rolling plan. The first week is more or less fixed; the second usually subject to change. Any new business comes direct to me, but to be honest, most of the Six Towns area is already covered, so there's not much new business coming through.'

Jo looked at the ledger again, and pointed at the entry for the following day, Saturday. 'It shows here that she worked on Saturday *and* Sunday, but no details of where she went.'

Josh furrowed his brow in thought for a moment.

'Yes, I remember. Saturday was the fifth of November and Phoebe said one of her care homes was thinking of taking a group to an afternoon firework display somewhere. She asked if she could hold on to the vehicle just in case. I said she could, of course.'

'Of course,' Andy said.

'She kept it until Monday. In the end the care home decided not to go to the bonfire, anyway. Foul weather or something.'

'Did she say which care home?'

'No, I don't think so.'

'So, you didn't ask?'

'Didn't need to, because if she had taken them, she would have provided me with full details and I would have included it in the ledger.'

'Do you ever check the mileage on the vehicles and reconcile it with the schedule?' Andy asked.

Josh bristled again. 'No, I don't. Look, we are a small outfit, I know all the drivers personally and don't have any doubts at all about their honesty. If I started checking up on them it would destroy the whole tone of the place. I can vouch for all of them individually. The fact that we are valued by an organisation like the NHS should speak volumes for the sort of operation I'm running here.'

'We were certainly not implying anything to the contrary, Mr Reeves,' Jo said. 'But we do have a missing person and we tend not to walk on egg shells in these circumstances when we're asking questions. One last thing, do the drivers use the same vehicle all the time?'

'Yes, so they can introduce any personal touches for themselves or for the benefit of the people they are transporting.'

'And is Phoebe's vehicle here now?'

Josh hesitated for a second. 'Well... yes. Why?'

'We'd like to see it, please?'

Josh looked from one to the other with just a trace of anxiety. He gave a nervous laugh.

'I can assure you she's not hiding in there.'

Jo held her arm out to the door. 'Please, Mr Reeves.'

Josh closed the ledger, taking his time to place it back in the desk drawer. His brow was furrowed as if he was deep in thought or pondering what to say next.

'Is something bothering you, Mr Reeves?' Jo asked. 'We'd just like to see where Phoebe spends such a lot of her time, that's all. We're not going to check if the tyres are still legal, or if the indicators work or anything. Given that the NHS has such a high regard for you, I assume we are safe in believing it is taxed and insured with a valid MOT.'

'I just don't understand what you can hope to get from seeing it. And it doesn't need an MOT; it's only just over two years old.'

'There you are then. So...' she gestured towards the door again '... can we go, please?'

Josh took a bunch of keys from a hook near the door and led the way out and across the yard to a corrugated-iron rectangular garage with large double doors the full height of the building. He unlocked a small pedestrian access door in the one on the left and they ducked their heads as they entered. The place was very cold; there were no windows and for a few seconds the only light was that which followed them in through the door. Josh threw a bank of switches and six neon strip lights flickered on to illuminate eight vehicles parked in two rows of four, their bonnets facing each other across a centre aisle with a shallow culvert running along the middle. All the vehicles looked well-maintained and clean, but the third one along on the left positively sparkled. It had silver bodywork with the words 'Non-Emergency Ambulance' in blue letters just under the windows of the passenger section. The window nearest the back of the vehicle was frosted; in what Jo assumed was a toilet.

'Let me guess,' Andy said, walking across to it. 'This one is Phoebe's.'

'That's right.' Josh sounded a little anxious. 'We take the opportunity at this time of year to give them all a face-lift so they start the new year on a high.' He gave a nervous little laugh. 'Started with Phoebe's. Top of the list.'

'That is some face-lift, Mr Reeves,' Jo said. 'Can we look inside please.'

'Well…'

'Now,' Jo snapped. 'Why don't you want us to see this vehicle, Mr Reeves, because that's what it's beginning to feel like? Are you sure you haven't got her tied up in there?'

'Or her body, perhaps,' Andy added. 'We could always get a search warrant, or arrest you for obstructing the course of an investigation.'

Josh fumbled with the keys. 'You said you just wanted to see the records. Well, we've done that and I've got other stuff planned at home.'

'And another seven vehicles to deep-clean before Wednesday,' Andy said. 'Or doesn't it matter for the other drivers? Just Phoebe, is it?'

Josh didn't reply. He selected one of the keys from the bunch and pressed a button on the fob to unlock the front doors. Access to the passenger seats was through a sliding door, which glided open at a second press of the same button. The interior was even more impressive, with fourteen luxurious seats in seven pairs, eight seats on one side, six on the other, set two steps higher than the driver's seat. Behind the line of six was a toilet cubicle and, at the very back, room for some luggage and folded wheelchairs.

'Very impressive, Mr Reeves,' Jo said when they stepped down from the ambulance. 'And in here?'

She indicated what appeared to be a space beneath the seat level. Josh sighed and reached down to slide back one of two doors revealing a large storage area, also sparkling clean.

'Christ, you could take the whole care home for a ride,' Andy said. 'fourteen in the top and another twenty in there.'

'It's real important that we deep-clean the buses on a regular basis. After a while they smell of piss. They can't help it, poor buggers, but a lot of them, you know, leak quite a bit. Each bus has a toilet but it's not easy for them to use it, especially when they're on the move. So, I guess they just try to hold it and sometimes can't. And I think some don't even know they've peed themselves. Sad, but I suppose that's where we're all heading eventually.'

'Well, that's cheered me up, Mr Reeves, thank you very much,' Jo said. 'What I don't understand, and I think DS Mills feels the same, is why this particular one has been so well valeted compared with the others.'

'Because, as I said, it's the first one.' Josh treated them to another bristle. 'You've got to start somewhere.'

'You mean they'll all get this same level of attention?'

'Yes, that's right.'

'And when will they all be finished, Mr Reeves?' Jo said. 'Because we'd love to come back and see them all sparkling in a row – I mean, in two rows. What if we came back early Wednesday morning?'

'Or was this meant as a special treat for your number one driver?' Andy asked.

'Look, I don't know what you're getting at, but I've got things I need to do at home, so unless you're planning to arrest me for over-cleaning one of my vehicles, I'm locking up and I'm out of here. Okay?'

'Okay, Mr Reeves, just one more thing. I assume the drivers each have a locker here on site? And if so, we'll need to see Phoebe's. *Now.*'

Josh sighed, shaking his head. 'For fuck's sake. Wait here, the keys are in reception.'

Josh was back within a couple of minutes. He led them through to a door at the end of the building into a sort of changing room, with a number of plastic stacking chairs lined up at one side and a row of ten lockers along the other. There was a table against the wall opposite the door through which they had entered, with a kettle and microwave on it and a wall cabinet above.

'Phoebe has two lockers,' Josh said.

'Only two?' Andy said, raising his eyebrows in mock surprise.

'She's just got more stuff,' Josh said, pulling open the two doors.

'While DS Mills checks these,' Jo said, 'can we have another look at the ledger? I'm sure he'll only be a few minutes and then he'll lock up and bring the keys back over to reception.'

'Well, I don't know…'

'I'll be sure to let you know if I find anything interesting or incriminating, Mr Reeves,' Andy said with a big smile.

'Look it's not really…'

'Come on, Mr Reeves,' Jo said. 'The ledger.'

They walked back to the front office where Josh made a great show of inconvenience lifting the heavy tome out of its drawer for the second time. Jo turned the pages, making a note of several of Phoebe's regular pick-ups along with dates, before Andy joined them. He looked across at Jo and shrugged.

'Well, thank you very much for your time, Mr Reeves. We'll be on our way so you can deal with this important business at home.'

They left the office, Jo briefly leaning back in.

'Oh, Mr Reeves, I almost forgot. Happy New Year.'

'Anything?' Jo asked after they had got into the car.

'I think we've found the answer to where our girl is moving her clothes to and from, given that we know it's not to her parents' house.'

Andy edged the car out of the yard onto the busy main road just in time to be stopped at the traffic lights. They were silent for a while before Jo turned to him.

'Did it strike you there was something missing from that conversation with our Mr Reeves?'

'You mean, he never once asked if there was any news about his missing star driver?'

'Exactly.'

*

The operations area contained twelve work stations in six pairs of two facing each other, and four small tables for impromptu meetings. Along one side of the room was a row of filing cabinets, little used in the now digital information environment. DCs Jodi Lawson and Kirsty Milner, both looking less formal than usual in close-fitting short skirts and trendy tops, had joined Eva at one of the tables and were deep in conversation as Jo walked through to her office to discard her coat. Andy joined the three women at the table.

'Not sure I can deal with all this hot femininity at close quarters,' he said with his hallmark smirk.

Jo caught the remark as she joined them.

'In which case, DS Mills, you can get the coffees.' She handed him the plastic tray with holes in it for six cups. She looked round the table. 'If my memory serves me right, that's three cappuccinos, one with sugar, and an Americano. And why not get yourself one while you're there?'

Andy stood his ground for a few moments as they all looked at him with wide smiles.

'Oh, yes, sorry – *please*,' Jo added. Andy shrugged, opened his mouth as if to say something, thought better of it, and turned and left the room. 'I have to admit, though, you two look like you're just back from or heading off to a party somewhere.' She nodded at Jodi and Kirsty. 'What do you think, Eva?'

'Definitely. I feel really dowdy alongside.'

'Going out for a meal later and came prepared for a sharp exit when the time comes,' Kirsty said.

'And we have a change of clothes in the event of any action,' Jodi added, with a smile, shared by the others.

'Well, I'll try and keep you out of harm's way,' Jo said.

Andy was back within three minutes, carefully placing the tray on the table with surprisingly good grace. They each took their cup.

'Okay,' Jo said, 'any news on the missing footage?'

'Mo said he has no idea what's happened, but it didn't matter because nothing showed up, anyway. I mentioned the possible mix-up with the trains – London or Sheffield. He said he was pretty certain it was the London train she got on, but he'll get them to resend the link from Piccadilly when he gets in tomorrow.'

Jo raised her eyebrows. 'New Year's Day?'

'That's what he said.'

'What's the issue?' Andy asked.

'Mo has been following this girl, you know the one on CCTV, and he was convinced she got on the late train to London that Saturday night. He checked all the stations through to Euston but she wasn't captured at any, including Euston.'

'Another disguise?'

'Seb thinks – well he's sure, in fact – it wasn't the London train, but the one to Sheffield.'

'And who is Seb?'

'My husband, and…'

'Your *husband*. He's working on the case now as well?' He waved his arm at the three DCs. 'There soon won't be anything left for us to do.'

'He's a surveillance expert.' Jo was annoyed at herself for feeling the need to explain, especially with a lie. 'Look, you all saw the footage. Can you recall seeing the CCTV coverage of her getting on the train?'

'Yes, definitely,' Jodi answered. 'Through the gate, along the platform; running to catch it. She only just made it.'

'Well, that part of the capture has been removed. Deleted, which makes me feel very uneasy.'

'But if it was a link,' Jodi offered, 'they'd have to delete at source. When you used the link again, it would just pick up what was left.'

'Which is why I wonder if it was a file downloaded from a link, if that's possible. But still doesn't explain why it was deleted when it was still part of an ongoing investigation. But if it *was* the Sheffield train she boarded, and if we *do* think this person could be Phoebe, then we need to check the stops between Manchester and Sheffield, and beyond, I guess. We'll leave that for DC Malik tomorrow, unless he remembers it's a holiday, because I assumed we would all be taking it off to recover from our hangovers.'

'That's if they haven't deleted it at source at the stations by then,' Andy said. 'Often kept for a week to ten days. We're day nine today.'

'Good point.' Jo turned to Eva. 'Can you get onto the Transport Police right away. We don't want to lose what could be evidence by delaying just a few hours. They don't need to do anything today except make sure to keep whatever they've got.'

Eva got to her feet. 'Right now, ma'am?'

'Right after DS Mills brings you all up to date with our tryst with Easy Rider. Sergeant?'

Andy leaned forward, elbows on the table.

'I think it's very possible that things are not quite what they seem at Easy Rider.' He took them through the interview with Mr Reeves, then leaned back in his chair.

'So, questions arising. Firstly, Phoebe Wright's minibus, ambulance, whatever, has been forensically cleaned. It will be interesting to check whether the other seven are given the same treatment. Somehow, I doubt it and, if I'm right, then why would he feel it necessary to do it to that one in particular?

'Secondly, throughout the whole time we were with him, he didn't enquire once if we had made any progress in finding her. So, either he doesn't care, which doesn't fit with his apparent worship of her. or he knows where she is or at least knows she's safe.

'Thirdly, we know the dates of two of the instances when Wright disappeared for a couple of days from the loving arms of Benny Morrison. On both occasions, she had use of the vehicle for a time but there's no record of what she was doing with it or where she took it. The first time, it was just part of one day, but the second time involved two full days – a weekend.' He looked across at Jo. 'We should check with Highfields if they keep records of these trips to confirm whether that did happen on that day.'

'Agreed, although I bet they don't,' Jo said. 'It's a pity we don't know which care home she claimed was considering sending their residents to a bonfire party. Except, of course, it could have been just an excuse for keeping the vehicle, especially as it coincides with her going AWOL from Morrison.'

'We could get a full list of all the care homes she visits,' suggested Jodi. 'There can't be so many that we can't contact them all. And even if they don't keep records, I reckon they'll remember any plans they had for Bonfire Night, or Bonfire Day, in this case, even if they didn't happen.'

'Good idea, Jodi. Anything else for now?' They shook their heads. 'I think we should pay Mr Reeves another visit, like we promised, on Wednesday – see how shiny the rest of his fleet is by then and get a list of Phoebe's care homes at the same time. Also, it might be an idea to get the SOCOs to do a job on her vehicle, just to check how thoroughly it has been cleaned. We'd need a valid excuse, but I'm sure we could come up with one.'

'He could hardly refuse, anyway, could he?' Andy said.

Jo furrowed her brow in thought. 'Just thinking,' she said, looking at Andy. 'If Reeves *is* up to something, those records don't mean a thing, do they? He could just write any old crap in the ledger while Miss Wright had the vehicle to do whatever she wanted with it. I think at some point we should commandeer the ledger and check *all* the recently recorded activity, not just the times when she went AWOL.'

This time there were nods all round. Jo checked her watch.

'Twelve twenty. Eva, you've got the short straw. Get in touch with the stations between Manchester and Sheffield and to where the train terminates. And if it's straightforward enough, and they can let us have the capture right away, it wouldn't harm having a look today. I'll be here for a while, going to contact Phoebe's parents and Benny with an update. Not much of one, it'll be same ol', same ol'. Nothing new but just to show we still care, and it might ward them off phoning me later.' She looked at Andy, Kirsty and Jodi. 'Unless you're desperate to stay, there's nothing stopping you getting an early finish here for an early start of whatever you're doing for the New Year.'

The three DCs got to their feet and returned to their workstations. Andy remained seated.

'Are you not leaving, Sergeant? Have I missed something?'

Andy stood up and stretched. 'Got an important meeting with

the Super at two o'clock. I guess I'll pop out and grab a bite to eat first. See you Wednesday.'

He walked from the room with Jo looking wide-eyed after him.

*

The call to Benny was painless. No anger or abuse, which she was half-expecting, just a resigned acceptance of the message, except for a quiet snort at Jo's 'no news is good news' comment. Words that slipped out, which Jo would have taken back immediately if she could.

She took a deep breath and scrolled to the next number. The phone was picked up on its second ring reminding her that they must be spending their lives in desperate anticipation of the right call.

'Hello, Phil Wright here.' The voice was loaded with both hope and anxiety.

'Mr Wright, it's DI Carter here, and to assure you right away, we have no news of anything bad having happened to Phoebe…' glass half full, she thought '… but neither are we much closer to discovering her whereabouts.'

'Oh, God.'

'We want you to know that we are following new leads and although it's too early to be anywhere near certain, nothing so far points to any harm coming to your daughter.'

'She's been missing for nine days. I'm not sure how *you* define nothing pointing to any harm, but from where we are it's difficult to come to any other conclusion. We just need… to *know*… so we…' His voice broke and Jo could hear his wife whispering to him with what she assumed were words of comfort.

'I know this must be incredibly difficult for you both, Mr Wright, but try not to jump to that conclusion. I understand it's natural to think the worst in order to prepare yourself, but as I said, there is nothing to indicate your daughter has come to any harm. Although I have no idea, or theory, as to *why* she has disappeared.'

'Well, what about this then?' Mr Wright had recovered enough to sound angry. 'We've heard that someone followed Phoebe when she left the pub that night. So, why hasn't he been arrested? You don't have to be Sherlock Holmes to put two and two together.'

'We know the person you mean, Mr Wright, and he has been part of our investigation. But he did not *follow* Phoebe home, he walked part of the way with her when she left the pub. And she was seen some time after that by a gentleman who was walking his dog. Please believe me, Mr Wright, we are following up every lead we get. I'm so sorry we have not been successful so far.'

There was a long pause, during which Jo could hear more whispering. When the conversation resumed, it was Mrs Wright's voice on the call.

'DI Carter, Helen Wright here. Thank you for taking the time to keep in touch. We really do appreciate it...' she gave a little chuckle '... even though it might not always seem that way. And if Phoebe gets in touch with us, we will, of course, let you know straight away.'

'Thank you, Mrs Wright. I hope our next conversation will be about Phoebe's *re*-appearance.'

'Goodbye, Inspector.'

She ended the call before Jo could speak. She leaned back in her chair and sighed again as Eva tapped on her door and opened it a fraction to peer in.

'Come in,' Jo called. 'Any luck?'

'Not sure yet. That particular train terminates at Sheffield and you need to change for anywhere else. It's an additional trans-Pennine service they're running just for the holiday period; all December through to mid-January. So that *would* be the train to get if you're going from Manchester to Leicester, but not *just* to Leicester, to lots of other destinations as well, including Sheffield itself, of course.'

Eva paused, as if to let the information sink in.

Jo frowned. 'Right. When I said, "any luck," you said you weren't sure, which leads me to wonder if you're going to tell me something else.'

'Well, the good news is I've got access to the CCTV capture for that train's arrival. And – more good news – as it's a through train, everyone who got on in Manchester had to get off there. I've got the footage from that platform ready to run; I wondered if you wanted to check it with me, or have I just spoilt your plans for an early exit home?'

Jo smiled. 'Yes, and yes.' She held up the empty Styrofoam cup. 'So, let's get a refill and start watching the movie.'

★

They found themselves sitting side by side again, legs stretched out in front of them, in their now familiar viewing position on the bed.

'So,' Seb said, as Jo began to run the footage on her laptop, 'if she got *on* the train in Manchester, and it was a through train, she must be one of the passengers getting *off* the train in Sheffield.'

'Seb, that's brilliant.'

'No need for sarcasm. You're getting paid for this, remember; I'm not.'

Jo laughed. 'I'm not being sarcastic, that's exactly the sort of incisive input I've come to rely on. No, really, Eva and I couldn't spot our girl, at least not how she was when she got on the train. But if she's changed her appearance once, she can no doubt do it again. So...' she nodded towards the screen, '...you managed to separate the face from the hair before. Let's see if you can do it again.'

'You're not suggesting we go through this now? We're supposed to be heading out to the pub with Sal and Jonno in fifteen minutes.'

'Of course not *now*. I thought I might take the laptop to the pub...'

'You're *kidding*.'

Jo laughed and elbowed him in the ribs. 'Yes, I'm kidding.' She swung her legs off the bed. 'Come on, let's get ready.'

★

The atmosphere in the Hare and Hounds in Holcombe Brook was, as to be expected on New Year's Eve, joyous and rowdy. The festive decorations, which always seemed superfluous a couple of days after Christmas, appeared to have had a new lease of life and the selection of pop songs from several decades clearly met the approval of celebrants of all ages who did their best to drown them out by supplementing the recordings with raucous voices. Sally and Jonno were staying over and they were all planning to leave the pub immediately after midnight and let the New Year in at the Carter residence where Roy and Bella awaited them; another family tradition not to be meddled with.

The noise in the pub made it difficult to sustain a conversation and there were periods when attempts to talk were happily abandoned in order to soak up the atmosphere. During these times, Jo's mind slipped back onto the case and the music receded to make way for thoughts and theories as she scanned the room for… she wasn't sure what. With her eyes focused on the screen of her iPhone, she was suddenly aware of someone speaking to her.

'What? Sorry. I missed that…'

Jo looked up. Seb was frowning at her, obviously waiting for an answer to a question.

'I said, do you want another of those or something different.'

'Something different?'

'Okay, what then?'

'No, that was a question. What do you mean, something different?'

'A different drink.' There was an edge to Seb's voice which was rarely heard. 'I'll speak slowly, stop me if I'm going too fast. You've… had… three…G&Ts… so… far… Do… you…'

'Want another? Yes, please.'

'What are you looking at that's so much more interesting than our company?' Seb sounded angry now.

'I'm sorry, but I'm sure I recognise someone over at the window table. Please don't all look now.'

Seb frowned. 'And that's why you're staring at your iPhone? Not sure I see the connection.'

Jo turned the phone so Seb could see. 'This is a still of the other girl who was captured on CCTV at…'

'Oh, for God's sake, Jo. We're out to celebrate New Year. Can't you leave it alone for one night?'

'Well, actually, *no*, Seb. And you know that or you *should* know that. She could be a key witness without realising it. So perhaps someone should tell her. What do you think?'

Seb sighed and looked at the image Jo was holding for him to see. He stood up, taking Jo's other hand in his.

He looked across the table at Sally and Jonno. 'Can you excuse us for a few minutes?'

'Oh, shit, I was really enjoying that,' Jonno said. 'Thought we were about to hear a few secrets.'

'Shut up, Jonathan,' Sally said. 'Don't be long, you two. I was really enjoying a bit of adult company for a change.'

Jonno shrugged and Jo laughed. They walked across to the door, giving Seb the opportunity to study the girl in question on the way. Once outside, they looked together at the girl on the screen.

'I'm one hundred per cent sure it's her,' Jo said. 'She looks like she might even be wearing the same outfit, and the bobbed hairstyle is an absolute give away. Question is, what to do right now? She's behaving like she's three sheets to the wind. Don't want to make a scene by waving my ID in her face, and there's bound to be people around who know Phoebe. Marlon Finch said she has lots of friends here. It could get awkward if they start throwing accusations around about us not doing enough to find her. But we really have to find out if she knew the other girl on her own outside the pub; the one who just *might* be Phoebe.'

'I guess so, because…'

'*Because*,' Jo went on, 'if she *does* know her and it *isn't* Phoebe, that changes everything. It doesn't necessarily mean we're now looking for a body, but the odds on that shorten significantly.'

They were silent for a few moments before Seb spoke.

'Let me have a word with Chris, the landlord. See if he knows her and where she lives or if he knows someone who does. Then we can go round to see her tomorrow. Because I think you're right, we don't want to risk a scene. What do you think?'

'I think you mean *I* can go round to see her tomorrow, not *we*. Otherwise, I think it's an excellent idea.'

They smiled at each other and kissed, with sudden passion. Hand in hand again, they went back into the pub.

'Sit here,' Seb said, pulling out the chair where he had been sitting. 'Then you'll have your back to the target and won't be watching her all the time. I'll get the drinks and talk to Chris. Don't tell Jonno anything, he can't be trusted.'

'Hey, I resent that.' Jonno frowned, then smiled, archly. 'Although, I don't deny it.'

Seb returned five minutes later, expertly carrying two G&Ts

and two pints, which he placed on the table, carefully unwrapping his fingers from the glasses.

'No luck, I'm afraid,' he told Jo. 'Chris says he's never seen her in here before. A couple of the other bar staff said the same. But we do know, don't we, that she's recently been in the Shoulder, so she may be known there.'

'Is someone going to tell us what's going on?' Jonno spread his arms in invitation. 'Or is it just too awful for our sensitive ears?'

Jo smiled. 'The girl with the bobbed hair at the table near the window is someone we saw on CCTV while we were checking Phoebe Wright's movements on the night she went missing. She's not part of the story, but we need to speak with her.'

'You mean,' Jonno glanced shiftily from side to side, 'to eliminate her from your enquiries? How exciting.'

'She's not part of our enquiries, but whatever turns you on, Jonno,' Jo said.

'Right,' Seb said, addressing Jo. 'Can we agree you'll check at the Shoulder tomorrow, so we can get on with tonight?'

'Okay,' Jo said. She got to her feet. 'Just need the loo.' She turned and moved quickly away. Seb looked across at the window table and noticed that the bob-haired head was missing.

★

'Clearly, you cannot be trusted to follow a simple plan.'

Jo and Seb, arms around each other, walked unsteadily along the icy surface of the narrow, terraced thoroughfare of Pot Green, where each of its cosy little houses still sported a twinkling tree. A row of cottages designed just for Christmas, as Seb's mum had described the street. Ahead of them, with the same inter twining of bodies and with similar unsteadiness, Sally and Jonno led the way home.

'It just happened that as I was looking in the mirror in the little girls' room, suddenly there she was, standing right...'

'It's a good thing you're not under oath, Mrs Carter, or I'd have you for contempt. What you mean is, you saw her heading for the loo and took your chance. Right?'

'Right, but I *did* look in the mirror and she *was* standing right next to me. So, no contempt. Not really. And one on one, with my advanced skills of diplomacy, it was easy to create a calm atmosphere for discussion. It also helped that I was completely wrong about her being three sheets gone. She's driving and was drinking tonic water. She was just enjoying herself a little loudly.'

'But no luck with her testimony.'

'No. She knows Phoebe, but not as a friend. Just someone who she sees occasionally in the Shoulder or in pubs in Bury. Says "hi" to her, that's all. But insists she wasn't in the Shoulder that night, and that, based on the CCTV image, the girl definitely isn't Phoebe. In fact, she doesn't remember seeing the girl in the picture either.'

'Although we know she was there, so not the most reliable of witnesses.'

'I don't know. You wouldn't expect everybody who was in the Shoulder that night to remember everybody else. And she may have been three-sheets *that* night because we know she wasn't driving.'

'In which case, we are no further on.'

Jo smiled up at him.

'Well, technically, *I'm* no further on, but thank you for keeping me company.'

They stopped and kissed again, with the same passion as before but for longer this time.

CHAPTER TWELVE

Tuesday 1 January

'God, who's idea was this?' Seb screwed up his eyes and peered out of the window at the sun dazzling off the thin blanket of snow.

'I recall that it was a unanimous decision,' Sally said, 'albeit made at a time and in a condition when we shouldn't have been deciding *anything*.'

The siblings were seated together at the breakfast bar in the kitchen. Jo had been down first, had finished her breakfast some time ago and had withdrawn to help Bella with preparations for their hike to the chimney above Ogden Reservoir. Jonno had not yet appeared.

Seb checked his watch for the umpteenth time.

'Nine-thirty. Who's up at this time on New Year's Day? No-one with half a brain who went to bed at half past two.'

'Unless, of course, they're going for a twelve-mile walk.'

'*Twelve* miles? TWELVE miles. You said six miles; I *know* you did.'

'I suggested we walk to the chimney and you said, how far is that, and I said, six miles.'

'I thought you meant there and back...'

'Oh, come on, Sebastian Carter, you know these moors as well as I do. You know it's more than that.'

Seb looked a little sheepish. 'Well, I admit it didn't seem quite right, but I just thought I might have got the wrong chimney.'

Sally sprayed out crumbs of toast with the burst of laughter. 'Priceless, Seb. Absolutely priceless.'

Jo entered the room looking as fresh as a daisy and making no attempt to contain her enthusiasm for the challenge ahead. She held up four rucksacks, two in each hand.

'Ready when you're good to go.' She leaned them against the wall at the side of the door. 'Butties, crisps, chocolate, Christmas cake, fruit, water, coffee, and something a little stronger for when *we* feel a little stronger.' She reached into one of the sacks and lifted out a half bottle of Laphroig. 'This is the only one, by the way. There isn't one in each sack, just mine.' She checked the clock on the kitchen wall. 'Nine-forty. Shall we say ten o'clock for setting off? Where's Jonno, by the way?'

'I fear we may have one pack too many,' Sally said. 'Not sure if my other half will make it.'

'Oooh, yes, he will.' The pantomime cry came from the hall a couple of seconds before Jonno appeared in the doorway. 'No way am I going to be ridiculed all day in my absence, then all evening in my presence.' He turned to Jo. 'Ready when you are, Inspector. Just a thought, though. How about we walk to the garden centre instead.'

'That's about half a mile,' Sally said.

'Really?' Jonno frowned. 'I guess we could always get a taxi back.'

Jo laughed. 'Seriously, Jonno, if you don't feel up to it, no point in making yourself miserable, so…'

'Clever stuff, Jo, knowing there's only one way I'd respond to that. I repeat, ready when you are.'

'Good for you, Jonno,' Seb said. 'Ten o'clock start. Just about time for you to grab a bit of breakfast.'

'That really would be pushing my luck. I'll put my faith in Jo's lucky bag for refreshments on the journey.'

'Bella's lucky bag, to be accurate,' Jo said. 'She put them all together.'

Bella appeared in the doorway. 'Now you be careful today, it's bound to be slippery in places, You especially Sally; don't want you falling down in your condition. Anyway, enjoy yourselves. I'm very impressed actually; I really thought you'd change your mind.'

'I was sort of hoping…' Seb said.

Jo checked the clock again. 'Right, in the hall in fifteen minutes.'

★

They set out at a few minutes after ten o'clock taking the same route as they had the previous Saturday on their way to Jo's cottage, along Miller Street and the station platform to the railway bridge. Once under the bridge, they followed Railway Street past the garden centre and on to Robin Road. They reached the row of terraced cottages admired so much by Sally and Jo, who spent some time deciding which of them they would choose to live in.

'Why not choose one each, then we could all live here,' Jonno said.

They continued on the riverside path then along Woodhey Road reaching the large detached houses close to the end.

'This is more me,' Jonno said, pointing to a large, modern, sandstone-bricked property. 'Room for lots of kids and a garden big enough for them to play in so they won't disturb me watching the rugby on Sky Sports.'

'Who said we'll have lots of kids *or* Sky Sports?' Sally said.

'Well, I only need you for one of those,' Jonno answered, 'so the question should be "who said we'll have a lot of kids *and* Sky Sports?"'

Jo and Seb laughed. 'You two are like an in-house sitcom,' Jo said. 'Do you rehearse this stuff?'

They crossed Bolton Road to where the Hare and Hounds was opening its doors to welcome the lunchtime crowd.

'I wonder if they're doing breakfast,' Jonno said. 'I'm starving.'

'You had your chance before we left,' Sally said. 'And you don't want to spoil your appetite for Mum's lucky bag, do you?'

They headed past the pub up Holcombe Old Road, taking the same cobbled lane at the fork up to the Islamic College, where they turned left to join Moorbottom Road. They stopped for a breather and half-leaned, half-sat on a crumbling dry-stone wall.

'You okay, sis?' Seb asked.

'Of course, why do you ask?' Sally smiled and raised her eyebrows in mock confusion.

'Because Mum told me to,' Seb said.

'I should have known. Anyway, that's supposed to be his line.' She gave Jonno a nudge.

They rested for a few minutes longer, taking a drink of coffee and sharing two of the chocolate bars between them.

'Okay, let's go, Seb said. 'Next stop, the Pilgrims Cross.'

'Oh, great, that's more like it,' Jonno said. 'Do they serve breakfast?'

'It's a trick, Jonno,' Jo said. 'It's not a pub, just a bloody big stone.'

Jonno sighed. 'So I guess the answer's no, then.'

They regrouped and set off again.

'God, it's beautiful here,' Jo said, as they climbed the narrow path to the moor top, the snow stretching in all directions as far as they could see. They continued to the Pilgrims Cross, climbing Bull Hill, which drew more gasps of appreciation from Jo, joined this time by Jonno.

'You're right,' he said. 'This is really special. I'm definitely going to bring the kids up here. *All* of them.'

Sally rolled her eyes. 'Best crack on,' she said. 'We've a long way to go yet.'

They continued down the hill along the narrow path to where a more distinct one crossed it running east–west, with a waymarker telling them they'd reached the Rossendale Way. They turned left, following the path westward. Their boots had so far penetrated the two or three centimetres of snow through to where the path was stoney, and the going had been easy enough. However, as they dropped down to where Alden Brook trickled its way through rocky banks, the path became a series of large flat boulders, eventually crossing the stream and doubling back to rise steeply up the opposite side. Jonno viewed it with some trepidation.

'Is this a good idea?' he asked. 'This could be dangerous if they're slippery, especially for Sal.'

'Oh, for goodness' sake…'

'No, he's right, Sal,' Seb interrupted. 'I'd forgotten about this bit. I bet this was what Mum was thinking about when she said be careful.'

'Well, *I'm* going across,' Sally said. 'But if you two knights in shining armour want to check it out first, Jo and I will wait here and admire your bravery.'

Five minutes later, they had all crossed the brook, although it took a while longer for the expression of smug satisfaction to leave Sally's face. The way followed the contours of the hillside to reach Great House Farm, where it doubled back across a flatter section and through a couple of farm gates on to Maiden Moor. Eventually, they turned due north, still following the RW waymarkers.

'Last leg,' Sally said. 'Watch out for buffalo.'

'Buffalo?' Jo said.

'Along here we often came across some cows. And they always parked themselves on the path, so we had to drop down the hill to get past them. We used to pretend they were wild buffalo.'

'Well, wild or not, buffalo or not, I'm heading back if we meet any,' Jonno said.

'My hero,' Sally said. 'Anyway, we won't today. They'll most likely be inside somewhere.'

'In which case, I wouldn't mind joining them. How much further is it? We must be nearly in Scotland by now.'

'Two or three more miles,' Seb said.

'What?' Jonno's eyes opened wide in disbelief and panic.

'Perhaps a little less.' Seb winked at Jo.

Ten minutes later, the way curved to the left and the stone chimney appeared before them.

'Behold,' Seb announced, 'Musbury Heights Quarry, our destination and lunch venue.'

The chimney rose above the ruined buildings, which covered a wide area but whose walls were mostly less than a metre high. Sally and Seb began to wander through the site in a state of excitement pointing out to each other where they remembered playing on their visits there as children. Seb turned to Jo and Jonno who had been watching in silent amusement.

'Come and see this.'

They walked over to where a small stone and wood-shored tunnel had been constructed under a man-made incline. It looked anything but stable.

'This slope here was for a tramway taking stone down to Haslingden to make flags. The tunnel was made later for access to the parts of the quarry that would have been cut off when they built the Ogden Reservoir.' He held up his hands. 'Don't ask me any questions; I only know that because I read it in the leaflet. I can't work it out here on the ground. But anyway, Sal and I were forbidden on pain of death to go in here, so we took it in turns to watch out for the old folks while the other went through.'

'Well don't even think about it today, Sally, dear,' Jonno said. 'And you won't fit through anyway. Seb.'

'No, I think our tunnelling days are over. So let's eat, over by the tarn.'

He waved his arm towards a small pond a few metres away.

'Don't tell me,' Jonno said, 'this is where you always had your picnic when you used to come here as children.'

'Why, *yes*,' Seb said, in mock surprise. 'How did you work that out? You should have been a detective. What do you think, Jo?'

The air was colder up on the Heights and the wind much stronger, but they found just enough shelter to enable the enjoyment of Bella's feast to offset the discomfort, helped by Jo's administering generous measures of Laphroig to each of their coffees As they neared the end of their repast, Sally looked across at her brother.

'I can't put my finger on it but something's different.'

'No flies,' Seb said. 'We always came up here in Spring or Summer when the tarn was covered in flies. It always spoilt it for Mum, I remember.'

'That's right. Of course. Although I'd take the flies right now for a bit more warmth.' She checked her watch. 'Ten to one, better get going.'

They retraced their steps back to the point where they had joined the Rossendale Way, continuing on the same path to the track that is Moor Road, leading to Holcombe Old Road and heading south. They were now walking in their marital pairs, with Jo and Seb leading.

'What's that giant biscuit tin doing over there?' Jonno shouted to them.

Their eyes followed his pointing finger.

'That's an MCV,' Jo said. 'Mobile command vehicle The base for the search of the moor after Phoebe Wright's disappearance. I'm not sure why it's still there,' she added, half to herself. 'I guess this would have been Phoebe's route if she is the girl on camera.'

Seb nodded but said nothing.

The track led down to Lumb Carr Road, joining it at the Shoulder of Mutton, where they waited for Sally and Jonno to catch them up.

'Right, I suggest Sally, Jonno and I stop for a drink, while Jo carries on back home.'

'Hey, wait a minute...!'

'Can we trust you to behave and not start waving photographs around?'

Jo smiled and placed her hand on her heart. 'I promise.'

'Right,' Seb said. 'Let's get in there.'

★

By the time they stepped out of the pub, darkness had descended. The overcast sky had warmed the air and the earlier covering of snow had already turned to slush and was now melting to a slippery wetness.

'Let's walk back on the pavement,' Jonno suggested. 'That's enough off-roading for today.'

'Good idea, but no sliding on the way down,' Sally said, wagging a finger at her husband.

'If I do, it won't be on purpose.'

They set off together with Jo and Seb close behind. Jo's phone rang and she fished it out of her jacket pocket with much cursing as she fumbled with removing her gloves. She checked the caller.

'Don't tell me,' Seb said. 'That's Mum checking we're alright, now it's gone dark.'

'I wish,' Jo said, sliding the green disc on the screen to take the call. 'Hello, Mr Wright.'

Jo stopped walking, allowing Sally and Jonno to get further ahead, and pressed the speaker button so Seb could listen. They could hear the sound of an agitated exchange taking place in loud whispers before a female voice addressed them.

'DI Carter? Look, I'm sorry, we shouldn't have called you, not after we'd spoken yesterday and the day before. But Philip is all over the place, doesn't know where to put himself. We agreed we wouldn't call, then I caught him just now...'

'Please don't apologise, Mrs Wright. I quite understand. You are both holding up really well, considering. Feel free to call me any time, but as I said, I'll be in touch as soon as we have some news to tell you.'

There was a silence before Helen spoke again.

'So, no news yet?'

'No, I'm afraid...'

'I just wondered if she'd made a dramatic appearance for New Year. Silly, really.'

'Not silly at all, Helen. And I'll wait until we find her to wish you a Happy New Year.'

Jo ended the call.

'Have they seen the CCTV coverage yet,' Seb asked. 'They might be the most likely people to ID Phoebe, even in disguise. They might recognise the coat.'

'You're right, of course, but I was hoping not to have to do that. Not to have to put them through it. If they're convinced it's *not* her, that's a massive disappointment. And if they think it *is*, then... well, I'm not sure what they'll think and how they'll react.'

'At least they'll know she got off the moor safely.'

'They'll know she was still alive ten days ago a few hours after leaving their house, you mean, and that she got on a train to Sheffield later. I can't see they'll sleep easier for knowing that, can you?'

'No, but...'

'You're right, though. I'll get Morrison in first and then the Wrights afterwards to check it. Tomorrow.'

★

'Jo, I need to get going.' Seb popped his head round the corner of the dining room where Jo was sitting at the table speaking on the phone. The evidence of a meal recently finished was present in the form of a Christmas cruet set, unused napkins, half-drunk glasses of wine and coffee cups. Seb had left them about ten minutes ago to prepare for his journey home and Roy and Bella had vacated the room to allow Jo to take the call. Sally and Jonno had just left to return to Altrincham.

'Okay, just coming,' she shouted. 'Got to go, Mo. Listen, it's after eight. Just go home, for God's sake.'

'Your God or mine, ma'am?'

'Very droll. Just tell me you're leaving or I'll turn this into a disciplinary.'

'In which case, I'm leaving.'

'Good. See you in the morning for the showing with Morrison and the Wrights. Goodnight, detective.'

'Goodnight, ma'am.'

'Jo,' Seb again.

'Coming.'

They stood together, arms around each other, next to Seb's car as he prepared to leave for the long drive to their cottage in the tiny village of Kenswick, close to Leicester. They held each other in silence for a long time before Jo pulled back a little to speak.

'Seb, you remember when we were checking through the CCTV capture – on the bed?'

'Oh, I won't forget that for a long time.'

Jo laughed. 'Me neither. I said, perhaps Malik had stumbled onto something, and you said, unless he *knew* it was her, or something like that. Why did you say that?'

'I'm not sure.'

'Thinking back, it was like you were suggesting he was keeping something from us. Which sort of implies he was somehow linked to the disappearance.'

'I don't think I was suggesting that. It was just another reason why he might be so focused. What's made you think about that again now?'

'It's like he can't leave it alone for a minute. He's been at the station all day, best part of twelve hours. It's not like today is a *religious* holiday; it's a *bank* holiday. So, no reason for him not to take advantage of it. Sure, we all know it's important to find Phoebe; that's a given. I'm sure Jonesy already thinks we've spent too much time and too many resources on the case, and he's right, given the number of similar cases like this which result in the sudden, voluntary reappearance of the fugitive. He's just obsessed; like it's really important to him that he, *personally*, finds her.'

'Perhaps he fancies her.'

'It did cross my mind.'

'Not that I understand what he could possibly see in her. There again, my standards are so high.'

'Just make sure you keep them up there...'

'And, anyway, she's a bit young for me.'

Jo dug him hard in the ribs. 'There you go again.'

Seb laughed, and pulled her close to him again. 'I love you so much, Mrs Carter, but I really will have to go. Send me through the link to the Sheffield CCTV footage and I'll check the passengers off the train. Sorry we didn't get time to go through it together, but I much preferred what we did instead.'

'Me too. You take care now; drive safely.'

'I will.'

They kissed long and passionately, then hugged again, Jo's head nestling against Seb's chest. He finally stepped away and squeezed into the driver's seat, turning on the engine and lowering his window.

'You take care, too, and get that cottage sorted before I come back. I don't want to be wasting time in future waiting for the old folks to go shopping.'

Jo laughed. 'Okay, that's a promise. See you in ten days – fingers crossed.'

She waved as he pulled off the drive, peeping his horn as he drove away. She watched him until he was out of sight, wondering why, after the past twelve perfect days they'd spent together, the niggling doubt about their future still remained.

CHAPTER THIRTEEN

Wednesday 2 January

Jo got to her feet as Eva stepped to one side and waved Benny Morrison into the small meeting room. It was one used regularly for informal meetings between the public and the police designed to be less official-feeling than the standard interview rooms. This one was carpeted with pale yellow painted walls and was furnished with a rectangular beech table with six matching chairs around it. A large wall-mounted monitor screen faced along the table.

'Thank you for coming in, Mr Morrison. Please take a seat.'

Benny sat down on the chair offered, Eva taking the seat next to him.

'Are your daughters still with you?' Jo asked.

'Still in bed. I'm taking them to the station this afternoon.'

He looked anxious and tired. His clothes were creased and he looked as though he'd dressed in a hurry with no thought for his appearance.

'What's happened?' he said.

'We'd like you to look at some CCTV images and tell us whether you think any of the people could be Phoebe. If it is her, she has disguised herself, so no use looking for a woolly hat and long blonde hair. Okay?'

Benny sighed. 'I guess. I thought you got me here to tell me something; not for another grope in the dark.'

Mo entered the room and sat down close to the screen. He clicked the mouse and the screen came to life, showing a still image of the car park at the Shoulder of Mutton.

'Okay, roll them, Mr Malik.'

Mo set the image moving, adding his live commentary.

'I guess you recognise where this is, Benny. Outside the Shoulder on Lumb Carr Road. This is that same Saturday evening, the twenty-second of December at around eight o'clock. There's a bus into Bury due in a few minutes. These guys smoking outside will be joined by more from inside. Watch carefully, and tell me if you want me to pause the action.'

They remained silent for a few minutes focused on the screen, watching the people board the bus. Benny turned to Jo as the bus disappeared from view and shrugged.

'Is that it?' he asked. 'I don't recognise any of those people. What are they supposed to have done?'

Jo nodded to Mo to continue.

'Let's jump forward,' he said, moving to the next sequence. 'These are the same people, getting off the bus at the Interchange.'

He paused it again as the door to the room opened and Andy Mills walked in.

'More movies?' He screwed up his eyes at the screen. 'Nope, same movie.'

'We're just taking Mr Morrison through the capture to see if he can ID anybody,' Jo said. 'Grab a seat.'

Andy dropped onto one of the chairs, slouching low and spreading his legs.

'Everything ready out there?' Jo asked him.

Andy nodded, his eyes already fixed on the screen. Mo restarted the sequence. They watched in silence again as the passengers disembarked, all but a couple of them hurrying through the entrance to the Metrolink. When they had all disappeared, Mo stopped the action and Benny leaned forward.

'Can you go back to the bit with the bus stopping at the Interchange. And then go slow?'

Mo restarted the sequence on half speed. As it finished, Benny leaned back and drew in a breath.

'Again?' Mo asked.

'No, that's okay. One of them from the Shoulder is missing.'

Jo raised her eyebrows. 'Really? Not too surprising, I suppose. I'm sure some would have got off at earlier stops. Which one exactly?'

'A woman in a baseball cap, glasses, puffer jacket.'

Jo smiled. 'If you're right, Mr Morrison, I'll be very impressed. DC Malik, can you join the dots for us?'

Mo changed the screen to show another sequence.

'This passenger is getting off the same bus on Bolton Street.'

The footage showed the same woman step down onto the pavement. Two more cameras picked up her image as she walked to the Interchange and disappeared through the Metrolink entrance.

'Full marks, Mr Morrison,' Jo said, smiling, 'and, as promised, I'm very impressed. Is this person known to you?'

'Never seen her before.'

'So, how did you pick her out?'

'Well, you wanted to see if I could ID Phoebe from the CCTV, and there were only two females on their own getting on the bus at the Shoulder, so I assume it's one of those you're interested in. Easy to remember what they looked like for less than two minutes until you showed me the next shot, and only one of them got off the bus at the Interchange.'

'Perhaps you should have been a detective, Mr Morrison,' Jo said, failing to hide her disappointment.

'Well, I watch a lot of television.'

'You're sure you don't recognise that woman?'

'No, and it's definitely not Phoebe. I mean, her hair is nothing like for a start, and she doesn't even *move* like Phoebe. She sort of stoops; Phee struts her stuff like a model on a catwalk. Also, I understand, according to that Grimshaw guy, she was wearing the same clothes as in the pub.'

'And carrying a full rucksack, which was later found empty on the moor. We believe one possibility is that she changed into clothes that were in the rucksack and...'

'Permed and dyed her hair. I think you watch too much television as well, Inspector. With respect,' he added.

'As I've said before, we are not discounting any possibilities in our search for clues, *except*, you'll be relieved to know, that she permed and dyed her hair. But there are things called wigs that can be used to change one's appearance. Do you happen to know if Phoebe possesses a wig – or wigs?'

'Why would anyone with hair like hers consider wearing a wig?'

'Why? Well, if they wanted to disguise themselves, Mr Morrison.'

Benny paused and smiled thinly. 'Yes, okay. I'm just really disappointed that this meeting wasn't to share some news about her. And as far as I know, she does not possess a wig or wigs. There are none in *my* house, anyway. You'll have to check with her parents.' He leaned back in his seat and nodded at the screen. 'So, what happened next to this woman?'

'She got the tram to Piccadilly,' Mo said, moving forward to the sequence showing the same woman buying a ticket and walking quickly along the station concourse. The coverage stopped, changing to a black screen. 'From there, she boarded a train, we think to either London or Sheffield.'

'Do you know if Phoebe has any connection with Sheffield? Any friends there?' Jo asked.

'Not that I'm aware of. Not now, anyway. She did Performing Arts at A Level at Holy Cross and started doing drama or something at Sheffield Uni. Only stayed for one term. She came back at Christmas and started her current job in the new year, just one year ago.' He paused. 'Actually, she's mentioned a couple of times recently that she might give up her job and go back to uni and try again. I hope she does. I'm told she's a really good actress and she certainly has the looks to go with it. But as far as I know, she hasn't kept in touch with anyone. I guess she wasn't there long enough to make any real friends.'

'But she does take regular bus loads of people over there for days out, to Meadowhall Shopping Centre?'

'That's right, but...'

'I just wonder why go all that way when the Trafford Centre is right on the doorstep. Phoebe's boss tells us that many of the people possess a bladder which doesn't... shall we say... travel very well.'

Benny leaned forward. 'You know, I asked her exactly the same thing. She said it's about the whole experience, not just the shopping destination. Hardly a day out, crawling along for eight miles on the M60. That's what she said – in those words, more or less.'

'Certainly less exciting than twisting along the Snake Pass whilst trying not to piss yourself,' Andy put in, raising a laugh from the other four.

★

Jo and Andy returned to her office whilst Eva escorted Benny from the building.

'So, one last sweep of the area and we can get the MCV moved off. How long, do you reckon?'

Andy shrugged. 'As long as a piece of string. But I suggest we make it as soon as possible.' Jo raised her eyebrows in question but remained silent. 'The boss is not happy with the resources and time we're putting into this. And the number of personnel, for that matter.'

'Please explain.'

'He believes this case is not exceptional enough to be focusing so much time and energy on it; and cost. He mentioned the MCV as an example. I understand as well that he's going to block the temporary relocation of personnel to Haslingden library. I mean, it's not even on our patch.'

Jo felt her jaw clench in her determination to remain calm, as her sergeant's enjoyment at imparting this information became obvious.

'And exactly when did our leader share these thoughts with you?'

'Couple of days ago, New Year's Eve after we'd been to see Reeves at the depot. I told you I had an important meeting with the boss.'

'Well, I think he's right about Haslingden library.' Jo adopted a tactic she had used many times before, based on the popular theory of the best form of defence. 'I think the focus has moved away from there. It was only ever a provisional arrangement, anyway, for if we needed to do more work there. Have you told Kirsty yet?'

Andy's expression changed from self-satisfaction to confusion.

'Well... no... I thought...'

'Can I leave you to tell her then, and I'll phone the library myself later to thank them for their offer. And as for the MCV, again I think he's spot on. In fact, I assumed when you took it upon yourself, unilaterally, to terminate the search, you'd have arranged for it to be removed, given that was the *only* reason it was up there. When I saw it on our walk yesterday, I was amazed it was still in place.'

'Yes, but...'

'As to resources, not sure I'm with him there. What we have is a girl who sets out across a deserted moor at night in the direction of her parents' house and never arrives, disappearing without trace except for items, which we can be confident she had with her, scattered around on her route. Further investigation has revealed this person *regularly* goes missing, albeit for shorter periods, and I think we can be sure that on those occasions someone *will* know where she went. Finding the person or persons with that knowledge will, I'm sure, help us solve the mystery surrounding this girl. For the record, I believe this case goes much, *much* deeper than we first thought, and I am rarely wrong about these things.'

'Now, look...' Andy half rose from his chair.

'Sit down, please. We're not finished.' Andy sat down again, very slowly.

'So, for that to be "not exceptional enough" you must all lead very exciting lives up here. I'll have a chat with my *immediate* boss to hear his rationale.'

She leaned back in satisfaction, not having raised her voice above a conversational level throughout.

'Okay, *now* we're finished. Could you ask Eva to join me please on your way to the MCV.'

She picked up her iPhone and switched it on, frowning at the screen. Andy jumped to his feet, noisily pushing back the chair.

'I don't have to listen to...'

'To what?' Jo said, without looking up. 'Better get going. Don't we get charged for that thing by the hour. Not a moment to lose.'

Andy stormed from the office, slamming the door on his way out. Ten seconds later, Eva popped her head into the room.

'You okay, Boss?'

Jo frowned in mock confusion. 'Yes, absolutely great. Why?'

Eva smiled. 'Oh, nothing. You didn't call him a wanker again, did you?'

'I didn't call him a wanker before. Did he just ask you to come in here?'

'Not as such. He sort of twitched his head in this direction.'

'Good enough. Look, I'd like the e-fit guys to have a play with the CCTV images. Take the girl's glasses off, give her long blonde hair, but make sure to preserve the features as they are on the capture. See if that shows up anything. Can you get the techies working on it? And make sure to tell them to preserve the features. We don't want them just trying to make her look like Phoebe.'

'Okay.' Eva turned to leave.

'Oh, and ask them if they'll do it as a freebie and not charge our section.'

'Sorry?'

'I'll explain later. Right now, I'm going along to Easy Rider to take another look at Phoebe's locker and Mr Reeves's sparkling ambulances – or non-sparkling, I shouldn't be surprised. We need to speak to the other drivers as well; try to find out a bit more about our errant beauty's work habits. Hopefully we can catch a few before they head out. First day back, they may be slow off the mark. And I think it's about time DC Malik got some fresh air. He can ride shotgun; in fact, he can drive.'

★

Mo pulled the car into the depot yard and stopped alongside a new black Jaguar SUV parked in a space marked 'Reserved for JR' near the entrance to the office. They got out of the car, Jo nodding at the expensive vehicle.

'Someone's doing okay. The NHS must pay their contractors well. Interesting that when Mr Reeves *knew* we were coming the other day, he turned up in an eleven-year-old Fiesta.'

Jo pushed open the door and stepped into the reception area. Josh Reeves was behind the high-topped counter with his back to them taking something from a wall cabinet. He turned at the sound of their entry.

'Oh, hi…'

He looked at Jo, then seemed to tense when he saw Mo, his eyes briefly wide and questioning. Jo caught the expression.

'This is DC Mohammed Malik,' she said. 'I don't believe you've met before.'

'No, definitely not,' Josh said. 'You just took me by surprise. It's a different combination of detectives.' He gave a little laugh. 'How can I help?'

'Well, out of curiosity, we'd love to see the gleaming set of ambulances you promised us before, but our main reason for dropping in on you again is to have another look at Phoebe's locker, or lockers, should I say.'

Josh looked from one to the other then shrugged.

'Fine. The last person to check the lockers was your sergeant. No-one has taken anything out or put anything in since your last visit.' He reached under the desk and brought out two keys with fobs labelled P1 and P2. 'I'll take you over.'

They left the office and Josh led them across the yard to the garage.

'I'll have to disappoint you about the gleaming vans, I'm afraid. Valeting company let us down. They told us they'd got enough volunteers to work New Year's Day to get them all ready – *treble* time, for God's sake, and no-one turned up. All you ever hear from people is how short of money they are, and when they get the chance …'

The double doors were open and they walked in to the sound of water jets at the far end of the two lines of ambulances. All eight were still where Jo and Andy had seen them a couple of days ago, and the two furthest from the double doors were being hosed down. The condition of Phoebe's vehicle looked almost unreal in comparison to the others. The hoses were turned off and Josh opened the door to the room at the end of the building and waved them through.

'You know where to look, don't you?' he said. 'You won't be needing me.' He held out the keys to Jo.

'We'd like you to stay for a while, Mr Reeves, in case we have any questions. Could you open the lockers, please?'

'I've told you, nobody's been in there since, so why do you need me?'

'Even so, just for a while. Thank you.'

Josh looked across at Mo and sighed.

'Oh, and can you let us have contact details for the valeting company,' Jo asked.

'Carshine? What for? You're not going to start harassing them as well, are you?'

'Harassing? *Harassing*? Believe me, Mr Reeves, you'll know when you're being harassed. No…' she nodded at Phoebe's vehicle

'... I was just thinking we might get the same firm to come and clean ours. Now, please, the lockers.'

Josh stepped forward and unlocked them, pulling open the doors.

'Can I just go and check the guys valeting through there?' he asked.

'Very soon,' Jo said. She turned to Mo. 'Off you go, DC Malik. See if you can find anything a bit interesting.'

'Where are your drivers, by the way,' Jo asked. 'We'd like to speak separately to each of them as soon as possible. I thought you were all back at work today.'

'I sent them home while we got the vehicles cleaned and ready. No point paying them for just standing around.'

Jo sighed. 'Then it looks like we'll be back with you again, Mr Reeves. Tell, you what, while we check the lockers, could you get us the names of the care homes Phoebe looks after. I think you said each driver has their own list.'

Josh snorted a laugh. 'You don't think she might have moved in to one of those, do you? Or perhaps you think one of them is holding her hostage?'

'You seem very amused about the disappearance of your driver, Mr Reeves. It's almost as if you don't really care.'

'Hey, now look ...'

'We'll collect the list on our way out,' Jo said, turning away.

Mo started in the P1 locker with the shelf above the hanging rail, moving around what seemed to be a random selection of small items, mainly of clothing: woollen hats, gloves, a baseball cap, a fleece buff, packets of tissues. Moving to the rail, he examined the four hanging items: two light outdoor jackets, a hi-vis vest and a fleece gilet, looking a little lonely next to half a dozen empty hangers. Below, at the bottom of the locker, he searched through a number of dusters, cleaning cloths and fluids, a couple of aerosol cans and a dustpan and brush, which shared the floor with pairs of shoes, trainers, and boots. All functional, non-dressy.

'Nothing even a bit interesting, I'm afraid.'

'Well, I'm very disappointed, DC Malik. Try in here.'

She nodded to the second locker. Mo took a step to the side and started his search of P2.

'More of a wardrobe than a locker, this,' Mo said.

The rail held a selection of dresses, skirts, smart trousers, jeans, and tops squashed tightly together in the relatively narrow space. The bottom of the locker was filled with shoes and boots. Jo reached past Mo and picked up one of a pair of emerald-green high-heels.

'Jimmy Choo. God, these must have cost a fortune. And some of this gear, as well.' She ran her hand along the line of clothes. 'She must pick up a lot of money in tips from her admiring customers, or from somewhere else.'

Mo was already checking the shelf above the rail, which was packed with items of make-up, tissues, and face wipes, plus a small box containing two packs of condoms. At the back of the shelf were two more woollen hats, a pair of sheepskin mittens and a number of scarves. He reached behind them and picked something out, examined it and tossed it into the bottom of the first locker.

'This must be her "rave cave",' he said. 'For when she gets ready to join the action.'

'Her what?'

'My elder sister had a separate wardrobe where she kept all her sexiest party gear. She called it her "rave cave". She's in her thirties now and I doubt if any of it would still fit her, but when I first joined the police, she was in full swing and I had to warn her that if I ever caught her outside in some of the stuff she had, I would have to arrest her for indecent exposure.'

Jo laughed. 'It has been a long-time trend for girls to go on nights out wearing as little as they can get away with. Even back in my partying days.'

'I won't risk my career by asking if you followed that trend, ma'am.'

'I'm very pleased to hear it, detective. I wouldn't want to have to lie to you.' She peered into the bottom of the first locker. 'What was that you chucked in there?'

'A duster in the wrong place, I think. Or a mop-head or something.'

Jo picked it out and examined it; a mass of thickish brown threads, each between fifteen and twenty centimetres long, spreading out from a fine mesh base. With a stretch of the imagination, it could,

Jo conceded, be mistaken for the head of a mop; at first glance, perhaps, but then only by someone not familiar with using one.

'Obviously, you're not big into housework, DC Malik.'

*

Back in the busy operations room, Jo stopped to beckon Eva and Kirsty to join her and Mo in her office. Mo grabbed an extra chair on the way to add to the two positioned across the desk from Jo's. Eva and Kirsty followed them in, each carrying a Styrofoam cup of coffee.

'That can't be right,' Jo said. 'The senior officer not having something to drink. We've got something to show you but only if one of you gets me a flat white, and one for DC Malik.'

'I'll go,' Mo said. He left the room and returned a couple of minutes later placing the two cups on the desk. Jo held up the trophy for their appraisal.

'So, class, this is what we found in one of Phoebe Wright's lockers. What does this tell us?'

Eva raised her hand like a child in school.

'Yes, Eva?' The teacher's prompt.

'That Miss Wright has at least one wig.'

'Correct. And if you look at locker number two...' she held up her phone to show a photograph of its contents '...it's easy to see how she could fool Benny into believing she was moving clothes from home to home, when it was actually Benny's home to work and back. And more to the point, why would she need a rave cave at work, anyway?'

'A what?' Kirsty asked.

'Mo will explain.'

'When my sister was into night-clubbing, she...' Mo began.

'Mo will explain *later*,' Jo interrupted. 'Eva, how soon will the guys have the new image from the CCTV capture?'

'They said they'd get started on it right away. You seem to be a big hit with them, ma'am. We usually have to negotiate for a couple of hours before they'll commit to "tomorrow-at-the-earliest". That's if we're lucky.'

'So, when?'

'After lunch, they said.'

Jo checked her phone. 'Twelve-fifteen. And when do they have lunch?'

'They didn't say.'

'Right, I'll drop in on them now. It might help if one of us was there anyway, to guide them along to an objective end product rather than an attempt to recreate Phoebe. Tempting, the latter, for any red-blooded male.'

'Then we're in luck,' Eva said. 'This red-blooded individual is female. Leanne Purvis. She's very good.'

Jo smiled. 'Excellent. Has anyone seen or heard from DS Mills?'

Eva and Kirsty shook their heads, with just the hint of a smile each.

'When he gets back, would you ask him to come through?'

She turned and left the room.

*

Leanne Purvis was in her late forties, with a hint of grey along a centre parting of otherwise auburn hair. She was dressed in a loose sweater and baggy trousers and greeted Jo with a friendly smile.

'Thanks for getting on to it right away, Leanne. That was a lot quicker than I expected.'

'That's because it was easy, ma'am. As you know, we're used to creating faces from witness descriptions or reconstructing them from long-dead bodies. This was very straightforward. We used a still from the footage on Bolton Street. Full face, good lighting.'

They were looking at a wide-profile monitor screen displaying three faces. On the left, the mystery girl from the Shoulder of Mutton; in the centre Leanne's new image created from the same picture by removing the glasses, and replacing the baseball cap and curls with Phoebe's long, slightly-wavy blonde hair; and on the right, a full-face photograph of Phoebe herself.

'So, what do you think?' asked Jo.

'Well, the hair's a straight copy-and-paste, so we can ignore that for comparison purposes.' Leanne enlarged the three images to allow the faces, from hairline to chin, to fill the screen. 'So, the features: forehead, cheeks, eyes, nose, chin, lips. Not all that easy making the comparison when the expressions are so different. Phoebe smiling at the lens, anticipating the photograph; the other female caught unawares on camera; blank expression, looking a bit distracted.'

'You said, "the other female". Does that mean you don't think it's Phoebe?'

'I guess I really meant "the other *picture*" at this stage. We'd need more time to analyse the individual features before making a definitive judgement.' Leanne leaned back on her chair and sighed. '*However*, if you pressed me right now for an answer, I'd say it isn't the same girl.'

Jo screwed up her eyes at the screen. 'When I'm on a night out with the gang or with my husband, I look a lot different to other times of the day.'

Leanne laughed. 'Same here. But you can only do so much with make-up. Eyelashes, eyebrows, lips, skin – even ears if you wear different style earrings. The main thing to look for, facially, is shape. Forehead, cheeks, nose, chin.' She leaned forward again, pointing at the screen. 'Forehead, half covered by hair, but very similar, I'd say. Cheeks… well, what do you think, ma'am?'

It was Jo's turn to sigh. 'Much fuller cheeks. No doubt about that.'

'Nose, possibly a bit broader then Phoebe's, and the chin,' Leanne said, 'sticks out more just below and at the side of the mouth. The face is a different shape altogether, round as opposed to heart-shaped. Similar colour eyes, as far as you can tell through the lenses of the glasses, but Madam X, I'm afraid to say, is a lot less beautiful than Miss Wright.'

Jo stretched her arms then leaned back, her hands behind her head. She remained silent for a while.

'When we showed Benny Morrison, Phoebe's partner, the moving CCTV pictures, he said the girl was definitely not Phoebe and he based that to some extent on the way she moved. I guess that observation is extremely valid coming from someone who knows her intimately, but was something I chose to ignore until now. Leanne, could you, or whoever, check out those individual features as soon as possible. Because if this *isn't* Phoebe… then the whole picture, and potential outcome, looks a lot darker.' She checked her watch. 'And with that right at the front of my mind, I have to sit down with Phoebe's parents in an hour and ten minutes' time and take them through the CCTV capture from that Saturday evening.'

*

'Come in.'

Jo pushed open the door of Detective Superintendent Jones's office and stepped inside. The room had retained some remnants of the season, none of which Jo had noticed before. A number of greeting cards were displayed along the top of the filing cabinets and on one of the shelves of the bookcase. Sprigs of holly, sporting red berries, were tucked on top of several of the framed certificates on the wall behind the desk. Compared with the operations room, it was positively brimming with Christmas cheer.

'Hi, Jo.' Mal beamed and got to his feet, stretching out his hand. 'Happy New Year.'

Jo smiled back and took his hand. 'And to you, sir. Good time?'

'The usual. Quiet. Didn't make it to the end of Jools Holland for about the fourth year running, and I think I slept through the fireworks as well. You?'

He sat down again and waved Jo into the chair opposite him.

'We managed to see the New Year in at the Hare and Hounds. Then, yesterday, we had a long walk up to Ogden Reservoir, and back past the MCV.'

Mal's expression changed from a benign smile to a curious frown.

'The MCV?'

'Yes, the Mobile Command Vehicle, the one we've been using as a base for searching the moor. The one I believe you think is a waste of money... sir.'

'I'm sorry, Jo. I'm not sure... What did you want to see me about? Obviously not just to wish me a Happy New Year.'

'I just wanted to let you know that my sergeant has shared with me your concerns about how I am spending the Bury Division's budget irresponsibly and wasting their resources. And how you feel the disappearance of a nineteen-year-old girl is not all that important.'

Mal sprang to his feet, causing his chair to shoot backwards on its castors into the wall behind him.

'Not all that important.'

Jo was momentarily shocked. 'Sorry, I mean, not *exceptional* enough to be using up these valuable resources. Look, sir...'

'No, *you* look, Jo.' He turned to retrieve his chair and sat down again. 'If you've come up here for an argument, that's fine. When I requested your being assigned to us it was not based on your reputation as a shrinking violet, so I fully expect you to express any concerns you might have without pulling any punches. And I respect you for that. But can we have the discussion without cynicism and sarcasm, and without accusations and recriminations until we fully understand both sides of the argument. I think that's called *mutual* respect.'

Jo looked down at her hands resting on her lap.

'Yes, sir. Absolutely. I apologise.' She smiled. 'And I won't disappoint you by pulling any punches.'

'Good.' He leaned back in his chair. 'Just before you arrived, I was about to visit the little boys' room, which I will do now before we start again. That way I won't have to interrupt your flow once you come out swinging. And on the way back I'll get us some coffee, without which, it seems, meetings cannot begin these days.'

More relaxed now, and their having taken some tentative sips of the piping hot beverage, Mal nodded to Jo.

'Punch away.'

'Right. Last Saturday afternoon, when we met in this office, and after DS Mills had left, you told me you would be changing things around but not before the New Year. You said you hadn't yet decided who would take over my role in this case, although I admit you mentioned DS Mills as likely to be involved. What you *didn't* say, but what I took for granted, was that when you did decide, I would be the first to know. Decide who and when, I mean.'

Mal put on an exaggerated frown. 'Forgive me. Jo, but I don't recall taking you off the case in the past three days. I must have missed that somehow.'

'*Now* who's being sarcastic... sir? I'm referring to the communication. When I arrived here for the meeting on Saturday at exactly the time you requested, you and Mills had already finished your start-up coffee. Given how bloody scalding it is out of that machine, I concluded, being a detective, that you'd been together for some time. In fact, you told me that Mills had already presented you with a pretty damning picture of the status of the investigation.'

Jo raised her hand as Mal leaned forward. 'Please, sir, hear me out, then you can tell me if this is logical reasoning or paranoia.

'Two days later, on Monday, I asked him if he'd had a good weekend and he said, with that fucking stupid smirk on his face, "let's just say, *promising,* and leave it at that". Later that same day, as I was dismissing the troops for an early start to the festivities, Mills informed me, same smirk, that he had an important meeting with the boss at two o'clock, or whenever. Now, I had been with Mills almost every second of the working day up to his saying that, which leads me to believe the meeting had already been arranged before the day started. Which, in my fevered mind, put his choice of the word "promising" into a literal context. That is, he had been "promised" something.'

Jo paused.

'Is it my turn now, DI Carter?'

'Not yet. This morning he breezes in – different smirk this time, self-satisfied rather than mocking – and shares with me what I assume are the minutes of that meeting. As follows, bullet points only, over-spending, over-resourced, over-stated in terms of importance and – here's the kicker – wrong personnel. And all these comments attributed to you… sir.'

'Well, DS Mills had no right…'

'Oh, and he also told me, joyfully, that you were pulling the rug from under the possible temporary relocation of members of the team to Haslingden. But this is not a complaint about DS Mills, sir. He was just passing on to me what he had been told by *my* boss. If I allowed myself a more generous appraisal of my second-in-command, I might believe that, given the hierarchy within this station and, hence, the clear lines of communication, he would assume I already knew all this because you would obviously tell me first.'

Mal remained silent and relaxed as Jo caught her breath.

'Anything else?'

'No, sir.'

'Right, then…'

'Except…!'

'Go on.'

'I just want to say, I don't disagree with the points made. I am aware we are spending more time and resources than normal on a missing person when there is no evidence even of a crime being committed. And I had already decided to remove the MCV *and* cancel plans for a temporary incident room in Haslingden. The point is…'

'Yes, please get to the point, Jo, or else your bloody scalding coffee will be stone cold.'

Jo leaned back and gave just the hint of a smile. She took a sip from her cup.

'It's not really a point, sir, more of a question. Why, knowing the tension between me and Andy, did you choose to provide him with the means to humiliate me? Or *try* to humiliate me. In fact, I thoroughly enjoyed clearly winning the encounter and that pisses me off, because I thought I was above that sort of thing.'

Jo sat back and looked down at her hands again.

'*Now* is it my go?'

'Yes, sir. Thank you for hearing me out.'

'First let me say, I still harbour hopes that I can turn DS Andrew Mills into a good, a *better*, police officer. He is not behind the door when it comes to incisive, creative thinking in the line of duty. But that aspect of his work still frequently comes across as secondary to his need for points scoring and, shall we say, impact on his female colleagues. As if his job is just a vehicle for achieving some sort of legendary status within the station.'

It was Mal's turn to hold up a hand to ward off an interruption.

'I firmly believed I was making progress with him as we built a close working, and personal, relationship. The personal part, I'm a little ashamed to admit, being a means to an end rather than a genuine liking for the man. This has led me to trust him with what might be regarded as privileged information sometimes bypassing the usual top-down route. He has never abused that privilege in the past, encouraging me to think I was achieving my ambition for his… his… rehabilitation, shall we say. That all changed when you arrived.'

Jo was close to replicating Mal's springing to his feet, stopping short of that but with a similar angry outburst.

'Oh, so this is all *my* fault?'

'Fault is the wrong word. It implies you did something wrong and, the shout of "wanker" aside, that's not the case. It's not your *fault*, but you're the reason; plus, an unfortunate accident of timing. If you hadn't been the first person into the section on Christmas Day, you would never have been involved in the case and it would have been picked up the next day by someone else or, more likely, someone from Lancashire Division. As it was, I agreed that you should run with it as it was your first contribution to the team. If I'd have decided differently, you and DS Mills wouldn't be engaged in this tug-of-war over who heads it up now.'

'With respect, sir, none of which answers my question as to why you told my sergeant before telling me.'

Mal frowned. 'Really? I thought I'd covered that. But if you want the details, our chat prior to your joining us on the twenty-ninth did include DS Mills expressing an opinion, in answer to a direct question from me, that you were not making any progress. That is, you – the team, not you – DI Carter. There was nothing personal against you in his remarks, and I certainly made no comment or gave any indication of likely changes of personnel allocated to the case. Nor did DS Mills broach the subject.

'Later, I sort of regretted the way I'd abruptly dismissed him from the meeting and phoned him on the pretext of clarifying a detail relating to a case earlier last year. I said one of the other guests at the dinner was bound to ask and I wanted to be prepared. And I used the opportunity to suggest we got together for a quiet drink in my office on New Year's Eve afternoon.' He reached into the drawer of his desk and held up the half bottle of Famous Grouse. 'So, as you can see, that was very much a personal, not work-related, get-together.'

'Being non-work-related, then, I assume nothing was said at that little jolly about the use of resources and a change of leadership? So, Mills made the whole thing up, did he?'

Mal sighed. 'I may have shared with him a few initial thoughts – none of which were in any way critical of you or your team – in an unofficial, off-the-record conversational way over a wee dram.

Nothing definitive, so Andy must have drawn his own conclusions based, I suspect, on what he wanted to hear rather than what he actually heard.'

'Nothing definitive…'

'Which is why, as I started to say before, he had no right to share with you his own spin on a very different message. He has, it seems, betrayed a trust, and if that has caused you concern and embarrassment, DI Carter, then I am sorry. An error of judgement on my part. But, as I said, he has never previously abused that trust, which, on reflection, is probably because he has never felt the need to. He has had behavioural counselling in the past: I read the report and it goes into the theory of consequentialism and nonconsequentialism, all of which went over my head because I just couldn't relate it to the person in question. But basically, when I asked for clarification, she said his principal focus is on actions. In other words, if he feels like doing something, he'll do it without worrying about the consequences.'

'Which is not a comfortable thought when applied to a serving police officer,' Jo suggested.

'She also said,' Mal went on, 'that he likes to be in control. I could have told *her* that. And he invariably is, or should I say, invariably *was*. Since you arrived, he seems to have lost the plot.'

'So, he *has* shared with you his concerns about me, sir. Was that officially or over a wee dram?'

'Neither, he hasn't said anything. But I'd have to be deaf and blind not to pick up the tension between the two of you. It's so tangible you can almost touch it. And that goes for all the team – the section, in fact. The best thing is for me to separate you and get you both on the right, and the right *level*, assignments; for the greater good of the department.'

For the greater good. Jo reflected on those words, ones she had heard before in a very different setting and displayed in Latin on a wall plaque.

'So, the plan for reassigning the case to Lancashire, sir. Any advance on that?'

'I've had a word with Crossley's Super and, as usual, we got straight into budgets. Would this mean they'd have to pick up the cost of the whole case, or just going forward? That sort of thing.

But he agreed in principle it made sense, so, hopefully, we'll resolve the financial issues.'

Jo nodded. They sat in silence for a few moments.

'Forgive me for asking, sir, but does DS Mills know my main reason for being here?'

Mal opened his eyes wide.

'Of course, he doesn't,' he almost shouted, 'and I'm not sure I *do* forgive you for asking. Only you and I, plus the Chief Constable. Not even the guys between me and her. And, of course, Detective Superintendent Livingstone at GMP. Plus Seb, I assume.'

Jo frowned. 'Not Seb. I thought I shouldn't share this with anybody outside the people you just mentioned. I haven't told him.'

'Well, I'm a bit shocked, Jo. I don't believe there should be any secrets between spouses, or partners. And he isn't just "anybody" is he? He's the most important person in your life.'

'You're right about the last bit, sir, but I'm not sure how comfortable he'd be knowing what I'm really here for, spying on my fellow officers.'

'I know what you mean, but I have no issue at all if you decide you want to tell him. Anyway, going back to your initial question, DS Mills does *not* know precisely why you're here.'

Jo smiled. 'My apologies, sir. I must be getting a bit paranoid, wondering what range of subjects you cover in your off-the-record chats.'

Mal gave a chuckle, taking Jo by surprise. 'I bet you'd like it to be him, wouldn't you?'

Jo thought for a moment before smiling herself. 'Yes, probably. It would certainly fulfil a promise I made to myself. But it isn't him.'

★

It was a little after 2.15 p.m. when Eva led Helen and Philip Wright into the same meeting room and seated them in front of the TV monitor screen. Eva departed briefly to get coffees, and tea for Helen, while Jo introduced them to Mo and went over again Eva's explanation as to why they were there.

'Thank you for coming in,' she said. 'We won't keep you long but, as we told you a few days ago, we are following up a number of leads including the possibility of Phoebe leaving the area. As you know she was last seen by your ex-neighbour at around seven-thirty on Saturday, the twenty-second of December. If she *did* leave the area that same evening, one possibility is that she travelled by bus to Bury then on from there. We are as sure as we can be that she is not staying with any one of her close circle of friends in or around Bury.' Jo paused as Eva entered with the drinks. 'We have some close circuit television footage of people boarding a bus at the Shoulder of Mutton at ten past eight on the twenty-second. If Phoebe was planning to leave the area that would be one means of transport, so we'd like you to watch the recording and tell us if either of two women boarding the bus could be your daughter. Okay?'

Helen gave a little whimper and removed a tissue from her handbag as if in readiness for either a revelation or a disappointment.

'Okay, Helen?' Jo asked again. Helen nodded. 'Good. Mo, take us through.'

The steady image of an empty pub car park and the deserted picnic tables began to change with people moving into view in twos and threes, mostly smoking.

'This is the scene at just after eight o'clock,' Mo said. 'The bus will be arriving shortly and more people will leave the pub itself to board it. We'll point out the two women we want you to see, but let me tell you in advance that neither looks like Phoebe. If either of them is Phoebe, then she has deliberately disguised herself.'

Philip raised his hand and frowned angrily. 'Just stop a minute.' Mo paused the feed. 'You've brought us here to see a woman who looks nothing like Phoebe on the off chance we might say it *is* her. Am I right? Because if I am, this sounds like pure desperation on your part.'

'You *are* right, to a point, Philip,' Jo said, 'but I did say we were following every possible lead, and these women are in the most likely place Phoebe would be at that time if she was planning to run away. As you know, Phoebe took a full rucksack onto the moor with her that night, which we found empty a few days later. Given how well known she is in these parts and how easily recognisable, it's possible she may have tried to change her appearance to avoid being noticed. The rucksack may have contained clothes that she changed into before making her… let's say, escape.'

'Escape from what?' Helen wailed. 'I mean…'

'It's only a theory,' Jo said, 'but we are determined to follow up every possible lead and you are more likely than anyone to recognise Phoebe, even in disguise.' She paused. 'Can we continue, Philip?'

Fifteen minutes later, after a quarter of an hour of further whimpering from Helen, Mo stopped the feed. The result was the same as with Benny; they were convinced neither woman was their daughter.

'What an absolute waste of time,' Philip said, his face red with anger. 'To put us through this…'

Helen reached across and patted his hand.

'Everyone's doing their best, Philip.' Her voice was shaky and her face lined with tears. 'They can't do any more.'

'It must be so frustrating, Philip,' Jo said, 'but it's not necessarily a waste of time. As I said, we are following several lines of enquiry, so every possibility we discount means we can allocate more time and resources to the others, which hopefully gets us closer to finding Phoebe.'

Philip turned his head away in disgust.

'While you're here we want to ask you about Phoebe's acting. We hear she was doing drama at Sheffield University and doing very well. Did she tell you why she gave up the course after just one term?'

'What on earth has that got to do with anything?' Philip snapped, his colour still rising. 'That was a year ago. You're not suggesting she's gone back to uni and just forgot to tell anybody. Because it wouldn't surprise me if…'

'Don't be silly, Philip,' Helen cut in, recovering her composure and taking charge. 'Phoebe was, *is,* a very talented actress. Right through school, from reception class to GCSEs, she showed a natural aptitude for drama. Always the drama queen, we used to say.' She sniffed a little laugh. 'She went on to college to do Performing Arts, but lost her way a bit with having to work from home through COVID and although she got excellent grades at A level, I think she'd lost her… momentum. So she went to university half-heartedly and because, I suppose, it was the obvious thing to do. But she certainly wasn't fully committed, so it wasn't a big surprise when she gave it up. A disappointment, certainly, but not a surprise.'

'Did she appear in plays and shows other than at school and college?'

'Oh yes. She's been a member of PADOS since she was at primary school, and...'

'Pados?'

'Prestwich Amateur Dramatic and Operatic Society. She was a leading light, always one of the main characters since her mid-teens. The last one they did was just before lockdown when she played Annie Oakley in *Annie Get Your Gun*. She was only fifteen and made up to look a lot older, but everyone said she was brilliant, didn't they Philip?'

Philip nodded, his eyes tearing up at the memory.

'And she's also had parts, small parts, with quite a few of the travelling shows. *Les Misérables* at the Opera House a few years ago. Just someone in a crowd of people but with a speaking part. She would be asked to stand by as a sort of local deputy for anyone who might be unavailable for a performance; ill, for example. It meant she had to go to rehearsals and everything. We thought it was really good experience and quite a few of the main stars had encouraged her to take it up as a career. So she told us, anyway.' She paused. 'Such a waste,' she added, with a catch to her voice.

Jo gave her a few moments to recover.

'And do you know how she came to work for Easy Rider?' Jo asked.

'She said she'd bumped into somebody one day in Sheffield who was an ambulance driver for the company, taking parties from care homes for days out to the Peak District and Meadowhall. They'd got talking and he had mentioned they were looking for another couple of drivers and he'd put her name forward if she wanted. It was probably just a chat-up line, but I think Phoebe saw that as a way out and went to see them when she came back at Christmas, the Christmas before this one. And she got the job, started straight away in January and never went back to uni. I have to say, she seems very happy in the job, so we aren't too upset at her leaving.'

Jo paused for a moment and placed two A4-size photographs on the table.

'I'd like you to have a look at an image our technical team has created from the CCTV capture. Are you okay to do that?'

'I'm not sure what…' Philip began.

'Yes, of course,' Helen interrupted.

'Thank you,' Jo said, placing the two pictures side by side so the Wrights could compare them. 'This is a still from the CCTV coverage you've just seen, and this is the same image but with the glasses and cap removed and Phoebe's hair added. Now, given what you have just said about Phoebe's talent for drama, can you look again with that in mind, and tell us if it's possible that could be Phoebe acting out a part? You said, as did Mr Morrison, that the woman didn't move like Phoebe, didn't stand like Phoebe; but if she was trying to be someone else, wouldn't it be easy for her to adopt a different walk or stance, like in a show or a play? What do you think?'

They studied the pictures for a long time. Philip shook his head.

'I can't see it,' he said. 'Clutching at straws in my opinion.'

Helen was silent for a few moments longer, still focused on the images.

'Well, I can't say one way or the other with any certainty, but I suppose it's just possible. Remember, Philip, a few times when we've been to watch her in plays we didn't recognise her at first, even when we knew it was her. We thought we'd got the wrong character, but it *was* her and she'd become, as you just said, someone else.'

Jo nodded. 'Thank you, Helen. If you had to say one way or the other, based on your instincts, how likely is it that this is Phoebe?'

'Oh, for God's sake, what sort of a game are you playing putting Helen on the spot like that? She's just said that she can't be certain and…'

'I'm not asking for certainty, Mr Wright.' Jo's voice had an edge to it this time. 'But you are the only people around who have known Phoebe every moment of her life. I'm not asking for a definite ID, just an instinctive feel. If Helen isn't able to provide that, then no matter, we are no further back. Helen?'

Helen screwed up her eyes and studied the computed picture again. She looked up at Jo.

'Can I see the moving picture again?'

'Of course,' Jo answered. 'Mo, show Mrs Wright the sequence in Bolton Street. The lighting is best there, and that's where they took the still image from.'

Mo obliged and all five gathered round the screen in silence. After a long time, Helen leaned back and sighed.

'I'm sorry, but I really couldn't say. I'd like to help, but...'

'That's okay,' Jo said. 'It's been very useful, hearing about Phoebe's background and links to Sheffield. But I think it's time we got you home again.'

Philip was on his feet before Jo had finished speaking. 'I still don't see this has been anything but a waste of time. We'd appreciate it in future if you'd only contact us when you have something to tell us.'

'I can't promise that, I'm afraid, Mr Wright,' Jo said. 'It will depend on whether we need more information about your daughter. But I *can* promise we will only get in touch with you if necessary.' She turned to Eva. 'DC Johnson...'

Eva led them out of the room after Helen nodded a thank you to Jo.

★

'Anything forthcoming on the return journey?' Jo asked.

Eva had returned forty minutes later after dropping the Wrights off at their home in Hawkshaw. She was seated across the desk from Jo.

'Nothing in the way of information, but I'm not at all sure that the relationship is on a sound footing. Helen spent most of the time gently telling her husband how useless he was in a situation that required a cool head. There was no suggestion of a row or anything; he just sat there and took it.'

'Yes, well there are many ways to deal with adversity. A person must choose the way that's best for them. And if Philip's is to lash out and blame people, then you can't criticise him for that. I'm not sure what I'd be like in that situation, probably exactly the same. Anyway, given that we can't discount it being Phoebe, knowing she can change her appearance so convincingly, I'd like to get this out on the local evening news if possible, and online.' She handed Eva the still of the girl who had been at the Shoulder of Mutton, and read from a handwritten sheet.

'Police investigating the disappearance of Phoebe Wright would like to speak to this person, seen at the Shoulder of Mutton public house at around eight p.m. on Saturday the twenty-second of December, and later at Bury Metrolink station and Piccadilly train station. They ask that this person make themselves known at their nearest police station. Anyone who feels they may know this person should also get in touch with the police.'

She handed the sheet to Eva. 'I think that about covers it but tweak or add to it if you think of anything else to include, and add the contact numbers, of course. Main priority is to get it out there tonight.'

Eva stood ready to leave as Jo's phone sounded with an incoming call.

'Just hold on,' Jo said, waving her to sit down again. 'DI Carter speaking. Oh, hello, Helen. This is a little unexpected so soon. How can I...? I see. Let me put you on the speaker; I have DC Johnson with me.' She pressed the speaker button and placed the phone on the desk. 'So start again, please, Helen.'

Helen's voice held a trace of excitement. 'When we got in we checked the coats again on the hall stand and we're both pretty sure we remember the one she must have taken.'

'That's great, can you describe it for us?'

'It was one of those quilted jackets. You know, the ones with lots of circles of padding round them. Philip used to say it looked as though she was wearing a pile of tyres.'

Jo and Eva laughed. 'Good description,' Jo said. 'What colour is it?'

'Well that's it, it's reversible – grey one side, blue the other.'

'Short or long?'

'Short, I suppose. Just down to the hips.'

'And you're sure of this?'

'Well, we both agree, and that doesn't happen very often. Yes, very sure. She's had it for a while and we found some photographs with her wearing it a few years ago. That's what jogged the memory.'

'That's really helpful, Helen. It gives us something else to look for on the CCTV capture. We may need you to look at it again, but if we do, we'll try to arrange it at home so you don't have to turn out. Thank you again.'

She ended the call and paused for a few moments in thought.

'Let's go ahead now with the appeal then get back to the CCTV later. It might not move us forward, but, like Mo said, in the absence of anything exciting, something a bit interesting can grab you.'

★

Jo was getting ready to leave early to get home for 6.00 p.m. to catch the local news on ITV when her phone rang. She checked the caller's name on the screen before answering.

'Yes, sir.'

'Hi, Jo. I'm just about to leave, but could you attend a meeting in my office tomorrow morning at eight-fifteen? I want to pursue this change of accountability on the Phoebe Wright case. DI Crossley will be in attendance and, to save you asking, DS Mills *won't*. Okay?'

'Yes, of course, sir. But please don't exclude DS Mills on my account. As if you would,' she added, with an embarrassed little laugh.

'Indeed, as if I would. Anything to tell me before I leave?'

'We have an appeal for information going out on ITV local news at six o'clock, and BBC at six-thirty, if you want to catch it. I'm just leaving myself now to do just that.'

'Thank you, Jo. Just when I thought I was finishing work for the day.'

Jo laughed. 'It's not compulsory, sir.'

'Goodnight, Jo.'

'Goodnight, sir.'

CHAPTER FOURTEEN

Thursday 3 January

When Jo arrived at the Superintendent's office at just before the allotted time, there were two other people already seated around his spacious desk. Jo sensed the atmosphere in the room was relaxed and cheerful and felt it unlikely they had been discussing police matters up to that point All three got to their feet as she entered.

'Good morning, Jo,' Mal said. 'Introductions first. This is the oft-mentioned DI Al Crossley from Lancs Division CID in Blackburn. The one who's been dodging all the work on this case so far.'

Jo shook Al's extended hand. The DI wore a blue sports jacket, grey trousers and open-necked pale blue shirt. 'I knew they'd catch up with me sooner or later,' he said, returning Jo's smile.

'And this,' Mal went on, 'is Superintendent Livingstone, who is head of the region's Operation Revoke, fighting organised crime and, especially, drug-related crime. Gordy is responsible for co-ordinating the efforts of schemes across all towns in the Greater Manchester area. I know you two have spoken on the phone, so now you know where the voice comes from.'

Gordy Livingstone was tall, slim and in his mid-forties. His slightly greying hair was cut short and he wore an immaculate dark grey suit with a white shirt and navy tie. His chiselled features made him look more like a movie star than a policeman.

'Pleased to meet you, sir,' Jo said, shaking his hand.

'And you, too, DI Carter. I'm sure we'll have a lot to say to each other over the coming months.'

'I look forward to it,' Jo said, feeling a bit like a besotted schoolgirl.

'Let's sit down,' Mal said, waving Jo to the empty seat. 'I know you can't do meetings without a caffeine injection, Jo. Lucy will be entering within seconds to put that right.'

On cue, Mal's secretary entered with a plastic cup holder bearing four steaming drinks and placed them individually in front of each person, before leaving. Lucy Chu was a small South Korean woman of few words and, according to her boss, consummate efficiency.

'Thank you, Lucy,' Mal called after her. 'Silent and superb,' he added, as she closed the door. 'Just one item on the agenda for the meeting today, the leadership role in the pursuit of our missing girl. Gordy is here to meet with you afterwards, Jo, but I've invited him to sit in on the meeting, where he gets waitress service rather than having to queue in the cafeteria for his coffee. And this shouldn't take long. We three...' he indicated Jo, Al and himself '...have discussed this already, although not together. But for Gordy's benefit, the background to the change is this.

'Phoebe was reported missing by her parents, who live in Hawkshaw, which is in the Greater Manchester police area. And because of that, it was picked up by Bury – by Jo, in fact – and we have run with it since then. However, Phoebe was last reported seen on Holcombe Moor close to a feature known as Robin Hood's Well, which is within the Lancashire area. *And*, she lives at an address in Helmshore, which is also in Lancashire. With me so far?'

Gordy smiled and nodded.

'Given Jo's assignment is specifically to work with you, Gordy, as the Bury link to the GM-wide drug-trafficking crackdown, we believe it makes sense to place the case where it really belongs, on DI Crossley's patch, but working through the Bury team, headed by Detective Sergeant Mills. That's where all the information to date resides and all the contacts. This will release DI Carter to do what she was brought here for, and use Al's – and Mills's – *local knowledge* to the full.'

He stared at Jo, as if daring her to react to his last comment. Jo remained silent and impassive.

'Makes perfect sense,' Gordy said, 'and I'm delighted to have DI Carter fully on board.' He displayed a set of perfect teeth with his friendly smile.

'Good. I think Al is intending to spend the day with us. He and

I will meet Andy Mills when we've finished here. Jo, I believe the superintendent plans to give you a tour of what he believes is the nerve centre of the police world at the GMP HQ in Central Park.'

'If that doesn't interfere with what you have planned,' Gordy said to Jo.

'Nothing that's more important and won't wait, sir.'

'Good, and perhaps I could drive you there, it's not the easiest place to find if you're not familiar with the area.' He smiled. 'And, it goes without saying, we'll provide you with a lift back.'

'And hopefully I'll still be around when you get back, Jo,' Al Crossley said. 'I'd appreciate a full handover.'

'So we're all set,' Mal said. 'He shook Gordy's hand then turned to DI Crossley. 'And while I remember, whatever you do, don't call DS Mills a wanker.'

Gordy raised his eyebrows in surprise.

'I'll explain in the car, sir,' Jo said.

*

Jo was grateful for being a passenger once they had turned off the M60 at Junction 20 and headed towards the city centre. She was a confident and enthusiastic driver, but she had to concede that local knowledge did have its advantages, particularly at that particular motorway junction and at the roundabout near the Manchester Rugby Club that took them on to Lightbowne Road and the last leg of their journey. Throughout the drive, Gordy talked her through the background to his role with the GMP, the work of the National Crime Agency set up in 2013 by the Home Secretary to fight organised crime, and its success to date, much of which she already knew. But she was happy to sit back and listen to his gentle baritone voice and easy delivery.

'It's hard to put an accurate figure on what organised crime costs the UK public, but some put it as high as forty billion pounds per year. That's not only drug-related crime but child abuse, people-smuggling, cyber-crime, illegal immigration, and many other organised crimes. It's estimated there are more than six thousand OCGs operating across the UK. The good news for you is, you're not expected to put all that right...' He paused for a reaction.

'Phew, that's a relief, sir. You had me scared for a minute there.'

'Unless you feel you can, of course,' Gordy went on, with a chuckle. 'I wouldn't want to hold you back. We – you and I – will be focusing on drug trafficking in the northern sector of Greater Manchester.'

Jo rather liked the sound of 'you and I' and found herself looking forward to working with this man.

'And here we are,' Gordy said as they arrived at the HQ building which shared the site on Northampton Road with Manchester College and North Manchester Division Police Station. The building was a huge rectangle whose outer walls were mainly of glass. Gordy took her on a tour of the building, which they completed almost at a run, in order to visit all the different departments and sections. It was immense and impressive, with acres of glass, neat open-plan areas, plush offices and bright colours. He introduced her to numerous people on the way – names, positions, brief CVs – even some personal details here and there. So many, in fact, that Jo knew she had no chance of remembering even ten per cent of their names, let alone the other information.

Eventually, they settled in Gordy's office, a glass cube containing an L-shaped beech-topped work station with matching tilt-and-swivel behind it and several other dining-style chairs with padded seats and arms. Under the picture window, there was a long cabinet in the same wood on which stood a Pyrex coffee jug on a hotplate and a tray containing several mugs, a small jug and a pot containing sugar cubes. Gordy waved Jo to one of the chairs across the worktop from his. He walked over to the coffee percolator.

'This is always an anxious moment,' he said. 'Wondering whether you're going to ask for tea.'

Jo laughed. 'No, coffee, please. White, no sugar.'

He brought over two mugs and set them down, taking his seat opposite her.

'So what do you think of the nerve centre, as your boss calls it?'

'As he claims *you* call it, sir. Either way, it's really impressive.'

'Yes it is, but when we have members of the public in the building as part of an enquiry, or on a tour, they must look round and think the police service is awash with money. I had a friend who worked as a purchasing manager at a major food company in

Manchester, and they moved into a new purpose-built building, even more impressive than this. He said whenever a potential supplier entered the building they added a nought to their tender for the business, in the belief that money simply wasn't an issue.'

Jo laughed. 'It's certainly a bit different to Bury HQ, but I really like the station there.'

'It's a great little place. Whoops, there I go, a great *little* place. What I mean is, you know everyone and it feels a bit like home from home, if you'll excuse the cliché. Here, it's like one of those ocean cruises, where you're on a ship for a month with three thousand people and get to meet less than a hundred of them. And Bury is designed on the same principles, promoting new ways of working through open-area planning, which fosters more effective communication, and encourages teamwork, enabling greater flexibility to meet the ever-changing needs of the community they serve.' He laughed. 'I bet you can tell I've made that speech before.'

'It came out very smoothly, sir, but it all made perfect sense. And I think I'm right in saying that Bury had a good record for a while, until quite recently.'

'That's correct. It helped when – was it four years ago – Tom Brown, the then Home Secretary, decriminalised all users, encouraging them to come forward with information about dealers. His argument being you remove any link in the chain from OCG to user, and it breaks. So we are targeting middle level dealers and local networks of supply, while continuing activities against individual suppliers. And for local success, we rely on intelligence from surveillance, but mainly from whistleblowers. I guess you know all this stuff, Jo, and in Bury it was very productive as part of GMP's Operation Revoke's "Clear, Hold, Build" scheme. Seized over two million pounds' worth of drugs, near a quarter of a million in cash and made hundreds of arrests. That was up to about nine, ten months ago, when suddenly, based on the same sources of intelligence, we were turning up at places where no-one was home, and stuff was getting back on the streets again.'

He paused and leaned forward, resting his elbows on the worktop and steepling his fingers under his chin. He smiled. 'And so, we did the sensible thing and sent for Detective Inspector Jo Carter.'

PART TWO

PART TWO

CHAPTER FIFTEEN

On a bleak Sunday morning, in the shadow of the 128-foot-high Peel Tower, the headmaster stands, legs apart, hands clasped together behind his back and surveys the half-circle of eighteen boys in front of him. He is a large man, well over six feet, broad-shouldered and with a stomach that challenges the buttons on his heavy canvas coat. The brim of his battered trilby flaps in the strong wind, which threatened to lift it off his head. Behind the boys, a second man, another master, stands patiently waiting for the exercise to begin. He is much smaller, slim and wearing a long trench coat and flat cap that looks much more secure than his colleague's headwear. Both men are equipped with a large rucksack.

The boys, aged between thirteen and fifteen, are focused on the larger man, mostly on his hat in anticipation of its aerial departure. They are all dressed in the same jackets and trousers, the latter tucked in the top of thick, knee-length socks which themselves disappears into stout ankle boots. Each has a small bag slung on a strap across his chest and carries a hard-backed notebook. Three of the boys hold a larger folded sheet in their other hand.

'Alright, boys,' booms the headmaster. 'We will all progress as one group to the Pilgrims Cross, where we will split into our three teams and head off for our separate targets. Have the team leaders got the maps?'

The three boys hold up their folded sheets.

'You, Jackson. You're a team leader?'

'Yes, sir.' *The boy grins back. He is easily the tallest of the group with a confident air and mischievous eyes.* 'Democratically elected... sir.'

'Yes, well, make sure you show some leadership. Timepieces?' *He addresses the wider group.* 'Each team should have one?'

Three boys again hold up their hands, each holding a large watch, which almost filled his palm.

'You again, Jackson. Make sure you take good care of it, that goes for all of you. Before we set off, can anyone tell me what is unusual about the Pilgrims Cross?'

There is silence for a few seconds, then a voice from the group. 'It hasn't got a cross, sir.'

'Correct, Metcalfe. So, why the name, the Pilgrims Cross?'

Another voice. 'It had a cross until 1901, sir, then it was vandalised.'

'Good, Cropper. So what are we going to see?'

Cropper again. 'A memorial stone, which replaced the original cross, sir, with writing on it.'

'Writing telling us the history of the cross and the stone, including when it was placed there. Which was when?'

'Yesterday.'

'What was that you said, Jackson?'

'Twenty-fourth of May 1902, sir. Ten years ago.'

The man glares at the boy, who smiles back.

He addresses his colleague. 'Ready, Mr Armitage?'

'Yes, Headmaster.'

'Right, then I'll lead the way.'

It has been a wet September and the ground is boggy beneath the long clinging grass. The going is slow and it takes the group almost an hour to walk the mile and a half to the cross's memorial stone.

'Right, boys,' the headmaster says. 'We rest here for ten minutes. Have a bite to eat and Mr Armitage will provide you each with a drink. Then we'll split into our teams and head for our different locations. Wainwright's team, we'll call them Team A, will remain here at the Pilgrims Cross; Jackson's, Team B, will make for the cairn, and Fairbrother, with Team C, up there to Bull Hill.' He points to a path leading away from the memorial stone up a gradual rise. 'Mr Armitage, when you have distributed the drinks, please remind the boys of their objectives.'

The boys gather round in a full circle this time.

'You are to quarter the area around your target,' Mr Armitage says, in a voice an octave or so higher than the headmaster's, 'and record anything of interest you find or see and mark it on the map. These could be plants, flowers, birds – especially birds – insects, small mammals. Or large mammals,' he adds, 'although they are likely to be less numerous.' The boys laugh, politely. 'Then during the first session at school tomorrow, we will expect a report from each group listing and describing what you found, with the map coordinates, along with a sketch, or sketches of the area. I will expect to see some panoramic views from Team C, as the top of Bull Hill is by far the best viewpoint in the area.

'The purpose of the exercise is to test your attention to detail and your observation skills, along with your ability to describe clearly what you have seen. The time is now twenty minutes to midday. You have just over two hours to complete the task and we will expect you all back here at two o'clock. During that time, the headmaster and I will remain here so if you have any questions or problems, you know where to find us.'

He turns to the headmaster, who nods. 'Right, boys. Off you go and good hunting.'

*

'Are you just going to sit there, Arthur?'

'I'm the leader, Frank. I have to watch everyone else and see they are doing things right.'

Arthur Jackson is seated on top of the pile of stones which constitutes the cairn – the target of their mission. Frank Newton is a well-built, mature-looking youth with the first hint of stubble on his face. He is Arthur's closest friend and the only one of the group brave enough to challenge him. He is leaning on the dry-stone wall close by, his hands already covered in soil from his rummaging around in the undergrowth.

'And when did you become an expert on...whatever it is we're doing?' he asks.

'You don't have to be an expert to be a manager.'

'A leader is different to a manager. A leader sets an example by showing his people what to do.'

'That's not quite correct,' a voice from behind him says. A small boy with a spotty face has his hand raised as if he is asking permission to speak.

Frank looks round at the owner. 'What do you know about anything, Walter?'

'Well, a leader sets the objectives, then provides the means and support for them to be met. A manager then... well... manages the work involved to achieve those objectives.'

'What rot,' Frank says. 'Where did you hear that?'

'No,' Arthur says. 'I'm with Mr Lowden on this. You're absolutely right, Walter, so I'm going to sit here for a little while longer and come up with some leadership objectives. In the meantime,' he raises his voice, 'I want everyone to continue collecting anything that is likely to satisfy old Armitage. I'll keep the map here; you tell me where to put the crosses.'

A few minutes later he slides down off the pile of stones and calls over to one of the other boys. 'Denton. John Denton. Over here.'

A small boy with thick round glasses and slicked-down hair hurries over.

'Right, John. You fancy yourself as a bit of an artist. I want you to make a drawing of the cairn. Make sure you put in where the wall is and the clumps of gorse. Just like it is now. Okay?'

'Okay, Arthur,' he says, blinking in confusion but not prepared to risk a request for clarification. 'From here, okay?' he says, sitting on a rock a few yards away.

'From anywhere as long as you get the wall and the gorse in. It's got to show exactly where the cairn is.'

'Okay, right.' He takes a pencil from his bag and opens the notebook.

Arthur turns and shouts to the others. 'Gather round, everybody. I'm about to show you a bit of leadership, just like the boss told me.'

★

Frank Newton says what everyone else is thinking. 'This will get us into a lot of trouble.'

'Who will know it was us?' Arthur asks. 'You've seen Denty's drawing. If anyone asks, we show them that.' He walks round the group, stopping to tower over each boy and stare into his eyes. 'So, we're all in? Raise your hand for yes.'

Walter Lowden raises his hand, followed by the others. Last of all is Frank, a full half minute after everyone else.

'Good. Then let's go.'

CHAPTER SIXTEEN

Sunday 13 January

Seated on the sofa, in her new temporary residence, her legs tucked under her and sipping her second glass of Sauvignon Blanc, Jo contemplated the change of pace in her life since that first meeting with Gordy Livingstone. It had been ten days since his rallying call had filled her with enthusiasm for a new challenge and a new working relationship. Fitness-wise, she had decided, there was not a lot to choose between Gordy and Andy, despite the latter's ten-year-or-so advantage, but there the similarity ended. It was great to be able to focus on actual work and not be endlessly negotiating verbal exchanges and second-guessing mood swings.

Or, it *should* have been great.

In reality her 'actual work' during those ten days had involved pouring over e-files, statements and manuscripts, and catching up with past incidents, successful and otherwise. It occurred to her that if everyone's understanding of police work was based on TV dramas, the public had been grossly misinformed. Most of it involved sitting at a desk studying documents or staring at a computer screen. All you ever saw on TV were the rare 'eureka' moments when someone looks up from the papers or the screen and says, 'You need to see this, guv,' or 'I think we've got him, boss.' She smiled at the thought and conceded that it wouldn't make great television to show the ten hours of trawling through information that got them to that point.

More of an issue was that her new role had taken her away from direct contact with the CID team and her *raison d'etre* for being there. The return of Detective Inspector Ches Tidmarsh from an extended festive break with his family down under, had effectively closed off any conduit to enable her to even dabble in new matters arising in the Borough. She got on well with Ches, but he represented a barrier to the pursuit of her main objective. And the one promise of excitement during the past ten days had also failed to deliver. The previous Monday she had attended, as an observer, a drugs raid in the Moorside area of Bury, based on information received from a previously reliable source…

*

Jo's alarm had sounded at 3.00 a.m., and after a shower, a coffee and a cereal bar, she made her way to the station to join the uniformed officers of the neighbourhood team, supplemented by two members of Gordy's specialist drug squad, preparing for the hit. After donning her puncture protection vest, she took her seat in the back of one of the four police vehicles, and the small convoy set out at 4.00 a.m., creeping through the silent streets, the covering of snow acting as soundproofing for the engines and tyres.

It was not Jo's first attendance at such an event, and as they pulled to a stop, fifty metres or so away from the target, but with it in full view, she noted again that it was never quite what she expected. Not a large expensive detached property, funded by ill-gotten gains, or a run-down little terraced; just a normal mid-market semi. As they approached on foot, she noticed a child's bike lying on its side in the front garden and a trampoline just visible over the top of the back fence. Just props, of course, to add to the normality and cast doubt over any suspicion as to what went on within the four walls.

Once in place, the police sprang into action, hammering on the front door and windows. After two minutes with no response, one of the officers stepped forward with the Enforcer, a sixteen-kilogram hardened steel battering ram, which he swung against the door, bursting through the locks and shattering the patterned glass panels. The group of ten officers swarmed in, five covering the ground floor and the others racing up the stairs.

Lights were quick to come on along both sides of the road and curtains were pulled back. Several people ventured into the street, shouting complaints and abuse at the police. A couple of teenagers started throwing snowballs at them to the amusement and encouragement of their neighbours. In less than twenty minutes, it was over; no-one and nothing found. The sergeant in charge phoned someone to come and secure the front door, and one car stayed at the scene to wait for them. Jo returned with the rest of the troop and was back home by 5.30. She had set the alarm for seven o'clock and gone to sleep without undressing.

*

That was six days ago, and during that time, something else had happened. Or *not* happened. In fact, not happened *again*. No need to worry yet. It wasn't the first time.

She sighed and got up from the sofa, checking the time on her engagement watch. It was just after nine o'clock; thirty minutes before her daily catch-up with Seb. Although this was only the second weekend without him, it seemed like a very long time since they'd been together, partly, no doubt, as a consequence of the lack of activity or progress in her work. And still five more days to wait. Five more days for the germinating seeds of doubt to develop. It was all nonsense, she told herself. Nothing, absolutely *nothing*, pointed towards there being a problem with their relationship, but the misgivings were there, all the same. Perhaps everything was too perfect. Logic says that when things couldn't be better, any change, however small, meant they would be worse.

She drained her glass and took it through to the kitchen, then headed upstairs. She would take the call in bed; somehow that always felt right.

*

Afterwards, she checked her alarm time for the morning, placed the phone on charge on the bedside table, and switched off the light. She thought of Phoebe Wright. Twenty-two days now since she went missing and they were no nearer finding her, alive or dead. No sightings, no clues, no new information. No reports of a phantom hound. As she snuggled deep under the duvet, the phone pinged with an incoming text.

She checked the screen. A single digit – '8'.

CHAPTER SEVENTEEN

Monday 14 January

Jo arrived at the station mid-morning and climbed the stairs to enter an unfamiliar, desolate world, briefly wondering if this was some strange dream from which she had yet to awake. She recognised her closed office across the large, empty room and saw the congestion inside through the glass partitions before carefully pushing open the door to encounter it. Eva appeared suddenly and breathlessly behind her.

'Sorry, ma'am, I was hoping to explain before you collided with all the detritus.'

'Now that's not a word you hear every day. So, please *do* explain.'

'Well, as you know, we were due to have the operations area revamped, rewired, reorganised, re-just-about-everything'd…'

'Next week. Right?'

'That's what we thought, but Space Invaders thought differently.'

'Who?'

'SpaceStretchers, the contractors, renamed "Space Invaders" by the team. They had it on their schedule for *this* week, so we had to either put the whole thing back for a couple of months, apparently, or quickly make arrangements for them to get on with it today. We've moved most of the big stuff downstairs, so the individual offices have just got the more portable…'

'Detritus…'

'…on a temporary basis. The stuff in here is mostly from the MCV. We've never got round to moving it out of the main room, and, anyway, it's still part of work-in-progress, although not *your* work-in-progress anymore, ma'am, I'm sorry to say.'

'Well, I guess it's a little soon to think of it as truly nostalgic, but it will remind me of all the fun I had with DS Mills. So where will you lot be while this is going on?'

'In the cafeteria, which is not really just a cafeteria any more for a while.'

'Temporary, you said?'

'Yes, we should have cleared all the offices by the end of today or, latest, tomorrow. I'll get them to start with yours.'

'No rush, Eva. As long as I have an accessible chair close to my desk, which I have, I'll be fine. I hope it's worth it when they've finished.'

'Well, I guess we'll know a week sooner than we expected.'

'Glass half full. Well done, detective.'

Left alone, Jo found it strangely comforting to be surrounded by so much evidence of her work to date at Bury Divisional HQ, the clutter pressing in on her space generating a feeling of cosiness rather than inconvenience. Her eyes made a brief tour of the boxes, stack of chairs, and the trolley which had held the twenty-three items discovered during the initial search of the moor close to Phoebe's last sighting. The items were long gone from the trolley, stored in plastic bags elsewhere, and on it now was the folded enlarged section of the OS map of the area, the numbered stickers still in place showing where the objects were found. The whiteboard, listing the items one to twenty-three along with their grid references showing where they were located, had been placed in front of Jo's board on the same easel.

Jo lifted it down and leaned it against the legs of the easel so she could see her own board above it. Remembering the text she had received the previous evening, she checked her phone and added the latest digit, '8', to the five already listed on the board, saying them out loud to herself, '1,9,5,7,7,8'. The previous evening's message had been totally unexpected. It had been two weeks since she had received the fifth digit and this one was the first to arrive other than on an official working day. She sat down at her desk and was still staring at the sequence of numbers as the door opened and Eva appeared again with two Styrofoam cups of coffee. She put them on the desk and lifted one of the chairs from the stack, placing it across from Jo.

'Terribly rude of me barging in uninvited, ma'am, but just wondered how you were settling in to your new home and when we can expect the house-warming party.'

Jo laughed. 'Very well, thank you, and not any time soon.'

'Now that's a shame – the second bit, I mean. It's a really neat spot, isn't it? I had a nosey this weekend. I go to the park most Saturdays, when I can, with my sister, Kerys, and her husband, just for a walk round and some bird-watching. We usually park near the chimney in the centre, but curiosity got the better of me this Saturday and we used the lower car park so we could peek through the trees at your cottage. Has Mr Carter seen it yet?'

'Yes, both Mr Carters. Mr Carter junior wants to move some of the old furniture out while we're renting it and replace it with something more modern. He's more into late-IKEA than mid-Edwardian. Probably a wise move, actually. I'm not sure some of the chairs will be able to support him. He's not actually stayed there yet but, fingers crossed, he'll be back on Friday.'

'That's good. It feels like you're going to stick around for a while and I'm really pleased about that, along with a majority of all-but-one of the guys out there, I reckon.'

'That's very kind of you, Eva. I really appreciate that.' She smiled. 'And I'll check with young Mr Carter about the party when I next see him.'

After Eva had left, Jo booted up her PC, leaned back in her chair and sighed. She wondered how the guys out there would feel if they were aware of the secret currently known only to herself, Detective Superintendents Mallory Jones and Gordy Livingstone, and Chief Constable Emilia Crabbe. At best, it would reduce her majority to all-but-two.

★

The realisation hit Jo the moment she returned from a light lunch in the quick-break area on the second floor. The police cafeteria, which adjoined the now-deserted operations room, had been, as Eva had said, the victim of some collateral damage following Space Invaders' insurgence into the operations area. The dining tables had been repositioned to create temporary accommodation for the CID team, much to the amusement of the rest of the station personnel.

Casting her eyes again over her assigned collection of detritus her attention locked onto the first item of the twenty-three listed on the MCV whiteboard, and, in particular, on the six digits in the third column, the grid reference:

| 1 | Fleece buff (pink) | 769 190 | 8m from nearest object (item 6) |

Jo picked up the map from the trolley, unfolded it and spread it out on her desk. The small round stickers numbered one and six were close enough together to overlap, even on the enlarged map. Number one had a red sticker, indicating that the buff was relevant to the search, number six, a discarded plastic Evian water bottle, was green, deemed not relevant.

Jo's eyes went back and forth from the map to the whiteboard before she took a deep breath, realising none of this was part of her sudden revelation. *That* was displayed above on her own board in the sequence of digits she had received by text over the three weeks between Christmas Eve and yesterday. She stared at the numbers for a long time, just to make sure, then drew a circle on the map before re-folding it and stuffing it into her shoulder bag, which she grabbed along with her car keys. After throwing her coat over her arm, she raced from her office across the open plan area and down the stairs. She arrived, breathless, at her car and almost threw herself into the driving seat. Pulling out of the station car park and fastening her seat belt as she drove, she just made it to the green light to turn right onto the major junction at the end of Peel Way, before picking up the B6214, Crostons Road, to Ramsbottom.

In the excitement of discovery, she had to check her speed several times on the way, especially along the open stretch of road after Brandlesholme, past the left fork to Greenmount, and up to the turn-off for Summerseat, where the houses appeared again. After turning right then immediately left at the Hare and Hounds in Holcombe Brook, she got stuck behind a tractor climbing the long hill to the Shoulder of Mutton. She drummed her hands on the steering wheel in frustration.

'What the hell is a tractor doing out in the middle of January?' she asked herself.

Whatever its purpose, the tractor continued its climb, finally turning off to the right immediately after the pub to descend via The Rake into Ramsbottom. Jo stepped on the accelerator as if she had to make up the time lost in the wake of the farm vehicle, eventually pulling off the road onto the small and currently empty parking lay-by close to Stubbins. She got out of the car, taking her walking boots from the boot and changing into them. She opened the OS Locate App on her phone and, after checking her current position, she unfolded the map and spread it out on the floor of the boot.

The way to her destination was initially via a vehicle track heading off the road just south of the parking area. Jo set off clutching the re-folded map in one hand and her iPhone in the other. The start of the track was through a gate and she followed it up a long, steep incline to a kissing-gate opposite Chatterton Close, a large house, currently unoccupied. Jo was now on Moor Road, the old main road to Helmshore, not much more than a track itself at this point and one with which she was familiar. She and Seb, along with Sally and Jonno, had passed this way on their walk on New Year's Day.

She turned right along the old road, checking the map and the app and turning off to the left along the Rossendale Way after about two hundred and fifty metres. After a similar distance, she turned right onto the broader path that would lead her to the grid reference point. Ahead she could see, rising from the brown tufts of winter grass, what she assumed to be a stone gatepost, and to the right of it a pile of rocks. She remembered now that she had passed it, or close to it, before, believing it to be evidence of some ancient field access or drive entrance. Checking the app when she reached it confirmed that this was the correct location. The pile of rocks, now behind it from where she stood, was a few metres away, and a smaller collection of rocks formed a much lower and narrower stack close by.

Now that her attention was focused on it, Jo could see that it was not a gatepost but a rectangular, vertical stone containing the inset carved figure of a woman leaning to her left. The sculpture was eroded with age but clearly identifiable. There was something sad and vulnerable about the woman and Jo felt a slight shiver down her neck and back as she studied it. After several minutes during which she stared mesmerised at what she assumed must be some sort of memorial, she closed the app on her iPhone and scrolled through her contacts to Eva's number. Her colleague answered within a couple of seconds.

'Hello, boss. Are you okay?'

'Yes, why?'

'Well, you just sort of vanished.'

'You mean I'm still supposed to tell you where I'm going even though I've been kicked off the team?' There was silence from Eva. 'Just joking. Where are you right now?'

'In what's left of the operations room.'

'On your own?'

'Totally.'

'Right, go into my office and check out the two whiteboards. The one on the floor resting against the easel, and mine above it.'

Jo could hear a door open and close before Eva spoke again.

'I'm here, ma'am. What am I looking for?'

'On the MCV board, what's the number in the third column of item one.'

'The grid reference? 769 190.'

'Right, now read out the digits, ignoring the semi colon, of my mystery message on the easel above it.'

'That's...195 778. That eight is hot off the press, then.'

'Very well remembered, Eva. Yesterday, in fact. Now interchange the two groups of three digits and read it again.'

'You mean, 778 195? Oh my God. Where are you right now? Let me guess – at 778...'

'One-nine-five.'

'And what's there?'

'Well, it's a sort of marker, like a stone gatepost, which I thought it was at first. But it's got a carving on it of a woman and... hold on a second.' Jo crouched down close to the carving. 'Just under the figure someone has scratched the letters E and S into the stone. What does it mean?'

'That's the memorial to a woman called Ellen Strange. The victim of a murder on the moor centuries ago, around seventeen-sixty something if I remember right. It's what DS Mills was referring to when he said history repeating itself.'

'And this is where she was killed? Where the carving stands?'

'No-one's absolutely sure about that. It's the cairn that's supposed to mark the spot, but that was moved there by some school kids from its original site just before the First World War. An early example of adolescent vandalism. It can't have been moved very far, though, so it's as close to the murder scene as makes no difference. The carved stone was placed there a long time afterwards.'

'And how did she come to meet her fate? Who killed her?'

'There are two versions of the story; the myth and the truth. The myth's a lot more interesting but the truth is that after an argument with her husband in a pub called the White Horse, she set off across the moor to her family's farm in Hawkshaw. He caught up with her and killed her, then buried her body under a pile of stones.'

Jo continued to stare at the carving for a long time.

'Hang on a minute,' she said, pausing again. 'Have I got this right? A girl has a blazing row with her bloke in the White Horse, decides to bugger off across Holcombe Moor to her parents' house in Hawkshaw, he follows her and kills her at or close to the spot where I'm standing now, which is as near as damn it to where Phoebe Wright was last seen.'

There was silence for a few moments.

'Different White Horse pub... I *think*,' Eva said, 'but, yes, that's weird.'

'Which means these texts could be clues linked to the case. It's only weird if it's just a coincidence. And what's the other pile of stones for?'

'The other pile of stones? I don't know anything about those. There should only be one cairn. Can't be somebody's starting moving them again, surely.'

'It's not a pile like the cairn. It's a few metres away and a lot smaller; just a few stones high, about half a metre wide, two metres long...' Jo paused for a couple of seconds. 'Oh, please, *please*, no.'

'What's wrong? You okay?'

'The second pile of stones. It's the size and shape of a grave.'

★

The half-circle of four police officers watched the CSIU vehicle pick its way carefully towards them along the narrow lane-cum-track, which was the old road to Helmshore. With similar caution, one of the smaller vans from the dog unit followed it closely behind. The two vehicles stopped behind the police car already parked at the point where the Rossendale Way crossed the track, and five officers of the Crime Scene Unit got out from their transport, each taking a metal briefcase and small holdall from the back. Jo was surprised and dismayed to see Detective Superintendent Jones get out of the passenger seat of the dog unit van.

'Shit. This might now turn into a demarcation issue above everything else,' she said, half to herself. She had been joined by Eva and Mo along with uniformed Sergeant Geoff Brazendale, who had been in charge of the initial search. They watched the superintendent set off at an ambitious pace directly towards them across the uneven terrain, ignoring the paths. He lost his footing a few times on the way and Jo couldn't help thinking that with hindsight he probably wished he had stuck to the paths. She guessed this was not going to do a lot to lighten his mood. PC Seth Walker, the dog-handler, meanwhile, had clipped the lead onto the spaniel's collar whilst the CSIs donned their suits and boots, the whole group taking the less direct, more walker-friendly, route along the designated footpaths.

'Afternoon, sir. Didn't expect to see you here,' Jo said, trying to sound casual rather than curious.

'Wouldn't have come if I'd known the trip was going to be as bad as that. Haven't felt car sick since I was a kid until today.' He nodded to everyone before continuing. 'And why do we need Jess? I thought we used her for finding things. You've beaten her to it this time, haven't you, DI Carter?'

'Not by smell, sir. It's over three weeks since the disappearance, so if it is a body, we should be smelling it ourselves. Unless she was killed only very recently, of course. I want to see if the dog homes in on the stones, and if she does and this turns out to be the worst-case scenario, I don't see how she could have missed it before. *Unless* whatever's under the stones has been placed there since we ended the search, which seems very unlikely. So, that gives me hope that Jess *won't* detect anything, and we'll just be left wondering why the stones have been moved.'

Mal took a few moments to follow Jo's logic before nodding and walking over with her to where the crime scene tape fluttered round the new pile.

'Please, don't let this be what it looks like,' he said.

They all turned at the sound of a vehicle bouncing along the old road towards them. Unlike the two vans, the black Kia Sportage showed no respect for the state of the road and in spite of its pseudo-off-road credentials seemed to hit the ground with its underside several times in an almost frenzied approach. The vehicle did a passable impression of an emergency stop and the driver was out of the car the second it reached a standstill. Detective Sergeant Andy Mills bounded towards them, his face like a thundercloud.

Mal leaned in close to Jo. 'This is why I'm here,' he whispered.

'What the fuck...?' Andy's opening comments, delivered loudly from a distance well before he reached them, were abruptly curtailed as he spotted Mal, who turned to face him. The senior man gestured for Jo to accompany him and they walked forward to intercept him out of hearing of the rest of the group who watched with anticipation and amusement.

'A development, DS Mills. Glad you could join us.'

'So am I, sir. I don't want this to sound petty, but I thought this was *my* investigation now.'

'Well, that's unfortunate, sergeant, because it did sound petty. I understand DI Carter, here, tried to contact you but was unable to do so. She left a message with DC Milner, which I assume was delivered, and which is why you are here.'

'My point, sir, is why is DI Carter here at all? My understanding was that she is off this case.'

Mal held Andy's eyes until the latter looked away.

'Would you like to know why we are *all* here, detective sergeant, or is the plight of a missing person secondary to your concerns about who does what?'

'I would, sir, of course, like to know. And, in fact, DC Milner did provide me with some details, about the possibility of something being buried near the cairn. But, how come she just happened to be out here on her own? It's not exactly on the way to the Ladies, is it...sir?' Ho looked at Jo for the first time.

'An anonymous tip-off, Andy; in the form of a grid reference. DI Carter decided she needed to check it out before mobilising the full team. Which makes perfect sense to me, by the way.'

'Not to me.' He continued to glare at Jo whilst still referring to her in the third person. 'She should have at least shared the information from the tip-off with me *before* she checked it out.'

'Well, she didn't, and I'm not wasting my expensive salary presiding over a childish tantrum, sergeant. If you don't wish to be involved in the next episode of this drama, then please return to the station and we'll discuss it later in a formal interview. Right now, I want to know what, if anything, is under those stones.'

He turned and walked away, Jo close behind. Andy waited several moments before following them.

'Right, let's proceed,' Mal said. 'What's next, Jo?'

'We have the buff from the original search, sir. This is a long shot, but we'll give Jess a scent of it then let her sniff around. It's been a long time since Phoebe was last up here, but I'm told Jess is a superstar. Whatever happens, we need to move those stones.' She looked across at Andy. 'Right, DS Mills?'

'Absolutely right,' Mal answered before the DS could reply or fail to reply.

Geoff stepped forward with the sealed evidence bag and crouched in front of the dog, which by now was trembling with excitement. He removed the buff with a gloved hand and held it out to her. Seth loosened his grip on the lead and Jess buried her nose into the fleece material. The handler unclipped the lead from the collar and bent low to whisper in the dog's ear.

'Good girl, Jess. Go find.'

There was a feeling of palpable tension in the air as the twelve officers watched the dog run through the grass in a wide circle, stopping from time to time to sample a scent. Gradually, she spiralled inwards, concentrating her attention ever closer to the cairns, spending several seconds in one place on occasions, before moving on to another spot close by. Steadily and inexorably, she edged towards the rough rectangle. Finally, mission completed, she came to a stop with her front paws on the stones. She looked up and across at Seth, whining softly.

No-one spoke for several long moments, each wrestling with

their thoughts. Sergeant Brazendale broke the silence, waiving the station's unwritten rule of not using expletives in front of Police Superintendents.

'How the fuck did we miss this?'

'Not sure we did, Geoff,' Jo said, as the group emerged from their temporary stupor. 'And we don't know yet what's under the stones.'

'Place your bets,' Andy said. 'And hope to lose,' he added, as the senior man turned to glare at him.

'Okay, Matty,' Mal said, turning to the Senior CSI, Matt Crenshaw, 'let's get the tent up and move the tape further out. And get forensics here, whoever's on today. Should be Doc Wiseman, I think. Let's move quickly.' He checked his watch, which told him it was five minutes to three o'clock. 'Not much daylight left, so let's get the lights here as well; do what we need to do before the weather closes in. One good thing is we're not likely to get many people out for an evening walk in the cold and dark.'

'Except it was an evening walk in the cold and dark that started all this,' Jo said.

★

An oppressive darkness had fallen before the meticulous task began of unveiling the contents of what was designated the 'dig site', the Super having forbidden the use of an earlier reference to 'shallow grave'. The arc lights, however, provided a more than adequate substitute for daylight even through the thin fabric of the tent and the main concern for the gathered group was the forecasted approach of arctic conditions heading their way on a strong northerly wind.

They had been joined by another team of CSIs along with more uniformed officers from Bury and Blackburn, ostensibly to protect the perimeter of the wider taped-off area, although there seemed little chance of intrusion given the hour, and the coldness and isolation of the place. The only threat to their privacy was the possibility of passing motorists on the B6214 being tempted to investigate the mysterious presence of bright lights on the moor. The on-duty forensic scientist, Dr Sylvia Wiseman, had been contacted and was on her way from Accrington, no doubt aggrieved, Mal suggested, that the call had reached her just fifty minutes before the end of her twelve-hour shift.

The tent, at five metres square, was large enough to accommodate the combined Crime Scene Investigation Units of five male and five female officers with room enough in addition for all five detectives, although Matt had requested that only two be allowed as observers as they began their slow and painstaking task. Andy and Eva had drawn the short straws as the others retired to the relative comfort of the small caravan, which had arrived with the influx of uniforms from Bury. They warmed their hands and their throats on welcome mugs of strong coffee.

With the arrival of Dr Wiseman a few minutes after 5.00 p.m., the ten CSIs began their search of the site, working inwards, shoulder to shoulder, from around the circumference of a circle scored in the ground at a radius of two-and-a-half metres from the centre of the stones. An earlier survey of the area outside the tent had revealed no clear shoe or boot prints; not surprising given the density and coarseness of the vegetation. They moved forward, the beams from their head-torches often crossing as their eyes swept the ground in front of them, picking up and bagging small objects out of the grass after a photographer had recorded each find in situ. Sylvia studied each item before it was logged and the bag placed in a metal storage container.

By 7.30 p.m. the strengthening wind was battering the sides of the tent and the falling snow was being driven horizontally into a blizzard. Jo and Mo replaced Andy and Eva as observers to enable the latter pair some relief from the conditions. In spite of the sedentary nature of the search, there was an energy about the group that could not be shared by mere watchers, even with the anticipation of discovery. The relieving pair took with them flasks of coffee, received gratefully by the CSIs, who used the break to arch their backs and stretch their limbs.

'Nothing significant so far,' Sylvia said. 'Half an hour and we'll be at the stones. Then we'll start excavating at the end where your little canine friend stopped to take the plaudits. No smell at all for us, even now we've confined the site. Means one of two things. She's either not under there, or she's been killed recently enough for there to be no time for decomposition. It would be slow in any case at these temperatures.'

'So... gut feel?' Jo asked.

'Don't do gut feel. Just do wait and see. Or wait and hope in this case.'

'You and me, both.'

The circle of CSIs had reduced from the initial ten to just six as the perimeter of their search moved closer to the pile of stones. They worked now in staggered shifts of fifteen minutes each to allow time to ease aching muscles and to warm themselves with coffee and movement. They completed the search of the surrounding area at just before 8.15 p.m. The team all got to their feet and turned to Sylvia.

'Just give me a few minutes, guys,' she said, kneeling down in front of the stones. 'Perhaps you'd like to stretch your legs outside.' She tilted her head to one side as if listening carefully. The wind roared against the side of the tent. 'Or perhaps not.'

The group laughed as one, deflected briefly from the gravity of their task. Sylvia began turning over the stones, beginning at the end of the rectangle where Jess had posed for her handler and working her way along. From time to time she selected one for closer scrutiny and scraped something off the surface into an individual evidence bag, which she handed to Matt for logging and storage. Throughout, she kept up a running commentary into a recorder placed on the ground in front of her whilst the rest of the group watched in complete silence. Finally, she got to her feet, still looking down at the stones.

'Right, team, time for the truth. Steady as we go.'

Matt crouched down to one side at the head of the rectangle, nodding to direct one of his team to the other side. Together they began to remove the stones, one by one as if they were as fragile as birds' eggs, placing each singly on the ground at arm's length behind them. It took only a few tense minutes to uncover what they were concealing.

'I think we need to get the Super.' Sylvia's hushed voice could only just be heard above the storm as they all stared in silence at the upturned toes of a pair of leather boots.

CHAPTER EIGHTEEN

Tuesday 15 January

Squeezed in amongst cabinets and chairs temporarily stored in the briefing room during the refurbishment of the open plan area, the assembled group awaited the arrival of their senior officers. As if the main topic on the agenda was sacrosanct until they were present, the talk so far had been about the logistical challenge of getting off the moor and home the previous night. Conditions had reached a point where local farmers had been mobilised to help move the police vehicles using a couple of tractors and an ancient but highly effective Land Rover Defender.

Jo's perceived advantage of parking on the main road had been offset by the difficulty of retracing her steps without the benefit of clear paths, followed by the treacherous conditions on the two-kilometre stretch of untreated road back to the junction with The Rake at the Shoulder of Mutton. The Bury contingent had regrouped for a brief review of the evening's events in that same room, along with Dr Wiseman, who later faced the prospect of heading north again to Accrington. Jo had finally arrived home at a little after two o'clock, and after a brief call, full of apologies, to her anxious spouse, had fallen asleep fully clothed on the bed. That had been five and a half hours ago.

Present in the room were Eva and Mo, Sergeant Geoff Brazendale, Jess's handler, Seth Walker, along with Matty Crenshaw and Lou Bakewell, CSIs from the Bury unit. They were joined at 7.45 a.m. by Jo, Andy, and Mal, and a young man who looked as though he ought to be getting ready for school, and who busied himself at two monitor screens at one end of the meeting table.

'This is George, one of our techno-whizz-kids,' Mal said, 'who is about to link us by some sort of magic to Doc Wiseman in Accrington and DI Al Crossley from Lancashire Division in Blackburn.'

Right on cue, the two screens came to life at the same moment, revealing the head and shoulders of each party.

'Thank you, George,' Mal said, 'and good morning to you both.'

They replied in kind together and Mal ran through who was present at the Bury end of the meeting.

'Pleased to see you must have made it home, Syl. Can't have been much fun.'

'Not as bad as it was getting back down into Bury from the dig site earlier; that was a bit like the Cresta Run. Dropped down to the M66 when I left you later and then onto the A56. Gritters had been out all the way, although I believe it's the snowploughs that have taken over this morning.'

'Well, thanks for joining us so early on the screen. And welcome to Bury, Al. I hope you slept well last night while we were doing all the work.'

DI Crossley laughed. 'Like a baby, thank you, sir. I still don't quite understand what got you all out there.'

'I've asked DI Carter along to explain. Jo…'

'Good morning, everyone,' she began. 'I received an anonymous tip-off in the form of a series of numbers – six in all in two groups of three, 195 followed by 778. If you reverse the two three-digit groups, the sequence becomes 778 195. When we did the search of the moor, immediately after Phoebe's disappearance, we recorded grid references for each item we found, and GR 778 195 is right in the middle of the search area. I didn't want to set a lot of hares running before I checked it out, so I drove up there yesterday afternoon and it led me to the memorial cairn of Ellen Strange, and the stone carving. *And*, the new set of stones close by, arranged in a rectangle.'

'How did you receive the tip-off?' Al asked.

'By text. Burner phone we think. The techies are checking mine now.'

'And when did you get it?'

'Well, it came as a series of single digits over a period of time. I received the first on Christmas Eve, then another every day or so up to five digits, and finally the sixth just a couple of days ago. It suddenly struck me what it was when I saw all six digits together alongside the list of grid references. They just needed swapping round.'

'Why would somebody do that?' Al again asked the question.

'No idea, at least no idea at first, which is why I didn't mention the texts earlier. I assumed it was someone having a joke with the new girl. And it seems it was, given where it led me and what we found.'

Mal turned to Andy. 'Detective Sergeant, for DI Crossley's benefit, just recap the events of last night, not forgetting to emphasise the appalling conditions we had to work in.'

There was laughter at all three locations reflecting a levity across the group, which could hardly have been imagined twelve hours ago. Andy leaned forward towards the screens.

'First, let me emphasise the appalling conditions that *some of us* had to work in whilst others drank coffee in a warm caravan.' There was more laughter at the comment and at the superintendent's expression of wide-eyed innocence. 'Responding to DI Carter's tip-off we had the site checked out with the dog who clearly got scent of something under the new set of stones. We called in reinforcements from Bury, along with some of your guys, including an additional CSI unit, and contacted Doc Wiseman, luckily catching her just minutes before the end of her shift.'

'Yes, thank you for that. Most kind. Although I have to say, I'm glad I was there. Go on, Andy.'

'Long story short, we checked out the area around the stones then started lifting them and saw the toes of our misper's boots sticking out. I guess we all felt a bit sick at that point until we went a bit further and deeper and realised there were no legs in the boots. It was *only* the boots. And I don't know about anybody else, but at that moment, in spite of what was happening outside, it felt like the sun had just come out.'

The laughter was mixed with a sense of astonishment this time.

'That's very poetic, detective sergeant, and more than a little out of character,' Mal observed. 'I remembered us all standing staring at the boots in a rapt silence, finally broken by the sound of DC Malik's phone going off. Made us all jump out of our skins.'

'Yes, I'm sorry about that,' Mo said. 'My dear wife, wondering when I would be home. I stepped out of the tent to take the call and I can assure you, the sun had *not* come out.'

Mal raised his hands to bring an end to the jollity, which threatened to take over the meeting.

'We have a few more questions to address following this episode, but let us not forget we still don't know what happened to Phoebe Wright and where she is now. At the moment we discovered her empty boots last night, that was very good news given the alternative outcome, but the reality is we are no closer to finding her.'

There were a few moments' silence broken by Jo.

'It seems to me the big question is what the link is between the grid reference, the boots and Phoebe's disappearance. Is it meant to provide a clue as to what happened to her by linking it to the fate of Ellen Strange?'

'How do you mean, Jo?' Sylvia said.

'Two hundred and sixty years ago, Ellen Strange had a bust-up with her bloke in the White Horse and set off across the moor for her parents' home in Hawkshaw. He followed her and killed her where we found Phoebe's boots last night. It was a different White Horse, in Haslingden, not the one in Helmshore, but it could be that…'

'Someone's pointing the finger at Benny,' Al suggested.

'It's a possibility.'

'Hold on.' Andy was flicking through pages of his notebook. He turned to Jo. 'When on Christmas Eve did you get the first digit?'

'Not sure of the exact time, but it was before Phoebe was reported missing, if that's where you're going.'

'Exactly. If the link to Ellen Strange is meant to point us to Phoebe's fate, then the person who sent the first number, and presumably all the subsequent numbers, knew she was missing before we did, and that was a full day before we started questioning people. Which suggests they were complicit in her disappearance, or perhaps a witness.'

'More likely a witness than the guilty party,' Eva put in. 'A perp would be unlikely to send clues to help people find him.'

'Or her,' Andy said.

'Or her,' Eva conceded.

'So where does that leave us?' Mal asked. 'Any further on? And if not, what have we got that's new?'

There was silence for a few moments. It was Seth who spoke first.

'The boots must have been buried there *after* the search had been terminated, otherwise there's no doubt Jess would have sniffed them out during the search. And also, the team would have noticed the new pile of stones. Do we have drone footage that might help us establish when the stones were moved and the boots buried?'

'Good point. We'll check.' Mal nodded to Eva who made a note. 'Anything else? What about you guys, Matty and Lou? Any thoughts?'

'It seems likely that the person who sent DI Carter the grid reference is the same one who buried the boots.' Matty smiled, a little embarrassed. 'I hope that wasn't too blindingly obvious. So if the Doc's team can ID someone who handled the boots, that takes the pressure off the techies checking for the burner or burners.' He paused. 'Only if it *is* the same person, of course.'

'Good again. Lou?'

'Well, just a thought, but if someone sent these cryptic clues to point the finger at Benny Morrison, why didn't they just come forward and tell the police what they know? Unless the guy doing the pointing is the real perp and wants to stay out of the picture.'

'Thanks, Lou. All good points. Answers, comments, anyone. Or, if not, any more questions – as if we haven't got enough already.'

Jo raised her hand. 'The link to Ellen Strange does seem to be suggesting something similar happened to Phoebe. But there's no evidence to support that. If she was killed on the moor on the twenty-second of December why haven't we found her body. Who's going to carry a dead body off the moor at that time of night and to where? There's no way she could have been buried – the ground would have been rock-hard. And if she'd been abducted and then killed somewhere else, why was all her stuff found near where she was last seen? And if all those small items were found, how come her boots were missed? We know they weren't initially buried at the cairn, so where and why would they have been hidden elsewhere. And by whom? Presumably by the person who was planning to stage that event last night and flagged it by sending me the clues, like Matty said. So given I received the first clue before she was even reported missing, last night's plan was in place for a long time.'

There were several moments of silence as each took in the tangle of questions arising from the previous evening's discovery.

'Al, I'd like you to stay on point with DS Mills,' Mal said, 'given that this latest development is on your patch, and the only new addition to the case for over a week. Geoff, as soon as possible, share the discovery of the boots with the initial search team and get their ideas as to why they were not found along with the rest of the stuff and, to DI Carter's point, where they could have been all this time. It's just possible, I suppose, that they *were* found, but not recorded and saved, but I don't understand how that could happen.'

Matty raised his hand.

'One thing, sir. For the boots still to be carrying Phoebe's scent after all this time, they must have been kept in a sealed container until very recently, so you could be right about them being initially found and bagged.'

'Right, let's make sure we share that point with the search team as well,' Mal said. 'At least this gives us something to do. Okay, sergeant?'

'Yes, sir,' Geoff said.

'So, over to you, Andy. Let's have a chat later this morning about how much, if anything, we share with the press, and what we tell Benny and the parents. It would be good to have something new for the media so we can raise the case's profile again. In the meantime, bring everyone who needs to know internally up to date and keep on top of the techies checking DI Carter's phone. I assume she'd appreciate getting it back as soon as possible. Sylvia, I'm sure you'll get back as soon as you have anything from last night's collection.'

'I'm on it, mate – as they say in *Line of Duty*,' she replied, raising the final chuckle from the gathering,

'Thank you for that, Doc, and thanks, everybody – for last night, in particular.'

★

The new development in Phoebe's disappearance, albeit not directly helpful to the cause, had truly set the hares running. Jo, herself, with the luxury of standing back from the immediate surge of activity, followed its course almost as a spectator. She had to admit to herself, with some reluctance, that DS Andy Mills was showing an application and interest that had been conspicuously missing whilst she had been heading the case. Perhaps the Super was right, and why wouldn't he be, that she was half the problem. Apart from his temporary meltdown on the moor when righteous indignation seemed to override reason, his behaviour and attitude towards her, personally, had improved to the point of genuine cooperation. And, bearing in mind the focus and ferocity of his meltdown, she had to concede it was unlikely he had been the sender of the cryptic clues which had led her there.

Taking advantage of her low-profile role as interested observer as the wheels of investigation whirled about her, Jo left the station mid-afternoon to return to her new home in Stock Street. Snow had been falling steadily throughout the day and the drive down to Burr's Country Park needed concentration and care. It felt good to get inside early enough to light the log-burning stove in the sitting room which had been waiting a long time, fully loaded, for just this moment. As the flames grew and the whole ambience of the property seemed to change for the better, Jo promised herself that she would get home earlier more often to enjoy this wonderfully primitive form of heating. For the moment, settling herself at the breakfast bar in the neat little kitchen, with a cafetière of coffee and a tube of Pringles, she opened her laptop and revisited the notes she had compiled so far on the primary objective of her assignment.

There were plenty of notes but they represented very little progress. In truth the distraction of the grid reference and the boots had been a welcome interruption to a thankless task. After an hour or so, having emptied both cafetière and tube, she closed down her notes and Googled 'Ellen Strange'. After trawling through a number of references, she downloaded the booklet *'ELLEN STRANGE A moorland murder mystery explained'* by John Simpson, a local historian. Printing it off, she took it through to the living room, kicked off her shoes, and curled her legs underneath her on the sofa. Within a couple of minutes, she had changed her position to lie full length with her head propped against a cushion and her legs stretched out. A further two minutes, and she was asleep.

She was awakened by a knocking on the door, loud enough to suggest it may not have been the first attempt at making someone hear inside. She shuffled her feet back into her shoes and opened the front door to two smiling young men in branded hi-vis jackets. Jo checked her watch.

'Five o'clock.' She smiled back at them 'Right on time. You did well to get here at all. Fancy a brew?'

★

'Hi. Where are you?'

'Hi to you, too. At home, where else would I be at nine o'clock at night?'

'At the station, on the moor, skating on Calf Hey reservoir, sipping tea at the Summerseat garden centre cafeteria…'

'The last of those is closed and two of the remaining three are dark and snowbound. Actually, I'm curled up on the sofa and wishing I had some company with which to try out the new sheepskin rug in front of a roaring fire.'

'Well, don't you be testing it until I get there, d'you hear?'

'Okay, boss. It came today, along with the two reinforced wing chairs and the double bed, and two very nice young men who stayed for tea. Well, a cup of, anyway. And I don't think we'll need the double bed; the rug's easily big enough for both of us. Must have been an enormous sheep.'

Seb laughed. 'Can't wait. Rough day yesterday?'

'Not really rough. Long certainly, and listen, I am sorry for phoning you so late. Just didn't have chance earlier.'

'No problem. I'm pleased you did. What a strange development – no pun intended, by the way. Any idea what's behind it or who? Your toxic sergeant still seems the most likely candidate, don't you think?'

'I'd say yes but for one thing, and that was his reaction when he joined us on the moor. He went positively ballistic, like I was trying to steal the case back off him. If he *is* the one who sent me there, then he puts Tom Hanks in the shade for acting ability.'

'So, who else? One of Benny's crowd, do you think? But how would they have got your number before you started handing out your cards?'

'And how would they get hold of the boots? It must be someone on the inside. Whoever it is has raised the stakes with the footwear trick. Sending me a few numbers anonymously is one thing; getting thirty police out from two different regional forces at night in the middle of a blizzard is something else. I wouldn't be surprised if the person who did this is wishing they hadn't right now.'

'I bet whoever it was didn't reckon on the terrier instinct of their target. That's a compliment, by the way, before you jump in and accuse me of calling you a dog.'

Jo laughed. 'You know me so well, don't you?'

'So, any developments through the day, other than your tea party?'

'Well the tea party was the high point of the day to be honest – until this phone call, of course. We checked what drone footage of the search area was available, but that only covered the period of the search itself. It confirmed what we already knew that the new rectangle of stones was not there then, but we've nothing to show when it *was* put there. Only, it must have been recently for Phoebe's scent to have survived on the boots.

'Nothing from forensics up to the time I left the station, which was around three, but that was what we expected. No prints found on the boots except Phoebe's and, unless the boot thief tried them on with bare feet before burying them, unlikely any DNA traces to come either. They still have the tent up at the site in case they decide to carry on looking, but it's been snowing heavily all day so I doubt if anyone will be keen to return yet. Geoff Brazendale, the guy who led the search team, has had them together again for a meeting to get any ideas on where the boots might have been and how they could have been missed, but nothing forthcoming from that, apparently. Eva texted me just before I called you. The text said "Brazendale" and a thumbs-down emoji. A woman of few words, our Eva.

'The only other thing of note is a new appeal on local TV and in the regional press. This will include the photo of Phoebe and a CCTV still of the mystery lady at the Shoulder. Oh, and the combined image that our techies put together a couple of weeks ago. To date we've only shown that to Morrison and the Wrights. And they go out with a full bootees update in the *Manchester Evening*

News, *Sheffield Star* and *Yorkshire Post* tomorrow, and the *Bury Times* and *Bolton News* on Thursday. The Super thinks it's a good opportunity and the right time to raise the profile of the case again.

'So there you have it. All that was followed by the furniture delivery at *Chez Nous*, which arrived bang on *cinq heures*, then the tea party. And after that, I've been swotting up on Ellen Strange. Downloaded a booklet by a local historian, John Simpson, which is really interesting. I guess you'll be familiar with it all.'

'I know there's a poem about what happened that we read at school. If I remember she was followed onto the moor by a peddler she'd met at Haslingden Fair, who raped and killed her. In fact, weren't they already lovers who were usually accompanied by some other person to make sure she came to no harm, only this time they sneaked off together on their own?'

'What you've just described is the *legend* of Ellen Strange, which was what the poem depicted. The *truth*, as uncovered by Mr Simpson from records at the time, is that the killer was her husband, one John Broadley. But this is the spooky bit; they quarrelled the evening before the murder, she set off across the moor to her parents' farm in Hawkshaw, he caught up with her and attacked and killed her. At least that's what everybody believed, although he was acquitted through lack of any witnesses to the killing.'

'And the clues led you right to the spot where she was killed.'

'Well, the *exact* spot is not known for certain, and anyway, the cairn was moved about a hundred or so years ago by some kids from a local school. But they did take me to the marker and the sculpture.'

'Didn't they hang somebody on a gibbet on Bull Hill right after the murder?'

'The legend again, in which people believed the peddler had made a pact with the devil to escape. If he did, he was badly let down. Terribly unreliable, these devils.'

'You are a little swot, aren't you? I'm terribly impressed.'

'Not me, Mr Simpson did all the work. Anyway, it was a very productive couple of hours developing my local knowledge. DC Mills *will* be pleased. And right now, I'm looking at this rug and… can't wait for Friday.'

There was silence from Seb.

'You *are* coming Friday? Right?'

'Well... I can't say for certain yet.'

'Oh, come on, Seb. You were supposed to come last week.'

'Hey, let's not forget who it is that's away from home. I'm here at our home; *you're* the absent one. It's been nearly four weeks – in fact, four weeks tomorrow – since you were last here. I understand it's early in your assignment and important to be visible, which is why I've not suggested you come back yet. But you've not mentioned *once* when you *do* intend to come back here for a few days.'

This time Jo was silent for a while before replying.

'Point taken. We always said this would be a challenge, didn't we? Living apart, like this. And we agreed we'd call it a challenge and not a problem. Because love conquers all, right?'

'Right. And I'm not saying I won't be coming, just that I can't be certain yet.'

'So what's the source of the uncertainty? The weather?'

'Well... yes... but not in the way you're thinking.'

'Do explain.'

Jo could hear Seb take in a deep breath. 'Okay, here goes. If it's like it is now, I'll be coming, probably by train, but I'll be there. If the weather improves enough, then the fixture against Hinckley, which should have been played tonight, will be played on Saturday afternoon. I mean, we're flying at the moment, Jo. Heading for National League One, and I don't want to miss it. We don't have a scheduled game on Saturday, so it makes sense to...'

'I understand.' Jo's clipped interruption was made through gritted teeth.

There was a long, tense pause.

'I get the distinct impression that you don't,' Seb said.

'No, I really do. If it's a choice between rucking with the team or fucking with your wife, then... no brainer. Clear as a bell.'

'That's a bit coarse, Jo, and does you no credit.'

'I don't know what...'

'It trivialises something precious. I don't fuck you, I make love to you.'

'It's the same thing.'

'Not for me.'

'Well, perhaps we can debate the difference next time we meet, whenever that will be. Look, Seb, I don't want to argue and the only way I can see to avoid that right now is to end the call. Let's talk tomorrow.' She paused, and pressed the red button.

Jo sat staring at the screen on her phone for a long time without moving. It was the most serious fall-out she'd had with her husband, in spite of the 'challenge' they had accepted and embraced as part of their relationship. She felt tears pricking her eyes. She got to her feet and looked at herself in the mirror above the fireplace. Was this the start, the top of the slippery slope? And, if that missing something didn't happen, what then?

CHAPTER NINETEEN

Wednesday 16 January

Jo went through the motions of a light breakfast of coffee and toast without really noticing. Nor could she remember anything of her short journey to the station, consumed by thoughts of the conversation with Seb the previous night and the questions it had raised in her mind. She had lain awake for a long time, in spite of the fatigue, which had been building all day following her long night on the moor. The moment of her submission to sleep had closely followed her reaching a decision; one that had been forced upon her but which seemed simple and necessary under the circumstances. Now, in the light of a new day, it didn't seem as clear-cut. In truth, she was not sure whether she was looking forward to the next contact with her husband, or dreading it.

Inside the station, there was still a positive feel within the section as she edged her way past joiners and electricians crawling over the floor of the open plan area to take possession of her office. As Eva had promised, some of the items had been removed to alternative temporary locations, and the whiteboard from the MCV was back in the briefing room with its renewed status as a live item. She walked over to the window and stared at the screen on her iPhone as if willing it to ring or ping with a message.

Seating herself at the desk, a pile of documents awaiting her attention, she opened her laptop and leaned back in her chair. Why? she thought. *Why* was she waiting? What if Seb was staring at his own phone thinking exactly the same. Well, it was up to her. After all, she was older than Seb by a full six years and, as a consequence, much wiser or so she'd always claimed. She smiled at the thought, remembering all the mileage they'd got out of their age difference in the way of jokes and banter. She picked up her phone and went to her recent contacts. The iPhone pinged before she had time to make the call. The content of the text was not unexpected, and set up her own intended message perfectly.

'Sorry about last night. Have decided to miss match to see my lovely wife. You were right, no brainer. Will let them know tonight at training.'

It was the longest text she had ever received from Seb and she marvelled at the punctuation.

She replied; *'You'd better not do that!'*

'Why.'

No question mark, Jo noticed, with a smile, but she'd overlook it just this once. She typed in her response.

'Because I'm coming to watch you.'

Jo began shuffling the papers around on her desk with no real purpose. She looked around the cluttered room, her eyes taking in the random collection of items temporarily stored there and tried to focus on something to occupy her other than a return to the trawl of information. DC Kirsty Milner knocked and entered all in one movement. Jo looked at her phone, hearing the pinged reply but slipping it into her pocket.

'You'll want to see this, ma'am. Report just in.'

'Go on.'

'Body discovered this morning around ten-forty in one of those large wheelie bins in an alley back of the Lancashire Gate pub in Bury town centre.' She placed a single sheet of A4 on Jo's desk. 'Uniforms in attendance and the area's been cleared and sealed off. Traffic diverted.'

'How?'

'Multiple stab wounds, as far as they can tell.'

'Not hypothermia, then?'

'I guess that wouldn't have helped.'

'And the victim?'

'White male, probably late twenties to early thirties. No ID yet – the body's mostly covered by bin bags, apparently, and they haven't been able to check for a wallet or phone. They're waiting for us to see him first before they move him.'

'Do we know how long he's been there?'

Kirsty consulted the sheet. 'Bags of waste were put into that particular bin just after eleven-thirty last night and he wasn't there then, and there were people moving in and around the alley from six this morning, dumping rubbish, plus, we think, two deliveries further down past the bin. So, sometime between midnight and six.'

'Anything else?'

'Yes, a call came in last night around ten-thirty after a disturbance in the same pub. Carried on briefly outside but by the time our guys got there it was all over. So we don't know whether the death is related to the earlier fight.'

'Christ, Tuesday night, Kirsty. Hardly the time for heavy stuff like this. Or is this normal oop north?'

'Not on any day in the Six Towns, ma'am.'

'CSIs?'

'On their way.' Kirsty checked her watch. 'In fact, should be there by now.'

'And forensics?'

'Getting there as soon as possible.'

'Don't tell me it's Doc Wiseman. She'll never get down here from Accrington.'

Kirsty gave a little chuckle. 'No, not this time. Our very own Jamie Taylor.'

'Doctor Dish. Well, detective, let's get down there and give him some help. Has the Super been informed?'

'Yes, ma'am.'

'Great stuff, Kirsty, you've done everything but find the killer, so let's do that together.'

★

At a few minutes after one o'clock, Jo and Kirsty donned their white suits, gloves, and boots, and ducked under the crime scene tape across the entrance to the alley. The sky was still overcast and threatening but it had stopped snowing several hours ago. The large rectangular bin with its four heavy-duty castors was pushed up against the high wall which separated the pub's rear yard from the alley. The grey container was about one and a half metres high, the same length, and a metre wide. The Crime Scene Unit had assembled a metre-high platform around three sides to enable them better access by kneeling to reach inside, and had detached and removed the lift-up lid. A large tent had been erected around the bin and the team was currently searching the alley itself for clues to the incident. Matty was back in charge of the group and walked along the alley to join the two detectives.

'We can't go on meeting like this, Matty,' Jo said.

'Oh, really, ma'am? And I was just about to say we *must* go on meeting like this.'

Jo laughed. 'I didn't think you'd be back on shift yet.'

'Seven to seven. I just got unlucky yesterday with a seven to one-thirty. I say unlucky, but it's good to be part of something with a positive outcome for a change.'

'This will be a reality check for you guys, then. What have we got so far?'

'Interesting. There's no blood around in the alley. It should show up very clearly in the snow, even though its heat would partially melt it. There's a slight trace of blood on the rim of the bin where we assume the body's been lifted in but none showing on the bags covering it. No-one's touched or moved the body yet, by the way. It's exactly how it was found.'

'So, the lack of blood – you were saying?'

'Yes, it's almost certain the guy was killed somewhere else and dumped here. And no blood visible on the bags means they must have been taken out before the body was dumped, then put back on top of it, presumably to hide it. Fortunately, they didn't cover it completely. Well, fortunately for us, I mean, not for the guy in the bin. Also, there are tyre tracks along the alley, a couple of vehicles at least, that have been made since the snow stopped. We do know there has been at least one delivery made down there early this morning, but the tracks might give us something. I can't imagine someone – or more than one person – carrying a body around, whatever the time of night, so if he was killed somewhere else he was probably brought here in a car or van.'

'Great. Anything else?'

'I've spoken to a couple of the uniforms taking statements. The landlord says there was a fight in the pub last night. Started inside – just a couple of guys on each side, apparently. There weren't many punters in the pub, so it didn't escalate. He got them outside where it all calmed down, probably due to the weather. Bit of a shock to the system I imagine. Anyway, as far as the landlord was concerned it was game over, except someone in the bar had already phoned the police. But by the time they arrived it was all quiet.'

'So the earlier fight doesn't seem to be linked to the murder,' Kirsty said. 'Just a coincidence.'

'Any other reports of violence in Bury last night?' Jo asked her.

'Not that I'm aware of,' Kirsty said. 'It's hard to believe anyone would venture out at all.'

'So, just two incidents, both at the same pub. Can't be a coincidence. Have we contacted pathology?'

'Yes, Martin will be ready as soon as possible.'

Jo frowned. 'Martin? I don't think I've met him.'

'It's a "her", ma'am. Professor Chrissie Martin. Lectures part-time on pathology at Salford University, which is where she is and what she's doing right now. Her lecture ends at one, so she should just about be on her way by now. I told her that would be okay. I hope it is, ma'am?'

'Yes, that's fine. And here's Dr Taylor,' Jo added with a theatrical fluttering of the eyelashes.

'Right, I'll get on then,' Matty said, with an equally theatrical shrug. 'Can't compete with Jamie.' The two detectives laughed as Matty left them to return to his team.

The white-clad figure of Dr Dish was striding towards them down the alley, his gleaming white teeth smiling from his perfect face under his perfect hair, all atop a perfect physique; and with a twinkle in his dazzlingly perfect blue eyes.

'Good afternoon, ladies.' He rubbed his hands together and hunched his shoulders. 'A little chilly, don't you think?' he said, with deliberate understatement.

Jo resisted voicing the suggestion that perhaps they should huddle together for warmth, and felt sure that a similar thought would be passing through Kirsty's mind. The forensic scientist pulled the hood of his protective suit into place and slipped on his gloves.

'Are we ready to view the victim, yet?'

'DC Milner and I have just arrived,' Jo said, 'so we can look together.'

They walked down the alley and pushed into the tent where Matty's team had placed a plank lower down next to the long side of the bin to provide a step-up to the improvised viewing platform. The three of them knelt shoulder to shoulder and looked down at the body. It was lying half on its side but with the face upturned, eyes closed. As Matty had said, the bags placed on top of it had not covered it completely and it was easy to identify the sex and approximate age. Part of the chest was also visible, revealing the several stab wounds as individual crimson puncture-marks within the general blood-soaking of a lightweight hooded jacket.

'Hardly appropriate outdoor gear for last night,' Kirsty remarked. 'Assuming it was last night when he was killed. I suppose if he was dumped here afterwards it could have been earlier.'

'No smell yet,' Jamie said, 'so not much earlier. I guess Chrissie will let us know. Not much to do right now. I think we get the guys to move the bags in their own delicate way, then we can get down and dirty with our deceased friend in there.'

Jo turned to the senior CSI, her mind thinking of better places to get down and dirty with Dr Dish. 'All yours, Matty. Could you clear the bags, please.'

★

'I know you've already given a statement to one of our colleagues, Mr Manvers, but I'd just like to go over again what happened here last night.'

Jo and Kirsty were seated around a small circular table in the main bar of the Lancashire Gate with Jed Manvers, the landlord. It was easy to see how this man would be effective in breaking up a fight. Well over six feet tall, he was broad-shouldered and muscular, with battered features and enormous hands. His friendly manner and soft voice seemed to belong to someone else.

'Okay, but I told them all I know…'

'Yes, but we've now had time to examine the body so we may have a few questions that weren't covered before. It won't take long.'

'Do you know who it is?'

'Not yet, but I'm sure we soon will.'

'You're not going to ask me to identify him, are you?'

'Why would we ask you to do that, Mr Manvers?' Jo asked.

'To check whether he was in here last night. That's what this is about, isn't it? The fight and whether this guy was one of those involved.'

'Well, clearly there could be a connection, but we don't know that yet. How did it all kick off?'

'Everything was quiet and relaxed, then two guys came in around ten o'clock, looking for trouble, I reckon. Don't know whether they'd been drinking, though I have to say, they didn't *seem* to have been. I can usually tell. Should be able to after doing this job for as long as I have.'

'So you didn't know these two men? They weren't regulars?'

'I'd never seen them before.'

'How did it start?'

'Not sure exactly what kicked it off. I just heard raised voices. The usual hard man stuff. One of the guys said something like, "What are you looking at?" Answer, "Nothing much." That sort of thing. It's not a giant step from that to throwing punches, plus a chair in this case.'

'And who was on the end of all this? I understand it was just, like, two against two. Is that right?'

'More like two against one. Of the two involved who were already in the bar, one was trying to calm it all down. So, no more than a lot of shoving, a few punches, lots of language and threats, but no-one injured. Even the chair survived without any damage. Me and a couple of the regulars got them outside, without much effort to be honest, and I think the weather put paid to any further bravado. They seemed to be heading their separate ways, although there was a lot of shouting about it not being over, that sort of thing.'

'And the two guys involved, the ones already in the pub, do you know them?'

'They're not what I'd call regulars either, but they do come in from time to time, often with a larger group.'

'Names?'

'One's called Jack, and he was the one trying to calm things down. He comes in more than the other one. I don't know the other's real name but his mates call him "Knocker", which sounds a bit dated somehow. It's sort of an old-fashioned nickname for someone who looks like he's only in his twenties.'

'Knocker? Yes, I know what you mean. And have you had any trouble with these guys before – Knocker's crowd?'

'Of the two, Jack is the fighter, I understand, although not in here, thank goodness, except for once, some time ago. On that occasion he showed what he was capable of. Took three guys out, including putting one in hospital. He didn't start it, so he wasn't to blame, but he certainly bloody finished it. Jesus, I've never seen anything like it.' He paused to shake his head. 'In fact, from what I remember, it started pretty much the same as last night. Something out of nothing, but this time the two guys were lucky.

'Knocker can be a bit mouthy, but nothing really bad. A few arguments, usually on match days and never anything serious. It was all over before it began last night. I felt bad about the police being dragged out, especially on a night like that, but it was one of the other customers that called them. Can't blame the punter, I suppose; it might have turned nasty but we can usually deal with it ourselves, with the help of a few regulars.'

'So Jack and Knocker, had they had a lot to drink?' Kirsty asked.

'On their second pint I think. I don't really know why they were out at all. Tuesday night, terrible weather.'

'I don't suppose you know where they live?' Jo said.

'No. Pretty local, I think.' Jed frowned. 'Although I'm not sure why I think that. I know that quite a few of the crowd they're usually with are from Bury. Do you think one of them is the guy in the bin?'

'We have no idea who the victim is, Mr Manvers, there was no ID on the body, and it's unclear whether the altercation in here and the death are related at all. From what you've told us, I assume no-one was brandishing a weapon last night.'

'No – well, only the chair.'

Jo gave a little laugh. 'That doesn't count, Mr Manvers.'

'When will I be able to open again?' the landlord asked.

'Not for a while, I'm afraid. Certainly not for the rest of today. Our crime scene investigators will need to check over inside. Will you point them towards the chair used in the incident; they'll need to check it for fingerprints and possibly DNA.'

'I'm afraid they'll be wasting their time. One thing I did notice about the guy who threw it, and his mate, was that they were both wearing gloves, the whole time they were in the bar.'

★

Back at Bury Police HQ, the briefing room was the centre of activity again. Pinned to the large wall-mounted incident board were photographs taken at the scene of the discovery of the body, including the alley, the bin, the body – in situ from three different angles – the tyre marks, and exterior and interior views of the pub itself, next to a large-scale map of Bury town centre. A length of coloured string joined the photo of the bin with its position on the map. Alongside, on the same board, the timeline of the incident had been recorded from when the two antagonists arrived at a little after 10.00 p.m. the previous night to the discovery of the body at 10.40 a.m. that morning. Key moments noted between were the start of the altercation, arrival of the police, dumping of the evening's rubbish in the bin, and the two deliveries down the alley earlier on the current day.

Joining Jo, Kirsty, and Jamie Taylor in the briefing room were DS Andy Mills, DCs Mohamed Malik, Eva Johnson, and Jodi Lawson, along with PS Liv Parsons and PC Kieran Mallet, the two uniformed officers who had been first on scene that morning when the discovery was reported. Both officers had taken initial statements from staff at the pub and briefly by phone from the delivery drivers. Superintendent Jones was absent attending a Police Training Seminar, where he was the guest speaker at lunch, and Jo led the proceedings as the first senior officer at the scene.

'So, what do we know so far about what happened last night and overnight at the Lancashire Gate?' she began. 'Two incidents. Firstly, a fight inside the pub, which took place at around ten-thirty involving someone throwing a few punches and a chair, and which continued briefly outside. Secondly, a body dumped in a bin in the alley *behind* the pub sometime between eleven-thirty last night and six-twenty this morning. At this stage we can't say for sure that the killing took place last night, although if not last night, it must have been very recently. What we can say with some certainty is that it took place somewhere else. There were no traces of blood on the ground in the alley and none on the bags placed on top of the body, pointing to the fact that bleeding had probably ceased before it was dumped there.'

'Meaning he was dead when he was binned,' Andy said. 'I hope they put him in non-recyclable.'

'We don't know if the two incidents are connected,' Jo went on to cut across the laughter. 'We could ask the landlord to tell us by viewing the body, but obviously not before we've established who he is and informed next of kin. There was no ID on the body – cards or phone; we're checking his fingerprints right now. There are tyre tracks in the alley, which must have been made after about three this morning when the snow stopped, because there is no snow on top of where the tyres have compacted the earlier fall. We do know there were two deliveries down the alley this morning, at six-twenty and seven-twelve. We're checking tyres on each delivery vehicle to eliminate them, assuming that the body would have been taken to the bin in a car or van. However, it's not going to be easy or even possible to get any meaningful impressions.' Jo pointed to the photos of the alley and the tracks on the board. 'The alley is very narrow and the wheels of any vehicle would have to overlap any previous tracks. If the body *was* driven down there, its tyre-tracks would be covered by the first delivery vehicle.'

'CCTV?' Andy said.

'Checking now, but some of the cameras around the centre of Bury are out, they think because of the weather. We might get lucky.'

'Cause of death?' Eva asked.

'Five stab wounds to the chest, which we *assume* must have killed him, though not officially confirmed yet. There was also a minor wound to the left temple caused by a blunt instrument, but the pathologist doesn't think that would be a factor in the murder and might even be the result of a separate incident.'

'Like contact with a flying chair, perhaps?' Eva suggested.

'We'll know in time, and soon, hopefully,' Jo said. She looked across at Kirsty and Jamie. 'Would you like to add anything at this stage? They shook their heads. 'Okay. I have a few initial thoughts.'

Jo had been standing next to the incident board. She picked up the marker pen.

'There were a few things that Jed Manvers, the landlord, said when Kirsty and I interviewed him that struck a few chords. In isolation they don't amount to much, but added together I believe they raise a number of questions. Let me just list these so we can look at them together.'

She wrote:

1. *Why were they out drinking?*

'Manvers couldn't understand why the first two guys were there at all. I'm paraphrasing and Kirsty will keep me honest, but he said they never went in on Tuesdays and whenever they *were* in they had a good bit to drink. It was ten o'clock and they were only on their second pint.' Jo turned back to the board.

2. *Intruders looking for trouble – had not been drinking.*

'In my experience, and I'm sure in yours, violence in pubs and clubs is almost one hundred per cent fuelled by drink. On this occasion, it appears neither side had consumed enough to fit that pattern. Manvers said with all his years of experience he could tell when someone had had a lot to drink, and he reckoned the two guys who entered the pub at around ten had *not* been drinking. And yet within a matter of minutes they had started trouble with two already there. Jack and Knocker, by the way, according to the landlord.'

'Jack and Knocker?' Andy sounded incredulous. 'No-one's called Knocker these days. Are you sure that's not the name of another pub, the Jack and Knocker?'

'It may well be,' Jo said, 'but it's also what the two guys are called who were attacked in the pub. And I agree with you, for a twenty-something, Knocker is a bit of a cross to bear. But, reading between the lines, although Manvers didn't actually say this, it was like the second pair had gone in there with the sole purpose of confronting the other two.' She turned to Kirsty. 'Or is that a conclusion too far, detective?'

'No, I think that's right, ma'am.'

'Okay; next point.' Jo raised the marker again.

3. Fight easy to stop.

'Manvers said, and I quote, "It was all over before it began." Normally, if someone sets out deliberately to start a fight, it's usually a bigger deal that a few shoves and a chair, but it seems it was easily stopped by the landlord and one or two of the regulars, and when they got outside where there was *no-one* trying to stop them, they went their separate ways with just a bit of shouting. Even allowing for the fact that the landlord looks like a heavyweight boxer, it was a fairly weak capitulation.' She paused to think a moment then turned to the board again.

4. Jack tried to stop the fight.

'We asked the landlord if either of Jack or Knocker ever caused any trouble. He said no, they'd never *started* anything, but told us of one occasion when Jack was pushed enough to respond violently, and battered three guys, single-handed, putting one of them in hospital. And yet, last night, they were picked on by just these two guys and his response was, like, a peacemaker trying to prevent the fight. Doesn't quite fit, although again, it could be the drink – or lack of it in this case. Clear heads prevailing and all that. But, here's the kicker – for me, anyway.'

5. Both guys wore gloves all the time.

'It was cold last night, but well'ard guys don't usually go out drinking wearing gloves, and I can't ever remember seeing anyone wearing them *inside* a pub, unless they're part of a woman's outfit for a function or something. So what reason could these guys have for wearing them?'

Andy responded. 'Fingerprints. Which screams premeditation.'

'Exactly,' Jo said, adding to the list.

6. Knocker was targeted.

★

The team had dispersed to their temporary accommodation of half the cafeteria to pursue their assigned tasks, sharing the work with the wider group. It was Jo's first opportunity to check her last text message which had arrived at the precise moment Kirsty had told her about the discovery of the body.

'Brilliant darling but not sure good idea in this weather xx'

Punctuation and grammar had been ditched in the interest of spontaneity. Jo smiled, sadly, knowing everything had changed, anyway, in the last four hours and the chances of her getting time off at the weekend were virtually nil. What was needed next was a conversation, not another message. Talk, not text. It would have to wait.

Right now, she was sitting at the desk in her temporary storeroom, eyes glued to the screen of her laptop as she manipulated the street-level images on Google Maps of the area surrounding the Lancashire Gate. Kirsty had returned to the pub with Andy to speak with the staff again and compile a list of Jack and Knocker's usual crowd and any known addresses; their aim, to establish the current whereabouts of the two men through their regular contacts.

Mo was trawling CCTV coverage of the area, where functioning cameras permitted. The one camera covering the entrance to the alley had been operating throughout but showed a slow build-up of snow as it was blown directly onto the lens, and by 2.10 a.m. it was covered completely. Up to that time no vehicle had entered the alley. However, two other cameras close to Bury Interchange had recorded a black or dark-coloured Citroen Berlingo van, which had approached the pub at 4.15 a.m. along Haymarket Street from the traffic lights at its junction with Angouleme Way. The registration was not visible due to the number plate being covered, deliberately or by driven snow. Someone was compiling a list of all owners of Berlingo vans in the Bury area.

As expected, it was proving difficult to separate impressions of the tyres of the two vehicles that were known to have used the alley for deliveries that morning. However, there was evidence of a third vehicle that had pulled in close to the wall next to the bin. Moving to the side of the alley had partially separated its tyre tracks from the others. The tracks from this vehicle had been laid down prior to the two deliveries. It was a minor breakthrough, which would be enhanced if the vehicle itself could be located and the tyre treads matched.

Dr Dish's forensic team were finding little of value from the sparse pickings at the scene, except for trace samples of skin found on one leg of the chair that had been thrown in the pub. This may have been left by someone roughly handling the chair at some point, though not the attacker, who was wearing gloves. However, it could have been from Knocker, who had been struck by it during the altercation. If the latter, DNA comparison with the body would establish that the two incidents were linked. However, this could take a few days.

The glasses used by Jack and Knocker had, of course, been routinely washed the previous night after closing time, and there was such a confusion of prints on the chairs and table they'd used that there was little or no chance of anything useful to be gained from them. Fingerprints taken from the body were being checked against the two regional databases in the hope that the victim had previously been required to provide them. The search was at an early stage but so far there were no matches found against Greater Manchester and Lancashire records. In the absence of a hit, the next step would be to access HOLMES, the national database.

There had been no official report yet from Professor Chrissie Martin, except a brief message to confirm what they all knew anyway. Cause of death was multiple stab wounds to the 'upper frontal thoracic region of the body', or 'chest' as it was known to everyone outside pathology. The murder weapon, she believed, was a knife with a six-inch blade and one serrated edge.

Jo checked the time on the screen – 17.15. The late shift had arrived some time ago and would continue the quest for information. As the SIO, she had no expectations of leaving in the near future. The Super would be back soon from the seminar and would expect an update from her. She leaned back in the chair and stretched her arms above her head, then got to her feet and picked her way through the stored items to the window. It had started to snow heavily again and she reflected on how fortunate they had been not to be impeded earlier by adverse conditions. As she returned to her seat at the desk, the door opened and an excited Eva Johnson burst into the room.

'Got an ID, ma'am, and it seems you were right. The two incidents are connected. His prints are on file, taken after a fight in a pub three years ago when someone was critically injured. He wasn't the instigator or the cause of the injuries, but it was a serious incident and ended up at Manchester Crown Court. Everyone involved was required to provide prints. Anyway, our corpse is one Curtis Knox, aged twenty-nine. His address on our records is three years old so we are still checking that out. At that time he was still living at home. Maddie is putting together a full profile, but while we wait… well, Knox and Knocker? What do you think?'

'I think we have our man, at least our victim. Just the murderer now and we can all go home.' She frowned. 'Curtis Knox. That name sounds familiar.'

There was a tap on her door and Jo looked up to see DC Maddie Kemp, wide-eyed with her face up against the plain glass next to the door, and waving a sheet of A4.

'Come in, Maddie. That was a quick bit of data-gathering.'

'Haven't finished, ma'am, but I was sure you'd want to see this as soon as possible, you *and* DS Mills.'

Jo took the sheet from Maddie and read the few words typed at the top. Her eyes opened wider than Maddie's and she let out an audible gasp, before her face set into a frown. Eva was almost hopping up and down.

'Well, are you going to tell me?' she said.

Jo drew in a long breath. 'Yes, *all* of you. Go rally the troops before half of them push off home; get them back in the briefing room. Thanks, Maddie, and you're right, DS Mills needs to know right away.'

They left the room and Jo picked up her phone.

'Where are you, Andy?'

There were a few moments of silence on the other end of the call. Jo suspected her colleague was trying to recall the last time she had addressed him using his first name.

'At the Lancashire. Just leaving.'

'That's good, can you get back as soon as possible? We've had a bit of a development. I'm circling the wagons again, so could you come straight to my office and send Kirsty to join the gang in the briefing room.'

'Sounds exciting.'

'It is, but it might mean you and I are back working together again.'

'Perhaps exciting was the wrong word.'

'We'll see.'

★

The briefing room off the operations area was a buzz of excitement. Members of the incoming late shift and the day crew were present and all seats were taken around the table except for two at the end opposite the wall-mounted monitor screen, reserved for the two senior detectives. Some were standing behind the seats. And all conversation ceased as they entered the room along with Maddie. Jo checked the faces of those present in a silent roll call.

'Someone's missing?' She checked again. 'Where's DC Malik?'

'On his way, I guess.' Eva answered. 'I did tell him... I'll go and hurry him up.'

'It's okay, I'll go,' Jo said.

Mo was standing in front of his workstation in the cafeteria, staring at his phone. He must have heard Jo's approach.

'I'm *coming*,' he said, without moving.

'Good, whenever it's convenient, detective.' Jo said.

Mo turned. 'Sorry, ma'am. Just in mid thought. Didn't know it was you.'

Jo nodded to the phone.

'Not bad news, I hope.'

'Er, no. Not exactly. My... er... wife reporting another domestic crisis. The second time we've had our gas boiler service cancelled. And in case you're wondering, ma'am, I *received* the call.' He smiled. 'So I'll argue at my disciplinary hearing that I was not *proactively* wasting police time and resources.'

Jo smiled back, a little thinly. 'I'm glad to hear it. Let's go.' She stepped aside and waved him ahead of her, following him through into the briefing room.

'Okay,' Jo said, addressing the meeting. 'A new development, linking the events of the past two days. Maddie, tell us what you have found out about our bin man.'

'Well, two main points. The man's name is Curtis Knox, aged twenty-nine, last known address Clement Street, Tottington. So a possible link there to the man in the pub known as Knocker.'

'I'd say that's probable, rather than possible,' Jo said. 'But, sorry, go on, Maddie.'

'And he is currently...' she looked at Jo and smiled '... I guess that should be "was, until recently" employed as a driver for Easy Rider.'

A number of side conversations started spontaneously, mutually drowning any comments made.

'Okay,' Jo said, bringing the meeting together. 'So our victim is already linked to Phoebe Wright's case in that he was interviewed along with all the Easy Rider drivers, by…?' She paused and looked round the gathered group. Mo raised his hand. '… DC Malik. So, this just might be the most significant development since her actual disappearance. But we need to be careful what we decide it tells us.' She turned to the sergeant. 'Andy, share with us the point you made a few minutes ago.'

'Just that if there is a link between Phoebe's disappearance and Knocker's murder, and every instinct must tell us that there *is*, then I'm afraid it looks very bad for our golden girl. In fact, it rather points to the fact that she is dead as well.'

★

Terry Craven appeared much more focused on the fact that he 'said it all along' than he was on the distress of his partner, Eileen Knox. DI Jo Carter and PC Olivia Heywood, the team's family liaison officer, were seated together on one of the two facing, and severely sagging, sofas in the small sitting room of the terraced property in Tottington. Opposite them, the large personages of Terry and Eileen were squashed together on the other sofa. Eileen was leaning forward, her head supported on one hand, with a tear-sodden tissue squeezed tightly in the other. Terry was leaning back, one armed stretched out behind Eileen along the back of the sofa, seemingly relaxed and smug.

Jo leaned forward with some difficulty given the backward tilt of her seat.

'I realise this is very difficult, but anything you can tell us about Curtis's circumstances could be a big help. So, may I ask, Mr Craven what you meant by…' she looked down at her notebook '… "I knew it, I said it all along" when we told you of his death? Was Curtis in some sort of trouble?'

'Nothing special,' the man replied. 'Just never seemed settled.

Would never tell us what he was doing, who his friends were. Just drifted in and out when he wanted somewhere to crash, like when this was the easiest place to get to after he'd had a skinful. He just seemed to be heading for some sort of disaster.'

'So he wasn't living here? All the time, I mean.'

'No, just when it suited him. No warning, no notice, no asking, he'd just turn up and pass out.'

'Oh, for God's sake, Terry.' Eileen turned on her partner with sudden anger. 'Give it a rest, will you. Whatever he was like, he was still my little boy.'

She turned away and sobbed into her already-saturated tissue. Terry leaned forward and moved his arm gently across her shoulder.

'I'm sorry, Leenie. It's just that he treated you so badly.'

'He did *not*...'

'With no respect, then. Like he could just walk all over you and you never once pushed back.'

'I am sorry this is distressing for you,' Jo said, 'but do you know what Curtis's job was?'

They both looked at her in surprise.

'What's that got to do with anything?' Terry asked, his forehead wrinkled in a deep frown.

Jo shrugged. 'It's just that you paint a picture of someone with no apparent direction or stability. Which differs from our understanding of his situation.'

Terry and Eileen looked at each other then back at Jo.

'I don't know what you're getting at,' Terry said. 'I don't know what his job was. I just assumed he didn't have one. Well, not a regular one, anyway.' He turned to his partner. 'Leenie?'

'I never really thought about it,' Eileen said. 'It certainly never came up in conversation.'

'Conversation.' Terry laughed, mirthlessly, turning away. 'Can't ever remember having a *conversation* with him.'

'So what was his job?' Eileen was wide-eyed now with curiosity. 'Do you know?'

'He was an ambulance driver.'

Terry and Eileen stared at Jo in silence for a long time.

'You really didn't know?' Jo asked.

They shook their heads.

'But don't they have to have special training?' Eileen said. 'Like... medical qualifications?'

'Curtis wasn't a paramedic, if that's what you mean,' Jo explained. 'He drove a non-emergency ambulance, but an extremely important job all the same, with a great deal of responsibility for the care of very vulnerable people. I don't understand why he wouldn't have told you that.'

There was another long pause.

'Look I don't want to raise anyone's hopes here,' Terry pulled Eileen closer to him, 'but this doesn't make any sense. Are you absolutely sure you've got the right person?'

'Absolutely sure, I'm afraid, Mr Craven. It's a job most people would have been proud of, so I can't understand why he didn't make you aware of it. I'm sorry to ask at this time, Mrs Knox, but did he ever ask you for money?'

Eileen shook her head. 'No, never. In fact, in spite of what Terry says about him...' her voice rose in anger and she glared at her partner '... he actually gave me money from time to time. Quite often, in fact. Usually after he'd stayed over with us.'

'And what sort of amounts did he give you?'

'Well, it varied. Sometimes fifty pounds, sometimes more. Once he gave me five hundred but I said it was too much and I didn't take it, remember, Terry?'

Terry nodded and sucked in his breath, as if the memory of Eileen rejecting the money was a little painful.

'And did you ever ask him why he gave you the money or where he got it from?'

'No,' Eileen answered.

'And what about you, Mr Craven? Did you ever ask him where he got the money, given that you...' she checked her notes '... assumed he didn't have a job?'

'We didn't really talk, me and Curtis. But I would never have asked him that, because I'd be too worried about the answer.'

They sat in silence for a few moments.

'I'm afraid at some point we'll need you to identify Curtis, Mrs Knox. We'll arrange for someone to pick you up and take you to see him.'

'I'll do that for you, Leenie, if you like,' Terry said.

'No you will *not*,' Eileen replied. 'He's my little boy. I'll do it.'

'Thank you, Mrs Knox,' Jo said. 'We'll be in touch about it very soon.'

★

At Jo's request, Andy and Mo had stayed behind to await her return. Andy now sat across from Jo at her desk, whilst Mo continued his trawl of CCTV in the operations room. Olivia had remained behind with Eileen and Terry to discuss any assistance or support they may need before heading home in a taxi.

'Did you brief the Super?' Jo asked.

'Yes, he left but said to phone him if we needed him for anything, meaning to mediate, I guess.' He smiled, thinly.

'So, do we need him?' Jo raised her eyebrows.

'Not yet, I don't think.' He paused, then leaned forward. 'Look, off the record, *ma'am*, I have no doubt at all that I have the ability to lead a murder investigation; but not the rank. So, as the two cases are clearly connected, I accept it's you and me working together again, as you said. Exciting or not.' They sat in tense silence for a few moments. 'Anyway, you probably want to get the coffees in, so I'll get Malik and meet you in the briefing room in five, okay?'

'Okay.' She gave a little smile and looked round her store room. 'If they haven't taken the cup holder.'

Andy and Mo were sitting in silence at the meeting table when she entered with the refreshments. The DS looked relaxed and comfortable whilst Mo seemed anxious and detached.

'Cheer up, DC Malik,' Jo said. 'At least you can stay warm here.'

Mo frowned. 'Sorry, ma'am.'

'I said, at least you can… your dodgy boiler?'

He shook his head. 'Sorry, ma'am. I don't understand what… Oh, right. No, it's not broken down or anything, it's just due for a service, but it keeps getting cancelled.'

'Well, thank you for staying back, because, boiler or no boiler, I imagine you'd rather be at home. Close the door on the weather, snuggle together for warmth, all that good stuff.'

'Chance would be a fine thing. Wife's away on a course this week in London, so it's just me and the boiler.'

'I thought it was your wife who phoned you earlier to tell you about the cancellation,' Jo said.

'Yes, that's right. British Gas has her mobile number. She was passing on the message.'

'Oh, right,' Jo said. 'Let's move on. Anything else in from forensics or pathology?'

'Pathology have confirmed only a small amount of alcohol consumed in the hours before death,' Andy replied. 'Nothing on time of death yet, but the landlord has ID'd the victim as the guy in the pub known as Knocker from a photo taken at the time we took his fingerprints. So, that would put it sometime between ten-thirty Tuesday evening and six-forty Wednesday morning. No sign of the murder weapon but hardly surprising if the deed was done elsewhere. And too many footprints around the bin and along the alley to be of any use. Oh, yes – the van. Around midday today a black Berlingo was reported stolen from a street off Rochdale Road near Fairfield Hospital. That's the time the owner discovered it was missing. He parked it down the side street away from his house at around four o'clock yesterday afternoon, so doesn't know when it was taken. But earlier this morning a burnt-out vehicle was reported in a field on Blue Ball Lane off Heywood Old Road at Bowlee, since identified as a Berlingo. I think it's safe to assume it's the stolen van and, most likely, Knocker's lift to his final resting place.'

'Burnt out,' Jo said. 'So no chance of comparing tyre tracks, I guess. But you're right, it must be the vehicle used to move the body. Any CCTV around where it was parked?'

Andy snorted a laugh. 'I think they've only just got street lights. And nothing on Blue Ball Lane either. It's a favourite fly-tipping spot apparently; local residents nearby have been trying to get the council to instal cameras for years. The lane's unadopted; so nobody's responsible, nobody cares.'

'Speaking of CCTV,' Jo turned to Mo. 'Any luck around the Lancashire Gate?'

'Nothing more, ma'am. We've taken some stills from the footage of the van on Haymarket Street to show the owner of the stolen vehicle. But I'm not sure it's going to tell us anything even if he ID's it. Or if he doesn't, for that matter.'

'No, I'm not either.'

Jo thought for a moment before continuing.

'Liv and I had a very interesting talk with the victim's mum and her partner. They had no idea that Knox was working at Easy Rider as an ambulance driver. They didn't even know that he had a job at all and talked about him as if he was some layabout toe-rag. He didn't live with them but just dossed down there occasionally, when he was too drunk to get home. I'm paraphrasing what they said, but that's the impression I got. Now why would someone with a seriously responsible job choose to keep it a secret from the person closest to them?'

The two men shook their heads.

'What was your impression of him, Mo, when you interviewed him?'

Mo shrugged. 'Just an ordinary guy. Cooperative, certainly; answered all my questions, no edge to him. More polite than most of the people we get to interview.'

'Even so, I think there's more to Easy Rider than we know,' Andy said.

'Right, let's pay Mr Reeves another visit in the morning on the pretext of informing him of the adjustment to his workforce numbers. Thanks for staying back, time to catch up a bit more of that lost sleep. You two get going. I'll speak with the crew before I leave.'

She stood up to end the meeting and noticed that Mal Jones was waiting for her in her office.

'Sir?'

'Just to let you know, Jo, I've alerted the Major Incident Team at GMP Headquarters. Routine step when we have a major crime like this, flagging it in case we need extra resources. Academic at the moment because they're not able to assign anybody, and, as I'm sure you'll understand, if we can deal with this without calling them in, that would be my preference.'

'Oh, I can certainly understand, sir,' Jo replied, smiling. 'That's what I'm up against wherever I get sent.'

★

'Listen, I've got some bad news.' Jo's opening line to Seb sounded woefully inadequate. 'We've had a murder. Body found this morning behind the Lancashire Gate and I'm assigned SIO. I say assigned, but SIO-by-default might be more accurate. I was first there, putting it simply.'

'Which is how most SIOs are assigned, if I understand correctly.'

'I guess. Anyway, there's just no way I'm going to get over, unless we clear up the case in the next two days, which won't happen. And which means I'm likely to be working over the weekend, so I think you should stay there. Have you told them yet that you can't play?'

'Not yet. I was going to wait to see if it was called off, so I didn't have to.'

'I see. So are you saying it wouldn't look good if you just told them you weren't available?'

'Well, they wouldn't be delighted, but you're much more important than anything else. You know that – or you *should* know that by now.'

'I guess, but…'

'Hey, what's wrong? Look, I'll tell them tomorrow…'

'No,' Jo interrupted. 'I know this game is really important and, as I said, I won't be around much anyway. And the weather – I mean for travelling.' She gave a little laugh. 'It will give me longer to warm the rug for you.'

'The rug? Oh, yes, the rug. I think we can warm that up together, can't we?'

Jo was silent for a few moments.

'You okay?' Seb asked.

'I guess so. Really tired. I think that late night on the moor with Ellen Strange is catching up with me.'

'Best you get some sleep. Look, are you sure you don't mind me playing on Saturday? I guess I could come over afterwards and…'

'No point, Seb. As I said, I'm going to be tied up all weekend.'

It was Seb's turn to pause before replying.

'Well, if you're sure. Let's leave it for now and decide tomorrow. Okay?'

'Okay. Love you.'

'Love you, too. Take care.'

Jo turned on her side and began to cry. She had been lying

on her back on the sheepskin rug anticipating the usual 'talking dirty' exchange she enjoyed so much. *They* enjoyed so much. What had passed between them was a long way from that and when she mentioned the rug, it seemed he had almost forgotten about it. She went over the words again and could find nothing to suggest any softening of his feelings for her. Not in the words spoken, It was the words *unspoken* that gave the clues. She slowly got to her feet. This was ridiculous, she told her reflection in the mirror over the fireplace. She was behaving like a lovestruck teenager. But was a lovesick teenager any different to a lovesick thirty-something?

CHAPTER TWENTY

Thursday 17 January

The snow had stopped falling and the sky had cleared overnight. The resulting fall in temperature had left icy conditions on untreated roads, and traffic into and out of Bury was relatively light for rush hour on a working day. The prospect of more and heavier snow seemed to have deterred people from driving and encouraged them onto public transport; or to work from home.

Jo and Andy were already parked at the gates of the Easy Rider depot when Josh Reeves arrived in his Jaguar SUV. The manager treated them to his usual display of simmering hostility as he got out of his car to open the double gates. Jo lowered her passenger-side window.

'Good morning, Mr Reeves.'

'Now what, for fuck's sake?'

'Now quite a lot, actually,' Jo replied. 'We need to speak to you and your team about something. It might be an idea if we could get you all together to start with.'

'That won't be possible. Two have got their vehicles out for a couple of days and we're still missing one driver, thanks to you lot not doing your job. So, just tell me now what you want to say and I'll let the rest know when I see them.'

He made no move to open the gates. Jo and Andy waited out the silent inertia.

'Well, have you got something to say or not?' Josh said

'We certainly have, Mr Reeves, but we don't carry out our business from parked cars. I mean, we're not drug dealers, are we?'

Josh shot a glance up and down the road, then turned and released the heavy padlock. He pushed open the right-hand gate, the other automatically swinging back. Andy started the car and drove through, parking in the space marked 'Reserved for JR' in front of the office.

'Nice touch, sergeant,' Jo said, smiling.

Josh pulled up alongside, slamming his car door as he got out.

'Very amusing,' he said, scowling and nodding at their vehicle. 'Can't you read? That's trespassing, that is.'

'Then you must complain, Mr Reeves,' Andy said. 'We'll give you a number to call when we leave. Unless it turns out you'll be leaving with us, in which case you'll be able to complain in person.'

They followed him into his office.

'Look, just say what you have to say, ask what you have to ask. I've got a business to run and I'm down a driver.'

'*One* driver?' Jo asked.

'Yes. Don't you watch the news? She disappeared just before Christmas. Yes, *before* Christmas…'

'But just the one driver?'

Josh frowned. 'What's going on here? Yes, just one driver.'

'So everyone turned up for work yesterday?'

'*No-one* turned up for work yesterday. Don't you watch the weather forecast either? I told the drivers on Tuesday not to come in yesterday as all scheduled appointments and pick-ups had been cancelled. So we had no work to do. Two guys volunteered to take their vehicles home so they could be on call, but as far as I'm aware, they've not been needed.'

'And what about today?' Andy asked. 'Are you expecting the full crew – except your star performer, of course?'

'We've only got enough work for three drivers, so first three in get it and I'll contact the rest to lay them off for another day.'

'Curtis Knox,' Jo said. 'What can you tell us about him?'

'Why, what's he done?' Josh asked.

Jo nodded to Andy.

'What he's done, Mr Reeves, is got himself killed. We're sorry to inform you that you're *two* drivers short.'

'What?' Josh was wide-eyed. 'How? When?'

'How? – he died from multiple stab wounds. When? – sometime between ten-thirty on Tuesday evening and six-twenty on Wednesday morning. He was found in a wheelie bin behind the

Lancashire Gate pub. So, going back to DI Carter's question, what can you tell us about him?'

'Not much to tell. Did his job okay, not one of the most sociable of the drivers but we never had any complaints about him. Always punctual...'

'Not any more,' Andy said.

'Did he get on well with the other drivers?' Jo asked.

'I don't think he was real friends with any of them. I know he had his own group of mates he went around with. In fact, a couple of the drivers told me he was planning to leave, looking for another job. Jeez, I can't believe it. Was it a fight or what? I didn't think he was a fighter. He didn't come across like that.'

'Do you know of anyone called Jack who he was friendly with?' Andy asked.

'No. I don't know any of his friends. Quite a few of the other drivers are mates with each other – go out for a few after work, sort of thing, But, as I said, he seemed to have his own bunch of mates.'

'We'd like to see his vehicle, please, Mr Reeves,' Jo said. 'And his locker.'

'What now? Look, I've got...'

'Yes, now,' Andy interrupted. 'All this work that you have to do to run this business...' he looked around in feigned confusion '... whatever it is... can wait for just a few minutes.'

'Shall we go?' Jo waved her arm towards the door.

The snow had already started falling again as they walked across the yard to the garage, Josh leading, his shoulders hunched, a picture of put-upon reluctance. They stepped again through the small door to where six vehicles were parked, four on the left, two on the right. On this occasion, all the vehicles looked equally clean and well maintained. They checked Curtis Knox's ambulance and two of the others for comparison, finding them in exactly the same state inside and in the luggage storage compartments.

'And his locker?' Jo prompted.

'Look, that's private,' Josh said. 'Don't you need a search warrant or something?'

'I doubt if Knoxy will mind,' Andy said. 'And if he does come back from the dead and complain, I promise I'll tell him we forced you to do it. Now for God's sake, open the fucking thing.'

Josh jangled his bunch of keys in a staged show of inconvenience, finally selecting one and turning it in the lock.

'Open it, please,' Jo said.

Josh pulled the door open. The locker was the same design as Phoebe's with a hanging rail below a high shelf. It differed from hers, however, in that it was completely empty. Josh stared into it.

'What the fuck's going on?' he said. 'The little bastard's cleared everything out. He must have already decided to leave and just... took off. Some of the stuff in here belonged to the company – hi-vis coat, cleaning stuff. Why would he take cleaning stuff?' He turned to Jo, his surprise turning to anger. 'The little bastard,' he repeated.

'That's assuming it was Mr Knox who cleared the locker,' Jo suggested. 'It could have been one of the other drivers, if they knew he was leaving and he'd told them he wasn't coming back. He could have given them his key. Or, it could have been you and this is one big pantomime. Anyway, we can check because we'll be sticking around for your crew to arrive, and any who don't make it in we can get to afterwards. I'm sure you understand under the circumstances, we'll need to speak to each of them separately. I know we've interviewed them before, but that was a missing person; this is murder. Can you think of anything that would link Phoebe and Curtis? Something that they both had in common which set them aside from the others?'

'Not a thing. Chalk and cheese. She's the life and soul, he was... well... just the opposite.' He stopped to think. 'Except he was the one who most often gave Phoebe a lift home if she needed one.' He shook his head. 'Fucking hell. *Two* drivers down. This is serious shit.'

'And, of course, they do say these things happen in threes, don't they?' Andy said. 'In which case, you've still got one more to lose. I think if I was one of your drivers, right now I'd be considering killing one of the other five to make sure it wasn't me.'

★

It was early afternoon when Jo and Andy left the depot. They had spoken to the other six drivers, who had all reported for work in spite of the weather; keen, no doubt, to avoid another day without pay. All seemed shocked, and one or two a little worried, at the news, but none had anything useful to contribute. Nor had any admitted to raiding Curtis Knox's locker.

'So, any thoughts?' Jo asked as they turned onto Bolton Road for the short drive to the station.

'You mean other than I'm bloody starving?'

'Yes, apart from that. But let's address that one first. Station cafeteria or Costa in Tesco?'

'You're the boss, but I was thinking more of McDonalds, unless that's a bit downmarket for you.'

'Right, head for Woodfield. I'll trade a decent cup of coffee for an all-day breakfast McMuffin.'

'In the interest of solidarity with the lower ranks?'

'If you like.'

The crowded diner in the busy Woodfield Retail Park didn't lend itself to the sharing of opinions relating to a murder enquiry, so the meal was eaten in relative silence except for Jo's repeated comment about her coffee sacrifice.

'Remind me to bring a flask next time,' she said, to no response from Andy, whose focus on his Big Mac and fries was absolute to the exclusion of all else.

Back in Jo's office, looking even less like a storage facility now with more of Eva's detritus removed, she looked with something close to affection at the carton of vending machine coffee in front of her. Andy joined her and took the chair opposite.

'So,' he said, 'to your question "Any thoughts?" yes, I have a couple.'

'Go on.'

'First, I think we should get forensic to swarm all over Knox's wagon, before Reeves has it deep-cleaned.'

'Great minds,' Jo interrupted. 'I've just got Taylor moving on that. I assume you're thinking Phoebe's might have yielded more if we'd got to hers first.'

'As you said, great minds. And second, unless I'm too late with this as well, did you notice Reeves's use of the present tense for Phoebe; past tense for Knocker? Phoebe *is* the life and soul; Knocker *was* just the opposite. Probably nothing, just words after all, but reminded me of the last time you and I spoke to him. Remember?'

'I do. He didn't enquire about any progress on Phoebe, as if he knew something.'

'Exactly.'

They sat in silence for a while before Jo spoke again.

'Let's get the team together and see what they've got so far, if anything. Then let's run checks on the other six drivers. A fleet of minibuses running elderly people around is a great cover for something, especially when the vehicles have large luggage compartments that are never needed.'

'Not for luggage, anyway,' Andy added.

★

The full CID team was present in the briefing room including DCs Maddie Kemp, Glynn Thomas and Shelley Moston. At one end of the table, a TV monitor stood in readiness, currently displaying the static image of an empty chair facing the camera across a desk. Jo took the seat at the opposite end of the table facing the screen. The rest of the group settled into theirs.

'Okay, everyone,' Jo began. 'We have plenty to get through… I *hope*. DS Mills and I have had another interesting visit to Easy Rider, but let's start by covering what you've got so far. The empty screen, by the way, is for DI Crossley to fill when he arrives at his desk in Blackburn. So, who's first?'

The door opened and Detective Superintendent Jones poked his head into the room.

'May I join you?' he said, smiling at the group. 'I'll wait outside if you want to take a vote on it.'

The laughter was welcome and genuine as he took a seat at the side of the room away from the table.

'Right,' Jo said. 'I repeat, who's first, and don't all speak at once now you've got somebody to impress.'

Eva raised her hand. 'Not sure we've got much to impress with, ma'am. Door-to-door on the street where the van was stolen gave us nothing. No-one heard anything, which is not surprising, as the owner said the van wasn't alarmed. Also, the place where it was torched is not in line of sight of any properties. It was in a field where the ground is quite a bit lower than the lane that runs alongside it, so except at the height of the blaze, it's unlikely to have been seen, even by anyone driving past on the main road. Can't have been much traffic about, anyway, given the time and weather; the lane itself is used as a cut-through and, I'm told, is rough and heavily potholed. So, we don't know when it was taken *or* when it was torched. Not much of a start, I'm afraid, ma'am.'

'Thanks, Eva. I'm not sure that would tell us much now, anyway. Have we got anything from the pub yet on the two bad guys? Given we now suspect they targeted Knocker, we can reasonably assume they were involved in his death. Ten out of ten, perhaps, for the bleeding obvious.'

Kirsty leaned forward, holding up a sheet of paper. 'We checked with customers who turned up at midday today for a drink at the Lancashire. The pub's still closed, of course, but we pulled them inside for a chat. I've got the names of three people who were there the night of the fight, along with contact details.' She held up the sheet. 'Thought we could get them in, along with Jed Manvers, to check out some mugshots, or at least help with an e-fit.'

'Who's Jed Manvers?' the Super asked.

'Landlord of the Lancashire Gate, sir,' Jo said.

'When is the pub due to open again?' Andy asked.

'Down to us and forensics, I guess,' Jo said. 'Why?'

'Might be an idea to let them open today and a couple of us go down there and chat to the evening crowd. More likely to get some at that time who witnessed the fight and, if so, best while it's still fresh in their minds.'

'Makes sense,' Jo said, 'and can I take it you are volunteering for this arduous task?'

'I'll just do as I'm told, as always,' Andy replied. 'I know it'll be a shitty job, but, hey…'

'Okay, let's do it,' the Super cut across the ripple of laughter.

At the end of the table, the screen startled everyone by bursting into life. Al Crossley's substantial frame filled the previously empty chair.

'Good afternoon, everyone. Thank you for inviting me again like this, and sparing me the journey. Sorry I missed the start of the meeting.'

'DS Mills can cover off what you've missed later before he goes off on his bender,' Mal said. He turned to Jo. 'Go on, DI Carter.'

'Hi, Al. Nothing exciting so far, Just ticked a couple of "work-in-progress" boxes.' She looked round the table.

Glynn raised his hand. 'We've had some luck with Knocker's mate. A call came in at eleven-seventeen from the guy who had been with the victim in the Lancashire,' he said.

'Jack?' Jo asked.

'Actually, his real name is Denzel Chadwick, but he's known as Jacko, not Jack. I asked him how you get Jacko from Denzel and he said you don't. He's called that because he's really good at Michael Jackson's moonwalk.' Glynn shrugged and raised his hands. 'Anyway, he'd heard the news story about the fight and the body on local radio this morning and called in. He didn't know the guys who attacked them and said he left Knocker at the metro station to catch a tram straight after they'd left the pub.'

'*He* caught a tram or Knox did?' Andy asked.

'He did. Knox set off walking down Haymarket Street towards his flat on Manchester Road. Jacko said he didn't know his actual address, but thought it was near the junction with Radcliffe Road. He said he saw the other two guys go down one of the side streets towards Silver Street. The opposite direction.'

'And was that the end of it, as far as he knew? No-one doubled back or anything?'

'No, ma'am, not according to Jacko.'

'Okay, let's get him in and talk to him.'

'He was phoning from Preston and he's on his way here. I checked with him just before this meeting started and he was about to turn off the M60 at Besses' roundabout. So he should be here by the time we finish the meeting, if he isn't already.'

'What was he doing in Preston?' Andy asked.

'He's a delivery driver for a privately owned electrical supplies company based in Blackburn.' Glynn checked his notes. 'Lancashire Lectrix – with an "x". Very creative.'

'I know the company,' Al Crossley put in. 'Quite sizable for the town; employs over two hundred people. They came up on our radar once due to an employment issue related to pension provision. We got involved because a demonstration at the site turned a bit violent.'

'Okay,' Jo said. 'We'll talk to him after the meeting, and he's probably the best chance we've got with the mugshots. I assume we do have Knox's actual address from the information we got from Easy Rider?'

'Yes and no,' Maddie answered. 'He's on their records as living with his mother, but with Jacko's information, we're doing a door-to-door of all the flats around the junction with Radcliffe Road. They're mostly large, privately owned houses converted into apartments. The uniforms are still on it.'

'Good. Anything more from pathology?' Jo asked.

Shelley leaned forward. 'Prof Martin has sent her full report through which confirms her initial conclusions, including the murder weapon – six-inch blade, one serrated edge. But she also added that there was some minor bruising on the back of the right thigh, which would have been consistent with his being hit – fairly gently, she said – by a car. She emphasised this was in no way related to cause of death, but it had been very recent, probably within the twenty-four hours before his death.'

'Good. Mo...' she turned to DC Malik '...CCTV?'

'Cameras picked up the aftermath of the punch-up as it spilled into the street. A bit of posturing and pushing, then the four guys just separated almost as if nothing had happened. We can track Knox down Haymarket Street to the junction with Angouleme Way, then straight across along Knowsley Street, presumably heading to Manchester Road, which would check out with where Jacko says he lives. I say presumably because there's no CCTV after the Town Hall and as the road dips down he drops out of sight. Jacko went inside the Metro station, like he said, but then came out again and looked down Haymarket Street in the direction Knox had gone. Probably just to check no-one was following him,'

'Something to ask him later,' Jo said, nodding to Eva who made a note.

'After a few minutes he went back into the station.'

'And *was* anyone following him?' Andy asked.

Mo looked surprised. 'No-one that the cameras picked up – or Jacko, I guess, if that's what he was checking.'

'So how much more of the footage did you check after Knox dropped out of sight?' Andy again.

'Three, four minutes.' He frowned. 'I'm not sure what…'

'What I'm getting at?' Andy cut in. 'If the two guys did target Knox in the pub, they might know where he lived. They could have waited to make sure Jacko had finally gone into the station before going after him, which could have been a lot longer than four minutes. Did we track the two guys onto Silver Street?'

'Cameras were out in Moss Street where they cut through and I haven't picked them up again yet. Still looking.'

'What are you thinking, sergeant?' Jo asked.

'These guys hadn't been drinking, so might have had a car, or even a stolen van, parked on Silver Street or one of the streets off it. It's a popular parking area if you can get a space, and I can't see that being a problem on Tuesday night. We might pick up the Berlingo on a working camera if they did. If they were the ones that killed him, they would most likely follow him and pick him up before he got home. And to do that, they'd have to come either along Haymarket Street or onto Angouleme Way and into Knowsley Street.'

Jo nodded towards the map. 'Show me.'

Andy traced with his finger the two possible routes round the one-way system from Silver Street to Manchester Road.

'Either way,' he said, 'they would pass through the junction here at the Town Hall, and we know there was a camera working there.'

'That's if they were the killers and they had a car,' Mal said. 'What else is pointing to those two possibilities?'

There was silence for a few moments.

'Perhaps the fact that he may have been hit by a car,' Jo suggested. 'Professor Martin knows none of this…' she nodded at the map again '… so that conclusion is totally independent of Andy's scenario.' She looked round the group before addressing Mo again. 'Let's check inside the Metro station to see if Jacko really did catch a tram. Do we know where he lives, by the way?'

'I didn't ask him,' Glynn answered, 'on account of him coming in to be interviewed.'

'Okay,' Jo said. 'DC Malik, you've got some more digging to do. If we can place the Berlingo close to the scene around that time, it will help confirm a link between the murder and the pub encounter *and* establish it was premeditated.' She paused. 'Okay, our turn, I guess.' She nodded to Andy. 'DS Mills, take it away.'

Andy took the team through an account of their separate meetings with Josh Reeves and each of his six drivers.

'A few early thoughts,' he said. 'We believe Easy Rider is not what it seems, even apart from the fact that its drivers are going down like Ten Little Indian Boys, or eight in this case. And just for the record,' he smiled across at Jodi, '...that's ten little Native American boys.' There was a slightly uncomfortable ripple of laughter and a polite smile from Jodi. 'The DI has got Jamie Taylor's crew to check out Knox's vehicle. We feel that we were slow to get to Phoebe's, because by the time we did it had been forensically cleaned, begging the question – why? What were we likely to find in there? Unless, of course, we believe Mr Reeves that it was a routine valet carried out each year when the vehicles were parked up over Christmas. Well, *don't* believe it. You'd have to have seen Phoebe's wheels compared to the others to understand, and the valeting company tell us they carry out regular deep cleans throughout the year. So Mr Reeves is simply lying.

'The empty locker – that's interesting. That's something that is different to Phoebe's case. Her locker, *both* her lockers, were still full of her personal and work stuff. Reeves said some of the guys had told him Knox was planning to leave so it's just possible he never intended going back and emptied his locker. But things like cleaning stuff were missing, so we believe it was cleared by someone else. It might have been emptied by one or more of the other drivers, although they all deny it, or could be part of the deep-cleaning process that goes with disappearing drivers.

'Which raises another point. Reeves speaks of Phoebe in the present tense, and of Knox in the past tense. Phoebe *is*; Curtis *was*...'

'That's just semantics, isn't it?' Mal interrupted. 'Can't be relevant, surely.'

'May not be, sir, but when DI Carter and I last interviewed Reeves, a couple of weeks back, he didn't once ask how the search for Phoebe was progressing. What he did tell us was that she was the star of the show. Both DI Carter and I independently reached the conclusion Reeves knew more about her present situation than he was letting on. This episode served to add a bit to that feeling.'

'But it is just a feeling, and...' Mal went on.

'With respect, sir,' Jo interrupted, 'that's why we interview in pairs. So we get *two* feelings.'

Mal glared at her briefly before his expression softened again.

'Point taken. Carry on.'

'Right, let's move on from the facts and get some theories on the board. DC Malik, the marker's yours again,' Jo said, nodding towards the whiteboard.

'Okay,' Andy began. 'We asked Reeves if Phoebe and Knox had anything in common, and different from the other drivers. He said no, they were chalk and cheese, although Knox was the one who most often gave her a lift home after work. But they *did* have something in common – they were both considering leaving the job. Phoebe had told Benny she was thinking of going back to uni to pick up her drama course and may well have shared that with Knox during one of her lifts with him. Knox himself had mentioned his intention to leave to a few of the other guys and most likely mentioned Phoebe's plans as well. Reeves knew about Knox and probably his star turn, too.

'So, was that why Knox was targeted and killed? He was planning to leave and that did not sit well with his employer. And has that been Phoebe's fate – removed permanently for the same reason and, presumably, by the same agents of death. Or, has she disappeared of her own free will, knowing that would happen otherwise? We must hope for the best, but, as I said before, Knocker's murder rather points to the worst. Big question, of course, what is it about working for Easy Rider that makes it either a job for life or a way to death? That's assuming that we're right about the reason for the demise of the two drivers.'

Andy leaned back in his chair. Jo took up the narrative.

'Let's consider Phoebe's situation. She's been with Easy Rider exactly one year after giving up prospects of an acting career by leaving her uni course at Sheffield after just one term. Something very exciting and lucrative must have happened to make her do that, and, having returned home just before Christmas, she started work immediately in the New Year. Which suggests she must have been recruited in Sheffield for the position, and, according to her driver's log, Meadowhall in Sheffield is her single most frequent destination for the groups she looks after. Not Blackpool, not Chester, not the Trafford Centre – all of which are much closer and offer the same or more – but Sheffield.

'The vehicles they use are VW top-of-the-range, fourteen-seater, executive mini-coaches intended for people travelling further and for longer, with excellent toilet facilities and, more interestingly, a storage compartment designed to accommodate luggage for a full coachload. So why choose something in that price range to do a series of daily runabouts? And if the luggage compartment is not required, why is it regularly cleaned? Any suggestions?'

'Trafficking,' Jodi and Eva responded as one voice.

'Drugs? Guns? People?' Jo said. 'The storage area would take up to six or eight people in relative comfort over short distances.'

'Comfort, that is, compared to how some poor bastards are shipped around,' Andy added.

'Great cover for moving stuff about,' Kirsty said. 'Bunch of oldies on a day out. Not an obvious target for stop-and-search.'

'Presumably she would have time to do this,' Al asked, 'I mean pick-ups and drop-offs, while her passengers are occupied.'

'Yes, she doesn't escort them once they reach their destination. They have trained staff from the home or assigned at the site to do that.'

'So she has several hours to kill waiting to take them home?'

'That's right.'

'Plenty of nice shops in Meadowhall,' Kirsty said. 'Not a bad place to kill time. You said that was her most popular destination, so how often does she make the trip?'

'Average two, three times a month, and during the last quarter about once a week.'

'Not a big treat wandering around the *nice* shops that frequently, I wouldn't have thought,' Andy said. 'Or is that just a man thing?'

Kirsty shrugged. 'Probably not – I mean, not a big treat. Not, not a man thing.'

Jo turned to Mal. 'Sir, any thoughts?'

'If you're right about what might be going on at Easy Rider, well, it's not the sort of job you just move on from, is it? So that fits with the fate of Knocker Knox, and why Phoebe might want to make herself scarce. Does the scope of your theory include the other drivers – all or some of them?'

Andy replied, 'When we spoke to them earlier a couple of them did seem a bit worried about Knox's death. But it's hard to see how two or three out of a team of eight could be involved without the others at least knowing. And just knowing would probably lock them into the job, anyway.'

'He who rides the tiger…' Jo said. She turned to Mo, who had been writing on the board until just a few minutes ago. 'Your thoughts, DC Malik?'

Mo paused before answering, as if choosing his words carefully.

'I don't want to be the one that pours cold water on the excitement, but there are a lot of assumptions in that theory. And a big one is that there is something suspicious about the regular, diligent cleansing of the vehicles, which has led to the speculation that they must be being used for something dodgy – seriously illegal, in fact. These are old people who may not all be, shall we say, sanitarily efficient. I'm sure the NHS will have strict standards on the cleanliness of vehicles for the purpose of moving vulnerable, incontinent people around, especially in the aftermath of COVID. And the standard of the vehicles themselves – executive-class, etc – might be what was needed to get them the contract. I think it's a giant leap to use that to throw doubt on the legitimacy of a company that's been in existence for over five years and has never appeared on our radar once.'

There were several moments of silence before anyone spoke. Jo broke the spell.

'Well, it's good to have a balanced view, so thank you for reining us in, Mo. It's not what I expected , but…'

'Sorry, ma'am, I…'

'No apology necessary, detective. What I *did* expect you to say, was that this theory puts Sheffield right in the picture and justifies your careful tracking of the girl at the Shoulder all the way to the through train from Piccadilly on the day Phoebe disappeared.'

Mo frowned. 'But if Phoebe was planning to flee the… organisation, or whatever, she would be unlikely to run away to Sheffield. Based on your theory, the only people she knows there will be part of that same organisation, wouldn't they? She'd be running into the arms of the enemy… so to speak.'

'Which means?' Mal asked.

Mo shrugged. 'It's unlikely that it *was* Phoebe who was heading out there on the nine-fifty train from Piccadilly, or by any other means of transport for that matter.'

Silence descended again as the feeling of excitement generated by Jo and Andy's developing storyline dissipated.

'Okay,' Andy said. 'Let's test DC Malik's theory with the NHS's contract with Easy Rider. I'll be happy to follow that up personally.' He turned to Jo. 'If that's okay with the SIO.'

Jo nodded, with the briefest of smiles. She turned to Mo.

'If you could add the last couple of points to the board, Mo, including your own comments, then everyone take a copy and think about anything more you'd like to add. Glynn, can you check if Jacko has arrived and settle him into an interview room with a suitable beverage; and while DS Mills investigates the hygiene standards of NHS transport facilities, DC Lawson and I will join him for a chat – and perhaps a moonwalk demo. Thank you, everybody.'

*

Jo was having difficulty reconciling the person sitting across the table with the explosive incident involving his overcoming three assailants, one of whom had ended up being hospitalised. She had been expecting someone similar in appearance and stature to Jed Manvers. Denzel 'Jacko' Chadwick was a little above medium height, but slim, with a boyish face, which made him look considerably younger than his thirty-two years, and a ready smile. He wore jeans and trainers, and a tan leather jacket over a Manchester City replica shirt. It was true that he appeared physically very fit, but only his dark brown eyes, which managed to look friendly and intense at the same time, gave the hint of an inner steeliness, which might make someone think twice about upsetting him. And although he oozed charm and charisma, his benign outer appearance coupled with her knowledge of the violence which lurked within gave Jo a feeling of unease. The expression 'coiled spring' came to mind.

'Thank you for getting here so quickly, Mr Chadwick, especially in these conditions.'

'No problem under the circumstances. Anything to find the bastards who did this to Knoxy.'

'Bastards? Plural?' Jo asked. 'Why do you believe it involved more than one person?'

'Well, there were these two guys in the pub…'

'Okay,' Jo interrupted, holding up a hand. 'Let's start at the beginning. Why were you out that particular evening, Mr Chadwick? Tuesday night, foul weather? And a late start, I believe.'

Denzel shrugged. 'We didn't intend being that late, Knocker was planning on leaving Easy Rider and asked if there were any vacancies at Lancashire Lectrix, that's who I work for, doing the same as me. He wanted another driving job if possible, he said. So we'd arranged to get together earlier, sort of eightish, to talk about it, but I got delayed getting back from work. Fucking snow. Sorry…'

'No apology necessary.' Jo smiled. 'I think that describes the weather very accurately. But you didn't consider postponing the meeting?'

'I did suggest it because I was still trying to get home at the time we were due to meet up, but Knocker insisted. Well, not exactly insisted, just asked if we could make it later. So I checked with the girlfriend, who was round at her mate's, anyway, and arranged to meet him at nine-thirty. Still only just made it.'

'And this meeting was in the Lancashire Gate?'

'That's right.'

'So you drove there instead of going home?'

'No, went home first, then…'

'Where's home, Mr Chadwick?' Jodi asked.

'Radcliffe. Bury Road. Parked the van and got the Met into Bury.'

'So, where did you arrange to meet Mr Knox?' Jo again.

'In the Lancs. I got there just after him, he was still ordering a drink at the bar. He got us both one and we sat down.'

'And what time was that?'

'As I said, right on half-nine.'

'How did he seem?'

'Fine. Not sure I know what you mean.'

'Well, was he stressed, worried, distracted… anything different about him?'

Denzel laughed. 'Nothing different, he's always all those things. *Was* all those things.' He shook his head. 'Shit, I can't get my mind round this. I mean all this was less than... what... sixteen hours ago? The only thing on his mind seemed to be changing his job, apart from his obsession with this missing girl.'

'Obsession?'

Denzel gave a little chuckle. 'He fantasised about her all the time. Used to give her a lift home from work quite regular. Upset him quite a bit, her going missing.'

'Do you know if he was in a relationship with her?'

Denzel laughed out loud this time. 'He *wished*. But she was way out of his league, and if that sounds unkind, that's exactly what Knocker says... used to say.'

'So getting back to Tuesday night, tell us what happened.'

'There were only a few people in the bar, then around ten o'clock, these two guys came in, you know, sort of scowling and looking round.'

'Did you recognise them?'

'No, never seen them before.'

'Can you describe them?'

'Sure, pretty nondescript. White, about my age – bit younger perhaps. Medium height, hard faces. Both wearing black padded coats, one had a hoodie underneath with the hood up, the other had one of those caps with the pull-down ear flaps.'

'Would you recognise them again?'

'Reckon so. In fact, I hope I get to meet the fuckers again.'

'Then perhaps you could have a look at some mugshots when we finish, see if you can pick them out.'

'Fine, no problem.'

'Thank you. Go on, what next?"

'They ordered drinks at the bar, we kind of looked across then carried on talking. Next thing they're both standing over us. One of them pushed Knocker so he had to get up quick to stop falling off the chair. The guy said, "What the fuck are you looking at?" Knocker said, "Nothing much." It kicked off. A few punches, the second guy swung a chair at him – hardly touched him, nearly hit me...'

'So what did you do, Mr Chadwick?'

'Well, all that happened in a few seconds. I stood up and got between them; tried to break it up, and then Jed was there, arms around the first guy, just about squeezing the life out of him. Another couple of punters got up to help and we all ended up outside.'

'A bit unfair, really. I mean, you and Knocker weren't to blame; why didn't you get to stay?'

Denzel shrugged and smiled. 'Someone had phoned the police and, to be honest, I didn't want to be there when they arrived…'

'Because of the previous incident, do you mean? When someone ended up in hospital.'

Denzel opened his eyes wide in surprise. 'You didn't waste much time finding that out. Does that make me a suspect?'

'Of course not, but we did wonder why you didn't respond in a similar way on Tuesday.'

'Martial arts,' Denzel said.

'I see; well we did also wonder *how* you managed to beat up three guys in the previous incident.'

'I have to be careful how I use them, as you know, and it was in the Lancs when it happened last time.'

'But it's not illegal to use martial arts on someone in self-defence, no-one blamed you for what happened.'

'That's true, but it's the bit about, if I can remember the right words, "excessive and disproportionate use of force." That's the grey area. Get it wrong and it's criminal assault, and when you're a martial arts expert – like me – the crime is all the more serious. I just didn't want to hang around and have someone saying "oh, it's you again" or whatever. Not that I'm saying I wouldn't have done it different if it had developed into something else, but once we were outside, it all fizzled out. Too fucking cold for anything, so after a couple more shoves and a bit of finger-pointing we went our separate ways. But, before they disappeared into Moss Street, they shouted, "This isn't over tonight. Watch your backs," or something like that. And they meant it, didn't they? Fucking *bastards*.' The spring, Jo noticed, seemed to be uncoiling a little. 'I wish I *had* put them in hospital, or the fucking mortuary.'

Jo waited for a few moments to allow Denzel to calm down, which he quickly did with a shrug and a sigh. 'So what happened next?'

Denzel took a deep breath. 'Knocker set off walking home; I got the Met. It had been all a waste of time, and… of Knocker's life. I probably could have got him a job, as well.'

'So you just got on the tram and went home?' Jodi asked.

'That's right. Well, actually, no, not straight away. I went back out of the station and checked Knocker wasn't being followed; watched him walk past the Town Hall where the road goes downhill and he dropped out of sight. Then I went back into the station again and caught a tram.'

'About the attack, have you any theory as to why two strangers should walk into the pub and immediately pick on Mr Knox?'

'These things happen. Perhaps they thought he'd looked at them a bit too long, then we'd started talking about them. I don't know. You can ask them when you catch them.'

'But you believe these two… strangers… were incensed enough to kill Mr Knox later that evening, even though you checked that they weren't following him? Did Mr Knox know them? Was it some kind of vendetta, do you think?'

'I think it's your job to answer those questions.' The muscles in Denzel's jaw and neck visibly tightened. 'But Knocker said he *didn't* know them, if that helps. Look, it was just a pub fight that went too far…'

'You see, what I'm having trouble understanding,' Jo interrupted, 'is why the body should end up back where the incident began a long time after all the parties involved had gone their separate ways. Unless it was placed there to make us *think* the murder was the result of the random attack when in reality it was something much more personal and sinister.'

Denzel said nothing, his dark eyes suddenly angry and burning into Jo's. He shrugged.

'Can't help you there.'

'Just out of interest, how long have you known Mr Knox?'

'About three years, maybe four.'

'Was he a close friend?'

'We weren't *best* mates, exactly; more just part of the same crowd. But, yes, I'd say we were friends.'

'And yet you don't know where he lived.'

Denzel paused, tensing again. 'Not *exactly*, no. Somewhere on

Manchester Road near the lights at the corner of Radcliffe Road. But half the time I think he stayed with his mother.'

Jo leaned back. 'Okay, and thank you again, Mr Chadwick.' She turned to Jodi. 'Anything we haven't covered, DC Lawson?'

'Not that I can think of right now.'

'Okay, so if you don't mind, Mr Chadwick, we'll give you some pictures to look at. But before we finish is there anything else you want to tell us?'

'Only that I hope you get the bastards soon.'

'Oh we will, Mr Chadwick. I'm sure of it.'

★

Curled up on the sofa in front of the fire with a glass of wine within easy reach, Jo went through in her mind the interview with the moonwalking Mr Chadwick, feeling something didn't fit with his account of the events of two days ago. Exactly what, she was unable to decide.

It was clear to her that Curtis had been targeted and the whole incident was staged to look like something it wasn't; and pretty clumsily staged, she thought. Which made her doubt that Denzel *did* believe it was a random confrontation. Also, the idea that a potential killing machine would have the self-control to become an instant peacemaker when someone was chucking furniture at him, didn't ring true either, by a very long way.

One thought, which she quickly dismissed, was that perhaps the two assailants were part of Phoebe's crowd and suspected Curtis's obsession with her had turned into something more deadly. In her experience it didn't take long for people to put two and two together and come up with the answer they wanted. But surely there were easier ways to exact retribution than a complex set-up involving a stolen vehicle, a staged punch-up in front of witnesses and the logistical challenge of hiding a body in a wheelie bin, where it was certain to be discovered soon afterwards. Even so, she couldn't shake the thought that Phoebe was linked to this in some way. The Easy Rider connection wouldn't go away.

She sighed and reached for her glass of wine, almost knocking it over as she diverted her hand to her iPhone to take an incoming call. It was her third of the evening. Eva had phoned to tell her that Denzel hadn't fingered any of the mugshots; then, to her astonishment, Andy updated her on his night out in the Lancashire Gate, where customers' descriptions of the assailants and the action confirmed Denzel's account exactly.

This latest call was *not* work-related. Jo took a few seconds and a deep breath before she answered.

'Hi, there. Before we go any further, are you on the rug?'

Jo laughed. 'On the sofa, in front of the rug. How's my toy-boy tonight?'

'My evening has picked up considerably in the last thirty seconds. Are you ready to talk or do you want to assume the horizontal first?'

'No, I'm ready. The rug looks nice and fluffy; we can flatten it together – whenever. Look, let's decide now to leave it for this weekend, then we know where we are. *And*, we'll have longer to look forward to the rug ceremony.'

'Only if you're absolutely sure. I did say I could come over after the match.'

'I know, but you're only saying that to appease your ageing spouse?'

'It's the sort of thing I *would* do for the woman I love. Anyway, I understand they went to inspect the ground earlier today and couldn't find it under all the snow. But they're expecting it to be okay by Saturday afternoon.'

She laughed. 'So we agree, you'll play.'

'I'll play. So how's the hunt for the killer going? Any progress?'

'Not much to tell you, I'm afraid; I'll bring you right up to speed next time. But for now, do you mind if we talk dirty.'

'Okay, you go first.'

CHAPTER TWENTY-ONE

Friday 18 January

Jo had spent a restless night, her mind refusing to take a break from the thoughts circulating in her head following the interview with Denzel Chadwick. When she did snatch some sleep it was invaded by dreams of Seb and rugs and rugby all intertwined in the usual mish-mash of ill-defined and unresolved events. At six o'clock, she turned off her phone alarm, set for thirty minutes later, and after a shower and a hurried breakfast of cereal, fruit juice and coffee, she headed for the station, arriving at her desk shortly after seven.

The early shift had just arrived and were settling into their daily routine in the cafeteria. Jo left her office and went over to sit with Glynn Thomas at his temporary workstation.

'Okay, Glynn, can you bring up the CCTV feed DC Malik ran yesterday? I just want to check Jacko's movements again. Not his moonwalk, just what he did when he left the Lancashire Gate.'

Glynn laughed. 'No problem, ma'am. Can I ask why?'

'You can. He just came across a bit slippery in our interview. Nothing I can put my finger on and I might be doing him an injustice, but I'd like to check that he did what he *said* he did. And as you spoke to him first and took some details, I want us to check it together; you might just spot something.' She smiled. 'No pressure.'

'Okay,' Glynn said, 'here we go, starting with their exit from the pub.'

They watched as the action unfolded on Glynn's screen – the four men ejected from the main door, a few pushes and pointed fingers, the group dispersing, heads bowed against the driving snow, the assailants turning briefly to shout across at Jacko and Knocker before disappearing down Moss Street.

'Right, let's watch this next bit with Jacko very carefully,' Jo said. 'This in-and-out-of-the-Met routine doesn't make sense to me. Get ready to slow and zoom.'

Denzel and Knocker chatted for a few minutes, then parted with high-fives. Knocker headed down Haymarket Street and Denzel walked along to the entrance for the Metrolink, where he disappeared before re-emerging shortly afterwards to retrace his steps to where he and Knocker had parted. He looked towards the Town Hall, the direction his friend had set off walking.

'Stop it there,' Jo said. The image froze with Denzel standing, with his back half to the camera. 'Now zoom in and take it forward slowly.'

The image enlarged and moved jerkily forward. Denzel continued looking in the same direction for a half a minute real-time then turned half to his left so he had his back fully to the camera.

'Stop again. See his left arm, not by his side or in his pocket but now bent up in front of him. What do you think?'

Glynn took a long look before replying. 'He seems to be holding something up to his face. A phone, it's got to be a phone. He's making a call, with the speaker on, I guess. I didn't notice him taking it out of his pocket, though.'

'Run it again from where he came back out of the tram station, and keep zoomed in on him.'

Denzel skurried backwards like a rewind of an old silent movie. Glynn moved the action forward again with Denzel full screen.

'Zoom right in on his hands; now forward, a second at a time.'

The image was grainy and indistinct now with the extra magnification, but clear enough to show something in Denzel's left hand.

'He already had the phone out when he exited the station,' Jo said. 'Ready to make a call but not, it seems, until he'd checked where Knox was.'

'Unless it was Knox he was calling, checking he was okay.'

'Possibly, but why go into the station and out again and why have the phone out and ready? And what was the little turn to his left for before making the call, if he did make a call?'

They were silent for a few moments before Glynn spoke again.

'Assuming he *did* make a call, perhaps he only went into the entrance of the station to take the phone out of his pocket where we couldn't pick it up on CCTV. Which means he must be aware of where the cameras are. And that would explain why he turned his back to the camera and used the speaker rather than putting it close to his ear, so it wasn't obvious he was making a call.'

Jo was silent for a moment, then smiled. 'Mr Thomas, you're using up all my best lines. And that would mean – or at least *could* mean – he was letting someone else know where Knox was or where he was heading.'

★

The location of Attercliffe Police Station to the north-west of Sheffield city centre is on Attercliffe Common, conjuring up an image of a stately building set in a swathe of greenery. In reality Attercliffe Common, otherwise known as the A6178, is part of a busy route into the city from Junction 33 of the M1, passing close to the Meadowhall Shopping Centre. The police station itself is a large, rather bland, red-brick structure in the shape of a squared-off horseshoe stretching along the main road between, and down, the side streets of Whitworth Lane and Howden Road and adjacent to the huge and impressive English Institute of Sport complex.

The young police constable on duty in reception was destined for an exciting start to his day. His first impression of the young woman who entered the building at 8.45 a.m. was that she was exceptionally beautiful; his second was that she looked familiar.

'How can I help you?' he asked, giving her his best smile.

'My name is Phoebe Wright. I believe you've been looking for me.'

★

Jo looked up at the gentle knock on the door to see Eva's head halfway into her office.

'Come in, detective. Any news?'

'Yes, ma'am. The service provider has confirmed that a call

was made from Jacko's phone at ten-twenty-six p.m. on Tuesday evening.'

'Yes, and...?' Jo leaned forward.

'The duration of the call was forty-one seconds and we've got the number of the phone that received it. It's registered to a Gemma Ashton, address 6 Bury Road, Radcliffe, which is where Jacko lives.'

Jo leaned back and sighed. 'He was phoning his girlfriend. Any other calls around that time?'

'No. The one previous to that was to Curtis Knox's phone, a few minutes after eight o'clock, and just before then, a call to this same number. So that's consistent with... '

'Him calling the girlfriend to tell her he'll be out later, then confirming it with Knocker.'

'Yes, I'd say so.'

'Shit. And what did eagle-eyed DC Malik have to say about not spotting the call being made?'

'Not much, apart from being a bit pissed off at having it pointed out to him. Said it's the first thing he *has* missed so far, if indeed he *was* making a call. That was before we'd confirmed it with the service provider.'

Jo's desk phone rang. She lifted the receiver. 'DI Carter.'

'Ma'am, you have to take this call.' Kirsty made no attempt to hide the excitement in her voice. 'Putting it through.'

Jo repeated, 'DI Carter.'

Her eyes widened as she rose from her chair and turned to Eva. 'Just a moment, DI Watson.' Her voice was a little unsteady. 'I need to get someone else on this call with me.' She pressed the silent button on the desk set and turned to Eva. 'Where's DS Mills?'

'Just popped to the quick-break...'

'Get him in here *now*. Tell him we've got our girl.'

The door opened and Andy entered, summoned by another member of the team, his eyebrows raised in silent question. Jo waved him to a chair.

'Thanks for now, Eva. Meeting in thirty minutes, latest. Gather the guys together.'

She pressed the button again. 'Sorry, DI Watson; I've got Detective Sergeant Mills with me now. He's been closely involved in the search. I'll put you on speaker.'

A deep baritone filled the room. 'To save time while we're talking, I'm Kenny.'

'Jo and Andy,'

'Hi, Jo. Hi, Andy.'

'Hi, Kenny,' they replied in unison, Andy fidgeting a little with impatience.

'I believe I'm about to make your day. I'm with South Yorkshire Police CID team based at Attercliffe Police Station, Sheffield. At eight forty-five this morning a young women walked into our reception and introduced herself to the police constable on duty there. She claimed to be Phoebe Wright, your missing person, and has provided ID to confirm that. She is currently with a female uniformed officer in one of our interview rooms. We've made her comfortable but we've not formally interviewed her because we feel that is your prerogative. However, we have had an informal chat with her.'

'How does she seem?' Jo asked. 'Tense, depressed?'

'I'd say frightened as much as anything. In fact, she gave us the impression after a few minutes that she'd regretted coming in.'

'Has she said anything about where she's been?' Andy said.

'No. We asked her, of course, but she said she would not be revealing that to avoid getting someone else involved. We said, getting who involved in what, but she didn't answer. We didn't want to push her too far too soon. I'm sure you'll do that when you get her back, which I assume will be sometime today.'

Jo checked her watch. 'Nine-twenty. I guess we could be over with you later this morning, weather and roads permitting.'

'It's not the best day for travelling but you should be okay. Stick to the motorways – M62 then M1; we're only a couple of miles off Junction 33.'

'Is that the Meadowhall turn-off?'

'From the direction you'll be coming it's the second turn-off for Meadowhall. The shopping centre's right on our doorstep.'

'Interesting,' Jo said, half to herself.

'Why is that?' Kenny asked.

Andy answered. 'Wright is a non-emergency ambulance driver who takes groups of patients from care homes on shopping trips, and Meadowhall is a favourite destination. If she's been staying with someone close to there during the past few weeks it suggests she may have regular contact with them.'

'A friend or friends, do you mean?'

'We've lately had reason to suspect that Phoebe may have been moving more than just elderly people around,' Jo said. 'But that's just one of several lines of enquiry into her disappearance we've been following. Perhaps by tonight we'll have a fuller understanding of what she's up to. I'm sure you plan to do this, Kenny, but please keep a close watch on her until we get there. I don't like the sound of her regretting she's handed herself in. It could be that she's just worried about having to justify her disappearance to her parents and her partner – they've been beside themselves, as you can imagine. But if we're right in our suspicions, she might be facing something a lot more sinister.'

'Rest assured, we won't lose her again. I'll assign our PC on reception to keep watch over her. He's not been able to take his eyes off her since she walked in. And a woman PC for the toilet visits, of course.'

Jo gave a little laugh. 'Many thanks, Kenny. I'll let you know when the car leaves here and if you let me have the best phone number to keep in touch, they'll keep you posted on their ETA. Thank you again for your help.'

'No problem. Safe journey to whoever draws the short straw.'

They said their goodbyes and Jo and Andy sat in silence, taking in the new development.

'So,' Andy said. 'Who gets to go and retrieve the lovely Phoebe?'

Jo thought for a moment. 'Your call, I guess; your missing person. But I'd suggest perhaps Mo, plus Eva to cover the in-transit toilet visits, if necessary.'

'Okay, I'm cool with that, Mo and Eva. I'll try to come to terms with my disappointment.'

'I need us both here. Possible development on the Knocker thing. Anyway, she's too young for you.'

Andy leaned back in his seat. 'Oh, I'm spoken for right now; back with Eva. Didn't she mention it? I thought you girls had no secrets from each other. Just like there shouldn't be any secrets between partners. Eva and I have had some very interesting conversations recently. Your ears must have been almost catching fire.'

Jo stared at him in silence, not sure how to respond. Instead, she got quickly to her feet and nodded towards the door.

'Right, let's spread the joyous news – about Phoebe, I mean, not you and DC Johnson.'

One thing she *was* sure of. The smirk was back.

★

Following the briefing, Jo sat alone in her office and tried to recall the interactions and dynamics in recent days within the team, to identify any change in behaviour which might have pointed to the resumption of Andy and Eva's relationship. She was acutely aware of the potential for her clandestine conversations with Eva being shared with Andy in a careless, relaxed moment between lovers. Andy's comment about her ears burning all but confirmed they had been discussing her. Then there was the look which had passed between the two as she and her sergeant entered the briefing room to address the team; Andy's brief nod followed by the anxious expression on Eva's face.

There were more important things, she told herself. Like when to break the news to the Wrights and Benny. Gut feel said they should wait until they had interviewed Phoebe, or at least got her back to the station, but how would that look when they found out they'd had to wait longer than necessary for what they were desperate to hear. Andy's call, she realised, under the new division of their responsibilities.

She checked her watch and smiled. The analogue, self-winding Seiko was a man's watch; Seb's, in fact. One she'd always liked and which he had presented to her on her first visit to Bury two years ago. Her 'engagement watch', he had called it. She remembered how they'd gone to the Mill Gate Shopping Centre and he'd taken her to Timepiece, the little shop where they did watch repairs, asking the man to take out as many links in the steel strap as necessary to fit her wrist. He'd slipped on the watch, closed the clasp and they had kissed. The man was a little embarrassed until Seb explained.

'I've told her, up north that means she's agreed to marry me. So that was me kissing the future bride.'

The man had laughed and offered his congratulations. It was

an unorthodox and unexpected proposal, Jo having assumed they would live together as unmarried partners, but one she had accepted in her next breath. Somehow that recent memory put everything else happening around her into perspective. But even when recalling that moment of pure joy, she could not stop herself questioning Seb's motives for taking that step into marriage. Was it paranoia that caused her to wonder if it was just so there was no going back, not trusting himself to otherwise commit to a long-term relationship? The return to reality came with Eva's knock on her door and she shook her head as if to rid it of the thoughts.

'Come in.'

'Hi, ma'am. We're about ready to go.'

Eva seemed a little uneasy in spite of the normalcy of the message. Jo checked her watch again; it told her it was 11.40 a.m.

'Not before time. Two hours since we agreed with Sheffield that we'd pick her up. What's Mo been doing?'

'Making calls mainly, strutting about outside in the car park. Said he'd had a few things lined up to do today that he's had to change. But he's okay to go now.'

'Not sure what things would take him two hours to change. Gas boiler trouble again, perhaps. Anyway, safe journey, and stick to the motorways as advised. Here's hoping you get back for the weekend. Anything lined up?'

'Not tonight. Bridgewater Hall tomorrow. Halle Orchestra, Music from the Westerns.'

Jo smiled. 'Sounds great. Would that include the soundtrack of *Tombstone*? I'm sure you'll both enjoy that.'

Eva was silent for a few seconds, then sighed. 'I was going to tell you, ma'am, but then...'

'How long?'

'Just a couple of weeks. Didn't even know there was anything to tell based on last time. But recently, he's been... well...'

'Less of a knob? Yes I agree. I've actually found it relatively painless working with him.'

Eva smiled, sighing again, this time with relief. 'Exactly, so...'

'So, it would have been good for me to know in the light of previous *confidential* opinions we've shared about him. Otherwise, it would be none of my business.'

'Sorry, ma'am.'
'Off you go, and be careful.'

★

'So what were you doing for two hours?'

They were approaching the twin slip roads off the M62 onto the M1, making good time again after the slow drag over the Pennines where the heavy snow had reduced the carriageway to two lanes on a stretch from Milnrow to Brighouse.

'Is this you asking or is it what our leader has told you to ask?'

'Hey, where did that come from? I thought you got on well with her.'

Mo sighed. 'I do, mainly, but she's always making snide references to me phoning home. Like when I'm at work the rest of my world shouldn't matter.'

'That's just not true. I've been there when she's virtually ordered you to go home because you'd been at work so long. And she was genuinely concerned that you were coming to work on New Year's Day when everyone else was taking it off. That's hardly someone making unfair demands on your time.'

Mo took several moments to reply, concentrating on joining the flow of traffic onto the M1.

'You're right. I'm just a bit edgy right now. Don't know why.'

'It's like this case has got to you somehow. An obsession with this girl. Are you sure you don't know her?'

'What sort of a question is that?' Mo banged the steering wheel with the heels of his hands. 'You mean, have I been withholding information? Are you sure you've not become Carter's mouthpiece?'

'Carter. You mean the boss? What on earth…?'

'Witty; caring; empathetic; encouraging …' He drew in a deep breath. 'Sorry, Eva, just ignore me.' But he went on, 'At times she just seems too perfect. The job seemed to change when she arrived. We all had a *laugh*, for God's sake, which isn't what police work is supposed to be about… is it? But we've not actually *achieved* anything, have we? Phoebe's given herself up; we haven't *found* her. And since she's been off the case, I don't see any progress with the job she was brought here to do. I think that's why she's trying to link Easy Rider to the trafficking she's supposed to be investigating. Desperation! A substitute for getting a real result. Fuck's sake, it's all based on Reeves giving his fleet a good clean.'

'Hold on there, can I just remind you that I also believe there may be a link. And, more crucially, so does the sarge. I think we can agree, it's unlikely *he's* going along with her without really believing it. He's more likely *not* to go along with her when he does.'

'She can be very persuasive; I'll give her that. She's good in that sense; very credible.' He nodded to the Woolley Edge Services sign. 'Anyway, I need to stop here for a pee.'

Eight minutes later, after Mo had set the satnav for the remainder of the journey, they filtered back onto the motorway, completing the further twenty or so miles to their destination in complete silence, as if some verbal impasse had been reached.

*

Jo brought up the CCTV coverage on her PC and again ran the sequence from when Knox and Chadwick had parted company, through to the suspected phone call. It had to be something in those few short minutes if there was anything at all. It was after the third run-through that she leaned back in her chair and uttered a loud 'Doh!'

She paused the camera feed at the point when Denzel lifted his left hand, holding the phone up to his face. The six digits at the bottom of the screen showed 22.29.48; a few seconds before the half hour and nearly four minutes after the time of the call to his girlfriend. She checked her notes to be sure – 10.26 p.m., duration forty-one seconds. Unless the information from the service provider was incorrect or, even less likely, the time on the camera feed was out of sync, it meant Denzel had made two calls and from different phones.

She left her office and walked over to Kirsty.

'Can you contact Chadwick's service provider again for the exact time he made his call on Tuesday night, and, at the risk of annoying them, ask if there is any possibility it could be incorrect. We have it in the log as ten-twenty-six p.m. and if that *is* correct, we might just have a bit of a breakthrough.'

She turned to see Andy watching her from his workstation.

'Got a minute?' she said, nodding towards her office.

Andy followed her through, taking the chair across the desk from her. The faintest smile played around his mouth and eyes, as if in anticipation of a response to his earlier revelation about Eva. If that was what he hoped for, he was disappointed.

'Depending on what DC Milner tells us in the next minute or so,' Jo said, 'we may have something to work on.'

Andy's expression changed and he leaned forward as Kirsty appeared in the doorway. She read from her notebook.

'Call was made at 22.26.03; ended 22.26.44. They confirmed that the timing was accurate to one second. And the woman I spoke to *did* sound a little annoyed.'

'Don't care,' Jo said. 'That's what I wanted to hear.'

'And it means what, ma'am?' Kirsty asked.

'I'm not sure yet. We need a closer look. Thanks, detective.'

Kirsty shrugged and left, closing door behind her. Andy leaned further forward.

'So?'

'The CCTV capture near the Met on Tuesday night showed Chadwick making a phone call, whilst watching Knox walk away from him past the Town Hall. As you just heard, his service provider confirms that a call *was* made from his phone at ten-twenty-six p.m. to an iPhone registered to a Gemma Ashton, who lives at the same address as Chadwick and is presumably his girlfriend. *However...*' Jo turned the screen so they could both see, and pointed to the static image '... CCTV showed that the call we watched him make was nearly four minutes later, a few seconds before ten-thirty p.m., so *not* the call on record at the service provider.'

'So, he made two calls from different phones?'

'Must have. And the time he made the first call was during the ninety seconds or so when he was out of sight in the Met station.'

'Presumably from somewhere he wouldn't be picked up on camera.'

'I'd bet my life on it. Let's run the pictures again in the light of that discrepancy so we're not getting ahead of ourselves, because this is the second two-phone trick we've seen in recent weeks and Easy Rider seems to be the common denominator.'

★

To accommodate the addition of two more people, Phoebe and her watchers had been moved to one of the smaller meeting rooms, a much more relaxed and airy location with outside windows, a coffee machine, and six comfortable chairs around a rectangular, beech-topped table. Two uniformed officers, PC Glenda Rhodes and PC Cameron Davy, the latter having met Phoebe in reception, were seated on either side of their charge and got to their feet as Mo and Eva were waved into the room by the larger-than-life, smiling figure of DI Kenny Watson. Phoebe remained seated, hands on her lap tightly clutching a tissue, and looked anxiously from one to the other of the new arrivals.

'Hi, Phoebe,' Eva said in a quiet voice with a friendly smile. 'I can't tell you how pleased we are to see you. How are you?'

Phoebe didn't reply but looked down and raised the tissue to her eyes, her shoulders gently shaking. Glenda sat down again and placed an arm around her shoulders.

'Shall I get the coffees sir?' Cameron asked Kenny, moving over to the machine. 'Or tea?'

'Good idea,' Kenny turned to Mo and Eva.

'Coffee's fine for us,' Eva said. 'Both white, no sugar. Thank you.'

Mo, so far, had not spoken, his eyes fixed on Phoebe as if he couldn't quite believe he was seeing her.

'Before that, introductions,' Kenny said. 'I think you both know who this young lady is.'

Names and handshakes were exchanged between the officers, and the conversation turned to their journey, weather and road conditions until Cameron set the six Styrofoam cups down on the table. They took their seats and sipped their drinks.

'I have explained to Phoebe that she will be returning to Bury this afternoon,' Kenny said. 'She understands that she is not under arrest but she has not shared with us her reasons for leaving or her circumstances during the last few weeks. We believe the important thing is that she is safe and has, of her own free will, made herself known to us. I'm sure that once she has had time to think she will be more forthcoming.'

Phoebe spoke for the first time.

'I'm so sorry for all the trouble I've caused, and all the worry. Mum and Dad, Benny. What will they think of me...' She began to cry.

'We'll deal with all that later,' Eva said. 'For now, the priority is to get you home.'

'Even so,' Mo said, 'it is only right that Phoebe should know there will be consequences because of the amount of time and resources...'

'But we can face those consequences as and when,' Eva interrupted, glaring at Mo. 'After you've been reunited with your partner and your parents.' She turned to the others. 'Thank you for looking after Phoebe but I think we should start back as soon as possible.'

'That's right,' Kenny said. 'Just a few formalities before you leave. Let's go to my office. Won't take more than a couple of minutes. Then we'll get you home, Phoebe.'

Mo and Eva followed the senior officer to the open plan CID area, which looked like a copy of their own place of work, his small office at one end of the room a near replica of their own DI's.

'I'll just get the paperwork. One minute.'

Eva turned on Mo after he left.

'What was the point of that, for God's sake? Don't you think she has enough to deal with right now without threats of... consequences. I'm sure she realises she can't just walk back into... whichever home she decides is hers, and start work again on Monday. So I don't understand why...'

'She just needs to be aware of what a fuck-up this has all been. Her parents in tears on TV begging her to return. No point in pretending that all's well when, I hope, she'll be put through the ringer when we get back. Might as well be honest with her.'

Eva looked shocked. 'Put through the ringer? This isn't like you, Mo. I know you've been really focused on her disappearance, but I didn't realise it was with... what's the expression... malicious intent?'

Mo sighed. 'I don't want to fall out with you, Eva, but I don't think it's appropriate to be almost thanking her for showing up.' He put on a high, comic voice. '"Now we know you're safe, Phoebe, we can all get on with our lives again. It's *so* good of you to let us know you're okay." Sorry, but I can't go along with that.'

'It's not like that, as you must know. We need to understand why all this happened and, forgive me for mentioning, whether it *is* something more than just a break from mithering parents and boyfriend; whether it *is* about what's happening at Easy Rider. An hour with a captive audience on the drive back might see her loosening up if she thought she was among friends.'

'*Friends.* You can't be...'

'Sympathetic adults, then. Probably too late now.'

The door opened again and Kenny entered, holding a clutch of papers.

'Just a couple of signatures each.' He laid the sheets out on his desk, four in all, two copies of two. 'First to confirm you have taken charge of the... I nearly said "prisoner"... former missing person. And this second one for the contents of her bag, believe it or not. If you can both sign and add the date and time. My Super insists on the time being included. I think he's worried if Phoebe does another runner, he wants to make sure it's on your time not ours.'

Eva laughed. 'I can understand you wanting to get her off your hands.'

'It's not really like that, and I know at least one member of the team would like to keep her for a lot longer. Constable Davy is truly smitten.'

'I'm sure he'll get over her, given time,' Eva said.

'And don't be too hard on her,' Kenny said to Mo, placing a hand on his shoulder. 'My daughter's in her late twenties now and a loving mother of two wonderful kids, but when she was Phoebe's age she was all over the place. Got kicked out of uni – drugs, behavioural issues. She came good with flying colours.' He paused, 'Sorry about the lecture.'

'We'll be gentle with her, won't we, Mo.'

'Of course. But I'm sure your daughter had consequences to face, sir, as part of her recovery and rehabilitation.'

'That's a good point, Mo.' Kenny nodded his approval. 'Anyway, let's get her moving in the right direction.'

Twenty minutes later, after goodbyes and thank-yous, Eva and

Phoebe settled into the back of the car with Mo ready in the driver's seat.

'Just before we go,' he said, unbuckling his seat belt, 'need to pay a precautionary visit to the Gents. Won't be long.'

He got out of the car and they watched him go back into the building.

'Men,' Eva said. 'What are they like?'

Phoebe sniffed a token laugh and they waited in silence, broken eventually by Eva.

'DC Malik is right, Phoebe, that you will be expected to explain what has happened, and why; but I don't want you to worry about that now. All in good time. There are people whose lives will be able to start again knowing you are safe.'

Phoebe turned to her with a sad smile. 'Thanks for the words of comfort, but you really don't understand. You *can't* understand.'

Mo appeared before Eva could respond. She checked her watch as he got into the car.

'Twelve minutes, you've been. What have you been doing?'

'That could be regarded as an indelicate question,' Mo replied. 'But we've a change of plan. Problems on the M62 over the tops, stationery traffic due to snow and accidents, so it's the Snake Pass home.'

'Who told you that?'

'One of the guys back there. Next to me in the loo. Told him I was heading back to Manchester and he gave me the latest weather and road report. He said he's heading that way and had just checked. Lucky really, not often you benefit from a weak bladder.'

'Are you sure about the Snake Pass?'

'If I wasn't, I wouldn't go that way, would I? And as you pointed out, the priority is to get Phoebe home ASAP.' He set the satnav and buckled up. 'Seatbelts fastened? Let's go.'

They set off, with the wind whipping the snow against the windscreen.

★

Jo and Andy, along with Jodi, Kirsty and Damon, had just taken their seats in the briefing room when the door opened to admit DI

Alistair Crossley, having made his way from Blackburn on receiving the information about Phoebe's reappearance.

'Afternoon, all,' he said. 'I hope I haven't missed anything exciting.'

'Pleased you made it through the snow, Al,' Jo said. 'Let's get you a coffee to warm the blood. We're just about to start and we may have something.'

'Excellent. White, one sugar please.'

Damon went over to the vending machine to fill the order.

'Firstly,' Jo began, 'as far as Phoebe is concerned, DCs Johnson and Malik are on their way to pick her up from Sheffield.'

'I got a call from DC Johnson about thirty minutes ago,' Andy put in, 'from the motorway services on the M1 north of the turn-off for Attercliffe, so they're well on their way. We reckon they should be back within a couple of hours.'

'When she does return,' Jo said, 'I'm assuming that you two, Al and Andy, will interview her. We may need to get her checked over first by the doctor and I imagine yours won't be the final meeting with her. It might be some time before we get to the bottom of where and why she disappeared. I expect the Super will want to speak to her as well at some point.'

'She's told the police in Sheffield that she won't be implicating anyone else in her disappearance,' Andy added, 'which I suppose means she won't say where she's been. Well, we'll see about that.'

'That on one side for now,' Jo went on, 'I'd like us to focus on Curtis Knox's murder, if you'll bear with us, Al, where we might have something to work on. Earlier, I went through Tuesday evening's CCTV capture outside the Lancashire Gate and the Metro station. For those who haven't seen the footage, it shows the four guys being ejected, fairly gently, from the pub and heading their separate ways. What we didn't pick up initially was this.' She clicked on an icon on her laptop and turned to a large screen on the wall behind her, which came to life with a static image of the front of the pub. 'We'll go forward a bit.'

She paused the sequence at the point where Chadwick had returned to where he and Knox had parted, and went on to explain the discrepancy in the timing of the phone calls.

'So, any thoughts?' Jo looked round the group. There was silence for a few moments, then Damon spoke.

'Either, he didn't make the second call, changed his mind, perhaps or he made it from a different phone.'

'And we believe the latter,' Andy said. 'He held it up to his face for over a minute.'

'So we have two people linked to Easy Rider who have two phones,' Al said. 'Phoebe and Chadwick – although Chadwick's link is a bit tenuous. I mean, just through Knox.'

'Interesting too,' Andy pointed out, 'that Phoebe told her boyfriend that her second phone was a work phone only to be used for company business, but her boss, Reeves, claims he only ever uses her personal number. Just remind me, we checked her calls, and they seemed to cover *all* her contacts with Reeves relating to her work. That's right, isn't it?'

'That's right,' Jodi answered. 'Over half of the calls made and received were work-related, and the texts as well.'

The group were silent for a while, each with their own thoughts.

'So here's a scenario, some of which we've already been over before,' Jo said. 'Please feel free to interrupt if I'm straying into fantasy. Easy Rider is a front for trafficking – drugs, people, arms, but let's say drugs for now. It's a perfect set-up. I think it was you, Kirsty, who said, who's going to stop-and-search a bunch of oldies on a shopping trip? Not exactly PC but a very good point. And, by the way, to do that, *all* those involved will have to use two phones; a burner for the business end and a contract one for cover, which, as we know, is standard practice for drug dealing.

'Let's assume all the drivers at Easy Rider are involved. As someone has already said, even if they weren't involved in the actual trafficking, it's hard to believe they wouldn't know what was going on, so they're locked into the operation anyway. So what happens when someone wants out? We know that both Phoebe and Knox were considering doing just that. And we also know they spent time alone together, with Knox regularly giving Phoebe a lift home from the depot to Helmshore. A long enough journey to get into a meaningful conversation and share a few personal thoughts. Knox had mentioned his own plans to a few of the other guys and it had got back to Reeves. So more than likely the boss knew about Phoebe's plans as well. Phoebe disappears and somebody tops Knocker. Well, our golden girl wasn't done in, but is it likely she would disappear off the face of the Earth just because she'd had a row with her boyfriend and parents? And at Christmas? After all, 'tis the season to be jolly. More likely that she feared for her life, and when she heard what had happened to Knox, that prompted her to give herself up to police protection.'

'Unless, of course,' Andy said, 'she's decided to go back to work as normal, and it really was just a bust-up with her nearest and dearest. I don't believe that, by the way, but I guess we can't discount it.'

'But the other person with two phones is Denzel Chadwick. How does he fit into your scenario?' Al asked the question.

'We believe his involvement in the events of Tuesday night are more than a little suspect,' Jo said. 'Firstly, he was probably capable of killing the two guys who confronted them, but chose to play peacemaker. The landlord said the incident was almost a carbon copy of his confrontation with three guys some time ago, when he took all of them out, putting one of them in hospital. Secondly, having made such an effort to get to the pub he seemed happy to leave right after the incident was over. And, thirdly, the phone; was he checking where Knox was and then letting somebody know, possibly the two guys who attacked them in the pub?'

'So no significance attached to the call to his girlfriend, then?' Al said.

'Unless it was insurance against us picking up on CCTV his making the second call. He calls home using his contract phone from the entrance to the Met station, where there are no cameras. Then, immediately afterwards, calls the bad guys on the burner where he *could* be picked up on camera; so if we ask him who he was calling he says his girlfriend and his provider would all but confirm that. It's only a really nit-picky person, desperate for any semblance of a clue, who might pick that up.'

'And she did,' Al said.

'Eventually,' Jo said.

There was silence as people checked their notes. Damon leaned forward.

'But why wouldn't he just make the call with his burner in the Met station where he called his girlfriend from? Then he wouldn't have to stage anything?'

'Perhaps he needed to see where Knocker was when he made the call,' Jodi offered.

'Quite possibly,' Jo said. 'So, what next, and, in particular, how do we get more information about Easy Rider? Because right now, there's no justification for demanding anything from them. If we went in gung-ho with just a few tenuous suspicions, we wouldn't have a chance of getting past a half-decent lawyer and that would just have the effect of putting Reeves on his guard. DC Malik does have a point, deep cleaning NHS vehicles isn't a reason to start pulling the company apart. So, suggestions.'

Jodi said, 'We've already hit a barrier in checking out Knox's vehicle. Reeves is refusing to allow a forensic examination without us giving him a specific reason and presenting some evidence of an issue. His point being, what has the state of his ambulance to do with him being knifed after a pub fight?'

Jo shook her head. 'Did we get anywhere checking out Phoebe's care home list against her logged visits?'

'The care homes don't keep the same amount of trip data as Easy Rider,' Kirsty replied, 'so we were mainly comparing Phoebe's detailed schedule against notes on a calendar. They mostly tallied, but the care home managers admitted that some may not have been written on the calendar but stuck on with a Post-it note. After the event it would probably have been thrown away. The one place that did keep good records, Highfields in Whitefield, compared very closely with her log.'

'But that's just one, of course,' Andy said. 'I think we can assume that for such an operation to work, if it *is* an operation, the vast majority of the business they do must be legit. So, in effect, all the care home staff and residents, along with the day patients they ship around, are witnesses for the defence.'

Jo got to her feet and walked over to the whiteboard. She picked up the marker pen and wrote '*What we need*' on the board and underlined it.

'Let's forget what we can and can't do right now and concentrate on what we need, I'll kick off.'

She wrote, under the heading:

1. How many drivers at Easy Rider have >1 phone?

She turned to the group. 'Next.'

Damon raised his hand. 'Need to check bank accounts.' Jo added it to the list.

2. Bank accounts.

'*All* bank accounts,' Damon went on. 'If they're trafficking, they'll have to put the dirty money in a separate place.' Jo added "*ALL*" to the second point

'Home addresses,' Jodi suggested. 'I mean check out the actual places they live. What sort of properties. Like phones and bank accounts, they might have more than one.' Jo added:

3. Properties owned > 1.

'Same with cars,' Andy said. 'We already know Reeves has a clapped-out Fiesta for when he's expecting us and a new Jag when he isn't.'

4. Cars, went onto the whiteboard.

'Social media,' Jodi said. 'Facebook, X, Instagram. Check accounts and activity for mutual friends and any repeated, cryptic messages. Next best thing if we can't check drivers' email and phones.' Jo wrote on the board:

5. Social media.

'Are you offering to pick that one up, Jodi?' Andy asked. 'Sounds like a riveting job.'

Jo laughed with the others. 'I think we'll draw lots for that later,' she said, 'so as not to stem the flow of ideas. Any more?'

'Just a thought,' Damon said. 'They've got at least one vacancy for a driver right now. Would it be possible for one of us to get in there under cover? I know it's a long shot. They'll be looking for someone with special attributes, like a criminal mind, for example. But we know enough about drug trafficking to be able to say all the right things.'

'Sounds more exciting than trawling Facebook,' Andy said.

'And a lot more difficult as well,' Jo interrupted. 'Good thought, but I can't imagine Mr Reeves will be advertising in the *Bury Times* or putting up vacancy notices in local hospitals. If we're right about Easy Rider, I'm sure he'll have a good idea who to approach to fill the gaps. Worthy of a mention, though.'

She turned to the board and added:

6. Driver vacancy.

Jodi raised a hand. 'Just going back to number three, ma'am, about the houses. Would it be an idea to tail some or all of the drivers when they leave the depot to go home? Only six working now, so two unmarked cars a night would pick up all six over three days. Even if we scored only one hit that would be enough to tick that box.'

'And you think this will get you out of three days' checking social media?' Andy asked. He looked at Jo. 'Worth a try, I reckon.'

'Okay,' Jo said. 'From Monday then. For today, I think we have a decent list to go at.' She read from the board.

'How many drivers have more than one phone?'

'*All* bank accounts.

'Properties owned – do they have more than one?'

'Cars – again, do they own more than one?'

'Social media – mutual friends, any message pattern.

'Driver vacancy – long shot, we'll park this for now.' Jo paused. 'No pun intended.' She turned to her fellow DI. 'Anything you want to add, Al, before we send these good people scurrying away to fill in the blanks?'

'Not right now, but maybe in an hour or so when we've interviewed Miss Wright. Unless, of course, she provides us with all the answers to the above. From the little she's said so far, I'm not holding my breath.'

'Nor me. We'll see if Mo and Eva have managed to loosen her tongue on the way over. Okay, team, let's get working on this list and feel free to add to it if you think of anything else. Full steam ahead.'

'Like the *Titanic*, you mean?' Andy said.

★

'Did you get the name and address of the guy you met in the Gents?'

Eva was staring ahead with frightened eyes as the wipers struggled to clear the windscreen of heavy, driving snow which all but covered it again before the next sweep. Mo gripped the wheel tightly, the whiteness of his knuckles against his brown skin reflecting his own anxiety.

'No, of course not. He was just a voice next to me. Why?'

'Because if we get out of this alive I'd like to go round to his house and tell him to mind his own fucking business next time he feels the need to offer advice on how to die in an Arctic whiteout. Sorry about the language, Phoebe.'

Phoebe was looking out of the rear passenger window in the same position as she had been for the past fifteen minutes since they left the city behind and began their precarious journey onto the moorland of the Peak District National Park. Eva had managed to get a few words out of her when they first set off but silence had soon descended on the back seat of the vehicle. It was clear she hadn't heard the expletive or the apology.

'Oh, come on,' Mo said. 'It's not that bad.'

'Not that bad,' Eva responded. 'Please tell me how this could possibly be any worse.'

'We'll be fine, trust me.'

'How can we be fine? We can't see where we're going, for fuck's sake.'

'Foul language won't get us there any faster, Eva. Just get a grip. I'll stop up ahead and we'll wait for the snow to stop.'

'Wait for the snow… it's mid-January, Mo. It might not stop for another week… or more.'

'Well, until it eases off, then. It can't keep this up for long.'

'*It!* What's *it*? I repeat, it's mid-January. And where are you going to stop?'

'Snake Inn. Just up ahead. I need a pee, anyway.'

'What again? Well, I hope they've got some vacant rooms, because I can't see us getting much further.'

'They'll all be vacant. The hotel's closed during January.'

'That's great. So why are we stopping there? We've just passed the Ladybower Inn, haven't we? That didn't look closed. Perhaps we should head back there. Then you can have your pee indoors and we can all keep warm.'

'We'll be okay, believe me. Perhaps you'd prefer being stuck on the M62.'

'Definitely. No doubt about it. That's if it is still blocked, or ever was. At least you can be sure there are people working hard to get everybody home.'

They were both silent for a while as they continued, ever more slowly, into the blizzard. Phoebe continued to stare through her window.

'Look it's just up here on the right,' Mo said.

A large white building came into view, separated from the road by a picket fence and with a wooded hillside rising behind it. Mo turned in to the large car park and pulled to a stop close to the side of the inn.

'Now what?' Eva asked.

'We'll stop for a while, and if it doesn't get any better, then, okay, we'll head back. Anyway, I'm going in for a pee.'

'I thought you said it was closed.'

'It is, but it won't be empty. There'll be someone here. The owners, or pub-sitters. Somebody anyway. They won't have abandoned it just because it's closed for business. Stay here with Phoebe. I won't be long.'

Mo got out of the car. They were relatively sheltered, at least from the wind, close to that side of the building, but a few flakes swirled into the car before he could shut the door. He walked round to the front of the inn, disappearing from sight.

'Sorry about this, Phoebe,' Eva said, turning to their passenger. 'I guess you stick to the motorway on your trips to Sheffield.'

Phoebe seemed to come out of her trance, turning to Eva with a surprised expression.

'You know about those?'

'We know a lot about you, Phoebe, except, until now, exactly where you were.'

'The trips to Sheffield – you mean with the care home residents?'

'Yes, what other trips did you think I meant?'

'No. I mean, none.'

'So, I was just asking if this is the route you'd use or…'

'Sometimes, but Woodhead Pass, usually. It's more scenic than the motorway, and there's a parking area with toilets next to Torside Reservoir. A good place for stretching legs and emptying bladders.' She gave a little laugh, then turned to look out of the window again. 'I wonder if I'll ever see it again,' she said, half to herself.

'Why do you say that?'

Phoebe shook her head. 'As I said before, you wouldn't understand.'

Mo appeared round the corner of the building. He beckoned for Eva to join him. She opened the car door and stepped out into the snow. It was falling less heavily now and the wind had dropped a little.

'What?' she called.

'Just need a word. And they've opened up for us to use the loos, so might be an idea to have a precautionary pee, even if you don't want one right now.'

Eva ducked her head back into the car. 'Let's go inside, Phoebe. Stretch our legs and empty our bladders.'

'I'm okay, thanks.' She continued to stare out of the window.

'Well, I can't leave you here, can I?'

'Why not? I'm not going anywhere, am I?' There was an edge to her voice. 'Am I under arrest?'

'Well, no, but...'

'And did I come forward voluntarily?'

'Yes, although...'

'Then I'm not exactly a high risk, am I? And I'm no good at hot-wiring cars, so if you take the keys I won't be driving off either. Go and have your pee and I'll be here when you get back.' She gave a sickly smile and placed two fingers against her temple. 'Brownie's honour.'

'Eva,' Mo shouted. 'What's wrong? Come on, just want a word. The pee is optional.'

'I don't want to leave Phoebe and she wants to stay in the car.'

'Well, let her stay then. There's nowhere for her to go, is there, even if she wanted to.'

Eva placed a hand on Phoebe's shoulder and she turned towards her.

'Brownie's honour?' Eva said.

Phoebe smiled, more relaxed now, and saluted again. 'Brownie's honour.'

Eva closed the door and followed Mo round to the front of the inn and inside.

★

'Let's get back out there.' Eva was getting agitated at the amount of time they'd been staring at the Google map on Mo's iPhone.

'Right, okay, but are we agreed that we go back the way we came then pick up the A61 at Owlerton, then onto the M1 at junction thirty-six. Then M62, blocked or unblocked. Satisfied?'

'We've just been through all this, for fuck's sake, and *no*, I'm not satisfied, seeing as how you're asking. It's been a complete fuck-up. God knows what shit's coming our way when we get back. Now, *please*, let's get back to Phoebe.'

'Look, let's assume you and the boss are right and she's involved in something and dropped out of sight to save her own skin. And hearing about Knox, she's decided she's safer with us. Well, now she's raised her head above the parapet, she could be a target herself. So when that guy mentioned the motorway was blocked it occurred to me we'd have a better chance of getting her home safely if we took the Snake Road back, because no-one would expect that. That's if there is someone after her.'

'You're changing your story now, Mo. For starters, how would anyone know Phoebe had given herself up? Did this guy *really* tell you… ?'

'*Yes*. Okay, to be honest, I only thought of the rest of the rationale after we set off. But it makes sense. And the guy said he was heading for Ormskirk and he'd already decided to go over the Snake.'

'Well, you may just meet him again, then, stuck in a snowdrift or something, and I'll get the chance to fuck him off after all. Now let's get back to Phoebe. She probably needs a pee herself by now.'

They stepped out of the inn, thanking the manager, and walked round to the Subaru. The first thing they noticed was that the bonnet was at an unusual angle, rising slightly from the windscreen end. The second was the absence of the passenger. The third was a single set of footprints in the snow tracking round the back of the car from the passenger side and then round the front and away towards the road. And while they were noticing all this, a stream of anguished expletives issued loudly from both detectives.

★

'I don't fucking believe this.' The normally calm and relaxed Al Crossley was showing another side to his character, one fuelled by unrestrained anger. 'Four weeks, *four fucking weeks* this girl has been missing. She comes out of hiding and you manage to lose her in less than *four hours.*'

There was a pause and Eva pictured him coming down off the ceiling of the office he was using at Bury station next to DI Carter's. She hoped he had the door closed to limit the sound carrying across the abandoned open plan area to the temporary ops room in the cafeteria, and that Andy wasn't a silent party to this call. She was seated next to Mo on the bed in one of the inn's empty guest rooms, with her phone on speaker between them.

'She was on her own for just a few minutes,' Mo said. 'We had no way of knowing…'

'Exactly. *Exactly.* Which is why in situations like that we never leave them alone *because* we have no waying of knowing.'

'But she's not a criminal, sir. She *volunteered* to come forward. It makes no sense that she would change her mind and run away in the middle of a blizzard miles from anywhere.'

'So what are you saying, DC Malik? That she could have been taken? Because if so, this completes the circle back to when she was first reported missing and we didn't know then whether she had absconded or been abducted. We start again.'

There was a long pause during which time the DI's heavy breathing was the only sound they could hear. When he spoke again, his voice was more calm and, because of that, more chilling.

'So what have we done so far?'

'Alerted South Yorkshire and Derbyshire police, and Tameside,' Eva replied, 'and…'

'Which is why we've had calls from all three. Telling them what, exactly?'

'Well…what happened. We left her in the car for a few minutes whilst we decided how to proceed…'

'How to proceed. Yes, we'll come to whose brilliant idea it was to chance it over the Snake later. Go on.'

'Phoebe didn't want to leave the car and we thought it best not to force her. As she pointed out, she wasn't under arrest or anything. When we returned she'd gone. There were footprints from her door, round the car and towards the road. It's possible she could have got into another car because the footprints stopped at a churned-up slushy area where contractors' vehicles must have been manoeuvring, turning round or whatever, and we couldn't pick them up after that.'

'So we don't know whether we're looking for a girl on foot, or a girl in a vehicle?'

'No, sir,' they answered in unison. 'But,' Eva continued, 'most likely in a vehicle. Even if she set off on foot, I can't believe she'd have much difficulty hitching a ride, except that there's not much traffic on the A57 right now.' She glared at Mo as she spoke.

'Did she tell you anything about where she'd been and who she'd spent the time with?'

'Only scraps,' Eva answered. 'I thought she was opening up a bit when we first set off but she soon clammed up. Said she'd spent Christmas and New Year with friends, but they'd got a bit twitchy with all the appeals in the press and on TV, so she'd moved out a few days ago to stay with someone she'd met on some of her trips over there. No names, though. She said that's all she'd be saying; not wanting to get anyone into trouble for taking her in.'

'And you think it was her who disabled the car? Is that likely?'

'Yes, if she didn't want us to be able to follow her. Her boss says she's an excellent mechanic – self-taught, but really good. It would be easy for her to lift the bonnet and pull the right wires. The prints clearly show she walked round the back of the car from the nearside rear door, past the driver's position, where the bonnet release is, to the front of the car. Then away towards the road.'

'And possibly into another car.'

'Possibly. We've no way of knowing. But there were no other footprints around the car except Phoebe's, except ours of course, and ours were all on the driver's side. So if someone did pick her up there, they didn't force her out of the car. She must have been willing to go.'

'What a mess. What a fffff...*mess!* I think I know the answer, but CCTV?'

'None working, sir,' Mo answered. 'The place is closed for business; refitting inside and repairs outside during the off season, and the surveillance cameras are being upgraded as part of the maintenance programme. We had to talk our way in to have a pee. Wish I'd just wet myself now. I'm sorry, sir, but it was my decision to take the Snake, based on advice from someone whilst I was having the pee before that one. The guy said the M62 was blocked over the top, but the Snake was open.'

'I need to get on with co-ordinating all this with Sheffield and the others. They'll be just loving this. Christ, I thought the initial search was complicated enough with just two forces involved. How are you getting back?'

'The guy who's minding the inn said he can fix the car. He's on it now.'

'Well if he's charging you, make sure you pay him with your own debit card and don't try claiming it back.'

The call ended. They sat in silence for a long time, not looking at each other.

'Gut feel,' Mo said. 'Did she walk or was she snatched?'

'Gut feel. I reckon snatched, though don't ask me to explain the lack of footprints. But how did they know we'd be taking the Snake Pass?'

'And who was the guy who persuaded me it would be a good idea? One thing I can tell you for certain, there was no-one tailing us on the way here.'

'So perhaps she did walk. Let's see if we can pick up her footprints again on the other side of that mess of slush and mud. But if we're right about the snatch,' she added, 'there won't be any to find.'

★

Jo and the rest of the CID team were recalled to the briefing room to learn of Phoebe's second vanishing trick just six hours after Jo had imparted the euphoric news of her reappearance. The group around the table looked stunned, as if none could come to terms with the reversal of fortune. Showing commendable restraint, DI Crossley avoided sharing his displeasure with their colleagues on their mission of mercy and focused on the facts. Andy sat silently at his side, his jaw tight, staring down at the table top.

Al clicked a few keys on the laptop in front of him and a Google map of the High Peak area of the national park appeared on the large wall screen.

'We have both ends of the pass covered here...' he zoomed in to the western end of the road '...at Glossop Golf Club, and here...' moving the image across to the left '...at the junction of the A57 with the A6101 at Rivelin. There is very little traffic on the Snake Road, apparently, so the police will be stopping every vehicle. But don't get too excited, we have no idea whether she is in a vehicle. And even if she is, we may not have got the road checks in place in time. DC Johnson tells us there is no evidence that she was forced into a vehicle, so if she did abscond on foot, she would have had to hitch a lift, and at the risk of sounding sexist, having seen the photographs of her, I think it's highly likely she would get one. DC Johnson, by the way, is of the same opinion.

'There are a few roads off the A57 to the east of the Snake Inn before the junction at Rivelin – the A6013 south at Ladybower reservoir and a couple of minor roads north, here, near Hollow Meadows.' He enlarged the image to point them out. 'But we think it's unlikely any vehicle on the A57 will be going anywhere but Glossop or Sheffield, so hopefully the checks are in the right place. At this short notice, we can't cover every eventuality, and I think in getting them set up so quickly, the guys at both ends have done a great job.' He paused. 'I don't think they'll be saying that about us right now.'

He leaned back in his chair.

'When are DC Malik and DC Johnson expected back, sir?' Kirsty asked. 'Or are they part of the op out there?'

'They're not part of the op because they're stuck at the Snake Inn until the owner, or whoever, can fix their car. Otherwise it's an AA job and God knows how long the waiting time is in these conditions for a disabled vehicle in a safe parking area off the main routes. So in answer to your question re their ETA, I'd say sometime between tonight and early next week.'

He smiled, and the brief levity was welcomed by a collective chuckle. Jo noticed that Andy did not join in.

'We've sent two cars, four officers, to Glossop to help out with manpower and we have a police helicopter on stand-by,' Al went on, 'but in these conditions, the chopper would be of little use. And speaking of the conditions, we can only hope that if she did abscond on foot, she managed to get a lift quickly. With the light going very soon, someone could die out there overnight.'

He turned to his left. 'DS Mills, anything to add?' Andy shook his head, his jaw still set, his eyes still looking down at the table. 'DI Carter?'

'Nothing that will help right now. At least what we know now that we didn't yesterday is that Phoebe is alive. Let's hold on to that thought. For the moment, though, I think we have to focus our attention on the Knox murder until we hear of any developments.'

'Agreed,' Al said. 'So, get back to what you were doing and keep your fingers crossed for our slippery lady.'

'And don't forget,' Jo added, 'that Space Invaders will be putting us back where we belong overnight. So make sure you take everything home with you that might get lost in the relocation. Or should that be re-relocation?'

CHAPTER TWENTY-TWO

Saturday 19 January

Jo awoke at 6.20 a.m. and turned to where her husband should have been sleeping next to her. The late phone call, just before midnight, informed her that there was to be a pitch inspection early on Saturday and they were hopeful the game would go ahead. The christening of the sheepskin rug would have to wait.

Jo had calmed Seb's apologies with a reality check. She reminded him that it was her suggestion that they postpone his visit, and, anyway, Jo's leisure time over the weekend had been virtually wiped out by the events of that day. Phoebe's second flight for one thing, but that had been almost upstaged by an incident on the night of the murder which had just come to light. Around fifteen minutes prior to Seb's call, the station had phoned to inform her that someone had just contacted them with the report of a sighting which could possibly be linked to Curtis Knox's death. With no reason, or inclination, to pursue it at that late hour, Jo had resolved to get in especially early the next day. Now, as the wind rattled her bedroom window, Jo decided that around eight o'clock was especially early enough for a Saturday morning.

In the comfort and safety of her warm bed, and with the reassuring sound of the heating kicking in at 6.30, her thoughts went out to Phoebe. It put her disappointment at being robbed of a few fleeting hours with the man she loved into perspective. In spite of the amount of police time she had wasted, the anxiety she had caused her own loved ones, not to mention what criminal activity she might be involved in, surely she didn't deserve to be stranded out on the moors of High Peak in these conditions, or, even worse, in the clutches of the people she may have been fleeing from. With a feeling bordering on guilt, Jo got out of bed and headed for the shower. She decided she could easily beat eight o'clock after all.

As it turned out she made it with only a couple of minutes to spare. The journey of just under two kilometres had taken her around forty minutes, with traffic crawling along roads reduced to single track with snow heaped at the sides and on the pavements. The snow had stopped falling and the sky was clearing, but despite the best efforts of the gritters on the main routes, there were challenging icy stretches on the minor road from Burr's Country Park. Any feeling of heroism she felt in beating the elements was quickly quashed by the sight of DCs Lawson and D'Arcy already at their original workstations, along with DCs Dylis Knapp and Grant Hager, of the weekend crew, all focused on their PC screens. The operations room had been restored to its new normality and everyone seemed more relaxed.

'Morning, team,' Jo said. 'Good to see you back in your rightful places?'

'Morning, ma'am,' Dylis said, 'we've had an interesting development in the Knocker Knox case.'

'So I believe,' Jo said. 'Before we get to that, I don't suppose we've heard anything yet about Phoebe?'

'Nothing so far,' Jodi said. 'The road blocks didn't come up with anything, but the chopper's going up in…' she checked the time '…around twenty-five minutes, at eight-thirty. It's pretty clear over there, apparently. But whether they'll find anything…' Her voice tailed off. 'You sort of hope they won't, don't you? If she's been out there for, what, sixteen, seventeen hours…'

'We'll see,' Jo said. 'And what of our absent friends, DCs Malik and Johnson. Do we know where they are?'

'Eva phoned,' Jodi answered. 'They got the car fixed, but by that time the pass was .. well… *im*passable… so they spent the night at the Snake Inn.'

'How romantic. I thought it was closed for business.'

'It is. Eva said they made an exception under the circumstances.'

'A bit risky for the management, I suppose, chucking two police officers out with the chance of them freezing to death in a snow storm. So, Dylis, this interesting development? An eyewitness, is it?'

'Possibly. This person saw something which seems to fit with the timing. I've got the recording of the call, if you'd like to hear it.'

'Yes, please.'

Dylis clicked on an icon on her screen. A hush descended on the room as everyone turned to face her workstation. The first sound was that of a beeping, to indicate an incoming call.

'Time of the call is 11.23 p.m.,' Dylis said. The female voice on the recording picked up the story;

'Police, Bury Division.'

The response was almost drowned by the sound in the background.

'I'm calling about what I saw on Tuesday night.'

'Who is this speaking, please?'

'Davey Wilson.'

'I can hardly hear you, Mr Wilson. Where are you?'

'I'm on the Met.' The noise level noticeably reduced. *Just got off at Victoria. Heading into Manchester.'

'Okay, how can I help you?'

'I think I saw something in Bury on Tuesday night that might have something to do with that guy getting killed.'

'Go on.'

'I was driving into Bury between quarter to and eleven o'clock and I saw this guy kneeling on the pavement next to a car.'

'Where was this exactly?'

'Near the little park on Manchester Road close to the junction with Wellington Road, near Holy Cross College. There were two other guys helping him up. I assume they were from the car.'

The noise had increased again with the sound of shouting and traffic almost drowning his voice.

'Can you speak up a little, Mr Wilson, I can't...'

'I can't really shout this out. I'm in a crowd here.'

'Can you find somewhere more quiet?'

'Hold on.' They could hear Wilson in a brief conversation with some others before the background chaos receded again. 'Is this better? I'm back in the station again. I'll catch them up later.'

'Thank you. You were saying these men were helping him up.'

'Right. Well, I stopped alongside them and asked what had happened. They said the guy had stepped out in front of them and they had collided with him. They said he was okay; just a little shaken and very drunk, but they knew where he lived and they'd take him home.'

'Did they say where he lived?'

'No. Anyway, I drove on a bit then stopped and watched them in the mirror. They got him standing up and he seemed okay.'

'You said a car. Could it have been a small van, do you think?'

'Not sure, now you mention it. But it was black… or dark blue.'

'Did you see them put him in the vehicle?'

'Yes they sort of eased him into the passenger seat. No, they didn't, they put him in the back seat and one of the guys got in with him. So it must have been a car, mustn't it?'

'It would seem so. Can you describe the two men?'

'Didn't get a look at their faces. It was dark and snowing. They were both about the same height, dressed in black. One had a hood, I think; the other, one of those hats with pull-down ear flaps. And before you ask, no I couldn't identify them again.'

'Okay. We'll need to speak to you again, Mr Wilson, and take a full statement. I think what you saw could be relevant. May I ask why you haven't been in touch with us before?'

'Didn't think any more of it until tonight. I was in the same pub – the Lancs – talking about it with my mates and it suddenly occurred to me. Must be thick or something; sorry about that.'

'That's okay, Mr Wilson, but we'll have to see you as soon as possible, so perhaps…'

'You don't mean tonight? I've got stuff planned, and…'

'No, not tonight, but as early as possible tomorrow morning when you can meet the officer in charge of the enquiry. What is your address, Mr Wilson? We may be able to pick you up, especially if you're not fit to drive yourself. Although some people don't like the idea of the neighbours seeing a police car stop outside their house then drive them away in it.'

'Er… no, it's okay. I'll get in as soon as possible. I live on Manchester Road in Whitefield. I can get the bus.'

'Shall we say eleven o'clock?'

There was a long pause.

'Okay, I'll do my best.'

'Thank you, Mr Wilson. Enjoy your night out. Bye for now.'

'Bye.'

Dylis clicked on the icon to end the recording.

Jo looked round the group. 'It seems that DS Mills' theory of the car following him home could be correct. It could explain the minor bruising as well if it had collided with him.'

'I wonder if he was right about them putting him in the back of the vehicle,' Damon said. 'Because if he is, that rules out the link to the van, doesn't it?'

Jo thought for a moment. 'Not necessarily. If the incident in the pub was carefully planned, and if that meant parking a vehicle in one of the streets close to the pub even for an hour or so, it's unlikely to be a stolen one. Too big a risk that the theft had already been reported and details circulated.'

'So they'd use their own vehicle for the hit and the stolen one for the drop?'

'Very succinctly put, Damon. Yes, that's what I'd expect.'

'And it sort of points the finger at Jacko, doesn't it?' Jodi said.

'Go on,' Jo prompted.

'Well, if they were the two guys from the pub, how would they know Knocker would be walking along that road, unless someone told them?'

Jo nodded. 'And we believe Jacko made a call to someone just before then.'

They all turned as Andy arrived.

'The very man,' Jo said, without humour. 'I wonder if *your* ears have been burning.' She immediately regretted the emphasis on the possessive pronoun.

He took a seat at his work station without answering.

'Any news on Phoebe?'

'No sightings so far,' Jo answered, 'but the chopper is up now, so fingers crossed.'

'I don't like being the one stating the bleeding obvious,' Andy said, 'but if she's been out there all this time, she won't be doing any interviews anytime soon, if ever again.'

As he finished speaking, his iPhone sounded. He took it from his trouser pocket.

'DS Mills.'

They could hear the faint voice of the caller, but not what they were saying. The significance of the information reached the group through the expression on Andy's face, which changed from his usual detached arrogance to something approaching despair.

'When?' he said.

A brief reply.

'Where?'

The voice went on for another minute.

'Okay, I'll be ready.'

He ended the call and stared at his desk top, breathing in slowly and letting out a big sigh. He looked up and around the anxious group, who had already guessed what was coming.

'That was Crossley. The chopper spotted something around fifteen minutes ago at the bottom of a valley, couple of miles or so from Glossop. A body, they think. They're setting out to recover it now before the weather closes in again. Crossley is on his way to pick me up and we're heading out there. I'll contact Johnson and Malik and we'll meet them there. That's if they can get through from the Snake Inn.'

'Is it definitely Phoebe?' Dylis asked the question on everyone's mind.

'They can't ID it from the chopper. Apparently, it's lying face down and half covered in snow. But who else is it likely to be?'

'There are plenty of not-rights who go walking or climbing in this weather just to prove they can do it,' Damon said. 'So, fingers crossed.'

'Fingers crossed?' Jodi said, shaking her head. 'I find that quite ironic.'

'Meaning?' Andy asked.

'Well, hoping it isn't Phoebe means we're hoping it's someone else who's dead.'

Andy shook his head and got up from his chair. 'That's too deep for me. I need to get kitted up for a polar expedition and put SOCOs and forensics on alert. We could organise that with Derbyshire, I suppose, but I'd rather have our own guys on it.'

He left the room, which fell silent as people grappled with their thoughts.

'DI Mills is right, of course,' Jo said. 'I take your point Damon but, realistically, who else could it be?' She checked the time on her watch. 'Okay it's just coming up to nine-twenty. Let's apply ourselves elsewhere for now. An hour and a half before we meet Mr Wilson. Might be worth phoning him around ten-thirty to make sure he's up and about.'

As she finished speaking, Kirsty arrived with DC Danny Chu, a Hong Kong Chinese, another member of the weekend crew.

'Sorry, ma'am,' Kirsty said. 'Snow blocking the line between Radcliffe and Bury. They let us off the tram and we had to walk the last mile along the side of the track.'

'No problem,' Jo said. 'Just get settled. We have something to tell you.'

★

Al and Andy made the forty-five-kilometre drive from Bury Police station to the scene of the incident in just over forty minutes, assisted by the siren and blue lights and the earlier efforts of the gritters and snowploughs out of Glossop. They got out of the car, taking puffer jackets from the rear seat and pulling on woollen hats and fleece-lined gloves. Already filling a layby-cum-viewpoint about four miles from the Snake Inn on the Glossop side were three Range Rovers from Derbyshire police, two Land Rover Defenders with members of the Edale Mountain Rescue team, a fire appliance and an ambulance. The helicopter had returned to base as the wind increased and the snow fell heavily again, making it too dangerous to lower anyone into the valley. The Edale team had fastened a number of ropes to the metal roadside barrier and three of their members were lowering themselves down the steep sides of Holden Clough towards the icy waters of the stream at the bottom, securing them to trees and rocks at intervals as they descended. The senior officer from Derbyshire police introduced himself as Inspector Reg Barlow and the three men went over to the barrier to watch the operation unfold.

Twenty minutes after Al and Andy's arrival, the CSI Unit from Bury pulled up on the road next to the layby. Matty Crenshaw walked over to the three officers who were leaning on the barrier looking down to where the ropes disappeared into what appeared to be a bottomless abyss, with the swirling snow masking anything further than ten or so metres away.

'Morning,' Matty said, his eyes joining theirs in the search for some form of detail. 'I thought the adventure with that pile of stones was cold and exciting enough. Little did I know...'

'You're a bit ahead of yourselves, aren't you?' Andy said. 'I thought you were just standing by. We don't know yet whether or not this is a crime scene.'

'Well, perhaps we can help you decide. And, more to the point, the Super thought we should come.'

Al turned to Barry Major, leader of the rescue team.

'Can you just remind your guys not to get too close to the body and not to touch anything they might find on the way down. I know they've been briefed, but just a reminder.'

Barry spoke into his radio and passed on the message. They could hear the crackle of a response. He ended the exchange and turned to the detectives.

'They've found some stuff on the way down. A shoulder bag and some clothes. Also, they think, a phone. Just a corner sticking out of the snow, but they seem pretty sure. And they haven't touched anything,' he added.

'Thanks,' Al replied, with a smile. 'Can't upset Matty and his gang. I know they're dying to get abseiling down there.'

'Dying is probably the wrong word, sir,' Matty said.

'Any ETA yet for Malik and Johnson?' Al asked Andy.

Andy checked his phone. 'Message from Malik five minutes ago. They're going to follow a snowplough heading this way. He reckoned about twenty minutes, so that's fifteen from now.'

'We'll need to stop the plough well short of here,' Matty said. 'It's going to be sweeping snow down into the valley. Can't risk a mini avalanche until we've checked the descent and the scene itself.'

'Good point,' Al said. 'Reg, could you get one of your cars a quarter of a mile or so down the road to hold them up.'

As Reg left to speak to his crew, Barry's radio crackled into life again. After a couple of minutes he turned to the two detectives.

'They're close now, about ten metres away. The body's lying with its head in the stream so no doubt it's dead, but almost completely covered in snow and getting buried more every minute. They've extended the ropes to the bottom but I guess you don't want them going any closer.'

'No, that's great, Barry, thanks.' He turned to Andy and Matty. 'Well, I guess it should be us three first. If your guys can stay down there, Barry, just in case we need them.'

'No problem.'

'Right,' it was clear Al was trying hard to sound positive, 'let's go.'

The three men stepped over the barrier and grasped a rope each.

★

Davey Wilson arrived under his own steam just a few minutes before eleven o'clock. Jo went down to meet him in reception. She thought he looked remarkably well for someone who had been out until 4.00 a.m., as he was quick to tell her. Damon joined them in the interview room before popping out again to supply them with coffees.

'Thank you for coming in, Mr Wilson,' Jo said, when they had settled into their seats around the small table. 'You gave a good account to our colleague last night, but we'd just like you to go through it again in case thinking about it has made you remember anything else. Okay?'

'Okay. Where do you want me to start?'

'Firstly, tell us why you were out on Tuesday. You say you live in Whitefield, but at the time you were heading away from there.'

'I was staying at my girlfriend's. She lives in Tottington. If you want her address, you can check if you like.'

'Well, we'll have the address for our records but I'm sure checking your story won't be necessary. So tell us what you saw.'

'As I told the police last night, near the little park on Manchester Road next to Holy Cross, I saw this guy on the ground in the road.'

'In the road or on the pavement?' Jo asked.

'Well, sort of on the edge of the pavement, and two guys were helping him to his feet. I stopped and asked what was going on and they said he'd stepped out in front of them.'

'So they said he stepped out in front of them, but he was actually still on the pavement.'

'Well, yes.' Davey frowned. 'But I guess they could have just nudged him back onto it.'

'Possibly. Go on.'

'I asked what they were going to do and they said they knew where he lived and they'd take him home. And that's it really. I carried on to Lucy's – my girlfriend's.'

'You told our colleague that you stopped just after you'd driven off.'

'Oh, yes, that's right. Just to check that everything was okay. They were helping him into the back of the car.'

'Helping him? Not forcing him, then?'

'No, not really. He seemed a bit agitated, but you wouldn't be particularly happy, would you, if someone had knocked you down. Especially if you were pissed. I just put it down to that.' He paused and looked down at the table. 'But if he was the guy who was murdered and they did it, I guess I was wrong.'

'Well, we don't know yet if what you saw had anything to do with the murder, Mr Wilson, so don't worry about that. Can you describe the man who was knocked down?'

'No, sorry. He was being helped up with his head down. He had a jacket on with a hood which had sort of half fallen off his head.'

'You've probably seen this picture of the dead man on the news,' Jo placed a photo of Curtis Knox on the table in front of him. 'Could that have been the man on the ground?'

Davey studied the photo for a few seconds. 'Don't know. Could have been I suppose. It was dark, don't forget.'

'And what about these two?' She placed the e-fit pictures of the two men in the Lancashire Gate.

'Possibly. They had that headgear, definitely.'

'Okay, finally. did you catch a name, by any chance? When the two men were talking to each other or to the one they'd knocked down.'

'No. In fact I don't think they spoke at all except to me when I asked them what was happening.'

'Well, thank you, Mr Wilson. That's been very helpful. We'll have your girlfriend's address, if you don't mind, in case that's where we need to get in touch with you again. I hope the prospect of your early start today didn't ruin your night out.'

'Not really, although it was on my mind. What I saw, I mean, not the early start. It's kind of creepy thinking that I was seeing the start of a murder.'

'Well, as I said, we don't know that yet. Thank you again.'

Damon rose from his chair, a signal for Davey to do the same. They left the room as Jo reached for her iPhone.

★

The descent from the roadside to the stream was around sixty metres, the first fifteen of which were near-vertical. The layer of snow driven against the side of the clough gave a false impression of something substantial, but they would have had little control over that initial section without the ropes. As the slope became less sheer, they lowered themselves more slowly and halfway down came across the first of the objects littering the downward course. One high-heeled shoe, some items of clothing, a toilet bag; then the other shoe, a bottle of water, a torn shoulder bag and a number of smaller articles, including, barely visible, the corner of a phone. It was a basic model with buttons rather than a touch screen.

Matty had led the way past them to avoid disturbing the ground holding the collection and stopped briefly to alert the rest of the CSI crew to prepare to follow him down.

'Those rescue guys must have bloody good eyesight to spot that phone,' he said. 'Not sure I'd have seen it.'

'They were probably less focused on just surviving than we are,' Al said, as the three men below them came into view through the swirling whiteness. They edged their way down until all six stood together on a narrow ledge a few metres above the river. They could just about make out that the half-covered object close to the running water was a human being. The legs and torso were almost covered by snow. The stream was mostly frozen with just a narrow flow in the centre. The head was face-down, half under the water with the neck twisted at an unnatural angle. Matty led the way down, followed by the two detectives. Andy edged closer to the body and crouched down, gently brushing away the snow from the shoulders and neck.

'What the fuck?' he gasped, half to himself. 'Matty, get over here and give me a lift.'

Matty reached forward and they pulled the body from the river, carefully turning it on its back. At that moment, Andy's phone sounded with an incoming text.

★

The operations room was unusually full for a Saturday, with a number of people from both the early and late weekday shifts present. The atmosphere, however, was tense and subdued with what seemed like a sense of pending doom. To kill time, Jo had fallen back on the seemingly endless sifting of information and her text to Andy had been to appease her impatience as she waited for news of the recovery of the body. The instant callback was a surprise in itself, but the content was a major shock. She had some difficulty at first processing the information.

'A *uniform?*'

'Yes, as in uniformed officer,' Andy said.

'Not Phoebe?'

'Not unless she joined the police and had a sex change during the last twenty-four hours.'

'So who is he?'

'Good question. He's wearing sergeant rank insignia and his ID tells us he's Sergeant Shaun Milligan of South Yorkshire Police. *However*, they have no record of anyone of that name working on the force. So either they've got a shite HR department or the man's a fake. We'll know more when we've checked any cash cards and such.'

'And if he's a fake…?'

'I've not quite got my head round that yet, because there are a number of items spread around on the way down to the body, which could be Phoebe's. Including a burner phone, a bit smashed up and password-protected, which could probably tell us a lot if the SIM card isn't damaged, and what looks like bits torn off a jacket. Also a bag, which might be the one the girl at the Shoulder had with her on the twenty-second of December. Crenshaw's getting everything bagged to take back, so we could check the bag against the CCTV capture at the pub. Just hold on.'

Jo could hear Andy in conversation with someone for a few minutes before he spoke into the phone again.

'Crenshaw says there are signs that someone might have left

the scene heading east along the side of the stream. Said he can't be sure from any prints on the ground because of the snow cover, but they've found some bits of material stuck on thorns along the bank in that direction. They're bagging those as well.'

'Cause of death? Any theories yet?'

'Broken neck, almost certainly, and the mostly likely cause of that would be a fall. It starts off really steep here, almost vertical. Less of a slope at the bottom, but if you lose your footing higher up, it's not easy to see how you could get control again. The Edale gang reckon that's likely what happened. They've recovered two bodies before from close to this spot.'

'So our fake copper could have chased Phoebe down there and fallen to his death. Phoebe manages to survive and runs off. Is that what you think?'

'If the bits of material on the way down match those along the side of the stream, I'd say yes. Otherwise, someone could have thrown her stuff over the edge...'

'And forgot to let go?'

'I admit that theory doesn't explain the dead body at the bottom. And neither scenario explains how they got here.'

'Any sign of our two strays from the Snake Inn?'

'They should be here any time now. They were following a snowplough in the car but we've stopped that half a mile away, so they'll be walking the rest of the way through the snow. Serves them right.'

'That'll take the shine off Mo's shoes. How long do you think before we get everything back here? I take it forensics won't be coming out to you?'

'Crossley's call, but not likely. Anyway, Taylor's probably off somewhere auditioning for the next Bond movie.'

'Ooo! And they say that women are catty. Not jealous, are you, sergeant? Surely not afraid of competition; not with your bottomless pit of charm.'

'I'm absolutely fine, thank you, *ma'am*. Except that I've now got to get back up this fucking mountainside,' he added, half to himself.

He ended the call before Jo could respond, cursing herself for the second time in a couple of hours for allowing her mask of indifference towards him slip.

★

Detective Superintendent Mallory Jones was a picture of agitation and indecision as he prowled round his office. Jo sat on a chair in front of his desk and waited for him to run out of words.

'We can't really do much about it right now. We handed it over to Lancashire, and I know Mills is still active, but it's their accountability. So it's Crossley's call. But we've got a couple of nice people less than five miles away, waiting for some news, and just because it's not good news – well, I know it's not necessarily *bad* news – I mean, we know she's alive don't we?'

'Well, not exactly...'

'*Was* alive, then, yesterday. That's good news, isn't it? And we know she escaped and is probably still alive. I mean, she got away from the guy in the stream, didn't she, so she must be okay. Well, not *okay*, perhaps, depending on whether she got through the night.'

'But that's just...'

'Can you imagine the stink if the Wrights find out what's happened since yesterday morning with their daughter? If somebody let's something slip and the press get hold of it. I don't want them to hear about it on *The News Where You Are* this evening. I think we've got to tell the Wrights everything and risk a bollocking for standing on people's toes. We can't put an appeal out for information and possible sightings until we tell them what's happened, can we? I'd rather get it in the neck from Lancashire than risk that happening.' He sat down again opposite Jo, breathing heavily as if the rush of thoughts had taken its toll. 'What do you think, Jo?'

Jo leaned forward.

'I think we...'

'I am right in my understanding of what you told me? This guy picked up Phoebe from the Snake Inn, dressed as a uniform, which would explain why he could lure her away from the car rather than snatch her. Phoebe found out somehow and jumped ship. Or he threw her down the valley and fell down after her. Possibly went after her to make sure she hadn't survived. I am right, aren't I?'

'None of that...'

'That's what you told me.'

'Can I speak, please, sir? Just on the off chance I might have something to say.'

Mal nodded his head slowly and sighed. 'Yes, sorry, Jo. Go on.'

'None of that is *fact*. It's *all* theory. It does fit with what we do know happened, but there may be other scenarios that fit as well. Matty's initial conclusion is that the scraps of fabric along the side of the stream come from the same article of clothing as the ones snagged on the way down. So, yes, it looks like Phoebe survived the fall and got away. *If* it was Phoebe wearing it and not someone else.'

'Surely you're not suggesting...'

'That it was someone else? No, of course not, but we don't know for certain. Also, there must have been two people involved in getting her away. There had to be a vehicle involved, which was subsequently driven from the scene.'

Mal nodded again but remained silent.

'And as far as our little runaway is concerned,' Jo went on, 'whether she is still alive or not I'd put at no better than fifty-fifty. So I'm not sure what we *can* say to the Wrights, and Benny Morrison, in the way of any assurances. Or what we can say at all, in fact. Our best option, in my opinion, is to get the chopper up again as soon as possible, and carry on the search. If Phoebe is still alive, she can't have got very far away on foot from where we found the body. And as far as an appeal is concerned, the chances of anyone seeing her out there are minimal, anyway. In the meantime, we need to hope nothing gets out to the wrong person.'

Mal thought for a moment. 'What about the rescue team. Are they fully aware of where the body fits into the wider picture?'

'When they were first called in to retrieve a body, no names, no details at that stage. But they were first to spot the articles shed on the way down and were there to observe Andy's reaction when it turned out to be a cop, then *not* a cop. So they've been fully briefed and sworn to secrecy, if that's still the correct term. Big test is tonight when they're in the pub and getting pressed by their mates as to what's happened.'

Mal gave his third nod, this time with a knowing smile.

'Yes, you're right there. Let's circle the wagons here right now and make it absolutely clear that no-one speaks of this outside the station, on pain of death. Well, dismissal, anyway. That's if we're not too late already. And we should cover the late shift as well.'

'I'll do that. We should be getting everyone back here soon. I understand Johnson and Malik may even be putting in an appearance.'

'They'll wish they hadn't when I've finished with them.'

★

As Al and Andy finally hauled themselves up and on to the welcoming stability of the tarmac, they looked around to take in the changed scene around them. Several more vehicles had arrived since they had started their descent into the clough, and were now parked two abreast across the road. Thirty metres or so along the road to the east they could see two men wearing orange hi-vis jackets on the other side of the crime scene tape in agitated conversation with Eva and Mo. One of the men, the larger of the two, was waving his arms and shouting, directing most of his anger towards Mo with Eva trying to calm the situation. The confrontation was drawing a lot of attention from the police and rescue crew. Andy strode over to join the fray.

'What's going on?' he demanded, bringing the group temporarily to silence.

'Afternoon, sarge.' Mo's greeting was a little sheepish and Eva looked down at the ground.

'These gentlemen are clearing the pass and are waiting to carry on to Glossop,' she said. 'They were asking how long it will be before they can get moving again.'

Andy turned a mirthless smile on the drivers. 'That's easy. The answer is just as soon as possible.' He turned to go.

'That's not good enough,' the larger of the two men shouted after him. 'We're due to finish at half two. That's in ten minutes and we've got to get to Glossop to knock off.'

Andy turned and walked up to them, crowding their personal space so both men had to take a step backwards.

'Well, I'm sure that if we can bring back to life the poor bastard who has recently fallen to his death down there, he'll be quick to apologise for the inconvenience. In the meantime, I suggest you fuck off back to your snowplough and do a crossword or something. Oh yes, I almost forgot – thank you for your understanding and cooperation.'

He walked away, brushing the snow off his coat and trousers and shaking his boots. Eva smiled at the two drivers.

'We're all under a lot of pressure at the moment, so please forgive our sergeant's frustration. We also want to get through as soon as possible, and we'll make it clear to your supervisor that it was not your fault that…'

'I don't give a fuck about the supervisor,' the driver interrupted. 'I want to get to the pub in time for the match.' He turned to his colleague. 'Let's get back to the plough, Lenny. At least it's warm in there.'

They walked away. Eva and Mo exchanged glances and shrugged.

'Are you okay, Mo? You look a bit tense.'

'*Tense*. It's my fault she's out there. *Tense* doesn't come anywhere close. She could have frozen to death.'

Andy joined them again. 'Lost our snowmen, have we? Anyway, Crenshaw's finished and they're bagging up the body. Get back to the car and tell them they can carry on. We can all follow them into Glossop.'

★

'You've had an exciting couple of days,' Jo said. Eva was phoning in with an update as they passed through Glossop heading for the M67 link road to the M60. 'And I'm afraid it's not over yet for you guys,' she added. 'The Super wants to see you as soon as possible after you get back, which will be after your interview with me.'

'Understood, but my colleague here is planning to take all the blame. Right, Mo?'

Jo couldn't quite catch the mumbled reply, but the tone seemed to contradict Eva's statement.

'I don't think you should treat this too lightly,' Jo said, pausing to give the remark more weight. 'I believe the chopper is up again? Is that right?'

'Yes, the snow had stopped, but not for very long, and it's coming down again now. I can't help feeling that if we don't find her in the next hour or so before it's fully dark…well, I don't fancy her chances. Having said that, we've had a mysterious case of high larceny here while all this has been going on. Two ham-and-chutney sandwiches, a packet of crisps, a Snickers bar, a Yorkie and two cans of Pepsi. Taken from the cab of the snowplough, along with a flask of coffee and a hi-vis jacket.'

'Really. The driver must be a sound sleeper.'

'Drivers, actually, plural, and we assume the heist took place when they were with us complaining that we were making them late for the pub.'

'Poor lambs,' Jo said. 'So, are you saying it might have been Phoebe who took them?'

'It's possible, I guess. The pass has only just been declared open so there were no other vehicles near the plough at the time except ours, and we have an alibi. The chopper's concentrating its search in that area.'

'Are you bringing the body here or to Blackburn? Or should it be somewhere in deepest Derbyshire, or South Yorkshire? I can't get my head around who and what should be where.'

'Derbyshire agree that this is linked to Phoebe's disappearance so are happy to let it go – surprise, surprise. DI Crossley says Bury and has Jamie and pathology on standby.'

'Okay, I'll make sure Jamie's made comfortable while he's waiting for you all to arrive.'

'I thought your lovely hubby was over this weekend.'

'Postponed. So Doctor Dish can have my full attention.'

★

It was after 6.30 p.m. when Jo finally made it home. She reloaded the multifuel burner and managed to light it at the second attempt, promising herself more practice, and opened the fridge to check the dinner menu. Or, more accurately, what was available. Feeling lazy and hungry she chose a Tesco ready meal – cottage pie – and tipped the remainder of a bag of frozen peas into a Pyrex bowl. 'Busy, busy,' she said to herself, with a chuckle, whilst silently thanking Percy Spencer for inventing the microwave. She placed a dinner plate in the oven to warm and poured herself a glass of wine. As she began to pierce the film of the cottage pie, her phone pinged with an incoming text.

Hi. Getting together with the team tonight until late. Okay to phone early tomorrow. Perhaps not v early. Love you to bits. Seb xxxx

Jo read the text several times, trying hard not to find a hidden meaning within the words. Her ex-boss had always accused her of being addicted to conspiracy theories. They had laughed about it many times, but there was nothing funny if it was your own relationship under the microscope. She texted back.

No problem. Have a great time. Lol J xxx

It's just a celebration after all, she told herself. They must have got the win they needed. She frowned. So why didn't he mention it? She went through to the living room, opened her laptop and went to BBC Sport, Rugby Union, 'Scores and Fixtures'. She entered National League Two in the search box and scrolled down the list of fixtures to the 'West' section of the league. The fixture almost jumped out of the screen.

Leicester Lions v Hinckley
Postponed

Jo resisted the temptation to phone Seb straight away and congratulate him on the win, just to feel him trying to squirm his way out of that one. But her initial feeling of betrayal and confusion quickly gave way to anger, and she decided she would wait for his promised not-very-early call and mention it then, knowing anger was something she could deal with. She placed the phone on the kitchen worktop and carried on piercing the film on the cottage pie, this time holding the fork like a dagger and stabbing down very hard.

CHAPTER TWENTY-THREE

Sunday 20 January

When Jo arrived at the station at 8.30 a.m. she was surprised to find the operations room deserted. She had called ahead and spoken to DC Knapp asking her to arrange for the Sunday crew to be available for a briefing at that time. It was only when she had almost reached her office that she realised they had already gathered in the briefing room. She could see there was an expectant buzz about the group and all faces turned to her when she entered and took her seat at the table.

'Settle down, everyone,' Jo said, sensing the excitement and anticipating the disappointment. 'I'm not about to tell you anything earth-shattering. I just thought that, as much of the action was elsewhere yesterday, an update might be appropriate. All of you will know some of it and some might even know all of it. So bear with me and we'll get everyone on the same page.'

The group settled back in their seats and Jo went through the developments on the Snake Pass, and their implications in the search for Phoebe.

'So, the popular scenario is that she was taken from the Snake Inn car park on her way back to Bury with DCs Malik and Johnson, escaped her abductors and somehow survived a steep descent down the side of a valley, which one of them did *not* survive. The theft of the food and coat from the snowplough on Saturday afternoon suggests she may have survived until then at least. But we have no idea yet, of course, whether she has survived a second night, if indeed she did get through the first one and she was the snowplough thief.

'So, Curtis Knox. We were all hoping when Phoebe turned herself in that she would be able to shed light on the activities at Easy Rider and in doing so establish for certain the link to the Knox murder. Whilst we have strong suspicions of this link, we can't be certain and, as such, are not in a position to go too far with our investigations into the company. I'm talking about raiding it, as I'm sure you know. The press would love a story about the police coming down hard on a company whose main purpose is to enrich the lives of the sick and elderly.

'So, it's back to our hit-list for the time being at least.' She pointed to the incident board and the group turned to view it. 'Not in order of priority, because all are important.' She read from the list. 'How many of the drivers have more than one phone, more than one car, property or bank account? And any suspicious activity on social media? None of which is easy to check. So we need to carry on with that. Does anyone want to impress me before we get back to our desks?' Dylis raised her hand. 'Yes, Dylis,'

'Been checking social media along with DC Lawson. All the drivers are friends with each other on Facebook, as you'd probably expect. Most of their posts are shared stuff and the usual pictures of meals and such, and lads together in a club or at a match. But there are a few that finish with one or two words or numbers, presumably times, that don't seem to be part of the message. And every one of those has been liked by all the others very soon after they were posted. All of the ones with times are on weekends when they wouldn't be meeting up or crossing paths at work.'

'That was quick,' Jo said. 'I thought you'd have to go through Facebook's police liaison team and all that. I assume the posts are part of their private listing.'

'Not so, ma'am. They are shared to all. Facebook are providing us with information much more readily these days when a crime or suspicion of a crime is involved. So, could be the drivers think there'd be no point trying to hide stuff. In fact, it would draw attention to them whereas they're more likely to get buried in the general posts.'

'That makes sense,' Jo said. 'Examples?'

'We've put a list together.' She clicked on an icon on her laptop then turned to the large screen mounted high on the end wall. 'The chart shows a list of the actual posts, the times posted and the time of the final "like" from the group. They were all posted out of working hours, late Fridays and weekends. So, the first one, which is a picture of three guys in a pub and some comments about a football game, ends with "23.30". It was posted on Saturday the fifteenth of December at 11.46 in the morning, and the last one of the group to "like" the post was Phoebe, in fact, at 12.03 pm. So we figured it could have been a message that they were all waiting for. Confirmation of a meeting time, perhaps.'

Jo nodded. 'Very interesting. Although didn't Reeves say that his drivers socialised together a lot? Could it be confirming the start of a booze-up or party?'

'Possibly, but didn't he also say some, like Knox, didn't mix with the rest of them? And presumably Phoebe didn't go on booze-ups with them, even though she acknowledged the post.'

'Okay, and what about some of the words: Silver, Rock, Castle. What's the link there?'

'All names of streets in Bury town centre. So they could be venues for meetings.'

'And ED. What's that? We've got a few of those.'

'Five in fact, all added to the end of a follow-up post after the time. Could be an abbreviation, or a name.'

Jo was silent in thought for a few moments before speaking. 'Right, Dylis. Good stuff. You've given us food for thought. Jodi's coming in today so pick it up with her. Anything else for now? Yes, Glynn?'

'Just a reminder that we said we'd start tailing the drivers tomorrow to check any second cars or second homes.'

'All sorted. Uniforms are covering that – not *in* uniform, of course, and in unmarked cars. But they're the experts, so the right people. And for those who might not be up to speed with this yet, we'll be tailing each of the drivers when they finish work over the next three days – two on Monday, two Tuesday and two Wednesday. All the drivers' registered addresses and private vehicles are, shall we say, at the modest end of the spectrum. This is an attempt to find out if they might be living and driving more towards the other end. Following each for just one day is optimistic to say the least, but if we can catch just *one*, it might give us a lead to the others over time.'

She rose from her chair. 'Right, Thank you for some really good work. Let's get back to it.'

★

Jodi arrived with Mo at just after nine o'clock. Jo stepped out of her office as they settled at their workstations. Jodi was wearing her traditional 'weekend' gear of tight-fitting denims and a loose off-the-shoulder top which gave the impression of a small girl of twelve trying to look eighteen. Mo had dressed down to the extent of wearing a Hawaiian-patterned shirt under his suit. His shoes gleamed as brightly as ever.

'Hi, you two. Didn't expect to see you today, Mo. Didn't the boss put you on detention or something?'

Mo snorted a laugh. 'Not exactly, but, like you, he wasn't well pleased. I'm glad corporal punishment has been banned, let's put it that way. I think you and the Super got the message across. I'm really very sorry…'

'I know, enough said for now. Why are you here anyway?'

'Trying to find out more about this guy who sent me over the Snake. I've checked with National Highways records over the past couple of days. There was never any reports of closures on the M1 and M62, but there *was* a warning about the other cross-Pennine routes – Woodhead and Snake. So it's highly likely, with hindsight, that he was setting us up. My fault, though…' he held up his hands, '…I should have checked.'

'Yes, you should. It does suggest you were set up, but I'm not sure how you're going to find him, especially on a Sunday, unless Sheffield have got the right people in.'

'South Yorkshire are doing their own checks to try and ID him, so they might have something for me. Anyway, that's why I'm here, and if I have to make any decisions, ma'am, be assured I'll check with you first.'

'DS Mills, not me. But certainly if we can get him it would be a step forward, if not in finding Phoebe, certainly in finding more about the web she's got herself caught in.'

She turned to Jodi. 'You and I, DC Lawson, are about to tangle with the dangerous Mr Chadwick again if we can track him down. Dylis brought me up to date with what you've found on Facebook. Let's check if the dates of any of the posts, particularly those stating a time followed by "ED", coincide with any police operation or activity, either on the date of the post or during the following few days.'

'Will do, ma'am. Can I ask why?'

'Just a hunch. I'll tell you more later.'

'I'd be interested to know why as well, ma'am,' Mo put in.

'All in good time, DC Malik. I think you should stick with finding your rogue meteorologist for now.'

She checked her watch. 'Nine-twenty-five. Right, Jodi, for now, get your laptop and let's see if we can catch Jacko before he goes to church. You might want to put a jacket on over that top.'

★

'Is this really necessary? Couldn't it wait until tomorrow?'

Denzel "Jacko" Chadwick was not the same cool bundle of charm as he was at their first meeting. He blinked several times after opening the door, adjusting his eyes to the brightness, and it was obvious that their calling had woken him up. He was barefooted, and the crinkled state of his jeans and tee shirt suggested he had slept in them.

'This is a murder investigation, Mr Chadwick,' Jo said. 'The brutal killing of your friend. I thought you'd be pleased that we're working overtime to find, to use your own words, the bastards that did this to Knoxy. Can we come in?'

Denzel Chadwick sighed and waved them into the hall, then into a sitting room on the left. 'Yes, you're quite right. Sorry, just got a bit of a hangover from last night. A fucking *big* hangover, in fact. Haven't been in long to be honest. Girlfriend's still asleep, so can you keep your voices down.'

'We only shout when someone's not cooperating with us, Mr Chadwick, so I'm sure there'll be no need for that today.' She smiled at him. 'You remember DC Lawson?'

'Yes, of course. Would you like a coffee or something?'

'No, we're fine, thank you?'

'Please sit down.' They each took a separate armchair, leaving the small two-seater sofa to their host. 'So how can I help you?'

'A couple of developments, Mr Chadwick...'

'Please, call me Jacko, then I'll know who you're talking to.' He gave a little laugh. 'And what should I call you?'

'Detective Inspector Carter.'

Jacko shrugged and smiled. 'Fair enough. Go on.'

'We have a witness on the night of the murder,' Jo said.

Jacko's eyes and mouth opened wide as he seemed to struggle to process the information. He closed his mouth again, without speaking.

'We knew you'd be pleased,' Jo went on, 'but not to the point of being speechless.'

'Just took me by surprise. That's great news, isn't it?'

'It could be if it leads anywhere.'

Jacko frowned. 'Leads anywhere? You mean it wasn't someone witnessing the actual murder?'

'No, but we believe it may have been just prior to that. A driver passing along Manchester Road saw two people bungling someone into a car. It was shortly after Mr Knox left you and directly on his route home. The driver's description seems to match the one you gave us of the two guys in the pub.'

Jacko shook his head. 'So what's the big news? I said already it was the two guys in the pub who killed him, didn't I?' His piercing eyes seemed to go even darker and Jo sensed again the anger inside him. 'Just exactly what are you doing here? I must have been on the fucking Metro when that happened.' He was close to shouting.

Jo put her forefinger over her lips and pointed upwards with her other hand.

'Please, Mr Chadwick. The girlfriend.'

Jacko glared at her for a few more seconds then laughed, the anger seeming to leave him as suddenly as it had arrived.

'Look, just get to the point, will you, so I can get back to bed.'

'Well, we find it hard to believe that the same two guys just accidentally came across him as they were driving home. Much more likely, we think, that they knew where he lived. Or, if not where he lived, where he would be walking shortly after they'd left the two of you outside the pub. What do you think?'

Jacko shrugged again. 'I don't have a clue. Knocker said he didn't know them. I guess if it *was* the same two guys and they *did* have a car and it was parked near where they were heading when they left us, it's quite possible they'd see him. If they were heading towards Manchester, they'd *definitely* see him.'

'Strange though isn't it, if they were heading towards Manchester at that time. The landlord said he thought they hadn't been drinking before they arrived in the pub. So they get thrown out of the Lancashire without finishing a drink and then just leave town. You'd expect they'd just go to another pub, wouldn't you?'

Jo sensed the anger was rising again. 'Look, perhaps that wasn't Knocker, perhaps they weren't the same two guys; perhaps it was a couple of good Samaritans giving someone a lift home. What's this all about, for fuck's sake. What are you suggesting?'

'Absolutely nothing, Mr Chadwick... yet. But we'd just like you to clear something up before we go.' She nodded to Jodi. 'DC Lawson.'

Jodi switched on her laptop and logged on to the downloaded CCTV coverage on Haymarket Street on the night of the murder. She leaned forward and turned it so Jacko could see the screen.

'This is you and Knocker talking near the Metro station,' Jodi said, 'just after you'd been thrown out of the pub. The other two guys have just walked off down Moss Street. Then Mr Knox sets off walking towards the town hall and you walk down to the entrance of the station.' She paused the sequence. 'I'll skip forward a bit and pause it again. This is you back in the same place a few minutes later looking down Haymarket Street, presumably at Mr Knox. Right?'

'Well, yes, obviously,' Jacko said. 'I already told you I wanted to check he wasn't being followed. What's your point?'

Jodi enlarged the image so that Jacko filled the screen.

'Can you tell us what you were doing at that point, apart from watching Jacko?' Jo asked.

'Just *standing* there, for fuck's sake. What else?'

'Not making a phone call?'

Jacko hesitated and screwed his eyes up, peering at the screen. 'Yes,' he said. 'Phoned her-upstairs to tell her I was on my way home and I'd call for her at her mate's.'

'So that *is* you making a phone call?'

'Yes, you can check that out.'

'We did. And you did make a call to your girlfriend.'

'So, what...?'

'At twenty-six minutes past ten that evening.'

'So why are we discussing this? Is it a slow crime day in Bury or something? Well, that's good after what's happened...'

'Check the time on the screen, Mr Chadwick,' Jodi interrupted, holding the laptop closer to him.

Jacko leaned forward and screwed his eyes up again.

'Can't make it out.'

'Let me help you; it says 22.29.48, nearly four minutes after you made the call to your girlfriend.'

Jacko shrugged. 'Well one of those times is obviously wrong, isn't it? I only made the one call and you say you've confirmed that. What's the big deal?'

'We've verified both times, Mr Chadwick. It appears you made *two* calls.'

Jacko sprang to his feet, eyes blazing. 'I've fucking had enough of this,' he shouted, lifting up the laptop as if he was going to smash it onto the floor. He slammed it closed and all but threw it back at Jodi, 'You push your way in here on a Sunday morning throwing accusations around. *I* phoned *you*, remember, with information trying to help you. This is why people don't go to the police. They'll fucking turn on you if they can't find the *real* bad guys. So, if you're not going to arrest me on some trumped-up charge, then fuck off out of my face. Detective Inspector fucking Carter.'

Jodi was visibly shaken and clutched the laptop to her chest. Jo remained unmoved and waited for the tirade to subside. She sighed and got slowly to her feet.

'Very well, Mr Chadwick. Thank you for your time, and I think you have my number from our last meeting. If you can throw some light on that second call, please get in touch. We'll see ourselves out.'

Jacko flopped back down on the sofa as they went through to the hall. As they reached the front door, a voice came from the top of the stairs.

'What the fuck's going on down there?'

'Whatever it was, it's over now,' Jo said. 'We're sorry to wake you up.'

They closed the front door and walked the few metres to their car. As they were about to get in they heard a shout behind them.

'Ladies, ladies, ladies.'

Jacko was walking towards them, waving his arms and still in his bare feet on the snow-covered pavement.

'I am so, so sorry. Please forgive me. I made the call to Gemma while I was in the station, before I went out again to check on Knocker. I had my phone out because I was going to call him to see if he was okay and tell him to phone me when he got home. Anyway, when he did seem okay, I thought better of it. Again, I'm sorry for blowing up like that. Lot on my mind right now, including what happened to Knocker.'

'Well, thank you for clearing that up, Mr Chadwick – Jacko. That's all we wanted. Now you'd better get back inside before you get frostbite.'

They pulled away along Bury Road, heading back to the station.

'Well, that was interesting,' Jo said.

'And just a bit scary.' Jodi gave a little shudder. 'Did you believe what he said about not making the second call?'

'Did you?'

'I'd have to say no.'

'Me neither. And did you notice the look on his face when we told him we'd found a witness?'

'He looked shocked, if that's what you mean, but I couldn't really read him beyond that.'

Jo nodded her head without replying. They drove in silence for a while.

'For a moment back there,' Jodi said, 'I really thought you believed him.'

'Well, it won't do any harm if he thinks that as well.'

Jodi turned onto Manchester Road and drove past the small park on the right, almost certainly the last place Curtis Knox was seen alive, except by the men who killed him.

★

The quad bike slid and scrambled off the main road through the farm gate and onto the moor. The farmer struggled to control it in the deep snow that reached over halfway up its wheels. Behind it, the trailer, weighed down with a full load of hay bales, responded as if it had some sort of propulsion of its own working against the vehicle towing it. For several kilometres he had suffered the blaring horns and lewd gestures of motorists desperate to get past him on a road reduced to not much more than half its normal width by the snow piled high at either side. The relief at leaving the angry cavalcade was quickly snuffed out by his wrestling match with the bike and trailer, one he was in danger of losing. Eventually, he managed to get the two vehicles aligned and aimed at his destination a few hundred metres away. The sheep, he noticed, seemed very excited about something. More stressed than excited, in fact, so it was unlikely to be just the arrival of more food. He pulled the trailer across the front of the open field shelter and hauled the first two bales from the load. Grasping one in each hand by the binding twine, he entered the makeshift building.

At first sight, he thought she was dead. Her eyes were open but staring icily upwards at the roof of the shelter. Then, as he drew closer, the eyes flickered briefly in his direction. Whether she actually saw him or not, he couldn't tell, because they went back to their upward stare with no sign of recognition or understanding. He dropped to his knees beside her, pulling his phone from his coat pocket.

'Wake up, lass, wake up,' he said, gently shaking her, then into the phone. 'Police and ambulance, *really* quick. I've got a young woman here, looks like she's freezing to death; she's in a bad way.' He gave the location and more details as prompted, then got to his feet.

The woman was covered in hay which was wet with snow blown in by the wind. He brushed it off her and removed his coat, laying it over her and tucking it under her freezing body, talking all the time, trying to get her attention. She remained unresponsive and only the occasional movement of her eyes was evidence of her being alive. He remembered reading that the best way to warm someone with hypothermia was by using your own body heat directly against their skin. He decided he couldn't bring himself to do that, so he lay at her side with his arms around her, pulling her close.

The ambulance from Glossop arrived within ten minutes of his call, preceded a couple of minutes earlier by two police cars, that parked in the centre of the carriageway a hundred metres apart, closing the Snake road again in both directions. One officer from each scrambled up to the barn as quickly as the deep snow would allow, followed by two paramedics from the ambulance carrying a stretcher and medical bags. Above them, a helicopter circled the scene.

The farmer released her and got to his feet.

'I hope she's okay,' he said. 'I can't get her to say anything.'

'What's your name?' The first paramedic gave him a reassuring smile.

'Seth. Seth Bennett. I wasn't sure what to do; I...'

'You did great, Seth. I'm Tracy, this is Luke. We'll take over now. Would you be able to get a few of those bales stacked up to keep the wind off her? That would really help.'

Seth and the two uniformed officers, who introduced themselves as Constables Keely Marsden and Greg Pearce from Derbyshire constabulary, heaved a further half-dozen bales off the trailer to form a protective wall next to where she lay. After checking her pulse and covering her head, Tracy and Luke removed her wet outer clothing and wrapped her snugly in a fleece blanket, and then with a foil sheet. With a little help from Keely, they lifted her onto the stretcher. In spite of the medics talking to her throughout, the woman failed to respond.

On the road below, another police vehicle arrived followed by a doctor in an NHS-liveried SUV. The four uniformed officers in the car split into pairs to assist at the roadblocks and the doctor, an elderly man who looked somewhat daunted by the prospect of the climb ahead of him, set off slowly towards them. Entering the barn, he looked across at Tracy and raised his eyebrows with the unspoken question.

Tracy shook her head. 'She may be suffering from dehydration as well as hypothermia. We've been trying to get her to drink something, but she won't take it. What she needs is a fast trip to hospital.'

Dr Percival introduced himself and knelt down to examine the patient, confirming the urgent need to get her specialist help.

'Do we know who she is?' he asked.

The two police officers exchanged a look and shook their heads without speaking.

'Right, well, Tameside is closest and best by road from here I think,' the doctor said. 'By the time the air ambulance finds a place to land we can be halfway there and get her right to the door.' He turned to Seth. 'If we can quickly make a soft base in the trailer, that would be the best way to get her to the ambulance. She's not suffered any trauma, except for a few grazes and bruising so a few gentle bumps won't harm her further. God knows what she could have been doing out here. I guess that's for you guys to work out.' He clapped his hands. 'Right, chop chop! Let's get going and get her hooked up in the ambulance.'

DC Pearce walked a few paces away out of earshot of the group and took out his phone. 'It's her,' he said, when his call was answered. 'Our runaway.'

*

Jo spent the afternoon going over the case notes covering both Phoebe Wright's disappearance and Curtis Knox's murder, and noting the clear dovetailing of the two files. There was a real danger of duplication, but also that key points may be lost because of an assumption they were being followed up by the other side. She checked Andy's report following his call to the NHS Transport Section regarding their sanitation standards for contractors' vehicles. She added the main points to her notebook, reading them aloud as she did so.

'All contract vehicles used for patient transfer – weekly clean. Three-monthly inspection without notice by NHSTS.

'Standards high and clearly defined. One warning then termination of contract without notice.

'Easy Rider record v good. No inspection issues/no complaints to date.'

She closed the book and sighed. It did not explain why Phoebe's vehicle seemed to have been singled out for special retreatment but it did confirm Reeves's claim, and Mo's opinion, that there were stringent demands for their securing and retaining the contract. There was no mention of any progress towards an inspection of Knox's vehicle.

At least, not in the report. Jodi knocked and peered round the door.

'Excuse me, ma'am. Just to let you know, forensics have got the go-ahead to check out Knocker's ambulance. They're examining it in situ tomorrow then bringing it in.'

'Are you my fairy godmother, Jodi? I'm just reading here, this very minute, that we've made no progress on that and you've just made my wish come true. What made Reeves change his mind?'

'Don't know. I just called to follow it up and explained, again, that refusal to allow us access could be construed as him having something to hide. Same conversation as before, but this time he just said okay. He even offered to bring it in for us.'

'Which no doubt means he's had enough time to make sure it's been deep-cleaned, like Phoebe's.' She paused and frowned. 'We do have a record of which vehicle each driver uses, don't we?'

'Yes, why?'

'Let's make sure we check the number plate against the engine number. Eight identical ambulances; easy to switch plates and any personal effects. Just want to be certain it's Knox's we're checking.'

'Will do, ma'am.'

As Jodi closed the door, Jo's iPhone sounded an incoming call. 'Andy?'

'Oh, I'm flattered. You've got me on your contacts list.'

'Come on, what?'

'Phoebe's been found. Thought you'd like to know.'

Jo stood up quickly, sending her chair rolling away from her on its castors. 'Alive?'

'Barely. A farmer found her in a livestock field shelter not far from where the body was discovered. She must have spent two nights out there, so even barely alive is a big plus. She's in intensive care at Tameside Hospital. She's suffering from hypothermia and dehydration, but she's also in shock, and that's what they're most worried about. They said it's as if she's just shut down.'

'Can she be moved? Can we bring her home?'

'Not sure. I've told you all I know.'

'So, where are you now?'

'At home, though not actually *my* home. I've spoken to Crossley and he suggested I get over there without him to save time. I thought I might take DC Johnson with me, in a *work* capacity, of course.'

'Of course, except Phoebe seems to have had a bad experience of Eva.'

'Good opportunity to lay the ghost. That's if we get the chance. I believe there's no guarantee she'll get through this.'

'Okay, I guess it's your call anyway – yours and Crossley's. Keep me posted. I'll contact the Super and he can decide what to say to her parents and Morrison. He's been straining at the leash to tell them something. And we'll liaise with Crossley to get a press statement together, perhaps for tomorrow.'

She ended the call, stepped out of her office and clapped her hands to get the team's attention.

'I have some news. DS Mills has just phoned to say Phoebe has been found, alive, on the moor near where our phantom policeman met his end.' She held up her hands to quell the spontaneous cheers and clapping. 'It's not all good news, I'm afraid. She's in intensive care in Tameside Hospital, suffering from hypothermia and dehydration and is in shock. She's in a very bad way and they cannot say whether she will make it or not. We must pray that she does, and of course I'll keep you up to date as we hear more. Jodi and Damon, can you contact Kirsty and Mo.'

She went back into her office and phoned her boss.

★

The car slid to a halt in front of the terraced house in Crest Lane. The street was untreated, with the snow compacted by the passage of numerous vehicles. The roadside gutters were piled high where people had cleared the latest downfall from the pavement in front of their doors. Benny's front step and lower part of the door were still covered.

'It doesn't look like he's been out today,' Damon said. 'Not out of the front door, anyway.'

'No, it doesn't bode well as to what state he's in. Even so, I think we got the long straw here. I don't envy the Super and Jodi telling the Wrights about the past three days of their daughter's life.'

They got out of the car and stepped carefully up to the door. There was no knocker or bell. Jo hammered with her knuckles and stepped back. There was no answer.

'Perhaps he's away,' Damon said. 'That would explain…'

'Who is it?' An angry voice from above.

The upstairs sash window had been lifted open and Benny glared down at them. He was bleary-eyed and his hair was ruffled and matted.

'Police, Mr Morrison. DI Carter and DC D'Arcy.'

'What now? You just woke me up.'

'It's five o'clock in the afternoon, Mr Morrison. What are you doing in bed anyway? No matter, we have news of Phoebe.'

'Phoebe?' He spoke as if he wasn't quite sure who they meant.

'Yes, Phoebe. Your girlfriend?'

Benny shook his head hard, as if to clear it of sleep. His expression changed from anger to sudden realisation.

'*Phoebe.* What? Nothing bad, please God?'

'That's much better. Can we come in, please?'

The head disappeared, hitting the frame of the raised window on its way in. They could hear whispered voices before he pulled the window down, then the sound of Benny racing down the stairs. Jo and Damon exchanged glances with raised, questioning eyebrows, the door opened and Benny stood before them in a hastily donned dressing-gown. His eyes were wide and anxious.

'Is she...?' He faltered.

'Alive? Yes, she is. Shall we go inside?' She nodded towards the room where they'd met on two previous occasions.

'Oh, thank God for that. Yes, please go through. Can I get you a coffee or something?'

'Don't you want to hear about Phoebe first?'

'Yes, of course.'

They took their seats in the armchairs. Benny leaned forward, twisting his hands together.

'Phoebe gave herself up to the police in Sheffield on Friday...' Jo began.

'*Friday?* So why has it taken you two days...?'

'Let me finish, Mr Morrison, then I'll answer any questions you have. We sent two officers straight away to bring her back. We had decided to speak with her before we informed you and her parents. On the way back from Sheffield at the Snake Inn on the Snake Pass, she absconded again. That was mid-afternoon and although we began a search straight away, it soon became impossible in the dark.'

'How did she...?'

Jo held up a hand. 'Please, not yet. We began to search for her again at first light yesterday. I'm sure you can imagine what conditions were like in the area at that time. The road closed to traffic from soon after she disappeared, driving snow, high winds and freezing temperatures. Even so, although we didn't find her, there was evidence that she had survived the night and was still alive well into the afternoon.'

'Why are you telling me all this, now that she's been found alive?'

'Because I want you to understand why we didn't inform you two days ago. We couldn't risk telling you that she was alive when there was a serious risk she wouldn't *stay* alive. And it's not all good news, Mr Morrison. Phoebe was found a few hours ago by a farmer, who had gone to feed his sheep. She was in a field shelter suffering from hypothermia and dehydration. We believe she may have spent two nights there. She is also in shock, which seems to be what is worrying them most at the hospital.'

'Hospital?'

'She's being treated in the intensive care unit at Tameside and Glossop Integrated Care in Ashton-under-Lyme. At the moment, they can't say for certain if she will pull through. I'm sorry the message can't be more positive.'

They sat in silence for a few moments, interrupted by a thump on the ceiling from the bedroom above. They all looked up. Benny sighed and dropped his head into his hands. He remained still for a long time and when he looked up there were tears in his eyes and he wore an expression of guilt.

'An old flame, rekindled last night and this morning. It was four weeks ago yesterday when Phoebe ran away from me. Last week, I decided, whether Phoebe was alive or not, we were finished. If she was alive, and really loved me, surely she wouldn't be putting me through all this pain and uncertainty. And friends were always telling me that it couldn't last. She was too young and dazzling for an older, boring guy like me. I guess I always believed that anyway, but...'

'We're not judging you, Benny. You don't have to explain anything to us.'

'I know, but I want you to understand. So I called Janis, the woman upstairs. We used to be an item for a while, immediately after I split with Jill. She's a teacher at the same college as me. Textiles, not that that's relevant. We went for a drink after college on Friday, and I called her yesterday morning. We went out for a meal last night and...' He sighed. 'I understand why you didn't let me know as soon as you knew Phoebe was alive, but what's really ironic is that if you had, I would never have made that phone call to Janis yesterday.'

*

Detective Superintendent Jones and DC Lawson had already returned from their meeting with Phoebe's parents by the time Jo and Damon got back to the station. They were sipping coffee in the Super's office and looking a little bruised from their encounter.

'Can't blame them,' Mal said. 'I said to you Jo, didn't I, what will they say when we tell them it was two days ago when she came forward. Well, they had a lot to say, especially Mrs Wright, who seems to be very much the dominant force. But it wasn't that so much as their demanding to know how their daughter managed to... escape, I think is how they put it, when she had just handed herself in. I explained, of course, that she wasn't seen as a risk *because* she had handed herself in, as opposed to having being caught or found. She accused me of hiding behind – what did she call it, Jodi?'

'Fucking semantics... sir.'

'That's right. She went on to say that if Phoebe doesn't pull through, she'll be taking it to the highest authority and suing the police for manslaughter. What else, Jodi?'

'The press, sir.'

'Oh, yes. They're going to rubbish us as widely as possible in the media. Double centre-page spread in the *Guardian*, that sort of thing. So, I hope she does survive for *everyone's* sake.' He paused. 'Especially Phoebe's, of course.'

'I assume they're going to see her?' Jo asked.

'Yes, I've arranged a car to take them to Ashton. They should be there by now.'

'And I assume she's under police guard?'

Mal nodded. 'And there's a nurse in the room with her all the time checking the monitors. It might be best if they keep Morrison away from the room while the Wrights are in with her. I doubt if they let more than two in at a time anyway.'

'It seems it won't be a problem. Morrison didn't give any indication that he wanted to see her. He seems to have moved on with his love life. We caught him in a compromising position, or, more accurately, a compromising location. Upstairs in bed with a colleague from work at five in the afternoon.'

Mal shook his head. 'Can't really blame him, I guess. She's been gone a month and never thought to call him once. Add that to the fact that she's been lying to him about her absences since they got together, and there's little reason he should trust her, is there?'

They sat in silence for a few moments. Mal checked his watch.

'Twelve minutes past six. DS Mills is staying at the hospital. I've asked him to contact me and you, Jo, if Phoebe's condition changes, as well as DI Crossley. Is it still snowing outside?'

'Not when we came in,' Jo said. 'Sky was clearing.'

'Great, just ice, then.' He got to his feet. 'Let's all slide home while we still can.'

Jo went back to her office and checked the time. It was 6.15 and it occurred to her that Seb had not yet called. He had said 'not very early' in his text, but surely late afternoon went far beyond that definition. She checked for any missed calls or texts, but there were none. Going to her 'Recents' list, she was about to press his name when something made her change her mind. She picked up the receiver of her desk phone and dialled his number. It rang for a long time before the call was answered.

'Hello?' A woman's voice, and one which sounded familiar.

Jo remained silent, biting her bottom lip and fighting the thoughts that flooded her mind. The woman spoke again, this time turned away from the phone.

'Sebby, *Sebby*.'

Jo slammed the phone back into its cradle. She felt tears welling in her eyes and cursed herself for reacting in that way. Reaching into her bag for a tissue, she spotted the small pink carton.

'My God,' she said. 'What have I done?'

CHAPTER TWENTY-FOUR

Monday 21 January

Jo's iPhone rang out at 6.25 a.m. She swore at it, as always, as she reached to silence the alarm, only to discover it was an incoming call. Seeing the name on the screen, she let it ring until it stopped then checked through the missed calls. There had been eight from Seb, the first at 7.40 p.m. yesterday evening, the last, excluding this latest one, at 2.37 a.m. that morning. She also noticed one from Seb's parents around midnight and cursed herself for not checking the source of each call she had chosen to ignore. It was too early to phone her in-laws, but not too early to bite the bullet.

She picked up the phone and almost dropped it as it sounded. The alarm this time. She switched it off and called her husband, pleased to hear him answer after a single ring.

'Jo!'

'Good morning,' she said. 'Long time, no hear.'

'What's happened? Are you okay? I've been calling you all night.'

'But not yesterday.'

'I can explain…'

'Okay, but first tell me, did you win the match?'

'No, we didn't, but neither did they. Look…'

'A draw, then, was it?'

'No, it was postponed at the last minute. Well, an hour before kick-off, which is why, with all the team already there, we decided to make a night of it. Look, Jo, I'm not sure what's wrong, but …'

'Well, let's start with your "not-very-early" phone call to me yesterday. Just checked my missed calls this morning and the first one was seven-forty *p.m.*'

'And I've checked my missed calls as well, and you didn't phone at all, so I'm...'

'I did phone, actually... *Sebby*.'

There was silence for a few moments.

'So it was you. I didn't recognise the number.'

'And you weren't in possession of the phone, anyway, were you? It's a good job your friend was there to answer.'

'Well, you're absolutely right about that, as it happens.'

'Do explain.'

'I lost my phone – the previous day, as it turned out. It was a pretty heavy night with the guys. Well, heavy for me, anyway; it seems I'm way out of practice. I got home, early hours, and couldn't find my phone. I assumed I'd left it at the pub so went back and spent most of yesterday – well, from about midday, anyway, searching the place. Both bars, toilets, even the kitchen although I couldn't remember going in there. Then I remembered the last time I had it was when I texted you about half-six on Saturday, so I went back to the ground to check there. The woman you heard was the groundsman's wife, Karen. She had to open up for me and stayed with me to lock up afterwards. So we looked for the phone together. Well, I say together – I was checking out the Gents when my phone rang and Karen was in the locker room where the phone was in one of the waste bins. So, you're right, it was lucky she was there when you rang or we may never have found it.' He paused. 'Anything else you want to accuse me of before we go any further?'

'It's a great story, Sebby. Let's leave it as just that for now.'

'You don't believe me? Oh, come on, Jo. How could you think anything like that? I thought everything was just about perfect between us. I'm sorry I didn't call, but I've been going out of my mind this last twelve hours wondering what was wrong. If you really don't feel you can trust me, perhaps we need to decide whether this is right for both of us. We can talk it through calmly on Friday.'

'Weather and fixtures permitting, do you mean?' She paused. 'Delete that, Seb. I'm just knackered, and a bit stressed. We've got our missing girl back but she's in such a bad way that we may yet end up with a body. And the stink that will follow if she doesn't make it after turning herself in to the police. Well, it doesn't bear thinking about, does it?'

'It wasn't your fault, Jo, remember that. They took you off her case.'

'It involved my team, and that's the same thing, or near as makes no difference.' She was silent for a few moments. 'Look, could you call Roy and Bella for me. They phoned at around midnight – I assume that was after you checked with them if they'd heard from me. They'll be wondering why I didn't answer the call. Tell them I'm sorry and that my phone was switched off or on silent or something. I'm going round for a meal with them tonight and it would be best if you spoke to them beforehand. I'll phone you when I get back.'

'Okay.' He paused. 'Are we good, Jo?' His voice was not much above a whisper.

'Yes, but perhaps we should have that talk. Love you.'

'Love you, too.'

She ended the call. Sitting on the edge of the bed, she reflected on her fifteen years as a detective and how they had conditioned her to recognise a lie when she heard one. Until now it had just been a vague uneasiness about the difference in ages and the fact that circumstances did not lend themselves to fulfilling Seb's wish for a family. But now, it was all too real, because she knew that Seb was not telling the truth. She had never met the wife of the groundsman – or the man himself for that matter – but she was certain she had heard the woman's voice before.

★

Her second call of the day was incoming and reached her as she was parking at the station a little before eight o'clock. It was DI Crossley with an update from Andy.

'There's no change in her condition, but I guess it's good news that she made it through the night. They said when they took her in that the next twenty-four hours would be critical, and she's got through half that time already. They're not saying when they may be able to move her, assuming they *will* be able to at some point, but it's unlikely to be today.'

'Is she conscious?' Jo asked.

'She keeps coming round, but then quickly goes back to sleep.

Andy and DC Johnson have taken it in turns through the night outside her room, ready to speak to her when she's fully awake and *compos mentis*. Which has been frowned upon by the nursing staff and Mr and Mrs Wright, apparently, who believe, of course, that they merely want to ask her where she's been and why she ran away in the first place. Andy's not in a position to tell them it's more than that, of course.' He paused. 'I'm wondering whether I should send someone over to relieve them.'

'I can't really spare anyone off the murder enquiry, Al. In fact, I could do with DC Johnson back here. I'm sure Andy and Eva will be fine staying over there for at least the rest of today.' She smiled to herself.

'I guess so. By the way, I've been thinking how these two cases seem to have merged into one. I'm not trying to offload Phoebe, but perhaps you should be driving both of them. What do you think?'

'I've been thinking exactly the same. About the merging, I mean, not who leads it. But with all the working staff here in Bury, it makes sense. My briefings are already covering both Knox *and* Phoebe. Perhaps we should wait until Phoebe comes round and see what she tells us.'

'Okay, let's keep each other updated on both in the meantime.'

Jo ended the call and entered the station, making her way to her office. The full crew were already in the operations room. She said a general 'Good Morning', then stopped at DC Malik's work station.

'Hi, Mo. You okay?'

'Not really. Can't get my head round the fact that Phoebe was perfectly alright until I got involved, and now she might actually die. I don't know how I'll deal with that if it happens.'

Jo was unsure how to respond, knowing it wouldn't be just guilt he would have to deal with. 'She seems to be holding up so far,' she said. 'Apparently, the next ten hours or so will be key. Did you get anywhere with your search for the errant weather forecaster?'

'No. Didn't expect to really. I think I was just fooling myself into believing I was doing something useful.'

'Well, there's plenty of useful things you can do now. We need to brief the uniform guys on their surveillance of the Easy Drivers. Plan was, as you know, to pick up the first two on our list later today when they're leaving the depot for home. But if we could extend that to a full day's...'

'Sorry, ma'am, but they'd need at least three cars for each target to do that. And we did only request four men for a couple of hours. I can't see them having the resources...'

'Not if we *ask* for them, I agree. But if they thought it was their idea...'

Mo frowned. 'I'm not sure...'

'If we said something like, "thanks, guys, although this is a real long shot. Not sure what else we can do..." Let them think we've run out of ideas. Give them a chance to come up with something. They rarely miss an opportunity to get one up on CID.'

Mo shrugged. 'Okay, but I think that's a longer shot than finding out about any second homes.'

'Give it a try, anyway.'

She went into her office, discarding her shoulder bag, laptop case and coat, and left again in search of a coffee. Maddie followed her back in clutching a notebook.

'Excuse me, ma'am. Dylis has come up with something more on Facebook.'

'Come in, Maddie. Take a seat.'

'You asked us to check the dates of the posts that included the initials ED against police operations. Well, this is interesting. Starting at the most recent, on Sunday sixteenth of December at eleven in the morning, someone posted, "23.30 ED". We missed that one the first time we checked and that was the day before we had the abortive raid in Bank Street, following a tip-off of a drugs pick-up. So working backwards from there, on Saturday fifteenth of December, the day before, one of the *drivers* posted "23.30", the one we flagged up before. Same time but without the ED; and late on the previous day, Friday the fourteenth, the same driver added "Silver" to the end of a post.'

Jo frowned. 'Excuse my legendary lack of local knowledge, but what's the significance of Silver in this context?'

'Bank Street is off Silver Street.'

Jo opened her eyes wide. 'Right. So, it's possible that the first two messages could have been setting up the pick, and the third cancelled it, our new friend ED stepping in to save a hit. If indeed that *is* somebody's name. What do you think?'

'Well, I hadn't got that far working it out, but yes, it makes sense.'

'Can we ID who did the third post?'

'Not yet, ma'am, and probably not at all. Most likely a false name, no personal details. He seems to have taken a lot of care to cover his tracks.'

'Or *her* tracks,' Jo said. 'Which driver posted the first two?'

'That's another thing, ma'am. It was Curtis Knox.'

★

The doctor stepped out of the treatment room into the corridor. Philip and Helen Wright were sitting side by side just outside, with Andy and Eva at a discreet distance a few metres away. The doctor nodded towards the two police officers, then addressed the parents with a relaxed smile.

'Mr and Mrs Wright, could I see you in my office, please? Follow me.'

'Excuse me.' Andy had got to his feet.

'In a moment,' the doctor said, without looking back. He opened a door to a room off the corridor and waved them inside.

'Some news, I guess.' Eva said as Andy sat down again with a gentle curse.

'About time.' He checked his watch. 'Two fifteen. Let's hope it means they can take her home. I could do with a full night in a proper bed. Preferably yours.'

Eva gave a little giggle. 'Those hospital beds aren't all that comfortable are they? Could have been worse; we could have ended up four-in-a-bed with the Wrights.'

'Now you're talking. Bring it on.'

The Wrights re-emerged and resumed their seats without making eye contact with Andy and Eva. A few minutes later the doctor appeared and beckoned the detectives to join him.

'Please, be seated,' he said. 'I'm Doctor Barnes, head of ICU. It seems our girl has turned the corner. She's regained full consciousness and although in theory she's not out of the woods, I think she's on the mend. I'm recommending that she is well enough to be transferred to a hospital nearer home where they can continue monitoring her for a further forty-eight hours.'

'So when...?' Andy began.

Dr Barnes held up a hand. 'I strongly advise that she is not questioned until tomorrow at the earliest. I understand the circumstances, she has been missing for a month and you must be keen to know where and why, but she's not going anywhere, and I'm sure you can wait another day.'

'Actually, Doc, you *don't* understand the circumstances,' Andy said. 'We do want to ask her where she's been and why she ran away, but we have other questions which relate to serious crime, and it's imperative that we speak to her as soon as possible, and definitely today. So if you can prepare her for that...'

'As I said, she is not out of the woods and putting her under any pressure right now could affect her full recovery. I'm sorry, but I can't allow that.'

Andy leaned forward.

'When, then?' Eva cut across the exchange. 'I'm sure you're aware that time is of the essence when investigating serious crime. Trails go cold very quickly, leading unnecessarily to people getting hurt – and worse.'

Dr Barnes softened his tone towards Eva. 'And you are suggesting this is such a case?'

'It's impossible to say whether it is or not; we would only know that in retrospect. Our job at this stage is to limit that risk.'

The doctor sighed, looking from one to the other.

'I'm going to let her parents in now to talk to her. Then we'll see how she is in an hour's time. Okay?'

'Okay,' Eva said. 'Although I'm not sure that facing up to her mum will be any less stressful than talking to us.'

The doctor snorted a laugh. 'You may be right. By the way, Phoebe mentioned something about a partner. Kenny, is it?'

'Benny. Benny Morrison.'

'Has he shown up yet? I think she's expecting to see him as well.'

'I believe he's busy right now,' Andy said.

The doctor shrugged. 'I see. Pity, I think she would like to see him.' He got to his feet. 'Well, now she's awake and we have a plan, there's no point in your hanging round in the corridor. I suggest you take advantage of our excellent cafeteria and come back in an hour's time.'

Seated in the excellent cafeteria, Andy made a call to Jo with an update on Phoebe's condition and proposed return home.

'Fairfield would be best,' he said. 'We'll need a private room and twenty-four-hour security if she is linked to a trafficking ring.'

'If they are moving her back today, it may be better to wait to interview her here. She'll be more settled being nearer home and perhaps more cooperative. Not sure it's a good idea to have Eva in with her, anyway, in case she still thinks… well, whatever she was thinking when she ran away from her. No disrespect to Eva and I'm sure she'll understand.'

'Point taken, but as you said recently, my call.'

'Yours and Crossley's; who, by the way, thinks Bury should perhaps take back full responsibility for both Phoebe and Knox. He feels, like I do, that they are now part of the same investigation.' Andy remained silent. 'I did say this a few days ago, if you remember.' Still no response. 'By the way, did you enjoy the western night at the Bridgewater Hall?'

'Does the Super know Crossley is trying to bail out?'

'Nothing's been discussed yet. Why, don't tell me you have a problem with that?'

'Ask me again if it happens. *Ma'am.*'

He ended the call and cursed, less gently this time.

'What was that about?'

'Seems I'm back under Carter.'

She grabbed his hand across the table.

'And I'm back under you – well, some of the time anyway. And I'm not complaining.'

Andy smiled despite himself and pulled his hand away.

'Behave yourself. We're tough cops; we can't be seen holding hands. Come on, let's go back and sit outside Phoebe's room. Apply a bit of silent pressure.'

★

Jo studied the incident board which stretched along the full length of one wall of the briefing room adjoining the open-plan CID work area. The white, magnetic writing board displayed all the features and characters of the case, major and minor, including street plans, maps, location photographs, mugshots, along with several metres of string connecting related items and an anthology of text in a variety of handwriting adding context and significance where necessary. She smiled at the picture of Benny Morrison, taken at the time of his arrest after the fight at the White Horse, his face battered and bruised.

The latest addition was an Ordnance Survey map of the Peak District, folded into a landscape format section, to show the length of the Snake Pass from the Woodlands Valley, just east of the Snake Inn, to Glossop. The scene of forty-eight hours of high drama from the time Phoebe disappeared from the inn's carpark, through what she assumed were two nights in the freezing outdoors, to right now, in an ambulance with a howling police escort delivering her back closer to her loved ones. Her loved ones? She wondered whether she should still be including Benny on that list.

Andy had phoned again to say that he and Eva were following the convoy of three vehicles all the way to Fairfield Hospital where a room, medical staff, and a couple of uniformed officers awaited her. They had left Ashton-under-Lyne shortly after four o'clock up to which time they had not yet spoken to the patient. He was at pains to point out that this was not a case of following Jo's advice, but because the doctor had dug his heels in. He was hoping to have better luck with the doctor in charge at their destination. She checked her watch – a quarter past five. They'd be there by now.

Jo continued to ponder the mass of information in front of her. In the past, she had secured arrests and convictions with far less. Just one link in the chain seemed to be missing to pull all the porous theories and circumstantial evidence together into a watertight case.

The door opened and Maddie looked in.

'Just to remind you, ma'am, You said you wanted to see Dylis and me together about the social media posts. We've got some more information.'

'Right, let's go into my office. Mine's a white, no sugar.'

Maddie giggled. 'I think I know that by now, ma'am.'

When the three women had settled themselves round Jo's desk, Maddie opened a file on her laptop and placed it where they could all see the screen.

'Following on from what you said this morning, I've managed to get some information on police raids over the past seven months. We've had some successful ones during that period but also some other cock-ups; five, in fact, including the one in December. But this is really interesting, on all five of those occasions there has been the same or similar messages preceding the op, the final post always ending in ED.'

'So which drivers…?'

'Just coming to that, ma'am. All five postings were by Curtis Knox.'

Jo frowned and drummed her fingers on the desk. She leaned back in her chair.

'Now that's *really* interesting. And all these mini-messages were added to longer posts?'

'Longer posts with some image or other – a photograph usually.'

'Good work, you two. Go back further and see if you can ID a date when this pattern started. If we can link that to when any one of the current drivers started at Easy Rider, we might have even more.'

The two women left the office and Jo leaned back in her chair and looked up at the ceiling, or beyond, in gratitude, to somewhere higher. Perhaps Knocker's demise had less to do with his wanting to leave and more about perceived betrayal. It was just possible that the missing link had begun to be forged.

★

The snow had held off for the whole of the day, but with the clear skies the temperature had dropped below zero and the compacted snow on pavements and side-roads had made for some treacherous surfaces. Jo's ambitious plan for a moonlit, albeit torch-assisted, evening walk from her house through Burr's Country Park and along the River Irwell to her in-laws in Summerseat, had survived just a few hesitant steps along Woodhill Road. She had been invited there for a meal and persuaded herself that her main reason for abandoning the adventure was that Roy would insist on driving her home afterwards rather than her take a taxi. That would mean he couldn't have a drink and that wouldn't be fair, would it?

Bella answered her knock on the door and hugged her closely, holding her for a long time as if Jo had returned from the dead.

'We were so worried,' Bella said, her voice breaking a little.

'And I am so sorry,' Jo said, suddenly realising she was not aware of what reason Seb had given for the unanswered call. Not that it mattered, Bella took her coat and waved her through to the living room. Seb's sister, Sally, had been there for the afternoon and stayed for the meal. Jo hadn't seen her since their walk on New Year's day, but her bump was now just about showing and her hand constantly went to her stomach as if checking it was still there.

'It moved for the first time a few days ago,' she said. 'Took me by surprise; wasn't expecting to feel anything for a week or two yet. God, don't say it's going to be hyperactive like its dad.'

'So when is it due? July, isn't it?'

'July twentieth, counting forty weeks from my last period. So I'm only sixteen weeks gone. If it's moving like this now, it'll be doing circuit training by the end.'

Jo laughed. 'You're not checking if it's a boy or girl, then.'

'Opinion is divided on that point and also variable. I don't like referring to it as "it" and Jonno insists that we should always say "the baby" if we don't want to know the sex in advance. Like, "the baby is moving", "when the baby comes". He'd like to know, and I blow hot and cold on the idea. And I know it's become a sort of cliché, but as long as it's… I mean, as long as the *baby's*… okay, neither of us really care.'

After a delightful meal, and a baby-dominated chat, during which Roy complained about being outnumbered and generally excluded from the conversation, Jo said her grateful goodnight with a hug for each of them and drove home. It was nine-thirty when she arrived back. She took out her phone to call the station for an update, then thought better of it. Dylis or one of the late crew would contact her, as they had before, if anything significant turned up and needed her attention. Instead she went straight to bed, snuggling under the duvet. Then, taking her phone again, and with the conversation with Sally at the front of her mind, she called her husband.

CHAPTER TWENTY-FIVE

Tuesday 22 January

Andy Mills and Al Crossley arrived at Fairfield Hospital in separate cars but at the same time: 9.25 a.m. Andy's mood had not improved since the previous day, when he had been denied an interview with the patient twice within a few hours, first in Glossop and then on their arrival at the hospital on Rochdale Old Road. It had ended in a noisy exchange of words leading to an embarrassing confrontation with hospital security who had been called by a staff nurse unaware of Andy's status and purpose.

They were met in the waiting room of the ICU by the same nurse, who warmly greeted Al whilst ignoring his colleague.

'She's had a very restless night,' said the nurse, whose badge told them her name was Annie, 'which is a little surprising as we would expect someone in her situation to sleep long and well. That's normally how the body makes its recovery. She's managed to eat something, but we're continuing to feed her intravenously for the time being. She's now sleeping, although still fitfully.'

She spoke as if she was reading a bulletin from a printed sheet.

'I'll get Dr Lei, but I'm sure she'll say Phoebe's not well enough to talk yet. I'm sure *you* understand.' She addressed the remark to Al.

'Let's hear what the doctor says, eh, Annie?' Al gave her a friendly smile. 'Obviously we will do nothing that will slow her recovery, but we do need to speak to her as soon as possible.'

'Yes, we were made very loudly aware of that yesterday when she arrived,' Annie said, still not looking at Andy. 'I'll go and get the doctor. Please wait here.'

She left the room and Andy leaned in to Al.

'She's making it pretty obvious that she fancies me, don't you think? All that pretending to be mad at me. Who does she think she's fooling?'

'Well, me for a start.' Al gave a little laugh. 'Look, go easy, for God's sake. Making a contest of it means someone's got to lose, and it'll almost certainly be us.'

Annie returned. 'Follow me please.'

She led them to the room where Andy's anger had run amok the previous evening. The same doctor rose to her feet as they entered.

'Good morning, gentlemen. I'm Dr Lei, as half of you knows. Are we going to behave today or is this round two?'

Melissa Lei was a petite, pretty woman in her early thirties, of Far-Eastern ancestry. Her smile was friendly and welcoming although her intense deep-brown eyes added an element of steel to her expression.

Andy spread his arms. 'Listen, doc, I'm really sorry about that. Just frustrated, I guess. So close to getting answers to some *really* important questions.'

'Apology accepted. Do sit down.' She waved her arm towards the two chairs across the desk from hers. 'But understand, I will not be bullied out of doing my job, which is to ensure that Phoebe makes a full recovery. And I'm sure you're aware that I can't just say, "okay, go talk to her." *She's* got to feel well enough to talk to you, and to *want* to talk to you.'

'I'm sorry, Dr Lei,' Al said, 'but whereas we accept that she must be well enough to speak to us, I'm afraid at some point she will *have* to talk to us whether she likes it or not. It's not a case of wanting to.'

The doctor bristled a little. 'I don't want to get into semantics...'

'What if we arrest her?' Andy asked.

'I don't understand,' the doctor said, her expression clearly supporting the statement. 'Is that what you do to runaways? Treat them as criminals.'

'No, we don't.' Andy said. 'Not to runaways.'

'Well, then...'

'Tell me, doc, why do you think we have two big guys in blue uniforms taking turns outside Pheobe's room?'

Dr Lei shrugged. 'To make sure she doesn't disappear again... I assume.'

'You assume wrong. I understand you've got wires attached and tubes inserted in places where Phoebe probably didn't even know she *had* places. Unlikely she'll get far trailing that lot, don't you think?'

'What DS Mills means,' Al said, 'is that the two police officers are there for her protection. We are not able to say much at this stage, but Phoebe is part of an investigation into a serious crime – a *very* serious crime. Until we know more we're not at liberty to speculate and we're satisfied she'll be safe here in your care, but we must speak with her as soon as possible. This is not just about her running away.'

'I explained this to the doctor in Glossop,' Andy said.

Dr Lei remained silent for a few moments, looking from one to the other.

'I'll check on her condition when she wakes up and see what we can do. In the meantime, please make yourself comfortable in the café.'

'That's *exactly* what the doctor in Glossop said. I hope your coffee's better than theirs.'

★

Jo logged on and scrolled through the case file, clicking on to the forensics report on Curtis Knox's vehicle. Before going through it, she thought about the uncomfortable conversation she had had with Seb the previous night. It had lasted less than twenty minutes, much shorter than their usual calls and in spite of the same words being used, the same jokes being shared, there was something different. Jo's mind was a confusion of thoughts. The contentment of being part of the Carter family, reinforced by the pleasure of last night's visit, set against her belief that Seb was into something that would fundamentally change their relationship. She wished she could just accept what Seb had told her was the truth. After all, his story was feasible and fitted all the facts of the case. Circumstantial evidence; that's all she had against him, and not much of that. It may well turn out that she was the only one hiding a secret.

She gave her full attention now to Jamie Taylor's report, summarising the headline points in her notebook. The check on the engine number and registration plate confirmed that it was

Curtis's ambulance they were examining. Jamie had included a sarcastic comment about there being no evidence of the engine being recently swapped with another vehicle. The examination in situ, before it was forensically recovered, showed the vehicle had been 'deep cleaned' as Jamie put it. 'as if the driver had died of a deadly infectious disease.' The next few paragraphs described the standard procedure for vehicle inspection that comprised, more or less, returning it to its component parts. Jamie had saved the highlight for the end.

In the storage area beneath the passenger compartment, wedged between the rear offside wheel arch and the main chassis, was a single 9 x 19mm Parabellum bullet, the kind typically used in MP5s. It would have remained undetected without removal of the wheel arch, which explains why it was not disturbed by the cleaning process. It is unusual to find a single bullet anywhere as they are loaded via a magazine and not individually. Other than it having been deliberately put there, it is difficult to understand how it could have got into that place.

Furthermore, there is trace evidence of gun oil in the storage area. However, this type of oil has a wide range of other uses. It could, for example, have been used to lubricate the wheels of an invalid chair. So its presence alone does not suggest that the vehicle has been used for transporting arms. On the balance of probability, it would not lead me to that conclusion, although the presence of the bullet suggests it should not be dismissed.

Jo sat back in her chair and stretched her arms above her head, hands clasped together.

'Curiouser and curiouser,' she said, questions rattling around in her mind. Why would anybody plant a bullet in one of the ambulances, if Jamie was right in saying it was deliberately placed there? And why somewhere it was unlikely to be found? Was somebody trying to set Knox up? And if so, who? Surely not one of the other drivers or Reeves. That would only focus unwanted attention on the whole company. All her instincts told her this was an important step, but in which direction? And how could a bullet in someone else's vehicle possibly connect to the young woman in intensive care a few miles away?

Her thoughts were interrupted by the noisy arrival of Al

Crossley and DS Mills. Andy dropped onto his chair, slamming the palms of his hands down onto the worktop. Then, with a loud 'Fuck, fuck, fuck', he got to his feet again and stormed out of the operations room.

Al joined Jo in her office.

'Things not going exactly to plan for our sergeant?' she asked.

'No, and half the problem *is* our sergeant,' Al replied. 'He seems either determined to wind up every NHS employee he comes into contact with, or he's so obsessed with interviewing Miss Wright he just can't help himself. Neither of which is going to get us talking to her any time soon.'

'God, along with Mo, that's two obsessed with our blonde bombshell. Unless you are as well, Al, in which case it's three.'

Al laughed. 'Not me. Oh, and by the way, I took a call from your boss while I was at the hospital. He wants to see us both, that's you and me, at twelve o'clock.' He checked his watch. 'That's in… thirteen minutes.'

'Did he say what it's about?'

'No, but he asked if I was with Andy, and when I told him I was, he sort of cut the call short, like he didn't want him to hear.'

Jo frowned. 'I wonder if he's having the same thoughts about who leads the investigations… or, investigation, singular.'

'We'll find out very soon, no doubt.'

★

It was 12.20 p.m. before Mal was ready to start the meeting. He asked Jo and Al, separately, to bring him up to date with the search for Knox's killer and progress with Phoebe's recovery. When they finished, he leaned back in his chair.

'So, to summarise, we are no closer to finding the killer or to our runaway's explanation for her disappearance.' He held up his hands as both Jo and Al leaned forward. 'That's not a criticism, just a summary of what you've just told me. And I'm concerned that we may miss something by seeing these as separate cases.'

Jo and Al exchanged glances and smiled.

'What?' Mal looked from one to the other. 'You two got a secret?'

'No, sir,' Jo said. 'It's exactly what DI Crossley and I have been discussing recently. Yesterday, in fact.'

Mal spread his hands. 'So... thoughts?'

'I believe Jo should lead both as a single investigation,' Al said. 'It makes sense for Bury to take it on, or *back* on, as this is where all the work and case knowledge sits. I'll happily continue to liaise. I'm sure my boss would want that, anyway.'

'Jo?' Mal turned to his DI.

'I agree, and as soon as we get to talk to Phoebe, if she cooperates, then I think it's going to show an obvious link. Either that or I'll have to review my policy of not believing in coincidences.'

'Okay, so let's do it. Perhaps you should get your team together right away, Jo, and you and Al tell them the new arrangement.'

'I think it may surprise them to discover they've been working on separate cases, anyway. Just one thing, though...'

'DS Mills?' Mal offered.

'The very same,' Jo said. 'Our relationship has improved since he's been working with Al, and this could return it to where we were before, especially as the first thing I'll be telling him is that he is *not* going to interview Phoebe. I can handle that bit, but given he seems to be more comfortable with both of you, then...'

'It might be best if the change of leadership came from me and Al.' Mal nodded. 'In fact, let's do it right now.' He smiled at Jo and nodded towards the door. 'DI Carter, go get our man.'

Jo left and went down to the operations room. Andy's workstation was unoccupied.

'Jodi, where's DS Mills?'

DC Lawson looked a little uncomfortable.

'He's left for the hospital, ma'am.'

'Hospital?'

'Fairfield. A call came through to say Phoebe was awake and seemed well enough to talk.'

'And he just went? On his own?'

'He took Eva with him. She said he should let you know, but he sort of glared at her and then she went with him.' She gave a weak little smile. 'Don't like telling tales, ma'am.'

'You're not, Jodi. You're just answering questions.'

She turned and hurried back to the Super's office. She burst through the door, the two men looking past her expecting to see Andy.

'He's gone to the hospital. Got a call to say Phoebe was okay and he took off with DC Johnson.'

Al scrambled for his mobile and checked his messages.

'Shit. I got a text ten minutes ago to say to phone the hospital. Andy must have got the same one. Why would he shoot off without letting us know?'

'Why indeed,' Jo said. 'Seems DC Johnson said he should let us know, but… well, she went along with him, anyway. Look, from what Al says, we really don't want him barging in there. He seems hell-bent on forcing the truth out of her.'

'At least DC Johnson's there. That should…' Mal said.

'Normally, yes,' Jo interrupted, 'but remember, sir if our theory's right, Phoebe ran away from DC Johnson and DC Malik on the Snake. If she hasn't worked out yet that they're the good guys, seeing Eva again might set her back a bit.'

'Right,' Mal looked from one to the other, settling on DI Crossley. 'Al, you contact Andy and tell him to wait for you. I suggest you both go and decide on the way who speaks to Phoebe, but I think Jo's right; definitely not Mills.'

*

Al drove the five kilometres to Fairfield as if they were heading for a fire, and failing with repeated attempts on his hands-free to reach Andy, the calls going straight to voicemail. In the end Jo called Eva who answered in an anxious voice.

'Can you put DS Mills on, Eva? We need to speak to him urgently.'

'Sorry, ma'am, but he's gone in to see Phoebe and…'

'What, by himself?'

'Yes, ma'am. He said it would be better if just one of us went in so we didn't overwhelm her … or something. Shall I go and get him to speak to you?'

'No, we're just pulling up at the hospital now. We'll be with you in less than two minutes.'

They abandoned the car on a double yellow line close to the main entrance. They raced into the building and up two flights of stairs to the ICU, drawing some anxious looks from staff and visitors. Nurses pushing wheelchairs and guiding stretcher trolleys moved quickly out of the way. A number of the nursing staff called out to them to be careful, one challenging them to stop. Eva was clearly very agitated and looked relieved to see them when they arrived at the unit's reception area.

'Just along...' She turned to direct them.

'I know where she is,' Al interrupted, dashing past her with Jo close behind.

A uniformed policeman rose to his feet from a chair close to the door of the private room as they approached.

'Who's in there?' Al asked.

'Just the DS, sir, and Phoebe, of course. Is anything...?'

Jo had already pushed open the door and Al followed her in. Andy was standing at the side of the bed, holding a pillow. He looked round, his eyes darkening almost to black.

'What the fuck...?'

'What the hell are you doing?' Jo demanded.

'I'm talking to Phoebe.'

'And the pillow?'

'Oh, for fuck's sake, I'm helping her get more comfortable. She'd slipped down and I was just... What the hell's going on?'

'Andy, a word please,' Al's voice was loaded with authority.

Andy looked from one to the other, then down at the pillow in his hand. He thrust it hard against Jo then pushed past her and stormed out of the room. Al followed him out and the door closed behind them. Jo stood in silence clutching the pillow to her chest, breathing heavily and wondering if the last few moments had destroyed any chance of a meaningful working relationship with her sergeant in the future, and surprised herself by realising that she actually cared.

It took a few moments for her to remember she was not alone in the room. She looked across at the patient, who did look rather uncomfortable and in need of being propped up. In spite of her pallor and strained features, and with her golden blonde hair pulled back from her face in a ponytail, which lay on the pillow beside her, Phoebe Wright looked beautiful. Which made Jo wonder again why she would give up a promising chance of fame for the job she was doing now. Or *was* doing until a few weeks ago.

'Hi,' Jo said, with a wide smile. 'I'm Detective Inspector Carter.'

'Hi.' Phoebe's voice was faint but steady. 'What was that about?'

'Oh, nothing really. It's just that we have a rule that two people should be present with anyone we interview.'

'Andy explained that. Trying not to… swamp me, I think he said. He seems nice.'

So it's 'Andy', Jo thought. He hadn't wasted any time making a connection, or perhaps just putting her off her guard.

'And really fit, as well.' Phoebe gave a little laugh. 'Or aren't you allowed to comment on that?'

Jo laughed. 'Oh, yes. We're allowed.'

'So, what do you think? Fit or not?'

'I think you're right. Really fit.'

They both laughed.

'Listen, could you just help me sit up a bit? Andy was just going to when you…'

'Yes, sure,' Jo said, feeling more than a little foolish. She lifted her and placed the pillow behind her. 'That okay?'

'Yes thanks.'

'So, are you ready to talk to us, Phoebe? You're going to have to very soon.'

The expression on Phoebe's face changed to a fearful, hunted look, and her eyes moved from side to side as if checking there was no-one else in the room.

'I… I've got nothing to tell you,' she said, her voice shaking a little now. 'Except, I'm sorry for all the trouble I've caused. And the anxiety.' She swallowed and her eyes filled with tears. 'Benny's not been to see me yet. Not even left a message. I don't think he'll ever forgive me.' She began to sob.

Jo pulled a chair close to her bedside and took her hand.

'Perhaps he's just hurt. You know, you not getting in touch at all. But if you explain why you ran away and where you've been, then maybe he'll understand.'

'It was because of the arguments, with my parents and with Benny. I just got fed up, needed a break.' Jo said nothing. 'That's all it was.'

Jo shook her head. 'I don't believe you, Phoebe. I think you're scared of something.' She paused. 'But we need to do this properly, when you're ready to tell us the truth, *all* the truth, and when there are two of us in attendance. But please don't tell us you were just running away from your parents and boyfriend. I'm afraid that won't wash at all.'

While they were talking, Jo could hear raised voices outside.

'I'm going to leave you now. I understand you had a restless night. Try and get some sleep and someone will be here to talk to you in the morning. But please, be prepared to tell us the truth, because it will be the only way to draw a line under this episode.' She squeezed her hand. 'Bye for now.'

Jo left the room, closing the door behind her, to discover the raised voices were not those of Al and Andy, as she expected, but a male nurse and Benny Morrison. Standing alongside the couple, and towering over them, was the on-duty police constable, looking as though he was ready to break up a fight. Benny caught sight of Jo and spread his arms in relief.

'Detective Inspector, thank goodness. I'm trying to see Phoebe, but this guy won't let me.'

'Visiting time is between four and five for intensive care patients,' the nurse said. 'No exceptions.'

'I've got to be back to the college for a tutorial at four o'clock,' Benny insisted.

'I'm sorry, Benny,' Jo said, 'but I have no jurisdiction here. Hospital rules apply. What I will say...' she turned to the nurse '... from what Phoebe has just told me in there, seeing Mr Morrison might help her recovery. She is very anxious about the fact that he has not been to see her so far. I'll leave you to decide whether that is worth making an exception.' She turned back to Benny with a hard stare. 'That assumes, of course, that you are not here to give her some bad news.'

'No, no, definitely not,' Benny said. 'That's all been taken care of. I really must see her. What will she think of me?'

The nurse hesitated then addressed the policeman. 'Don't let him through that door.'

He hurried off along the corridor.

★

Al and Eva were waiting for her in reception. Andy was conspicuous by his absence. The DI was looking decidedly anxious.

'Just stretching his legs and cooling off,' Al answered the unspoken question.

Jo nodded, then turned to Eva. 'You might want to check he's okay.'

'Yes, ma'am.' Eva looked less than enthusiastic at the prospect. Jo waited until she had left.

'What ...?' she started to ask.

'I think we may have been a bit hasty,' Al interrupted. 'According to DS Mills, he seemed to have won her confidence and they had been having a nice friendly chat. What did the patient have to say?'

'Pretty much the same thing.' She sighed. 'As you said earlier, Andy is his own worst enemy. You find – well, *I* find – I'm always examining his motives for whatever he's doing. Just seeing him standing over Phoebe holding that pillow. I wondered...'

'Surely to God you didn't think he was going to harm her?' Al spluttered in disbelief.

'Well, I...'

'Why on earth would he do that? He's been relentless in the search for her. It's not surprising he's so keen to interview her, although there's no excuse for the way he went about trying. Setting us against the nursing staff and going it alone. God knows what he expected to achieve by that. Nothing she told him would mean anything if she changed her story later. But, Christ, Jo – go on, tell me – why would he want to harm her?'

Jo shook her head, wanting to share the thoughts inside it and knowing she couldn't. Not yet.

★

The two DIs drove back to the station in silence. Jo was grateful for the fact that Andy and Eva were in a separate vehicle. And whereas she always believed in tackling awkward issues at the earliest opportunity, she was not sure whether right now would be the best time to tell the sergeant of his new chain of command, even though he was half-expecting it.

When they arrived back, ahead of the other two, she went

straight into her office, picking up DC Malik on the way and giving her an excuse for not entering the potential cauldron with the Super and DI Crossley. This was not at all like her, she thought, running away from a confrontation, but at least her need to talk with Mo was genuine.

'So, detective, how did it go with the uniforms and the tailing of our easy riders?'

'As I thought, ma'am,' Mo replied, 'they'd only commit to what we'd agreed beforehand. Couple of hours at the end of the drivers' shift. Tried your idea of asking for advice, but no response. Looked at me as if I was mad, like I must be out of my depth or something.'

Jo shook her head. 'And their report? Can I see it, please?'

Mo looked uncomfortable. 'Well, it's not really a report, ma'am, just verbal feedback to me about what happened. One guy went straight home to his address in Breightmet and stayed there. The other to the Wellington pub on Bolton Road. He was still inside at the end of the two hours.'

'And they just drove away leaving him in there?'

'That's what they were asked to do, ma'am. Follow them for two hours.'

'Well, I want a *report*, Detective Constable. Not a few casual spoken words implying we're wasting their time. This is part of a murder investigation, for Christ's sake. I'll expect them each to have added a written account of their first burdensome two hours to the case file by tomorrow morning, along with the reports of tonight's watch. And some constructive remarks might look good when the Super and *his* boss dip into it to check where we're up to. Okay?'

'Yes, ma'am. They won't be happy, but…'

'*I'm* not fucking happy, DC Malik, and that's much more important to me than how *they* feel. You can tell them that as well.' She sighed. 'Have you seen the forensic report on Knox's vehicle? No? Well, while you put a bomb up our uniformed friends' collective arsehole, I'll round up the gang and we'll all share it together.'

They left the office, Mo scurrying off to deliver the news of his boss's displeasure and Jo addressing the room in general, still devoid of DS Mills. She noted that the office being used by Al Crossley was also empty.

'Briefing room in five – no, three – minutes.'

She strode through the operations room and took a seat at the end of the long table. Within a minute and a half, the full group had joined her, mostly seated, the last few standing around the perimeter.

'Right, DC Malik will be joining us shortly, but so we're all on the same page, a couple of updates from me plus anything more you have to share. Firstly, our surveillance of the Easy Rider drivers last night yielded nothing. One straight home, one straight to the pub and still there two hours later. So short of a possible drink-driving hit, which would have blown the whole surveillance plan, nothing in it for us. Secondly, Phoebe has recovered enough to talk, but is telling us that she simply ran away because of her being fed up with her parents and Mr Morrison. I think I speak for everyone when I say I don't believe her. More interesting is the forensic report…'

She paused as Mo entered the room and joined those standing against the wall.

'I was just about to say, DC Malik, that the forensic report on Knox's vehicle has revealed something of interest. You can read the report in full on the case file, of course, but a few highlights. The ambulance had been cleaned to the point of being almost disinfected. Even so, traces of gun oil were found in the storage compartment. Also, and this is the really interesting bit, a nine-millimetre Parabellum bullet was found stuck between the wheel arch and the chassis. Dr Taylor believes it must have been deliberately placed there but, like me, has no idea why. So,' she spread her arms, 'I open it up to the floor. Any thoughts, let me know.' She turned to Mo. 'Anything more from our followers last night?'

'Nothing, ma'am, except the full report will be on the file this afternoon.'

'Maddie, anything more from Facebook? That was really good work, by the way.'

'Thank you, ma'am. We've gone back another twelve months from the seven months we'd checked so far. The earliest cluster of messages we found was in February last year, eleven months ago. We could find nothing before that. Two of the drivers joined Easy Rider around that time, both in January. A guy called Rob Challinor, and Phoebe Wright. We can go even further back if you like, ma'am, but …'

'No, not if there was nothing for... what... eight months before that.'

'Just one other thing, ma'am. During that period of eleven months, in addition to the five instances where there was a third message posted ending in ED, there were thirteen instances of just the two messages with place and time.'

'Which means?'

'Well, one conclusion would be they only had to call off five out of eighteen. Which could mean the other thirteen went ahead as planned.'

Jo nodded. 'So we could have an informant on each side. Someone tipping the police off about a pick-up, and someone on our side, this ED, perhaps, warning them that the police know about it. Whoever "them" are. Can we follow up on Challinor. I'd like to know everything about him before, especially, and since he started at Easy Rider. Let's give that top priority over the next twenty-four hours, because I think we're getting close to paying them a visit, *en masse*, with search warrants and forensics.'

★

Jo checked her watch. Nearly 9.20 p.m. Ten minutes to phoning Seb. Her laptop was open in front of her and she had been seated at their dining table trawling through the case file and recapping on CCTV capture for the best part of two hours without a break. In truth, it was mostly pretence, having fled – that's how it felt – *fled* the station at a little after six in order to avoid getting into a confrontation with Andy, and possibly Al and the Super as well. She convinced herself that she just wanted some quiet time to collect her thoughts after the latest developments – and to decide how to proceed with the interview with Phoebe tomorrow. Or, perhaps, *failed* to convince herself. Nothing that had passed by on the screen in front of her had added any facts or theories to what she already knew and surmised.

It was the back of her mind that had been most active, wrestling with what she was going to tell her husband, if anything, in ten – now five – minutes' time.

CHAPTER TWENTY-SIX

Wednesday 23 January

Jo sat across the desk from Mal thinking that this is what a disciplinary hearing must feel like. The closest she had been to one in the past was following the incident Andy Mills had referred to at the start of their hostilities. The deaths of the Enderby family, who had absconded and drowned, tragically, just hours before their eight-year-old son was due to be questioned about his involvement in a fatal shooting. Back then, the subsequent interview, carried out by her immediate boss, DCI David Gerrard, had been relatively gentle, and loaded with empathy and understanding. On this occasion, her boss's frustration was spilling over into direct accusation.

'This is not going to work, DI Carter, if you automatically assume the worst of every move Andy makes.'

Jo was stung by his use of her title and the sergeant's first name. Symbolic, she thought, of where the superintendent's loyalties lay. She felt the anger rising within her.

'I thought my main job here was to think the worst of *everybody's* every move ... sir. I'm not sure if a *carte blanche* benefit-of-the-doubt approach would work. In fact, I'm sure that it wouldn't.'

Mal glared at her. 'I'm not sure what you're driving at, detective.'

'Well, how about this, sir, if you'll bear with me. Over the past eight months or so, the number of successful hits on drug drops in the Bury area has been – I guess you know.' Jo paused, and waited out the silence.

'Well, not exactly...'

'*Zero*,' Jo said. 'But the team has recently unearthed evidence, or at least a strong suggestion, that social media has been used to set up drug drops in and around Bury; a total of eighteen in the past twelve months. During that time...'

Mal held up his hands. 'This is important information, DI Carter, and I want to hear the full story, and soon. But right now it sounds like an attempt to deflect the purpose...'

'If you hear me out, sir, I guarantee it is no such thing. However, it's your meeting. Far be it from me to...' She sighed and leaned back in the chair.

Mal slammed both hands down onto his desk.

'Is this belligerence because you haven't had a coffee, DI Carter? How remiss of me. But I am totally pissed off with yours and DS Mills's petty squabbles, and I told him so yesterday afternoon just before you scurried off home. It was my intention to have this meeting with you then, so we could start afresh this morning on the comparatively minor issue of a murder enquiry. So can we deal with one thing at a time.'

He pressed a button on his desk phone and Lucy materialised in the doorway.

'Sir?'

'For God's sake, get DI Carter a coffee.'

'Yes, sir, and you?'

Mal sighed. 'And me.'

'I am not deflecting the course of this meeting, sir,' Jo said, after Lucy had left. 'It appears I may have been wrong in interpreting DS Mills's motives yesterday at the hospital, but...'

'*May* have been wrong?'

'Yes, *may* have been wrong. I am trying to explain here the mitigation, given what we have recently uncovered, so you will understand, or *may* understand, the reason for my action. Sir.'

Lucy entered with the two coffees, placing them on the desk between them.

'Thanks, Lucy,' they said, almost in unison.

'You know what is also pissing me off?' Mal said. 'Wondering what Phoebe must be thinking of us right now. She hands herself in to one lot of police. Then gets taken away from the first lot of police by another lot of police. Then kidnapped by a third lot of police and nearly dies. Then a fourth lot of police end up squabbling in her hospital room. She must feel like she's a vehicle for police incompetence. So go on, then. Explain to me the reason for your *action.*'

Jo leaned forward. 'As I was saying, sir, from what we've uncovered it appears there were eighteen drug drops planned over the past year set up through a series of messages on Facebook by drivers from Easy Rider. On five of these occasions the police were forewarned and mounted an operation to intercept, but when they turned up – nothing; nobody there. Prior to each of the five abortive raids, an additional message had been posted, which we believe was to call off the drop.'

'Ri-i-ight,' Mal said, drawing out the word. 'This is good stuff, but I'm still having difficulty linking it to this meeting's agenda.'

'It seems to confirm we have an informant on each side,' Jo continued, 'which we already knew, otherwise I wouldn't be here. Someone telling us when a drop is due to take place, and someone telling the droppers that we know about it and calling it off. The five drops that we were told about were set up by Curtis Knox.'

She paused to allow time for Mal to process the information.

'So, you believe Knox set them up and then informed the police. Someone on the inside then tells them to abort.'

'That's a possibility. Another is that someone else pointed the finger at Knox by informing the police whenever he set up a drop. Don't ask me why, because I don't know. But our Knocker's death might be more to do with his perceived betrayal than it was about his planning to leave. Having said that, someone is trying to get rid of Phoebe, and that may well be because she's about to leave and presents too much of a risk. And we must assume, painful though it is, that our man, or woman, on the inside, must be aware, and possibly even complicit in planning her demise.'

'Which is why, seeing someone leaning over her in a hospital bed holding a pillow, you thought the worst.'

'Yes.'

'You told me once, with some certainty I seem to remember, that DS Mills was *not* the one. Why exactly?'

'Because he's a maverick and makes no secret of his... cynicism, discrimination, defiance, if you like. You'd expect our man – or woman – to be a regular, toe-the-line goody-two-shoes. The perfect police officer, in fact.'

'And now?'

'I *may* have been wrong.'

★

Jo arrived down at the operations room at just after 8.30 a.m. Her 'disciplinary' had concluded, once the Super had got his agenda back on track, with what felt like a final warning over her behaviour towards her sergeant. She was aware that the next contact with Andy would be difficult and she was spared its immediacy by his absence from the room. She sounded as cheery a 'good morning' as she could muster and stopped at DC Malik's desk.

'Day two of the pursuit, Mo, any luck?'

'Not checked the report yet, ma'am, except to make sure it had been added to the file, but I met one of the uniforms on the way in and he said nothing doing.'

'Right, third time lucky, perhaps.'

'Fingers crossed.'

She went into her office and dropped into her chair. Jodi appeared in the doorway.

'Got some stuff on Challinor, ma'am.'

'Who?'

'Rob Challinor, the new driver – well, new*est* driver.'

'Oh, right. Come in, Jodi. Close the door.'

Jodi seated herself opposite Jo and opened her laptop, placing it at an angle so both could see the screen. She opened a file showing the list of drivers and clicked on the folder labelled 'RC'. A further click produced a full-face shot of a man in his mid-twenties with a shaved head and facial stubble, and a mouth set in a scowl. Next to it was the same face in profile.

'This is from Rob Challinor's police record,' Jodi said. 'Not the smiling friendly face we have on our file now. He was charged with people-smuggling in Brighton twelve years ago, found guilty, and sentenced to four years, reduced to two years on appeal. The rationale being that he had shown kindness and understanding towards the illegal immigrants he had helped into the country. It was claimed his motives had been compassionate, not wholly monetary.'

'Bless him, poor lamb. So what was he doing during the nine or so years between his release and joining Easy Rider?'

'He moved to Bournemouth and enrolled with a rehab group for a while, run by a local charity, and then got a job with the southern tourist board driving a miniature train along the seafront. *Allegedly*,' Jodi added with a little laugh, seeing Jo's wide-eyed expression of disbelief. 'He was dismissed after being accused of keeping quite a lot of the fares for himself. He denied it, was interviewed by the police, but not charged.'

'So not exactly in the same league as The Great Train Robbery,' Jo said. 'And then?'

'That was eight years ago, and since then, off the radar in that there is no record of his having been in trouble with the police.'

Jo sighed. 'So….'

'*However*,' Jodi continued. 'I spoke to Dorset Police, and got hold of a DI Brendan Clarke who was around back then and who seemed to have a bit of a thing about Challinor. He told me that although he seemed to keep his hands clean, he suspected he was working in the background, setting up meetings between dealers and arranging drops, but never appearing on the front line. He said he also spent about ten months in Amsterdam, before reappearing again, but he has no idea what he was doing over there.'

'Just remind me, have we got anything on the other drivers? They're all squeaky clean, aren't they?'

'Well, none of them have a record, if that's what you mean, ma'am.'

'That *is* what I meant and, of course, you're right to make the distinction. Did your new friend at the seaside say anything else?'

'Only that around two years ago Challinor disappeared off the scene altogether. He thought he'd moved north.'

'I think that's a fair bet or he'd end up in the English Channel.'

Jodi giggled. 'I guess so, perhaps that was DI Clarke's little joke.'

Jo leaned back and stretched, looking up at the ceiling for a few moments, deep in thought.

'Can you get back to DI Clarke and see if he has Challinor's last known address down there. If so, get it on Google Maps and pop back in here. Is any of this stuff on the case file yet?'

'All of it; I just put it on.'

'That's great. Good stuff, Jodi.'

When Jodi had left, Jo booted up her PC and brought up the file to check the surveillance reports from the previous evening. She glanced around the operations room and noticed Andy was now at his desk. She'd need to come up with a credible reason for speaking to him soon. Perhaps when Jodi came back with any further news.

The reports on the trailing of the two drivers were brief and unhelpful. The only point of interest was that Rob Challinor was one of the drivers followed. He had gone straight to the Tesco Superstore on Woodfield Retail Park, emerging after sixteen minutes and driving home to a mid-terraced property on Melbury Avenue off Walmsley Road. He hadn't emerged by the time the surveillance was over. The other driver had gone to the Wellington pub on Bolton Road like his work colleague the night before. He was still there at the end of the watchers' two-hour stint.

Jo checked Challinor's house on Google Maps street view. She discovered what could have been a neat little property in a pleasant, tree-lined location had it not been for some neglected house-fronts and the weeds, grass and nettles growing up out of every available crack in the pavement, with moss covering a large area of the pavement itself. She hoped, with no real expectation, that the chase this coming evening would yield something, so her angry insistence that the surveillance was included on the case file didn't look like an act of petulance. A complete failure to produce anything would have been best kept *off* the record.

Jodi popped her head round the door and Jo waved her in and to the same chair.

'Got the address, ma'am, and found it on Google.' She placed her laptop on the desk as before and clicked on a tab which brought up a satellite image.

'Willart Gardens, ma'am,' Jodi said, indicating a cul-de-sac close to the River Stour on the outskirts of Bournemouth surrounded by countryside and farmland. She clicked on another tab, which brought up the street view and drew a gasp from Jo. The prestigious pseudo-Georgian detached houses, each with an integral double-garage, lined a perfectly maintained road with neat manicured gardens to the front and brick-paved drives.

'And this is our driver's,' Jodi said, moving the arrow on the image along to the end of the cul-de-sac where four similar houses circled a private area accessed between ornamental brick pillars which separated the properties from the rest of the Gardens. Jo said nothing, but moved her PC alongside Jodi's to show the house on Melbury Avenue.

'And that's where he's living now. *Allegedly.* Let's get DS Mills in here.'

She walked over to the door. Now was the moment.

'Andy, got a minute.'

Andy turned towards her, then looked behind him in a show of wondering who Jo was speaking to. He turned back to face her without speaking.

'Need you to see this.' Jo went back to her seat, leaving the door open, and sat down again in front of the two screens, paying no further attention to her sergeant. After a long silence, during which she sensed the tension in the operations room, she became aware of a figure standing in the doorway. She looked up.

'Take a seat. What do you think of this?' She pointed to the two screens.

Andy seemed to give up on the passive drama and sat down, his eyes initially on Jo, before turning his attention to the street level images on the computer screens.

'Before and after,' Jo said. 'This is where our newest Easy Rider recruit lived down in Bournemouth. And this is his home now, or that's what we're expected to believe.'

Despite any intention of indifference, Andy leaned forward to study the two properties more closely.

'That's some sacrifice just for the privilege of living in Bury,' he said. 'I saw on file that he was one of the drivers we shadowed last night. I can see why he couldn't wait to get back home.'

'There has to be something else,' Jo said. 'Another property.'

'And another vehicle, do you reckon?' Andy said. 'A fifteen-year-old battered Freelander wouldn't have looked all that great parked in front of his seaside mansion. Where did this information come from?'

'Jodi's new friend in Bournemouth. Jodi…?'

'A DI Clarke with Dorset police. He had been keeping an eye

on Challinor following a jail term for people-trafficking, although he's never re-offended.'

'Keeping an eye on him?' Andy prompted.

'He thought he might be working behind the scenes setting up drops and meetings. But he never got close to proving anything.'

'Well,' Jo said, 'perhaps we can help him.' She turned to Jodi. 'Really good work, detective. Update the file and put these images onto the incident board. And can you run a check on both properties. Make sure Challinor doesn't still own the house in Bournemouth. And is he renting the terraced in Bury or has he bought it? He might be splitting his time between them. Then we need to decide how ready we are to take this forward.'

Jodi left the room leaving an uncomfortable silence for a few moments.

'Right, next step to see the Super, I guess...' Jo said.

Andy stood up to leave. 'Right, let me know...'

'*Together*,' Jo said. 'Then he can see we're not being naughty children. Because I believe we're close to paying Reeves and Co an official visit. What do you think?'

Andy shrugged. 'Your call. But Jonesy is going to take some convincing to sanction a raid on a company whose only purpose is to make elderly people happy.'

'Forgive me, but I thought you felt there was something dodgy about the company right from the off.'

'I do, but we're going to need more than a guy moving downmarket with his accommodation to justify it.'

'We *do* have more, a lot more. The Facebook posts, for example. That pattern of messages must mean something, especially when we can link the five with the extra posts directly to failed police action. You're up to date with this?'

'Right up to fifteen minutes ago when you... requested my presence. But all five were Knox's posts. He could have been just playing with us. Adding the extra post and then anonymously contacting us about a drop that was never planned. All eighteen might just have been about setting up parties, meeting points, booze-ups...'

'Oh, come on. You can't seriously believe that?'

'Never said I did.'

'And what about the bullet in the ambulance?'

'Knox again.'

'Why are you doing this?' Jo fought to stay calm. 'This isn't a U-turn, this is a…fucking backward somersault.'

'Look,' Andy leaned on the desk with one elbow. 'If we descend on Easy Rider and find nothing, and the press get the full story, rationale for the raid and all, what I've just said are the things that *they* will be saying, in bold, in print.'

'So what do you suggest? Wait outside the Wellington and try to get as many as possible for drink-driving?'

'We wait until we interview Phoebe, and we might get all the answers we need. And if I'm allowed to be a naughty child again, just one more time, that might have happened already if it hadn't been for someone pulling rank.'

'And you know that whatever Phoebe said to you one-to-one in that room would have been worthless if she'd changed her story later. In fact, your being in there questioning her like that would have been the focus of the defence in any future case we chose to bring against her. It may still be a factor, but if it isn't, you can thank me for intervening.'

They held each other's eyes in hostile silence across the desk, broken by the sound of Jo's phone. She checked the caller.

'I need to take this.' Andy got to his feet 'You might want to stay. Yes, Al. I'm with Andy, okay to put you on speaker?'

Andy remained standing. Jo pressed the button and Al's voice introduced a much-needed sense of normality.

'Hi, both. Doctor Lei phoned me this morning. Phoebe seems to have relapsed a bit and the doctor thinks she's suffering from PTS. Apparently, she hasn't got much sense out of her this morning. The doctor seemed surprised because after seeing Benny Morrison yesterday afternoon she appeared much brighter. I got the impression Dr Lei was a little concerned because she was anticipating a steady improvement over the last twenty-four hours.'

'So can we…' Andy began.

'Interview her?' Al said. 'She was adamant that Phoebe could not be questioned today. And she emphasised "today" meaning, I assume, *all* day.'

'Oh, for fuck's sake,' Andy said, half to himself.

'Anyway, I've told Dr Lei that all contact going forward will be through you, Jo, so you may want to get back to her now and get it from the horse's mouth.' He paused. 'Although I don't think I've met a woman who looks less like a horse than Dr Lei.'

'Thanks, Al, except for the bit about the horse. I won't take that personally. We'll phone her now, just to keep the pressure on.'

They ended the call.

'Let's not forget,' Andy said, 'this girl is a talented actress. Far be it for me to offer an opinion, but for someone like that, feigning PTS must be a walk in the park compared to convincing people that you're Annie Oakley.'

'Let's phone the hospital now; get the horse to talk to us direct.'

'Well, you won't need me for that; I'm totally incompatible with everybody in the NHS. Oh, and by the way, you need to work on your metaphors. When you do a backward somersault you end up facing the same way.'

He turned and left the room, leaving Jo to go over the gymnastic movement in her mind and come to the same conclusion. Allowing herself a little smile she reached for the phone and called Doctor Lei on the direct line number provided by Al, not expecting to get though at the first attempt. The phone rang out for a long time and just as Jo was about to give up, a breathless voice answered.

'Dr Lei's consulting room.'

'Good morning, I wonder if I could speak to the doctor. This is Detective Inspector Carter, Bury Police. I'm a colleague of DI Crossley and I need to speak to her about Phoebe Wright.'

'Hold on, please.'

Jo could hear a whispered exchange, then a new voice on the line, clearly annoyed at having to take the call.

'This is Dr Lei. We have spoken to DI Crossley less than an hour ago. We'll let you know when Phoebe is well enough to speak to you. You don't need to keep checking. We are very busy here and…'

'I'm very sorry if I've caught you at a bad moment, Dr Lei. My name is Jo Carter, and I'll be liaising with you going forward. I just wanted to make sure you had my contact details, because it is becoming increasingly urgent that we speak to Phoebe as soon as possible.'

'I understand. Your colleagues have made that, shall we say, *forcefully* clear. One of your colleagues, anyway. But…'

'Can I share something with you in confidence, Dr Lei?'

'I suppose that would depend on…'

'I'll take the risk in the interest of expediency,' Jo said. 'Phoebe Wright is an accomplished actress. Only as an amateur at the moment, but with great potential as a future star. Right now she is reluctant to talk to us about her involvement in activities which may help us in our investigations into organised crime. I understand from DI Crossley that you believe she is suffering from PTS. I am totally unqualified to offer an opinion on that, but would appreciate your reviewing that diagnosis in the light of her acting ability.'

'I think I can tell …' The tone made the step from annoyance to anger.

'And before you go all righteously indignant on me, Dr Lei, I have been a police officer for fifteen years and I have been duped on countless occasions by people pretending to be what they're not. And we are *trained* to be suspicious and disbelieving. All I ask is that you consider what I have said in assessing whether Phoebe is well enough to help us to, quite possibly, prevent people getting hurt in the future. That's all.'

There was a long silence before the doctor spoke again. 'Very well, DI Carter; you've made your point. Leave your phone number with my assistant.'

★

After a quick lunch in the cafeteria and only her second station coffee of the day, Jo set herself up with her third in the briefing room in front of the incident board. Andy was right, of course; they had one chance to expose Easy Rider. If that failed, the only losers would be the police, and Jo Carter in particular. As for Josh Reeves and the drivers, they had a legitimate business to run, linked to the NHS dealing with the most vulnerable section of society. They would be more than just survivors of a failed coup – they would be heroes.

She turned at the sound of the door opening to see Geoff Brazendale's head poking into the room.

'Excuse me, ma'am. Got a minute?'

'Of course, come in, sergeant.'

Geoff took a seat at the table.

'I'm not sure if this is relevant any more now we have Phoebe back safe and sound, and I don't want to waste anyone's time…'

'Go on.'

'Well, the boots we found under the stones on Holcombe Moor. One of our guys, who was on the search, has just told me he can remember finding them on the moor and putting them in a sealed bag. When he got back to the command vehicle with them, it was locked. So he put them out of sight behind the generator at the side. When he returned later, they had been moved and he just assumed they'd been taken in and logged along with the rest of the stuff.'

Jo frowned. 'How could they have been logged without his input on the grid reference point? And how come it's taken him, what, nine days to remember this?' She shook her head. 'You're right in that it doesn't matter anymore in terms of the case, but… well, I think he needs to answer those questions, and probably a lot more. At the time, the missing boots were a big factor in building a picture of Phoebe's possible fate.'

'I know, I know. Jovi, Constable Kamba, is a new officer. A lovely lad, really keen, a breath of fresh air. And he genuinely believed the boots had been logged and saved, I'm sure of that. Then, when they came to light weeks after and we had all that crowd out in God-awful weather and it turned out to be a false alarm, he was afraid to come forward. And you know what it's like ma'am. If you don't come clean right away, the longer you leave it the harder it is.'

Jo nodded. Something rang very true about that. 'Look, Geoff, I'll leave you to do what you think is best. No real harm done. I have to ask, however, is it possible it could have been this young man who put the boots under the stones?'

'No way, ma'am. And I doubt if he'd have come forward if he had.'

'And his name is…?'

'Jovi Kamba, as in Bon Jovi. He's Kenyan, so I assumed that was the origin of his first name. But apparently he was named after the group, because his mum liked them so much.'

Jo gave a little laugh. 'It's a good job she didn't like the Boomtown Rats.'

'Or the Sex Pistols,' Geoff said. They laughed as he got up to leave.

Small victories, Jo thought. Solving the mystery of the boots was just about the only part of the whole case deserving of a tick in the yes box. As she turned back to the board, the door opened again.

'Hi, Jodi. More revelations about our miniature train driver?'

'Not about him, ma'am, but about his house in Bournemouth. In fact, it's not *his* house after all.'

'Go on.'

'The house is now owned by an Asian family who moved in when Challinor left. But they bought it two years ago off a woman called Margaret McGann, and she'd been the owner for over five years before that. But I double-checked with Brendan and he said that was definitely Challinor's known address.'

'Oh, so it's *Brendan* now, is it? We've moved on from DI Clarke. He'll think you fancy him.'

'I'm not sure he wouldn't be right,' Jodi laughed. 'In fact I think he's asked me out.'

'You *think*?'

'Well, we got talking. He wasn't sure where Bury was so I described it to him and he told me about where he worked, and I said it sounded great. Then he said he'd show me round some time. Asked me if I liked ice cream.'

'Well, as chat-up lines go, that's pretty original. Anyway, do we know anything about Mrs McGann?'

'Not yet; and still checking whether he's renting the terrace in Melbury Ave.'

'He might have been living with his parents, of course, which would blow the theory behind the downgrading out of the water. Check with handy Brendy, I'm sure he'll know. Good work, Jodi.'

★

Exactly five hours after she had left, Jo was back in her boss's office. This time at her request.

'I'd like to make the big move on Easy Rider, sir, and as that would be your call, I need to know what *you* need in order to give the go ahead.'

She paused.

'Go on,' Mal said.

'You don't sound surprised, sir. Were you expecting this request?'

Mal hesitated for a moment. 'Well, yesterday, when I had my chat with DS Mills...' Jo failed to stop her loud intake of breath. 'There you go again, DI Carter, leaping to the conclusion that supports your case. It's a good job you don't do that in your day job or you'd never have made CID at all, never mind inspector. Andy – is it okay if I call him Andy? – did exactly what you did this morning and went off on a tangent, or what initially *seemed* like a tangent, talking about the details of the case. He mentioned the proposed raid on Easy Rider as an example of what you and he *agreed* should happen. This was in defence of my accusing you both of prejudicing the outcome by spending too much time bickering.

'So the answer to your question is, yes, I did expect such a request at some time soon. What I told him was that we needed more than we had at the moment, because if we get nothing from the hit and the press get wind of it... well, I don't have to spell it out, do I?' He paused. 'Have you discussed this with your sergeant yet?'

'Yes, sir, and he said exactly what you just did. Only he made it sound like he was back-tracking, like *he* didn't want to go ahead with it.'

'Well, perhaps he doesn't, now I've made my position clear. I mean, heaven forbid that anyone should take my opinion seriously. Look, Jo, I believe we're making real progress, I really do. But, think of this; if we gather the troops together for a raid, with our insider problem they're going to know about it in advance. We need to keep digging, quietly, and I believe we'll get there without the trumpets and the bayonets.

'I want to focus on Knox's murder...' he held up his hand to stay Jo's interruption '...and, like you, I believe it is linked to Easy Rider. But what have we got so far on that? A stolen Berlingo, a phantom phone call, two guys helping someone into a car, and precious little else. No clear motive, except a tenuous link to a few dodgy posts on Facebook. We need to close a loop, somewhere in all this, a eureka moment, a missing link. Then we'll go in, with just you and I setting up the operation and briefing the troops on the way there. But right now, out there...' he pointed to the window '...the people we serve want a killer or killers off the streets. That's what they're looking for us to do. They don't give a shit about Easy Rider.'

★

As Jo lay in bed, watching the time on her iPhone approach nine o'clock in anticipation of Seb's call, Geoff Brazendale's words echoed in her mind. 'If you don't come clean right away, the longer you leave it the harder it is.' Perhaps tonight was the right time. The phone trilled. On the other hand, another forty-eight hours wouldn't make much difference, would it?

CHAPTER TWENTY-SEVEN

Thursday 24 January

Jo's first call of the day came on the hands-free as she pulled into the car park at the police station. She pressed the button with the green handset symbol on the steering wheel.

'DI Carter.'

'Good morning, DI Carter. This is Dr Lei from Fairfield Hospital. Just to save you time phoning in for an update, I thought I'd let you know that Phoebe had a much better night but woke up feeling confused and anxious again. At the moment, I must continue to insist that she is not disturbed and upset by being questioned by the police today, but I have taken on board your points from yesterday, and I will monitor her closely. We took the unusual step of installing a camera in her room while she was sleeping so we can watch her behaviour when she is alone. It's something that we do routinely for critically ill patients or those who may try to self-harm, so I can just about live with the intrusion. But her welfare is my number one priority. Helping the police with their enquiries is number two.'

'I fully understand, Dr Lei, and I'm very grateful to you for taking the time to keep me up to date and also for the surveillance of your patient.'

Once inside, Jo did a quick check of those present, noting that Mo was not at his desk yet but, to her surprise and relief, DS Mills was focused on his laptop and taking down notes from the screen. He failed to respond to Jo's cheery 'good morning, everyone' but Jo couldn't remember one single occasion in the past four weeks when he had. By the time she had placed her bags and phone on the desk and hung up her coat, he had followed her into the office along with DC Lawson. Jo waved them to the two chairs in front of her desk. Jodi sat down; Andy remained standing.

'What can I do for…?' Jo began.

'We seem to have a hotline to Bournemouth,' Andy said, nodding to the DC.

Jodi smiled. 'DI Clarke again, handy Brendy, I spoke to him last thing yesterday about Mrs McGann, the previous owner of the property in Willart Gardens. He's got back to me this morning to say that she is Challinor's mother. She changed back to her maiden name when she and his father got divorced. Not what we wanted to hear because it sort of scuppers our theory about why he's gone downmarket. Oh, and we've found that he is renting the property in Melbury Ave.'

Jo sighed and looked at Andy. 'In my meeting with Detective Superintendent Jones yesterday afternoon, he said something about me leaping to the conclusion that supports my case. I guess he's right.'

Andy shrugged. 'Don't we all? Have you seen the report on last night's surveillance?'

'Not yet.'

'Well, I can save you the trouble. Both drivers went straight home and stayed there, so nothing again.'

'And the directive from the aforementioned senior officer is that we focus on the murder. All this excitement with Miss Wright has deflected us a little. So…' she checked her watch '… it's eight forty-six. Let's get the gang into the briefing room at nine. Jodi, could you check with everyone to make sure the board is up to date for then. Thank you.'

Jodi left and Andy sat down.

'Any news from the hospital?' he asked.

'Yes, but no change. I spoke to Dr Lei yesterday and raised your point about her being a good actress, so to watch her closely and critically.'

'I hope you didn't tell her it was my point.'

'No, I forgot to mention that, but Dr Lei took it on board and they've installed a camera in her room to watch her when she's alone.'

'A secret camera, I hope. If she knows it's there it's going to play to her theatrical bent.'

'Yes, a secret camera. But it seems unlikely we'll get to speak to her today.'

'And in spite of what Jonesy says about focus, I have a feeling she holds the key to everything.'

They sat in silence for a few moments until Jo spoke again.

'When the time is right, I think you and I should interview her together.' Andy's eyebrows shot up in surprise. 'She's met us both, and she seems to like you.' Jo shrugged. 'Clearly her ordeal has affected her judgement, but we might be able to take advantage of that.'

Andy managed a little smile. 'I thought I was banned from her bedside.'

'*Alone* from her bedside. With a responsible adult, you might be okay.' She checked her watch. 'Five to nine. Let's get in there.'

The CID team of Eva, Jodi, Kirsty, Damon, Maddie, Glynn and Shelley were already in their seats when they entered the briefing room with Mo close behind.

'Okay,' Jo said, 'so let's get started.'

It was clear from the beginning that focusing on the murder of Curtis Knox to the exclusion of what was happening at his employer's was not a realistic option. The team's hard work over the past week had been inescapably drawing the two together. Jo's attempts to steer them down the narrow path of Knox's death had stalled discussion and caused confusion. After forty minutes, she held up her hand for silence, embracing the mood of the group whilst drawing on the words of her boss.

'Our prime concern at the moment, our number one priority, is to find out who murdered Curtis Knox. To quote the big man upstairs, the people we serve are looking to us to remove a killer, or killers, from the streets; they don't give a shit about Easy Rider. Whatever it is that's going on there, it's been going on for some time. However, it is clear from this meeting alone, that separating the two issues is impossible. There are too many cross-over points. So let's accept that as a given, but try to sieve out the more relevant points in establishing what happened that night.' She walked over to the incident board, whose information was threatening to fill the whole wall. 'Let's concentrate on the two assailants in the pub who, up to now, we have *assumed* are the killers. Let's park that assumption for now and recap the facts. What have we got?'

There was silence for a few moments, then Damon raised his hand.

'Just yell out, Damon,' Jo said. 'You only need to raise your hand if you need the toilet.'

The laughter seemed to break the tension and loosen tongues.

'They entered the pub and specifically targeted Knox. Which means they must have known he was going to be there.'

'Even so, the attack seems to have been a token gesture,' Eva added, 'in order to provide a motive for the killing later.'

'If the later incident reported by Mr Wilson is related, then they must have also known where he was heading when they parted,' Damon again.

'Or were *told* where he was going,' Kirsty said. 'And we believe Jacko made a call to a person unknown as Knox was heading home.'

'We've carried out door to door on Haymarket Street and both sides of Manchester Road along his route home,' Jodi said. 'No-one had seen anything. But if Mr Wilson had been right in that the pick-up had happened alongside the park, near the corner with Wellington Road, there are fewer houses there and their view would be masked by mature trees in the front gardens.'

'How do you know that?' Andy asked.

'I went along and had a look.'

Andy shook his head. 'I'm impressed. And what it must mean is that they'd hung back until he reached that spot.'

Damon raised his hand and quickly lowered it again. 'Wilson said Knox was a bit shaken but got into the car that knocked him down without resisting. Could that mean he knew the two guys in the car? They told Wilson they knew him… which means nothing, of course, but if it was the two guys from the pub, you'd expect him to be fighting like hell.'

'Excellent point,' Jo said. 'Pathology said it was only a slight bruising on his leg, and he hadn't been drinking, so he wouldn't have been helpless or disorientated. I wonder if we missed something here.'

'Unless they were holding a knife – six-inch blade, serrated edge – against a vital part of his anatomy,' Andy said. 'I'm thinking throat, by the way. That would probably persuade me to go quietly.'

'But if Damon is right,' Jo said, 'then we have a possible four, or five, guys involved.'

'Which raises again the question of motive,' Andy said. 'Two possible motives, in fact. He was leaving Easy Rider and they couldn't risk letting him go, or, they believed he had tried to set them up by arranging drops then informing us.'

'Which brings us right back to Easy Rider either way,' Jo said.

'So the guys who picked him up on Manchester Road and, presumably, killed him, could be two of the drivers,' Eva suggested. 'Except that Mr Wilson's description of them coincided with that of the two guys in the pub.'

'But it would be easy to do that,' Damon said. 'Dark outdoor clothing and the same headgear, to create a similar description for any casual witnesses who wouldn't be taking too much notice of them at the time.'

'But why go to all this trouble?' Eva asked. 'Five people, two vehicles, just to bump off one guy.'

'I guess because with it happening just after Phoebe went missing it was important to separate the two events,' Jo said. 'It had to look like the escalation of a bar fight so the Easy Rider connection to both would seem like a coincidence.'

'Didn't work, did it?' Andy put in.

'Even so, it's a big step from moving drugs around to premeditated murder,' Jodi said.

'Unless they're Class A drugs, and you think of what they've got to lose,' Damon said. 'Their freedom... indefinitely, if not permanently.'

'Damon's right,' Jo said. 'With Tom Brown's New Justice Regime and the NCA's war on organised crime, when it comes to sentencing, murder is no worse than hard-drug dealing.' She paused. 'Here's what we do, starting right away, I want all six of the drivers, plus Reeves himself, interviewed about where they were on the evening of Tuesday the fifteenth of January and who can vouch for them. Play it as standard procedure; in order to eliminate anybody with any connection to the case.' She turned to Andy. 'DS Mills, anything to add?'

Andy shook his head. Jo checked her watch.

'Ten-thirty-five. Let's start the ball rolling this afternoon and pick them off as they get back to the depot. Andy, can you take Damon, Eva, and Kirsty and get on to that. There's no point in trying to set it up in advance with Reeves. If we're right about Easy Rider, even if we're wrong about any direct involvement in the murder, he'll just warn them in advance to give them time to get their stories together. You okay with that, Andy?'

Andy nodded. 'Fine.'

'Okay, before we finish here, any responses from the descriptions of the guys in the pub? TV, online, press?'

'Nothing so far, ma'am, and not looking like we will,' Kirsty said. 'Uniform did a circuit of the pubs and clubs as well, but with no reliable e-fit and only a description of what they were wearing, it was a real long-shot. A few responses, but mainly mischief, they reckon. You know, dropping a mate in it just for a laugh. So no two people fingered the same two guys.'

'Right, okay. I guess that trail has gone cold now anyway. Anything else? No? Then I'll leave you guys to get sorted for this afternoon.'

As they all got up to leave, Jo called Jodi over.

'I need you to get back to Brendan Clarke. I hope you don't mind.'

Jodi shrugged. 'Well, if I *have* to, I suppose.'

'That's the spirit. Find out what you can about Margaret McGann, and in particular, where she is living now. And don't be lured down there by promises of ice cream just yet. I need you up here.'

★

Seated in her office, Jo looked out over the half-deserted open-plan area. The four detectives heading out later to the depot were back in the briefing room, planning the logistics for intercepting the drivers. She drummed her fingers on the desktop, and went over in her mind the dynamics of having an insider operating in the station.

It was hardly surprising that the tailing of the drivers earlier in the week yielded nothing. With the involvement of a wider group, which included the uniform section, it was more than likely that a message had got out to the drivers to make sure they each went to their 'official' home, either directly or via somewhere innocuous. That was assuming they had a choice of homes, of course, which was a big assumption. And if, God forbid, the insider was present at their meeting just now, word would get to Reeves and his crew before the detectives could check their whereabouts on the fifteenth.

She logged on to the Knox case file again and went through it from the beginning for the umpteenth time. She leaned back in her chair and exhaled loudly. Leaning forward again, she revisited the file listing the drivers and opened the folder on Rob Challinor. She flipped open her notebook and began to add a few bullet points. At the top of a new page she wrote *'Rob Challinor'* and underneath:-

1. *Joined ER January.*
2. *Facebook messages started February.*
3. *Prior – 2 years for human trafficking – Brighton.*
4. *No further police involvement for 8 years, but suspicion of organising drug deals and drops – Bournemouth.*
5. *10 months Amsterdam?*
6. *Lived in 'seaside mansion' in Bournemouth – owned by mother (Margaret McGann).*
7. *Moved north 2 years(?) ago.*
8. *Lives in rented mid-terrace in Bury.*
9. *Owns 15 y/o Freelander.*

She read through her notes a couple of times to satisfy herself there was nothing missing, then went to grab herself a coffee, stopping at Jodi's desk on the way back.

'Any luck with Maggie McGann yet?' Jo asked.

'Brendan's out at the moment, due back at twelve-thirty. They said could anyone else help, but I said I'd phone back. Saves explaining what's happened before to somebody else.'

'Right, and we don't want to upset him, do we, what with all that free candyfloss at stake?'

Jodi laughed. 'Ice cream, you mean. Seriously, ma'am, I'll chase it up with someone else if you like.'

'No, we can wait another hour or so.' Jo looked round the room. 'Where's Mo?'

'He's just popped out to Gregg's to get our lunch. Thursday is hot-sausage-roll day.'

'Yummy, one of my favourites. I'll keep my door closed until you've eaten them. The smell will drive me mad.'

'He's only just gone, ma'am, I can phone him and ask him to bring you one – or two.'

'Okay, but just the two.'

Jodi smiled and picked up her phone, jabbing a few keys. She raised it to her ear just as an incoming call sounded a few desks away. They both looked across at the ringing iPhone.

'That's Mo's,' Jodi said. 'He's forgotten to take it. Sorry about the sausage rolls, ma'am.'

'I'm sure I'll survive with the door closed.'

★

Andy and his team left for the Easy Rider depot at just after 3.00 p.m. in two cars in what was effectively a stake-out awaiting the return of the drivers. Jo felt a bit like a spare part, with the rest of the group fully occupied on laptops and phones, each drifting in and out of the briefing room to add more data to the already crowded incident board. At around 3.45 her iPhone pinged with an incoming text, an update from Andy. The first of the drivers was back and Kirsty and Damon were about to 'ambush' him, as the DS put it. They were planning to conduct the interviews in the police cars as a means of separating them. Good idea, Jo thought, she couldn't imagine Josh Reeves making a comfortable room available for them in the offices, if indeed one existed.

As she replied, 'Thanks', Jodi poked a frowning face into the room.

'I recognise a puzzled look when I see one,' Jo said. 'Come in.'

Jodi took the offered seat across the desk from her boss.

'This is a bit weird,' she said, 'but I'm not sure if it moves us forward or not. Brendan has checked out Mrs McGann, and she was definitely the seller of the property, but she moved into warden-assisted accommodation in Eastbourne ten years ago, which is four years before she bought the house in Willart Gardens.'

'So she remained in the care home after she acquired the property?'

'Well, it's not a care home, it's just a flat with emergency access to an off-site monitoring centre. You pull an orange string and someone asks if you're okay, that sort of thing.' She gave a little laugh. 'Quite fancy one of those myself.'

'With Brendan on the other end of the string, you mean.'

'That would be nice. But to answer your question, yes, she remained in the same flat.'

'While her son lived in the house. Anything else?'

'The flat is on a council-run complex so nothing very grand, in rather stark contrast to her property in Willart. Which begs the obvious question…'

'Why did she buy it?' Jo said. 'Or *did* she buy it? Thanks, Jodi. Get that on the file and the board right away.' She paused. 'On second thoughts, leave it just between the two of us for now, until I check something out. Don't discuss it with anyone else.'

Jodi opened her eyes wide with the unspoken question. Jo smiled.

'Nothing sinister, detective. I think I might have something to add to it, that's all. Great work, and please pass on my thanks to DI Clarke, and you can tell him I like ice cream, too.'

After Jodi left the office Jo turned to her PC and opened the same file again, writing a number on the next blank page in her notebook. Closing the file, she picked up her shoulder bag and coat and headed for the car park.

*

From where she had parked, in front of the line of terraced properties on Ainsworth Road close to the junction with Bolton Road, Jo had a clear view of the entrance to the depot. She kept herself low in the driver's seat, watching the ambulances arrive, with the occasional glance at the car registration number on the page of her open notebook on the front passenger seat. Not that she needed it – only one of the six drivers possessed an old Freelander.

At just after five o'clock, the vehicle that was the objective of her mission pulled out through the gates and turned left towards the main Bury–Bolton road. She followed at a discreet distance through the major junction onto Bolton Street, then along Peel

Way, passing Woodfield Retail Park on the left. The roads were clear of snow and ice after two days without precipitation and a rise in temperature, and rush hour was back to its chaotic worst. Jo was thankful that the Freelander was an easy target to follow, coupled with the fact that she had a good idea where it was heading. At the end of Peel Way, they filtered left onto the A56 heading north, soon passing Clarence Park on the right and turning into Melbury Avenue.

About forty metres into the avenue, cobbled alleys went off it to the left and the right giving access to garages at the rear of the properties on the main road. Jo pulled into the side just before the alleys and watched the Freelander continue along the familiar-looking roadway, stopping in front of Number 14. The driver's door opened and Rob Challinor got out. Instead of entering the house, he began to walk back along the avenue towards where Jo was parked. She turned in her seat, reaching down into the footwell at the passenger side as if she was looking for something, and hoping he wouldn't recognise her from the visits she'd made to the depot. When no-one passed the car, she looked up again. Challinor had disappeared.

She moved the car forward up to the alleys and saw him walking along the one to her right. Waiting until he was close to where it joined the next avenue, she steered the car into it and crept forward after him. He turned right at the end of the alley and Jo accelerated through, edging out into the avenue. Challinor had disappeared again, but a car was pulling out from the side of the pavement heading for the main road a few metres away. Jo edged forward to check the vehicle before it joined the traffic. It was a silver Audi SUV, registration RC 89. Eighty-nine, Jo reminded herself, the year of his birth; and slightly upmarket from his means of transport so far that afternoon since leaving work.

The Audi turned left onto the main road, heading back into the centre of Bury. Jo followed, forcing herself into the traffic to the sound of a few angry motor horns. At the junction with the end of Peel Way they turned left on to Bell Lane. Jo stayed a few cars back as they continued along the B6022 under the M66 motorway and past Fairfield Hospital. As they headed towards Rochdale town centre, the Audi made a left turn, leading Jo through a zig-zag of streets, and making her wonder if she would find her way back. She noticed they had picked up the B6377 heading north before turning off left at a sign for Dell Road and the Healey Dell Nature Reserve.

Jo was forced to hang back as they negotiated the narrow road, with no other cars to screen her pursuit. After about half a kilometre, the Audi turned through a pair of metal gates on the left leading onto the forecourt of two large detached houses. Jo had no option but to drive on and within a few metres the road became single track with passing places. With no roadside lights, she slowed down, cursing at the winding road until at one of the passing places she decided to risk a rapid three-point turn, which became a five-point turn.

On the way back, she slowed down to identify the property from where the Audi was parked on the drive next to a two-seater sports car, and noted the house number. She checked the time on the dashboard clock, 17.35, and wondered if Jodi was still at the station. She smiled to herself, thinking that might depend on whether DI Clarke had gone home or not in Bournemouth. She tried her on the hands-free.

'DC Lawson – oh, hi, ma'am. Where are you?'

'I'm at Healey Dell.'

'*Really*? It's lovely there, isn't it?'

'Not at the moment, it's pitch black, but I'd like you to check a property for me on Dell Road. I'm heading back to the station, I mean I *hope* I'm heading back to the station, if I don't get lost. I followed Challinor from the depot and this is where he brought me, *via* Melbury Avenue.' She gave Jodi the house number. 'As before, can you get the street view so we can look at it together when I get back. It's not quite as grand as Willart Gardens but not far behind. And can you check out this car – an Audi SUV, reg number RC 89. Owner, model and price tag. Are you okay to stay until I get back?'

'Of course. I wasn't planning to go yet anyway.'

'Great. Having said that, I think I've already taken a wrong turning, so I'm not sure how long I'll be. If I'm not back by, say, tomorrow lunchtime, you'd better go home.'

Jodi laughed. 'Okay ma'am.'

★

It had taken Jo, following the Audi, twenty-five minutes on the outward journey. She made it back in thirty-five, and was feeling very pleased with herself when she entered the operations room, hoping to see a look of surprise and admiration on DC Lawson's face. The operations room, however, was empty. Andy and co were back from the depot and the whole team were assembled in the briefing room. Jo placed her bag and coat in her office, picked up her laptop and notebook and pushed open the door to join them.

'Evening, all,' she said. 'Not planning a mutiny, I hope.'

Andy sighed. 'You've gone and spoilt our surprise.'

'Just getting our notes together from the interviews,' Eva stepped in quickly.

'Excellent. Good idea about using the cars, by the way. How did it work out?'

The gang of four exchanged glances, ending with the three DCs looking at Andy.

'The responses were all spontaneous,' he said, '*too* spontaneous, as if they'd rehearsed what to say. No hesitation, no indignation, just a churning out of information. They all claimed to have alibis, and with the exception of one driver, the others seemed to have been socialising in twos.'

Jo frowned. 'Meaning what exactly?'

'Six of them allegedly spent the evening in three pairs, four of them at two different pubs, the other two at one of their houses. Pretty neat. Except, that particular night the weather was so bad it's hard to believe they'd be out drinking, on a Tuesday, with somebody they see every day.'

'So, conclusion?' Jo asked.

'They had their alibis prepared in advance just in case, or… somebody tipped them off that we were coming. Or both.'

'But that can't be right,' Eva said. She looked round the table. 'You're not suggesting it was one of us? These are the same people who were in the earlier meeting.'

'Prepared in advance, then,' Andy conceded.

'I guess we can check with the pubs,' Jo suggested.

'Planning to do that tomorrow,' Kirsty said.

'And the billy-no-mates?' Jo asked.

'At home with his wife and in-laws all evening.'

'And which two were housebound together?'

'Reeves and Challinor. No way of checking that,' Damon offered. 'They both said, separately, that they'd just chilled with a few bevvies.'

Jo shook her head. 'Very convenient. What does it tell us, do you think?' She addressed the four.

'That we're no further on,' Andy said.

They sat in silence for a few minutes before Jo spoke.

'Well, in the absence of anything *directly* linked to the murder, we have something of interest relating to Mr Challinor. Jodi?'

Jodi turned to her laptop, clicked on a few keys and projected her screensaver circled by icons onto the large screen at the end of the room. The first image she brought up was of Melbury Avenue on Google street view, looking down its length from the main road.

'This is where Challinor is living now…' she moved the arrow along the avenue and turned it to show a particular house '… at number fourteen. And this is where he used to live before he moved up north.' The first image was replaced with the picture of his house in Bournemouth, the reaction of the group being similar to that of Jo's first impression. 'Except, that this is his mum's house. A lady called Margaret McGann. At least it *was* his mum's house until she sold it a couple of years ago.'

'So he lived with his mother while he was down there?' Eva asked.

'No, as far as we know, his mum never lived there. She's lived in a warden-assisted property in Eastbourne for the last ten years.'

'So, what…?' Eva began.

'There's more,' Jodi interrupted, clearly warming to her leading role. 'The boss followed Challinor today from the depot, and he led her to the terraced house in Melbury Ave, which is the address we have for him. Once there, he switched cars to an Audi RS Q8, personalised number plate "RC 89", two years old, current price around one hundred and twenty thousand pounds.'

There were a few gasps and murmurs around the table.

'He then drove out of Bury to Rochdale and onto Dell Road, the way up to Healey Dell. And to this house…' The new picture showed a large modern detached house with bow windows to the left of an enclosed porch and a single integral garage to the right. The property was one of two, fronted by a brick-paved driveway and well-tended lawns, separated from the road by a low brick wall and accessed via a pair of metal gates.

'Not quite in the same league as the Bournemouth house,' Damon said, 'but not far away.'

'So he owns two houses up here?' Kirsty said.

'The thing is,' Jodi replied, 'it seems he doesn't own any. He rents the terraced house in Bury, and…' she turned to Jo '…this is the bit you don't know yet, ma'am. I checked the land registry, and the house on Dell Road is owned by Margaret McGann.'

There was silence for a long time as they wrestled with the implications of Jodi's report. It was finally broken by Damon.

'So what does all this tell us?'

'That Rob Challinor has gone to a lot of trouble to hide the fact that his lifestyle is a lot different to what people are being led to believe,' Jo said. 'And if not his lifestyle, then his wealth. I mean, the car alone…'

'Unless it's his mum's,' Andy put in, to a ripple of laughter.

Jodi's phone rang and she checked the screen, her face creasing into a smile.

'Don't tell me,' Jo said. 'Handy randy Brendy.'

'I'd better take this,' Jodi said. 'Excuse me.' She left the room and returned within a few minutes.

'That was, indeed, DI Clarke and he seems to be working with us full-time at the moment. He's had someone visit Maggie McGann at her home in Eastbourne and, apparently, she has no knowledge of ever having owned a house in Bournemouth. She said she lets her son, Robert, handle all her finances; she just has to sign a few papers every now and again.'

'This lady must be extremely well off if she's got so much money, she can overlook a major spend like that,' Kirsty said. 'Is she confused? Dementia, perhaps?'

'The place where she lives is a modest, council-run complex, apparently,' Jodi said. 'It's not a care home, just a secure place for potentially vulnerable people. And as far as I'm aware, she's perfectly fine as far as her mind is concerned.'

'So who *is* buying the houses and the car?' Damon asked.

'I think we know the answer to that one,' Andy said.

'It's a pity Brendan's been so quick off the mark,' Jo said. 'They could have asked her about the house in Rochdale.'

'Although I think it's safe to assume she knows nothing about that either,' Andy said.

They lapsed into silence again. Jo checked her watch.

'Seven-fifteen. Just goes to show, time flies even when you're *not* enjoying yourself. Good work, though, all. Jodi, you'd better get on the phone and tell Brendan it's okay for him to go home, and you might want to mention the bit about Maggie's new house in Rochdale, anyway. Tomorrow we check the pubs for a sighting of our two pairs of drivers on the night of the murder, and decide how we move forward with Mr Challinor. Or, fingers crossed, Phoebe might be ready to clear up everything for us so we can all get away early for the weekend.'

CHAPTER TWENTY-EIGHT

Friday 25 January

Jo awoke feeling more positive than for a good few awakenings. The day had arrived when she and Seb would sit down and sort everything out. Though she might not be confident that everything would work out for the best, at least decisions would be made and they would move on with their lives, separately or together. As she walked the short distance from the car park to the police station entrance, her phone sounded with an incoming call. She checked the screen and smiled.

'You're early. Don't tell me you're on your way already.'

'I wish,' Seb said. 'Just the opposite, I'm afraid.'

'Don't tell me you're not...'

'Coming? You bet I am, as soon as possible, but not prematurely, if you know what I mean.'

'I do, but explain what you mean by just the opposite.'

'Might be later than expected. We have a visit from a dignitary at six o'clock, the Mayor of Leicester. That's the *City* Mayor, as distinguished from the *Lord* Mayor, you'll be interested to know. This guy actually makes important decisions, without the aid of a heavy chain round his neck, and he's big into supporting the police. So they want all the best-looking police officers to attend to create a good impression.'

'So you're out back working in the kitchen.'

There was a moment's silence. 'How the hell did you know that?'

Jo laughed. 'Just a wild guess.'

'There's a reception afterwards – Pimm's and vol-au-vents –

but, of course, I won't be attending. Not for long, anyway. But if I don't make it for midnight, Cinderella, please, *please*, don't turn into a pumpkin.'

'No promises, but I'll do my best. And don't you go rushing. Seriously, Seb. It's a long drive after a long day.'

'Difficult not to rush when I know who's waiting for me, but I'll take very special care.'

'Make sure you do. See you later.'

'Love you.'

She realised the doubts were never far below the surface and they emerged again. Was that really why he was going to be late? Thankfully, there was no way of checking this time on the BBC Sport webpage. Just as they were ending the call, the phone had buzzed with a missed call. Jo checked her Recents list, but it showed 'No caller ID.' She checked voicemail. No message had been left, but as she entered the operations room, Shelley called across to her.

'Morning, ma'am. Just taken a call on your landline from Fairfield. Phoebe's doctor seems to think she is almost ready to talk to you. Could you call back.'

There was a buzz about the room as those present absorbed the information with smiles and nods.

'Thanks, Shelley,' Jo said. 'I'll speak to her right away.' She closed the door and sat down at her desk, taking the iPhone to return Dr Lei's call. After few moments' hesitation, she entered a number. It was answered before the third ring.

'Good morning, DI Carter.'

'Good morning, sir. Have you got a minute?'

'Let's see,' Mal said. 'It's eight-twenty-three. I'm due on a conference call at eight-forty-five, so I've got twenty-two minutes if you'd like to come up now. And bring a coffee with you this time so we don't have to deflect Lucy from important work.'

Jo gave a little laugh. 'Right you are, sir. Shall I bring you one?'

'Got mine already. See you in a minute.'

Mal got to his feet when Jo entered and waved her to a chair.

'So? Have you found the murderer or murder*ers*? Is that what you're in a rush to tell me?'

'No, but Phoebe seems to be ready to talk, so we just *might* be getting a bit closer.'

'Well, that's good news. When will you see her? I'm assuming it will be you with A N Other, but *not* DS Mills.'

'I have to call back. The message passed to me was that her doctor *thinks* she is *about* ready to talk to me. So it might not be right away. And as for DS Mills, Phoebe seems to like him, so I think he might be the right person to do the interview with me.'

'Your call, Jo, so why did you want to see me now?'

Jo shifted in her seat. 'Just to bounce something off you, sir. Yesterday we had a meeting of the full CID team and decided to interview the drivers and Josh Reeves about where they were on the night of the murder, and…'

Mal held up his hand. 'But the guys who attacked Knox in the pub can't have been two of the drivers. Knox would have recognised them.'

'I know, and that's not what we're thinking. We've so far assumed that the two guys in the pub were the same ones who were seen picking up Knox on Manchester Road and who drove him off and killed him.'

'And that makes sense, doesn't it?'

'Yes, except that our drive-by witness said Knox appeared fairly relaxed about getting into their car. Well, perhaps not exactly relaxed, but certainly not resisting. And as Deecy-D'Arcy pointed out yesterday, you'd expect him to be fighting for his life if they were his two attackers. So it raises the possibility that Knox knew the guys who picked him up. But that line of enquiry is still early work-in-progress, and not what I wanted to see you about.'

'Go on, then.' He checked his wall clock. 'You're running short of time.'

'Andy and three of the team went to the depot yesterday afternoon, just a few hours after the meeting to grab the guys as they finished work, which they did – all six of them *and* their boss, Reeves. But they said the drivers had their alibis carefully prepared and just churned out the story, like it was rehearsed. Given what we know about our insider, the most likely scenario is that someone tipped them off that they were going to be interviewed.'

Jo paused for effect. Mal frowned, choosing his words carefully.

'What you're saying, Jo, if I'm not mistaken, is the insider was in the room when you planned your visit. One of the CID team, and *that* is quite an accusation.'

'Technically, it's not an accusation, sir, because I've no idea yet who it could be, and I'd really appreciate your coming up with another conclusion so I don't have to believe it.'

Mal swivelled in his chair from side to side, his brow creased in concentration.

'And the alibis, do they stack up?'

'Checking them out today, sir. Two of them say they were out together in one pub, two in another and two spent the evening at Reeves's house. The other was at home with a number of family members. That they all instantly recalled their movements on the night is suspicious in itself, but the fact that they all but one provided alibis for each other is almost a clincher, don't you think?'

'But, surely, if they were involved in the planning of this murder, they would have their alibis ready in advance, just in *case* they were asked to account for their movements.'

'Agreed, sir. That is the alternative conclusion that I want to believe. And my guess is, when we check out the two pubs, they'll confirm that the guys were there, because they'll have made sure they were getting noticed. I'm fairly confident that the one having a night in with the family will check out as well, which leaves Reeves and Challinor accounting for each other.'

'So there you are.' Mal checked the clock again.

'It was the *spontaneity* of the responses to the team's questions yesterday that concerns me. They didn't have to think, they just churned out the answers. I don't think we can ignore the unthinkable, that our insider is someone close to this investigation. And if they are, they know that Phoebe may be close to spilling the beans, which means by now the people who tried to take her on the Snake Pass will have also been made aware of that. I'd like to increase the security at Fairfield until we can move her out of there, which may be *after* we interview her.'

'Agreed ... look, I'll need to join the call in a couple of minutes, Jo, can I leave it to you?'

'That's the problem, sir, who do we add to the team at Fairfield when we can't be one hundred per cent sure of anyone?'

Mal paused, his hand already on the desk phone.

'Well, there's you, Jo. I think we're both one hundred per cent sure of *that* person.' His fingers flexed on the handset, then he paused again. 'See Brazendale, I'd stake my career on him.' He lifted the receiver as Jo got to her feet. 'Not that I'll have one left to stake if I don't get on this call.'

*

Jo found it comforting, sitting in the back of the first of two police cars, with sirens howling and blue lights flashing, as they raced along Rochdale Old Road. Sergeant Geoff Brazendale, who was seated beside her, had quickly 'raised a posse', as he put it, and four male and two female uniformed officers, along with Jo and Geoff, were on their way to relieve the two already on duty at the hospital. The occupants of the second vehicle included two officers from the centrally based Special Firearms Unit in Manchester.

Jo, on her call to Dr Lei, had informed her that she was heading out to the hospital with a police crew to take over from the two already there providing security. She didn't mention that this would involve five extra policemen and two semi-automatic weapons, and that they would be arriving with a light and sound show. Geoff had pointed out that such a high-profile display of force would encourage anyone planning to get to Phoebe to think again.

'We're there to protect her,' Geoff had explained, 'not use her as bait for catching someone.' Jo thought that sounded rather good and made a mental note to use it at the next opportunity.

Dr Lei was waiting for them in reception and looked shocked at such a show of force. Leaving two of the officers in the main entrance area, where they attracted some questioning looks from staff and visitors, the rest of the group set off in the wake of Dr Lei along the corridor and up the stairs to the Intensive Care Unit on the second floor. The doctor waved them into her office and squeezed past them with some difficulty to reach her chair behind the desk.

'I'm afraid this office is designed for a maximum of four average-sized people,' Dr Lei said, with the first hint of humour Jo could remember to date. 'So we had better make this quick before we run out of oxygen.'

'We just need someone to show us round this part of the hospital,' Geoff said, 'and we'll leave you in peace. Access points, corridors, walkways, empty rooms… that sort of thing.'

Jo noticed the doctor's expression change from surprise to fright.

'Why, what...?' she began.

'It's just a precaution, Dr Lei,' Jo said, with a reassuring smile. 'As we said before – several times, I think – Phoebe will be helping us with our enquiries into some serious crimes. And in doing so she will be making life very difficult for some dangerous people. We are just making doubly sure she gets that opportunity.'

Dr Lei picked up the phone on her desk and pressed a single button on the handset.

'Hello, security. This is Dr Lei in ICU, can you send someone along please to meet with some police officers. Thank you.'

With Geoff and his crew following a fresh-faced young man, who quickly embraced the idea of his own importance as he led the five officers off for a building tour, Jo settled into a seat whilst the doctor left briefly to return with two coffees from the nearby vending machine.

'So, about Miss Wright,' Jo said, 'what can you tell me?'

'I believe she is extremely anxious, and frightened. And to be fair, the hidden camera didn't reveal any different behaviour when she was alone. I don't know the background to her absconding, and I understand that you can't tell me much at present, possibly ever, but I think she knows this is all going to be life-changing for her and that is why she is putting off talking to you for as long as possible.'

'I'm afraid she is right about it being life-changing, if we're right in what we believe. As soon as I can, Dr Lei, I will share as much information with you as I'm allowed. I think that's only what you deserve for being so co-operative. Do you know when we can speak with her?'

'What she has requested is that she speaks with you, *only* with you. She mentioned that when you saw her briefly earlier in the week, you said there had to be two police officers in attendance.' She smiled. 'And I think she quite fancied the loud, argumentative, but undeniably attractive one who was with her before you arrived. But she insisted – well, let's say, requested – that it would be just you. I hope you can make an exception in Phoebe's case.'

'I would need to check that with my superior. It has implications, you see, if we need to take anything further with Phoebe. *Legal* implications. We would have to take advice on that. But I, personally, would be happy to go ahead with her alone.'

'That's good. And as for when, well although she is still in the same room, she is not officially under intensive care anymore so we have more flexible visiting hours. Her parents and Mr Morrison are due to visit her tonight, separately. Could we arrange for you to see her early tomorrow morning, say nine-thirty. I'm sorry it means waiting another day, but she talks about these visits as if they're some sort of watershed. Almost like she plans to tell them in advance what she'll be telling you afterwards.'

'I think one more day won't make a difference. If you could move her to a different room, that might be advisable from a security point of view, but please let Sergeant Brazendale know if you do. And if I do interview her here, perhaps we can position that as a preliminary meeting rather than anything formal. But as soon as possible afterwards, we will need to move her from here. And when I say as soon as, I mean later tomorrow, if you can sign her off by then.'

'I can do that, and thank you for your understanding.'

★

After a brief meeting with Geoff, followed by a tour of the building to see the deployment of his troops, Jo was given a lift back to the station by the two officers just relieved of guard duty, but without the excitement of the previous audio-visual accompaniment. She arrived just as Kirsty and Damon were leaving to check out the two pubs allegedly visited by the drivers on the night of the murder. She checked her watch.

'Twelve-thirty,' she said to the rest of the room. 'Just going to grab a bite to eat then I'll bring you up to date with Phoebe. Let's say, one-fifteen, briefing room.'

She arrived back in her office by 12.50, calling Andy in on the way. He assumed his normal posture of indifference, slumped down on the chair opposite Jo, sideways-on, with his legs stretched out in front of him.

'We've all been wondering where you were,' he said. 'No message…'

'I decided to add some more bodies to the Phoebe-watch at

Fairfield. Brazendale's out there with a few uniforms, checking all the entrances and hiding places.'

'A bit extreme, don't you think?'

'I believe it was you who first raised the theory of an insider forewarning the drivers yesterday. Well, if you were right, then it's possible, don't you think, that the same insider would know Phoebe is ready to talk. Shelley shouted it out to me across the room this morning, before you arrived. And as someone has tried to silence her once already – assuming that was their intention on the Snake – then they could try again. Better safe.'

'And when are we seeing her?'

'Well, she has requested to see just me initially. I don't like that, for the same reason I said before, but if it's the quickest...'

Andy swivelled round so he was facing Jo and leaned forward, elbows on the desk. His dark eyes were blazing with anger.

'And can you explain how that is different to what I was doing when you came bursting in all fire and venom? Because I can't for the life of me see the difference, unless it has to be a woman and it has to be an inspector.'

Jo was aware of the open door and kept her voice low.

'I thought we'd got past all this, DS Mills. If you just listen to the actual words instead of twisting the message into what you want to hear, I said *Phoebe* has asked for this and *I* don't like it. It was the doctor who passed the message on. I didn't get to speak to Phoebe myself.'

'Oh, the doctor. How do you know it isn't her idea to keep me away from her?'

'Christ, Andy, why would she do that? If I was the doctor, working somewhere with police swarming all over the place, I'd want to move her out as soon as possible. And anyway, before we agree to anything, we need to clear it with the man upstairs. Interviewing her with just one officer present could prejudice a future case against her unless we can position it as a preliminary meeting or something. One thing I think we do agree on is that she probably holds the key to everything.'

Andy stood up. 'So let's go see him now.'

'*I'll* see him after our meeting.' She checked the time. 'Which starts in five minutes.'

Andy turned and walked out of the office, through the CID room and towards the stairs.

*

Andy's outburst, clearly audible through the open office door, and his absence from the meeting had led to some tension within the team. At a time when optimism should have lifted everyone's spirits, Jo could feel a distinct cooling of the atmosphere. Eva, in particular, had an anxious look about her and failed to meet her eyes. Jo was aware that the continuing feud with Andy was in danger of polarising opinion within the team, with Eva likely to choose the opposite side. And she was conscious of the uncomfortable possibility that she was about to share information that could soon be passed on to someone on the outside. Pressing on regardless, Jo played it straight and positive.

'Phoebe has agreed to speak to me early tomorrow. She insists that she meets with just me to begin with. That is not what I want, it goes against all my instincts, but she has made it clear that is the only condition under which she will share any information. Before I go ahead with speaking to her one-to-one, we need to take legal advice as to whether that may prejudice any action we take against her in future. I'll be speaking to the Super after this meeting to get his view on how we respond to Phoebe's request.'

'And if the advice is not to go ahead one-to-one, ma'am?' Mo asked.

'I don't know. I assume we will need to proceed more formally and hope that she opens up, anyway. But it could delay any progress on the situation regarding Easy Rider, and possibly Knox's murder if indeed they are linked. In the meantime, we have increased the guard on Phoebe at the hospital. I'm not expecting anything dramatic to happen to her, but person or persons unknown have already tried to get her once, and we don't want to take any chances. I'm sure uniform will be praying for a relatively quiet Friday night at the pubs and clubs, with key personnel effectively hospitalised at the moment.'

The comment drew a few quiet laughs from the group, and Jo ended the meeting there, not exactly on a high, but on a 'not as low as it could have been'. She headed up to see Mal, with a sinking feeling born of having to explain her latest fallout with Andy. She decided a show of empathy with her second-in-command might mitigate further chastisement.

'I can understand how he feels,' she said, after much tutting, head-shaking and sighing by her boss, 'especially after I virtually threw him out of Phoebe's room because he was in there on his own. And I'll gladly stand by any advice that says we need two officers for the first interview. Because one-to-one is not the way I would choose to proceed, and I had already told Andy that I wanted him in with me when we got round to talking to her. So what I'm asking, sir, is not for you to mediate between Andy and me, but to provide advice on what we do tomorrow morning. I have a date with Phoebe at nine-thirty, and it is my intention to take Andy along with me and try to persuade Phoebe to meet with us both. And we can force that, of course, but it might further our interest more to get as much information as possible as soon as possible.'

Mal had got to his feet and was pacing up and down behind his desk. After a long silence, he took his seat again.

'I won't be taking legal advice on this, Jo…' he held up his hand to prevent an interruption '…but I *will* give you the go-ahead. We need to speak to Miss Wright as soon as possible be it one-to-one, two-to-one, or ten-to-one. I don't have to tell you which I prefer because we're all on the same page, but I'll leave it to you to achieve the best outcome. This Easy Rider, Knocker Knox thing is becoming an embarrassment and we can't afford to leave any stone unturned. If we can handle it ourselves without the MIT swarming all over it, that's what I'd like. So you have my permission, and my backing if it goes wrong. I hope you know that.'

'I do, sir, and thank you.'

*

Andy had returned to his desk by the time Jo got back to her office. He made no move to explain his absence from the meeting or to mention their earlier exchange, but Jo noticed that he had adjusted his position at his workstation so he had his back to her, presumably, Jo thought, so there was no chance of her catching his eye. If she wanted to speak to him, she would have to get up and walk to his desk. She couldn't help a little smile to herself at the petulant show of open defiance in the posture.

At just after three o'clock, Jo looked up to see Kirsty and Damon at her office door, just as her phone pinged with an incoming message.

'Come in,' she said. 'Back early from your pub crawl.'

'Yes, ma'am, and with nothing very surprising, I'm afraid,' Jodi said. 'Same story in each pub. They were remembered by the landlord because they weren't regular drinkers there. In fact, they didn't think they'd been in before. One of the pairs began to pick a fight – with each other, apparently – but calmed down and apologised after the landlord threatened to throw them out.'

'So just enough of a disturbance to make sure they'd be remembered,' Jo said.

'Yes, that's what we thought. And the other two spent the evening chatting up a couple of the bar staff. They actually got round to exchanging phone numbers. Only one of the women was in today, and the phone number she was given checks out with the one we've got on file for this driver. So, pretty conclusive, we think.'

'I think, too,' Jo said. 'And as you say, nothing surprising. And we have Reeves and Challinor cancelling each other out of the equation. So, if the two guys who picked up Knox, literally, were from Easy Rider, it has to be those two. What did Wilson say about the car they were driving?' She turned to her keyboard and brought up a file. 'Black or dark blue, small car. Reeves has a black Ford Fiesta, which he seems to use sparingly. Special occasions. I guess knocking someone down as a step towards killing them could be regarded as special. Different, anyway.' She sighed. 'But that conclusion is a bit of a leap, even for me. I guess one thing this does tell us. The fact that the whole crew went to the trouble of setting up alibis on that night, points to them all being involved in whatever is happening at Easy Rider. Okay, guys, get it on the file and board and get one of the others to bring you up to date with Phoebe. Good job.'

She checked her watch, 3.25 p.m., then remembered the text alert. There was no sender ID. The message read:

1 26 1761 00.03

She looked at it for a long time, trying to fit it into context with the previous series of digits. She looked up and around the operations room. Everyone was at their workstations focused on their PCs or reading from notes. She checked the time of the text, 15.08, over fifteen minutes ago. She couldn't remember if anyone was out of the office at that time. Was this early-onset paranoia, she wondered. Looking at the team individually, she couldn't imagine any of them would betray a trust or play games with her at a time like this. But the text hadn't sent itself. She got up and walked across to her whiteboard, still on its easel and still displaying the earlier sequence:

195; 778 – which she now knew to mean *778 195*.

She added the new eleven-digit message underneath, and stood back to study it. One thing was certain, this was no map reference. The *1761* seemed vaguely familiar, but she could not recall its significance. She continued to stare at the board until the sound of the desk phone brought her out of her trance.

'DI Carter,' she said.

'Geoff Brazendale here, ma'am. Nothing exciting, just an update. I've called in a favour from Rochdale and they're sending three officers so we can cover through the night. That will give us ten uniforms, five on, five off; four-hour shifts. Only proviso is, it's Friday night and if necessary they could be called away. We could probably get by, anyway. Only time will tell, but everything's quiet here.'

'Have they moved Phoebe to another room?'

'Yes. It's quite a way from the ICU and easier to police the approach. Only the doc, a couple of nurses, and the police team know she's been moved – and you, ma'am.'

'Good. Let's keep it our secret outside the hospital, Geoff. I'll be over at around nine o'clock tomorrow morning. See you then if you're still there.'

She took her laptop and notebook through to the briefing room and sat in front of the incident board, which had just about reached its capacity.

'You're going to need a bigger board,' she said out loud to herself, smiling as she remembered Roy Scheider's quote from *Jaws*, when he saw the monster for the first time from Quint's fragile fishing ketch. Except it was 'boat' then, not 'board'. She added a few of the later comments to her own files and notebook and returned to stare again at the cryptic message.

At 5.30, she gathered her things together and left the office, calling 'good night' to those of the team still there. As she passed Andy's workstation, she stopped to speak.

'I'm heading for Fairfield at eight-thirty in the morning so I'll meet you here. Hopefully, I can persuade Phoebe to let both of us invade her personal space.'

Andy continued to click the keys without replying. Jo waited out the silence as all eyes watched from around the room.

'I'll be here,' he said, without looking up.

Jo went out to her car with little optimism about the following morning's link-up with her sergeant. As she was about to turn on the ignition, her phone sounded with an incoming call. She checked the name on the screen.

'Hi, Kenny, this is a surprise.'

'Not a shock, then,' DI Watson said with a chuckle. 'Well I'm glad about that.'

Jo laughed. 'Not at all; what can I do for you?'

'Two things, firstly, I was wondering how Phoebe was, mainly so I can reassure PC Davy, then perhaps he'll get on with some work. He's been in a dream since she walked into reception a week ago.'

'He's not got over her yet, then. Well, you can't fault him for taste; she's a beautiful young woman. And if it's true love, it's probably a bit soon yet to be putting it behind him. But you can assure him that she's fine and I'll be seeing her tomorrow morning. And tell PC Davy I'll be sure to mention he was asking after her.'

'I'll do that. Thank you.'

'You said there were two things.'

'Yes, this next one is a bit more delicate.'

★

The prospect of Seb's arrival after nearly four weeks' absence filled Jo's mind and gave it a break from the contrasting fates of Phoebe Wright and Curtis Knox. She should have felt like an excited school girl about to meet her pop or screen idol, but the prospect of the awkward conversation she needed to have with him some time over the weekend overshadowed any delight at his pending arrival. Given that she would be leaving him early the following morning, she persuaded herself that tonight wouldn't be the right time to have that discussion. Not that she needed much persuading.

She prepared a light tea of scrambled egg on toast with cheese, mushrooms, and tomatoes, followed by yogurt and coffee and chanced an early glass of white wine, knowing that alcohol would certainly flow in some form or other once Seb arrived. Afterwards, she took her glass and settled with her notebook on the sofa in front of the expectant sheepskin rug and blazing logs to prepare for her meeting with Phoebe. After completing that to her satisfaction, and going over it again twice, she sneaked a look at her watch to discover it was only 9.25. The time seemed to be going so slowly. As she was about to take her glass through to the kitchen, her phone sounded with an incoming call. The name on the screen surprised her.

'Hi, Eva.'

'Hi, ma'am. Sorry to bother you, but I thought you would like to know. Following up this latest theory about the two guys from Easy Rider being involved in Knox's murder, I've been checking through the CCTV again. Mo checked before, but we were looking then for two guys on foot and the cameras were out on Silver Street where we would have picked them up. I've looked further down where it becomes Manchester Road leading on to Angouleme Way, and the camera outside St Marie's Church picked up a black Fiesta parked along that stretch with one driver and one front seat passenger. You could just about make them out but in no detail because of the street light reflection on the windscreen. It moved off at ten-thirty-seven. I checked the number plate against DVLA records, and that registration is not currently in use. It was last registered to a Ford Transit four years ago.'

'So false plates, and Reeves has a black Fiesta and no alibi except a possible partner in crime. That's excellent, Eva, but why, at twenty to ten on a Friday evening, are you checking CCTV? Shouldn't you be out with DS Mills clubbing, or in with DS Mills doing… something else?'

'That would certainly be my preference, ma'am, but he's got a real cob on him at the moment. Said he wants some time to think stuff through on his own. Don't know what that means... and don't much care. Well, actually, that second bit isn't true, but...'

Jo detected a catch in her voice. 'I'm afraid you can blame me for that, Eva. We had yet another fall-out today over what was probably a misunderstanding this time.'

'We did detect a *slightly* raised male voice in your office just before the meeting today, and its owner was very noticeable by his absence from the meeting itself.'

'I'm assuming you're not at work right now.'

'No, been checking the capture on my laptop at home. So I'm quite snug, on my third glass of wine and awaiting the delivery of a pizza. So it's just possible I might survive the night without Mr Mills.'

'Well, great work spotting that Fiesta, detective. I'll pick up on that in the morning before I head out to see fly-away Pheobe.'

She rose from the sofa after ending the call and, resisting the temptation to top-up her own glass, she placed it on the worktop near the sink and busied herself tidying up the accumulation of magazines, newspapers and other reading material from the floor, chairs and table-tops in the living room and dining kitchen. It was when she picked up John Simpson's pamphlet telling the story of Ellen Strange that she was reminded of the significance of *1761*. It was the year she was murdered on Holcombe Moor. She picked up her phone and opened the text message, writing it in full in her notebook.

1 26 1761 00.03

So what was the significance of 1, 26 and 00.03? She returned to the sofa to read the pamphlet again, but long before she reached the relevant passage, the meaning had come to her. The date, reversed, like the grid reference, *1 26*, meaning *26 1* – the twenty-sixth of January, the date Ellen's husband killed her close to where the moorstone stands as a memorial. And *00.03*, the time of death, close to midnight. That solved the meaning of the message, but not the reason for its being sent. Was it another invitation, like the last sequence of digits, directing her to the site? Now, this message, which seemed to be sending her a time; *reminding* her of a time.

Well, the twenty-sixth was tomorrow, so she'd have the opportunity to discuss it with Seb and decide what to do and who to involve. That would have to wait until after her meeting with Phoebe in the morning.

She went through to the wardrobe in the bedroom, looking along the hanging rail for a suitable dress for welcoming home her toy-boy. It occurred to her how inexpensive the collection was compared to the relatively few dresses in Phoebe's locker at work. She allowed herself the thought that, if everything turned out right between her and Seb, she wouldn't be wearing it for very long, anyway. She thought about Eva, alone at home, being messed about by Andy again and, suddenly, something occurred to her.

She felt herself go cold.

Andy had missed Eva's birthday because he used the American format for abbreviating calendar dates; month followed by day. 9/11, not 11/9. Which was how the date was set out in the text. 1 26, not 26 1. So if it was Andy who had sent this latest text, it seemed likely he would have sent the others. Or did it? Perhaps she would find out tomorrow. But if she was right, how could she go through with meeting him tomorrow morning? Should she challenge him or pretend she hadn't seen the text? Or didn't care about it? She hoped Seb would come soon to take her thoughts away from the dilemma or at least help her work through it.

She checked her watch again – her engagement watch, she reminded herself. It was 11.05. Then she looked again, not at the time, but at the small square window on the right of the dial at three o'clock which showed the date. Except right now, it wasn't displaying one date. It was halfway to changing to tomorrow's date. From the twenty-fifth to the twenty-sixth. She cursed herself for getting it wrong. Three minutes past midnight on the twenty-sixth was not tomorrow night; it was in less than sixty minutes' time.

She looked out of the window, the curtains not yet drawn together, at the clear starlit sky, the moon throwing down a blanket of pale light. An easy drive up to Chadderton Close. She knew now how to get closer to the stone by car, by opening the gate off the road and driving up the steep lane she had breathlessly walked up before. She needed to make a decision; any delay and it would be made for her. She wouldn't get there in time, if indeed that was what she was supposed to do. It was as if something other than her conscious mind was deciding for her as she grabbed her keys and phone, pulled on her puffer jacket, woolly hat and gloves and rushed out to her car.

*

The wall clock chimed the quarter hour. It was time to make a move. He opened the bottom drawer of the dressing table and felt behind the rolled-up pairs of socks wedged in and filling every cubic centimetre of space except for that allocated to the revolver at the back. He took it out, a Smith and Wesson Model 29 .44 Magnum, and rotated the barrel. He juggled the gun on his forefinger, spinning it back and forth, side to side, high and low, before bringing it to rest in the shooting position. He looked up at the mirror over the dressing table and aimed it at his reflection.

'Do you feel lucky, punk? Go ahead, make my day.' He smiled. 'You're mixing up your movies,' he told himself.

Pulling open one of the smaller top drawers, he took out a leather holster and strap and a box of cartridges, securing the holster in position just forward of his left hip facing across his stomach. He loaded the gun, placing it first in the holster, then practising a quick draw, again in front of the mirror. He checked the clock again. It told him it was 11.22; no time to lose. From the hallstand he took his coat and headgear and went down the stairs to the parking area where the Kia Sportage awaited him.

*

Jo pulled into the lay-by just past the lane up to Chadderton Close. By now, she was beginning to wonder if her dash to the memorial stone wasn't just a knee-jerk reaction without any real logic behind it. Nevertheless, she had changed her mind about driving up from the road to the old deserted farmhouse. It was too obvious an approach if someone was waiting for her. She got out of the car and checked the time on her phone – 11.39. Planning now to approach the stone via the path through the trees – the only alternative route to the track – she opened the boot and took out a torch and her walking boots. She put the phone on the roof of the car and the torch in her pocket and pulled on the boots. Closing the boot of the car as quietly as possible, she headed along the road past the parking area and through a kissing gate to join a woodland path.

It was easy finding the way along with the moon brightly shining through the bare branches, but the ground underfoot was slippery with frost as the temperature dropped below zero, and the protruding roots of the trees meant that great care was needed to avoid falling. She eventually reached another kissing gate, where the path joined the track that was Moor Road, the extension of Holcombe Old Road, and one with which she was by now very familiar.

*

Seb tried again on the hands-free; the fourth attempt at reaching his wife in as many minutes. He was close to leaving the M60 at the junction with the A56 which meant he was within fifteen minutes of making it home. It would be close to pumpkin time, he had planned to say, although it didn't seem at all funny anymore. He told himself that Jo was probably in the shower, or had popped out the back to get some logs; so there was no point in phoning continuously, it made more sense to wait a few minutes. No need to worry.

As he approached Bury town centre, he tried again, with the same result. Perhaps now was the time to worry.

*

Jo waited for a few moments at the gate, checking for any sign that someone was waiting for her. Satisfied for now, she eased herself through, staying as low as possible. She paused, hearing a sound like a distant trilling. Surely not a bird at this time. Anyway, it had stopped, that's if she hadn't imagined it in the first place. The whiteness of the frost reflecting the light of the full moon created a ghostly effect, making everything as visible as if it was daytime, and Jo thought this must have been what it was like on that fateful night two and a half centuries ago when Ellen Strange met her death not far from where she was standing now.

A few metres away from the gate the Rossendale Way crossed the track. Heading west along the clear way for a couple of hundred metres or so, still keeping low, she then turned right onto the broader path which would take her to the memorial stone. She continued until it came into sight, then, dropping down onto her front, she lifted her head and waited. She checked her watch; the date had almost clicked over to the twenty-sixth and the hands showed one minute to midnight. She reached for her phone to double-check the exact time. It wasn't there, at least, not in the pocket where she expected to find it. She tried another… and another, rolling on to her back to make it easier to search. Then she remembered the faint ringing some minutes ago that had pierced the silence. She said a silent 'fuck', realising to her dismay that she had left it on the roof of the car.

She rolled on to her front again and for a few more minutes she lay with her head down so her body was flat to the ground. It occurred to her, when she was sure the three-minutes-past deadline had gone, that she was going to feel very foolish standing up and finding herself alone at midnight on Holcombe Moor. She thought about Seb and what he must be thinking and in a moment of levity, she chuckled at the thought that at least she hadn't turned into a pumpkin. She got slowly to her feet. She was only a matter of ten metres from the stone. Standing just behind it was a figure dressed in black and wearing a ski mask.

CHAPTER TWENTY-NINE

Saturday 26 January

Seb felt the first wave of panic hit him as he pulled in to Stock Street to discover that Jo's car was missing. Given the build-up to this moment over the past few days, it seemed inconceivable that she wouldn't be there waiting for him without letting him know why. He went into the house, checking all the rooms. He noted that the wardrobe was open, but couldn't see any significance in that. He checked his phone in case he had missed a text or voicemail message, already knowing that he hadn't, before opening his 'Find My Friends' App to check her location. He had difficulty believing what it was telling him. In the living room, John Simpson's pamphlet about the history and legend of Ellen Strange lay open on the coffee table making the unlikely link to where the App was pointing.

He left the house and got back in his car, the wheels skidding through a three point turn as he set off, crashing the gears, up Woodhill Road towards the main road to Holcombe.

★

'Right on time, Detective Inspector.' The voice was artificially distorted by some device in the ski mask, making it sound almost dalek-like. 'I did wonder whether you'd come at all; whether you'd work it out in time. Easy to underestimate you. A mistake we've made but which we'll now put right.'

Jo was frozen to the spot. There was nowhere to run, no means of escape. Her thoughts again went to Ellen Strange and how she must have known her fate was sealed in the minutes before her violent death. But at the same time, in a single moment, Jo's mind distilled the wealth of information swamping the incident board into a picture of absolute clarity. She suddenly knew *everything*, including, most importantly, the identity of the person she had been brought in to find; the insider whose betrayal had gone far beyond the passing of information to complicity in murder.

With no place to hide, Jo began walking towards the stone, closing the distance between her and the man in black until she could see his eyes. Dark, intense, they betrayed his mindset, initially arrogant and confident, slightly confused as she approached, and then angry at her apparent lack of fear. She had seen those same eyes flash darkly in anger on more than one occasion. The man stepped out from behind the stone.

'Stop there,' the voice said. 'That's as far as you go.'

Jo stopped, noticing for the first time the gun he was holding in his right hand. She was level with the rectangle of stones which had concealed Phoebe's boots. He waved with the gun towards them.

'This time there will be someone for the dog to find.'

The eyes bored into hers, holding them in an almost hypnotic stare. Then, barely perceptibly, they moved to refocus on something over her right shoulder. At that same moment, she heard the faint sound behind her of someone approaching through the frozen grass.

★

Just before reaching the turn-off for Summerseat, it occurred to Seb that Jo might be with his parents for some reason. A family emergency, perhaps, that Jo didn't want to share with him whilst he was driving. He dismissed the idea as quickly as it came to him, speeding past towards the Hare and Hounds pub and the road to Helmshore. His mind was all over the place; how could she be there when her phone was somewhere else?

In spite of his expecting to find it, he had a sickening, sinking feeling as he pulled to a halt behind Jo's Toyota Yaris at the roadside parking area. He was out of the car almost before it reached a standstill and quickly checked inside. Taking out his phone, he tried Jo's number again and the sound of its ringing on the roof of the Yaris made him jump. He put it in his pocket and ran back to open the gate at the road end of the lane leading up to Chatterton Close. Reversing the car past the entrance with a squeal of tyres, he turned left up the lane towards the house. At the end of the lane was a car he didn't recognise blocking his way through onto Moor Road. He got out and felt the bonnet; it was still warm. Squeezing through a kissing gate, he turned right and sprinted along the old road towards its junction with the Rossendale Way.

It was just as he reached the path that he heard the first shot along with an unearthly scream. The second came a moment later. The third took a few seconds longer.

★

Time seemed to stand still, as Jo considered her options. Was this the opportunity to run, while the man had his attention divided? Should she turn and see who was behind her, or stay focused on the eyes behind the ski mask? She chose to stay still as the person behind drew closer. The eyes ahead of her were wide now with a look of surprise.

The new addition to the scene spoke with an American drawl, softly, but loud enough to carry.

'I'm your Huckleberry.'

He stepped forward, past Jo's right shoulder then moved in front of her like a shield, facing the man in the mask. It took Jo a few moments to process this latest development. Her protector was tall, broad-shouldered and wearing a long dark coat, unfastened, which hung loosely around him. But the most bizarre feature of his appearance was the black Stetson hat. He paused for a long moment, then edged forward diagonally to the right, pulling back the left side of the coat to reveal the gun in its holster and drawing the first man's attention away from Jo. He stopped after a few metres and the two men faced each other, leaving Jo as a virtual spectator to the unfolding drama.

'Who the fuck are you? Wyatt fucking Earp?'

'Close.'

The masked man had raised his weapon level with his waist; the other man's hand rested on the gun in its holster.

Jo shouted out. 'Not the best surface for moonwalking.'

The eyes behind the mask turned briefly towards her, registering surprise this time. When they looked back the second man's hand was stretched out towards him, holding the revolver in the firing position.

'Why don't you put the gun down?' The cowboy drawl again. 'Or you can die. Your choice.'

The two men were still for two more seconds, then the masked man raised the gun. The second man fired, the bullet hitting home in the man's left thigh, his own shot passing well wide as his leg was jerked backwards and lifted off the ground, sending him crashing onto his face. Crying out in pain, the sound hideously distorted through the device in the mask, he raised the gun, aiming at Jo. The second man fired again, the man's body twitching with the force of the round and becoming still.

Jo dropped to her knees, head down and shaking. She started taking in deep breaths to try to stabilise herself. The whole spectacle had been unreal from beginning to end. She looked up to see a hand outstretched towards her. She gratefully grabbed it and Andy pulled her gently to her feet. She looked at him and smiled.

'Thanks, Doc.'

'You're very welcome.'

Andy holstered his Magnum, took his phone from his pocket and crouched down beside the still figure of Denzel 'Jacko' Chadwick.

★

The air ambulance lifted off just before 1.00 a.m. with Denzel Chadwick clinging to life inside. A full uniform contingent sealed off the area with crime-scene tape, and Detective Superintendent Jones had arrived along with uniformed Superintendent Kevin Knightly. Jo and Seb sat together in one of the police vehicles that had bounced their way along the rough track to get as close to the scene of the drama as possible. Andy had surrendered his revolver to Kevin Knightly and was being interviewed by the two superintendents in another car.

'I have to go into the station, Seb, I'm so sorry, but...'

'I understand, I do understand. I just can't believe the risk you took. I keep thinking you would be dead now if Mills hadn't seen the message on your board and worked out what it meant. Both of those things, seeing it *and* understanding it, were real longshots. In fact, the other longshot was that you *both* survived. It was more likely that...'

Jo turned and kissed him, long and hard, full on the lips, taking him by surprise. She pulled away after a long time, her eyes teary and her lip trembling a little.

'I know.' The tears flowed now. 'And I can't stop thinking if that had happened, then...' She paused, unable to continue.

'What?'

Before Jo could answer, there was a tap on the window. Mal smiled in at them then opened the door.

'Sorry to disturb you two. Jo, are you okay? We need to get back to the station. Seb, you're welcome to join us there, but I think your wife will be tied up for quite a while, and I believe you've had a long drive. It's up to you. But we'll need to leave soon.'

He closed the door again.

'I'm coming...' Seb began.

'No.' Jo interrupted him. 'Go back so I have you to come home to. I would feel better thinking of you in our little cottage warming up the rug. I'll get back as soon as I can.'

Seb sighed and was silent for a few moments.

'Okay.'

She leaned into him with another passionate kiss. 'Go now.'

Seb squeezed her hand and got out of the car, and set off towards Chatterton Close, where he had left his own vehicle after pulling it through the gate to let the police convoy through. Jo watched him all the way until he went out of sight around a bend in the track. She turned to find Andy just behind her, still in his Stetson.

'They want to know if you're okay to drive. Someone can take your car back to the station and you can come with me.'

'I *am* okay to drive, but I'd welcome a chat, just you and me, before we get to the formal stuff.'

'I hope you're not planning to hit on me just because I saved your life.'

Jo smiled. 'The thought did cross my mind but, thankfully, at great speed.'

Andy snorted a laugh. 'Right, let's go chat.'

★

On the journey back to the station, Jo shared with Andy her 'lightbulb' moment, the final link in the chain of logic that she had felt was missing. Andy listened without speaking, nodding from time to time but remaining silent.

'What do you think about getting Eva in right now?' Jo asked.

'*Eva?*'

'Yes, *Eva*. Works in our ops room, tall, good-looking; got a boyfriend in the police.'

'Oh, *that* Eva. Why right now?'

'I need some things checking and I don't think you or I are going to have much time over the next hour or so.'

'Well, it's your call…'

'But she's *your* girlfriend, and she'll need picking up. I spoke to her earlier and she'd already had three glasses of wine.'

'Fine, but it would be better if you contacted her. I can't imagine I'll be very popular at the moment.'

'I'm not surprised, chasing off after another woman like that.' She paused. 'Perhaps when all this is over, you'll tell me why.'

Andy smiled. 'Perhaps by then I'll have worked it out myself.'

Jo took her phone and scrolled to Eva in her contacts. The phone rang five times before a sleepy voice answered.

'What? Oh, hi, ma'am…'

'Hi. I'm sorry for the call at this time but I need you at the station as soon as possible. We've had a significant development and need to move very quickly. Can you make it?'

'Of course, but… well, I had a fair bit to drink last night, and…'

'No problem. We can pick you up.'

'We?'

'I'm with DS Mills; he's driving.'

'What?'

'I'll explain everything. Fifteen minutes okay?'

'Thirty would be better.'

'Okay, thirty. Thanks, Eva.'

She turned to Andy. 'You've time to drop me off and pick her up afterwards. But no making up; straight back to work. Okay?'

'Yes, ma'am.'

Jo noted it was the first time her sergeant had used that form of address without sarcasm.

★

'Here's what we'd like you to do, Eva.'

The three detectives sat together in Jo's office. The operations room was deserted, and, except for Eva, would stay that way until the early shift arrived at seven o'clock.

'Get in touch with the service provider and check out the calls made by this phone on these two days, and especially between those times.' Jo pushed a piece of paper across the desk to her.

Eva looked at the number, dates and times, taking a while to absorb the instruction. She looked up and frowned.

'But, ma'am, this number…'

'I know. Can you get on to the provider now? Pull whatever strings you need to get the info. Threaten them with obstruction if you have to. This is *very* urgent, Eva, and say nothing to anyone yet, not even the Super. DS Mills and I will be upstairs occupying him for a while, anyway. Okay?'

Eva looked from one to the other, clearly shocked by this latest development. Then she opened her eyes wide, as if something suddenly made sense.

'Okay,' she said, in a small but determined voice. She got to her feet with a glance and a little smile to Andy. As she was leaving the room she turned back to them. 'When you arranged to pick me up, you said you'd explain everything. When is that going to happen, ma'am, starting with what went on tonight which had you both out on the moor at midnight?'

Jo smiled. 'Fair question, Eva. As soon as possible after we get the information from the server.'

Eva nodded and left without speaking.

★

Mal leaned back in his chair, swivelling from side to side as he did when he was deep in thought. He had chosen to speak to Jo and Andy together in his office before taking anything forward officially. The implications of what had occurred on the moor had not yet become clear in his mind.

There was the major issue of Andy's gun, his ownership and the fact that he had actually used it, although, given that in doing so he had certainly saved another officer's life as well as his own, it seemed unlikely that any damaging punishment would follow. He was the hero, and almost a victim, of the drama, not the villain; an interesting example of role reversal based on his previous record.

In so far as his DI was concerned, her penchant for creating a sensation on Holcombe Moor was almost on a par with that of Ellen Strange herself. Her brief explanation at the scene an hour ago was insufficient to satisfy his understanding of her race against midnight. Having said that, he had failed since then to identify any wrong she had done.

They arrived together in his office at exactly the scheduled time for the meeting at 2.00 a.m. In spite of the excitement and danger they had shared, he noted that he had never seen them more relaxed together during the month of Jo's assignment. He got to his feet as they entered and waved them to the two chairs in front of his desk.

'Jo,' he said. 'You haven't got a coffee.'

Jo gave a little laugh. 'I've just put one out, sir.'

'Good, I'd hate to have to call Lucy at this time. No doubt she'll be in the Northern Quarter right now, probably stoned – as in, inebriated, I mean. That's a joke, by the way. So, let's start with you, Jo. Tell me again what led you on to the moor.'

'I received another message yesterday, a series of digits, like before, except *not* like before. It wasn't the same format as the grid reference but turned out to be the date and time of Ellen Strange's death. So I went to check whether it was someone sending me a sort of invitation to be there at that same time. So…'

'Hold on.' Mal held up his hand to interrupt. 'Let me understand this. Believing someone might be luring you out onto the moor at midnight, you decided it would be a good idea to head out there by yourself, also believing it might be linked to a murder. Am I right?'

Jo shrugged. 'Well, put like that, in retrospect, it doesn't sound like the brightest thing I've ever done.'

'*Damn right*,' Mal shouted, slapping the desktop hard with the flat of his hand. 'What possessed you to...?'

'Because I didn't have time to think, sir. I interpreted it initially as pointing to late on the twenty-sixth before realising it was just a few minutes after midnight at the beginning of the same day. It left me no time to do anything but set off straight away if I was going to make it.'

'What I can't understand is why you were so sure that charging out there was what you were meant to do. Although, clearly, you were correct, as you were with the previous messages.'

'I was anything but sure, sir, but it was a possibility and I had no time to waste in checking it out.'

'And are we any closer to finding out who sent the original messages? Because without those, this one would have made no sense whatsoever, would it?'

Jo shrugged. 'I guess not, but I hadn't given much thought as to who sent them. Just a prank, after all, and no harm done.'

'Except for the frostbite,' Mal said. 'Well, perhaps we should start giving that some thought again. So carry on. What happened when you got there?'

'Well, I got close enough so I could see the moorstone then I lay down to wait until three minutes past midnight had passed. Nothing had happened, no-one had appeared, so I stood up and that's when I saw this figure – Jacko Chadwick, as it turned out – standing behind it holding a gun. He must have stood up when he saw me getting up. He was wearing a ski mask with a voice distortion device in it but I recognised him by his eyes. Dark and evil, you might say.'

'A bit like mine, you mean?' Andy said.

'Just a bit,' Jo said.

'And that's when the gunslinger arrived?' Mal addressed the question to Jo but was looking at Andy.

'Just in time,' Jo answered. 'Then the gunfight, at which point I expected to wake up and discover I'd been watching *Tombstone* on TV.'

'And you, what was all that about?' Mal turned his attention to Andy. 'And what does "I'm your Huckleberry" mean, for God's sake?'

'Well, it's real meaning is "I'm the one you want" or "I'm the man for the job." An expression used by the real Doc Holliday back in the 1880s ... sir.'

'Fascinating...'

'By the way, when will I get my gun back, sir? It is a legal firearm, licensed and...'

'We'll see. It may be licensed but you were certainly not authorised to use it. So, tell me how you came to be out there.'

'I went in to the DI's office after she had left to leave her a note about the meeting with Phoebe Wright tomorrow – well, later this morning – and I saw the message on the board underneath the grid reference for the memorial stone. Given that both messages referred to the killing of Ellen Strange, I came to the same conclusion that it was a summons to go to the stone at that time.'

'And the fancy dress?'

'Aimed to confuse, sir, and give an edge if, indeed, anything was going to happen. But the hat sort of goes with the gun and holster, and the coat – well, it's a modern puffer coat – just a long one.'

Mal shook his head and sighed. 'Go on.'

'I got there about ten minutes before midnight, parked at the top of the access lane to Chatterton Close, then set off for the memorial. They were facing each other near the stone. I approached, making myself visible, stepped in front of DI Carter, which was when I saw he was holding a shooter. I pulled open my coat to show him my gun and walked off to the side to take his attention away from her. She shouted at him, which divided his attention again and I drew the gun. When he looked back we each had a weapon trained on the other, though his was at waist level, and you can't hit a thing from there. I told him to put down his gun, but he raised it instead and I shot him, in the upper leg to disable him. He fired the gun; miles wide but he held on to it and aimed it at DI Carter. So I shot him again. He was squirming on the ground from the leg wound so I had no idea where I hit him, but he just twitched a bit and lay still.'

Andy spread his hands. 'End of story.'

Mal shook his head again. 'If only it was,' he said. 'Unofficially, that was a courageous thing to do, Andy, and I'm grateful for the action you took. *Officially*, I am recommending an investigation into the incident by the IOPC...'

Jo leaned forward. 'But, sir, surely you can't...'

'If I don't, Jo, there will be a *demand* for an investigation from elsewhere. And the very fact that I suggest it will send a message that I am confident of a favourable outcome.' He turned to Andy. 'I hope I don't have to tell you that you will have my full backing.'

'God, this is so unfair,' Jo said, finding her eyes tearing up in anger. 'It was my fault this happened. If I hadn't...'

'The Super's right, ma'am,' Andy interrupted.

'Look, will you please call me Jo,' she snapped. 'Until further notice, at least. You've just saved my fucking life, for God's sake. And now...'

'And now,' Mal interrupted, leaning forward over the desk and waiting until Jo's anger had subsided, 'I want you two to get out there and finish the job. Get whatever you can from Miss Wright and give me the last piece of the jigsaw so I can send the uniforms storming in to Easy Rider.'

'Before we do that, sir,' Jo said, 'we have unfinished business to deal with tonight and we'll need your help in raising some manpower.'

*

After the drama of the past few hours, there was an almost unreal calm in Jo's office as they sipped their coffees in silence. Jo was seated in her chair with Andy perched on the edge of her desk.

Andy checked his watch. 'Now?' he said.

Jo nodded and listened to his half of the conversation as he made the call. When he had finished, he turned to Jo.

'Right, now we wait.'

Jo nodded, and picked up her desk phone. 'Message sent,' she said as her call was answered on the first ring. 'Cars in position...? Great.'

She looked up at Andy. 'God knows what state we'll be in for meeting Phoebe.'

*

The unmarked police car edged out of the side road, the driver's attention fixed on the rear lights of the saloon as it pulled out of the driveway of the large Edwardian semi and headed for Manchester Road.

'On the move,' the passenger said into his radio. 'Target just turning left on the A56 towards the city centre. Drop in behind us.'

They followed at a discreet distance through Whitefield and the junction at Besses o' th' Barn. The second police car was now close behind the first as they reached the large roundabout which marked the boundary with Prestwich. The car took the third exit onto the M60, the leading police vehicle continuing on the A56 to make an illegal U-turn at the traffic lights at the Tesco Superstore, leaving the second to pick up the pursuit.

The passenger in the new leading police car spoke into his phone. Jo Carter answered.

'Heading along the M60, anticlockwise from junction seventeen. Do we intercept? Please advise.'

'Not yet. Let's find out the destination.'

'My guess would be the airport, ma'am.'

'Mine, too. Keep me informed.'

Even at that early hour of the morning, the motorway was relatively busy and it was not difficult merging with the traffic whilst still keeping the car in sight. It left the M60 at Junction 5, which linked to the M56, and the first pursuit vehicle took over again as the second did a circuit of the roundabout and dropped in behind it. At the second exit, the car turned off.

'Heading into airport complex, ma'am.'

'Pick up at first opportunity, before the target gets into the crowds on foot. Preferably straight out of the car.'

'Yes, ma'am.'

★

Jo placed the phone on the desk and shook her head.

'I'm not looking forward to this,' she said. 'I can't believe…' Her voice tailed off as Eva appeared in the doorway clutching a sheet of A4. She placed the information on the desk.

'Data from the provider, ma'am. Full list of calls, but nothing between those times...' she hesitated '...which is a bit of a surprise.'

'Thanks, Eva.'

'Another thing, ma'am. While I was waiting for the information, I checked again the CCTV capture on the night of the murder. I figured if the two guys from the pub weren't the ones who picked up Knox, well they must have gone somewhere. Most of the cameras were out but our friendly camera on Bolton Street picked up a couple of guys walking towards the Leisure Centre, away from the scene.'

'Friendly camera?' Jo asked.

'The same one that captured the woman from the Shoulder of Mutton getting off the bus on the twenty-second of December. There was hardly anybody around so they sort of stood out, and I'd swear they were the same two who were caught on camera when they were thrown out of the pub.'

'And the time was...?' Andy asked.

'Two minutes to eleven, around the time Mr Wilson saw Knox picked up on Manchester Road.'

'That's great work, Eva. Can you put that on the file and then you can get back home and sleep off the rest of the wine. Not that it seems to have affected your judgement.'

'I think I'd rather stay, if you don't mind, ma'am. I'd like to see this through.'

'I don't mind at all, Eva. If you two could make yourself scarce for five minutes I have a call to make to my anxious husband, then DS Mills and I will take you through what happened tonight.'

★

Jo checked her watch as she headed down to the interview rooms on the ground floor. It was 5.45 a.m. and it occurred to her that she'd had no sleep for almost twenty-four hours, and there was little prospect of that for several hours to come. Given the timespan, and the fact that during that period she had nearly been shot dead, she was feeling remarkably well; positive and energised. The man walking beside her was, after all, in the same situation, having also missed a night's recharging. The uniformed officer in the corridor nodded a greeting and opened the door to the interview room. Another officer was in the room standing just inside the door. The man seated at the table was nervously twisting his hands together, his face already showing the strain of the last hour. He looked up as they entered, his eyes fixing on Jo and opening wide with shock.

'Good morning, DC Malik,' Jo said.

'Wha… what's going on…?'

The police constable left the room and Jo and Andy took their places on the two chairs facing the detective constable across the table.

'What's going on, he says,' Jo said. 'I think that's my line, detective. You are asked by your sergeant to attend a meeting at the station early this morning and you decide to leave the country instead. And you think *we* have questions to answer. But before we go any further, we shall be recording this interview. I trust you have no objection.'

'I see, so it's an interview, is it? Well unless you're going to charge me with anything, then yes I do object to your recording it, *ma'am*. And if you insist on doing so, I think I should be allowed to have a lawyer present.'

'Very well,' Jo smiled, 'although I'm surprised you feel you *need* one. You don't know why we're here yet. We'll leave you to make the call.'

Jo and Andy got to their feet and made to leave the room.

'Okay,' Mo said, 'as it happens I *don't* feel I need a lawyer, so do what you like.'

They took their seats again. Jo turned on the recorder and stated who was in the room and that Detective Constable Mohammed Malik had declined to have a lawyer present.

'No recording would have been fine with me, by the way,' Andy said, 'because I'm always getting bollockings for swearing at people in interviews. So start by telling us, where were you fucking off to?'

Mo looked down at the table. 'Pakistan. My wife left me earlier this week. I was going after her. I'm sorry I didn't give the proper notice and all that, but she didn't give *me* any notice at all. I was planning to phone you from the airport when it was too late for you to stop me going.' He looked up from one to the other.

'Is this the same lady who phoned you on the fourteenth of January just after we found Phoebe's boots?' Jo asked.

Mo hesitated for a few moments. 'Oh, yes, to check when I'd be getting home for dinner.'

'Even though, according to you, she was down in London on a course at the time,' Andy said. 'What did she plan to do, talk you through how to make an omelette?'

Mo didn't reply for a long time, frowning in concentration, then shook his head. 'She went down the day after we found the boots, for the rest of the week.'

'Rumaisa, isn't it? Your wife's name,' asked Jo. 'That would be the name on her passport?'

'Yes, that's right. Look, do I get to ask some questions now, starting with why...'

'No, you don't,' Jo said, with a new edge to her voice. 'You get to answer ours, and to listen to what we think is going on. Let's stick with the phone call for now. You got that call at around nine o'clock, give or take, but here's a thing, there is no record of your receiving that call.'

Mo paused again before responding. 'Well there must be some mistake,' he said, angrily. 'You were there, for fuck's sake...'

'Yes, we were there,' Andy said, *'inside* the tent. You took the call *outside* the tent, in a sub-zero blizzard.'

'It was private...'

'Oh, I don't doubt that,' Jo said.

'And I use a different phone for private calls.'

'Not all the time though.' Jo looked down at the sheet of paper Eva had given her. 'On that same day you received two and made three calls to your wife from the number we have on your file.'

'And how did you get my wife's number?'

'It's the one we also have on your file for contacting your next of kin. Anyway, tell us what the number is for your *private* phone.' Jo waited, pen in hand, notebook open. Mo remained silent. 'Forgotten it, eh? Sometimes happens, not remembering your own number.' She looked at Andy and shrugged. 'You never call the number yourself, so it doesn't stick in your mind.'

Mo stared down at the table.

'But while we're talking about phones, on the day Phoebe turned up, you spent nearly two hours making calls, outside in the snow again, before you set off with DC Johnson to pick her up.

Private calls again, no doubt, because there is no record of them on your call list either.' She paused. 'We'd really appreciate it if you could remember that other number, so we could get the calls on that checked out.'

Mo made no attempt to respond. He seemed to be mentally detached from the exchange.

'There was no urinating weather forecaster was there, Malik?' Andy said. 'The calls you made from here that day were to set up a snatch. You went back into the station at Sheffield, not for a piss, but to let your mates know you were about to set off.'

'DI Watson at Sheffield told us they have a camera on the corridor outside the Gents,' Jo said, 'and they've clocked every person who went in and out of there, including you, on that day. And nobody used the loo from seven minutes before you went in to twelve minutes after you came out.'

'Then you ducked inside the Snake Inn ahead of DC Johnson to let them know you'd arrived,' Andy went on. 'Although she failed to mention it at the time, DC Johnson did wonder how you knew the Snake Inn was closed before you got there.'

'What is Phoebe going to tell us later this morning, DC Malik, that made it so important that she never made it back here?' Jo asked. 'With hindsight, it explains your obsession with finding her, the hours spent trawling through CCTV recordings. It was important that someone found her before the police did. And I think you were convinced that the woman at the Shoulder was Phoebe right from the start, which is why you tried to send us on a wild goose chase by claiming she got on the London train, even checking individual stations on that route to make it convincing. Then deleting the coverage of the woman boarding the train.'

'And yet with all that practice,' Andy said, 'you failed to spot Jacko making a phone call after the fight at the Lancashire Gate; failed to spot Josh Reeves's car on Manchester Road just before Knox was picked up; failed to pick up the two guys from the pub walking away from the scene on Bolton Street.'

'That's a bit harsh, DS Mills,' Jo said. 'I don't think he failed to spot any of those things. He just decided not to bring them to our attention.'

Mo had leaned back on his chair now with his arms folded and seemingly relaxed. Jo couldn't decide whether it was a show of surrender or defiance.

'Then there's Easy Rider,' Jo said. 'I should have clocked Reeves's reaction when you and I turned up at the depot. Not just surprise that it was a different detective, but shock and confusion because it was that particular detective. A bad miss, that.'

'And there's you always steering us away from Easy Rider,' Andy said, 'always casting doubts on the rest of the team's suspicions.'

'Hiding the wig you found in the locker,' Jo said. 'It didn't really help your cause, did it, once you'd decided on the identity of the girl at the Shoulder? You knew in your own mind it was Phoebe in a wig. It was best no-one else did. You even went as far as stating in one of our meetings that it definitely *wasn't* Phoebe. And then there's the murder and attempted murder.' She paused for a long time. 'We're not sure how you featured in those two incidents, so you can enlighten us, Mo. Or should we call you "Ed"? That's the other Brit diminutive of Mohammed, isn't it? Last two letters rather than the first two.'

DC Malik said nothing. A long silence was broken by a gentle knock on the door and the uniformed officer poked his head into the room.

'DC Johnson needs to speak to you, ma'am.'

Mo looked startled at the mention of his colleague's name. Jo paused the recording and left the room. She was back in within a couple of minutes. She took her seat and restarted the recording.

'It can't be easy having to face all this just a few days after your wife left you. Why did she leave? Was it because she knew, or found out, what you were involved in?'

'We'd been going through a rough patch. It was always going to happen.' His voice was flat and matter-of-fact.

'So she just upped and left without saying anything. When was that, did you say?'

'Like I said, earlier this week.'

'Surely you can be more precise than that,' Jo said. 'Let's say, when did you *discover* she had gone?'

'Tuesday some time, I found a note from her after I left work.'

'And how did she seem that morning?'

'Okay. Like I said, we'd been having some trouble, so not over-friendly. Look what has this got to do…?'

Jo consulted the sheet of paper she had just been handed by Eva.

'You see, a lady called Rumaisa Malik flew out of Manchester at eight-oh-five a.m. on Saturday the nineteenth of February, on an Etihad Airlines flight to Lahore, via Abu Dhabi. The one-way ticket was purchased the day before, by phone, at ten-twenty-five a.m., shortly after we received news that Phoebe Wright, with all her secrets, had turned up at a police station in Sheffield.' She looked up from the sheet. 'Quite a coincidence.'

'Okay, I got the day wrong. I've had a lot...'

Andy laughed out loud. 'Got the day wrong. Tuesday, not Saturday. Come on, Malik, you can do better than that. Perhaps she came back again on Sunday. Forgot her purse, or something, then went *back* to Lahore on Tuesday. There, has that helped you out at all?'

Mo stared at Andy; his demeanour had changed and his eyes were full of hatred. It looked for a moment as though he would leap across the table and attack him.

'I think what you did was quite noble, Mo,' Jo said. 'When Phoebe went to the police, you realised that there was a good chance that the balloon would go up...' she frowned '...or should that be, "would burst"? Your instinct was to make sure your wife was okay, so you shipped her off to her family in Pakistan, with a view to joining her if things didn't work out. And you must believe they won't, because you're booked on the same flight this morning.'

She paused and checked her watch .

'Six-forty. You've missed check-in by now, so you can take your time. Before you tell us what part you played in killing Curtis Knox and attempting to kill me, let's talk about the balloon that's about to go up, or burst. What is Easy Rider about? Drugs? People? Guns? All the above? We're going to find out very soon, probably within about four hours. It might help you in the long run if you told us now before you have to.'

Mo looked from one to the other with a look of defiance. 'I am saying nothing until I have seen my lawyer.'

Andy leaned towards him with a mirthless smile. 'Probably a sensible idea given the depth of the shit you're in, Malik.'

'DC Malik, you will be detained in custody for further

questioning. In the meantime, we can make available legal representation on your behalf, or you will be permitted one phone call to arrange your own.' Mo said nothing, but pointed to himself. 'For the benefit of the recording, DC Malik has indicated that he will arrange his own legal representation. Interview ended six-fifty-three a.m.'

★

Jo made it home by 7.20 a.m. planning to get at least an hour's sleep, a shower, and a change of clothes prior to her return to the station at 9.00, before setting off for Fairfield Hospital. Seb's insistence on helping her undress robbed her of fifteen minutes' sleep, although she felt that the trade-off was worth the sacrifice. Also, she felt the shower would have taken less time if she had taken it alone. Nevertheless, she arrived on time back at the station feeling invigorated with a strong sense of purpose and a healthy appreciation of what was important. Andy was already there by the time Jo arrived at just after nine. He had also been home, with Eva, to change and shower. Jo chose not to enquire what part, if any, the detective constable had played in his refreshment.

Kirsty intercepted them just as they were about to leave.

'There was an incident at Fairfield Hospital early this morning.' Jo's eyes opened wide in horrible anticipation. 'No, no… ' Kirsty continued, waving her arms to reassure her '…everything's okay. Geoff Brazendale phoned to report there'd been a disturbance, a fight, just inside the hospital grounds around three o'clock and he'd sent some of the police cover to deal with it. While they were outside someone had entered the building. They smashed some equipment in the room Phoebe was moved out of, Geoff thinks probably in anger because she wasn't there. He said to assure you that Phoebe has not been left alone since he set up the cover yesterday.'

Jo sighed. 'Thanks, Kirsty. We're heading there right now.'

'Let's hope that's the last attempt to keep Miss Wright quiet,' she said as she and Andy headed for the car park.

They drove in silence for the first few minutes of the four-kilometre journey to the hospital. It was Andy who spoke first.

'The boss may not be right, of course, about it being the same person who sent you all the texts.'
'Really. Why do you think that?'
Andy paused. 'It's not so much me *thinking* that.'
Jo let the comment sink in before replying. 'I see. Well, if I'm right in what I *think* you're saying…'
'And you usually are, I remember you telling me once.'
'You certainly didn't send the last one, although it was clearly meant to *appear* that you had – reversing the day and month like that.'
Neither spoke for a few minutes. It was Jo who broke the silence again.
'So, the obvious question is…'
'Why?' Andy said.
'And why the moorstone, and what about the boots, and… I can think of a few more.'
'And I'll answer them all.' He paused. 'I guess that's it for me now, anyway, one way or another. So you'll get your wish.'
'My wish?'
'I think I said before, there shouldn't be any secrets between lovers. Eva sort of let it slip about your intended legacy concerning Detective Sergeant Andrew Mills. Don't blame her, by the way, I can be very good at getting information when I put my mind to it… and in the right circumstances.'
Jo turned in her seat to face him. 'I thought we'd moved on from there, Andy, even before last night.'
'Perhaps, but it won't make any difference. Think about it. Cryptic, anonymous messages to my immediate boss, hiding evidence, dragging two police forces out into a blizzard, deflecting focus from a missing person investigation and shooting a major suspect in a murder case. I could lose about four careers on the strength of that.'
'Well, I'll be eternally grateful for that last transgression, I can tell you'.
They pulled into the staff car park at the hospital at exactly 9.20.
'What I'm planning to do,' Jo said, before they got out of the car, 'is meet with Phoebe on my own but suggest you join us. I'll say you'd like to say "Hi" and see that she's okay. I'd feel better if…'

'It's up to you, of course,' Andy interrupted. 'Just let me know.'

There were a few moments of tense silence, then Jo opened the door. 'Right, let's go.'

They were met by Geoff Brazendale in reception, who walked with them through to the room where Phoebe was waiting, filling in the details of the incident as they went, and confirming what Kirsty had already told them.

'So you reckon the two things were definitely connected – the disturbance and the gatecrasher?' Andy asked.

'Can't say for certain, but it's a bit of a coincidence if not. Bunch of guys fighting at three in the morning in the hospital grounds is weird enough. For it to happen at the exact time someone tries to pay a visit to Phoebe…'

'Right enough,' Jo said. 'Does Phoebe know about the incident?'

'No, I didn't see any reason to unsettle her.'

'Good,' Jo said.

They reached the room where Phoebe was waiting along with Dr Lei, and Geoff popped his head in to announce their arrival. The sergeant looked remarkably bright and focused given that he had stayed on duty all night through several shift changes. There was still a police presence in the form of an armed officer at each end of the corridor, which was empty of all other personnel. This was in sharp contrast to the areas they had just passed through which were bustling with activity. They could hear low voices through the door, which had not quite fully closed. The doctor stepped outside to meet them, her eyes resting on Andy with more than a hint of concern.

'Good morning. Phoebe did say very specifically that she would speak only to you, Detective Inspector. And she has just re-affirmed that to me, so…'

'And that's what we're expecting, doctor, but I'm hoping she'll change her mind after I've spoken to her.' She held up her hand to stay any objection. 'But I will not press her if she wishes to continue with just me. I will stress, though, that now Phoebe is well enough, she is likely to be facing consequences that will override any personal preference on her side. She might as well get used to that as soon as possible. Nevertheless, for today, we will go along with what she wants.' She turned to Andy. 'DS Mills, would you stay close and keep yourself available, if required.'

Andy nodded and turned to Dr Lei, with a wide smile.

'In the meantime, Dr Lei, could I suggest a peace offering in the form of a cup of coffee in your excellent cafeteria?'

The doctor opened her eyes wide in surprise.

'Well, I... don't see why not,' she said. 'Just excuse me a moment.'

She opened the door and leaned into the room.

'DI Carter is here, Phoebe.' She stepped back and waved Jo through, turning then to Andy with a smile. 'Let's go get that peace offering, Detective Sergeant.'

'Please, make that Andy,' he said.

★

The room was a step up from the private ward where she had first met Phoebe. The only suggestion of a medical institution was the hospital bed, and the pine bedside table with the anglepoise lamp deflected attention away from it. In front of the window was a mid-height coffee table surrounded by three wing chairs, one facing the window and one at each side. Along one side of the room was a cabinet on which stood a tray with a kettle, four China mugs, two ceramic jars labelled 'Coffee' and 'Tea', a bowl of sugar lumps and a couple of spoons. Above the cabinet was a large, wall-mounted television.

Phoebe was seated on one of the side chairs and got to her feet when Jo entered. She looked a different person to the one Jo had met previously; exactly like her photograph, in fact. It wasn't about make-up – she wore very little, Jo noticed – but all to do with the brightness of her smile and the twinkling of her eyes. Her hair was now hanging loose and slightly curled onto her shoulders. She was dressed in tight denim jeans and a light fleece top over a tee shirt.

'Good morning, DI Carter,' she said, reaching out to shake her hand.

'And to you, young lady. You look like a million dollars.'

Phoebe smiled. 'What, you mean all green and crinkly. One of Benny's jokes, please don't laugh.'

Jo laughed anyway, and they sat down opposite each other at the table.

'So how is Benny? And more to the point, how are you *and* Benny?'

'Okay to both questions. I mean there's a bit of tension still, but it's to be expected, and it's all my fault. It's not just my disappearing *now*, he's found out about all the other times I've told him I've been at my parents, and now he knows I was lying to him. Anyway,' she gave a little laugh, 'I'll get round him. I know *exactly* how.' She looked round the room. 'But I might move in here permanently. Great service, three excellent meals a day, doctors on tap, and some of them are *really* fit…' Her voice trailed off, and she slumped back in the chair. 'This is all pretend, you know; just a front, all this jolliness. I'm absolutely shit-scared.' There was a catch in her voice and tears filled her eyes. She choked out a little laugh and pointed to her face. 'This is why I didn't put any mascara on.'

'What are you afraid of, Phoebe?' Jo held up her hand. 'Before you answer, I understand you want to speak to me one-to-one, but DS Mills is with me. I think he's chatting up Dr Lei right now. He's keen to speak to you again, told me to say Hi to you, if you feel up to…'

Phoebe leaned forward, looking a little brighter. 'I'd like to see him again, actually, but can you and I talk first?' She smiled. 'It'll give him a better chance with the doc. I can't imagine she's much of a pushover.'

'Very well, but what we say to each other now can't be held in confidence. You have a lot of explaining to do, in addition to why you're frightened, and it's important that we know everything. So what you tell me can't stay with me, do you understand?'

'I understand, and I'm so sorry for all the trouble I've caused.'

'The main thing is you're back safe and, eventually, well. So let's go all the way back to when you left uni. But first, I'm going to make myself a coffee. Can I get you one?'

Phoebe sprang up from her chair. 'No, I'll do it. Sorry, no manners. What will you have?'

'White, no sugar – if you have any milk.'

'*Voila*.' Phoebe opened the door of the cabinet to reveal a mini fridge. She took out a milk carton and made the drinks.

'So,' Jo said, when they had settled back in their seats, 'start from what you think is the beginning of all this.'

Phoebe hesitated for a few moments. Then, as if a dam that was holding back the words inside her had been suddenly breached, she poured forth her story.

'When I was at uni in Sheffield I met this guy at a club. He lived in Manchester and worked as a non-emergency ambulance driver taking groups of people to hospitals and days out. He became a sort of boyfriend for a while and stayed with me a few times when he was over there, nothing serious, just… well, sex, really. Anyway, I'd told him I was thinking of giving up uni and going back home to Bury and he said he might be able to get me a job doing what he was doing. I said I was interested and he said how soon could I start. Just like that.' She shook her head. 'I must have been desperate, and naïve, because I grabbed his hand off. At the end of the term, the *first* term, I packed in the course and joined Easy Rider.'

'And who was this guy who recruited you?' Jo asked. 'And I'm afraid you will have to give us names…'

Phoebe hesitated, biting her bottom lip and looking away. 'Okay, his name's Des Saunders. He actually moved over to Sheffield shortly afterwards; he's who I was staying with in the few days before I got picked up by your guys.'

'So what happened when you first joined Easy Rider?'

'It was great, I loved it. Everybody was so nice, Josh, the other drivers, and the customers – we don't call them patients – were lovely. I got to drive this fantastic vehicle. Trips to the seaside from time to time, shopping days at the Trafford Centre and Meadowhall. A dream job, really. Even Mum and Dad seemed to approve when they saw how much I enjoyed it.' She paused. 'But it wasn't just people we moved around.'

She looked at Jo with wide, frightened eyes.

'Go on, Phoebe.'

'We were moving drugs. Josh explained it to me. He said they were all soft, recreational drugs, the ones legalised under the new regulations, but because they were now being controlled, there was loads of red tape between the supplier and the user. All we were doing was short-cutting the delivery process. This is what Josh said. He made it sound so innocent, like we were doing everyone a favour. The suppliers – they got their money quicker, the users

– they got their happy pills sooner, even the police, who had less paper-pushing to do. God I must have been so thick.'

She paused and shook her head, tears welling.

'Or perhaps you just wanted to believe it,' Jo said. 'And if that's *all* it was, then it's not such a bad thing, is it? After all, you were doing so much good, enriching the lives of the people who were your main customers. Take your time, Phoebe. Your coffee will be cold.' Phoebe reached for the mug and took a long drink. 'How did you pick up the drugs?'

'I never actually touched them. They were loaded into the luggage compartment while the vehicles were at the depot, except on some occasions when there was an arranged pick-up point, usually somewhere in Bury centre. But I was never personally involved in any of those And when we got to our destination, we had instructions where to park after we dropped off the customers and we just left the vehicle for an hour or so and someone came along to offload them. And vice versa, if they were loaded at the destination and offloaded back at the depot. I guess, it's the classic case of turning a blind eye, except I didn't need to because I didn't see anything anyway.'

'And who was the main man in all this, Phoebe? Who organised the movement of the drugs?'

'At the beginning it was Josh, but a couple of weeks after I started, this guy called Rob Challinor joined the company, and he seemed to have more and more say in what was going on. I overheard him once having a real stand-up row with Josh. I thought it was going to end in a fight, and it was Challinor having a go at Josh, not the other way round. He seemed to be taking over.'

'While all this was going on, were you ever aware of someone with the police being involved?'

'Oh, yes, it was a bit of a joke. Our man in the cop shop. Somebody called Ed, or known as Ed.'

Jo nodded. 'None of this so far seems too intimidating, Phoebe. Nothing that you'd run away from. So what happened?'

'As I said, Challinor seemed to be taking over, bit by bit, and it had stopped being so much fun. For the first half of the year, the drugs were sort of incidental. It was just part of an ordinary day; I hardly thought about them, and it wasn't every day; most days it was just the customers. The "core business" as Josh called it. Then last April I started going out with Benny and although he never tried to push me or anything, I know he was disappointed I hadn't committed myself to the course at Sheffield. I knew him from school, you know. He was my art teacher and we always got on really well together. No funny stuff; he was just a really nice guy.' Her eyes took on an abstract look. 'People ask me what I see in him, and it's just that. He's a really good person.' She looked at Jo. 'Did you think that? "I wonder what she sees in him", when you met him?'

'It's not for me to think...'

'It's okay; my choice, my decision. And I've treated him like shit. That big scene in the Horse, not getting in touch...' Her eyes were filling up again.

Jo waited until she had composed herself.

'Can we carry on, Phoebe? You were saying how things were changing.'

'That's right. I mentioned about leaving to Josh on one occasion and he got real nasty, which he'd never been with me. Said something about me just having to put up with it, we're all in too deep to do anything about it. That was just after I'd moved in with Benny and by then Josh had us all using two phones – a burner for arranging pick-ups of drugs and the contract phone for everything else. And secret posts on Facebook. He had us all checking out times and places and "liking" the posts. We had to do it.'

'Why was that, Phoebe? We know about the posts but if you weren't all involved in every pick-up, why did you all have to okay them?'

'Curtis said it was Rob's way of pulling us in, implicating us in everything that went on. So it looked as if we were more involved than we were. Even then I didn't catch on. I thought it was someone just playing the big man. You know, making more of it than necessary. God, I was so fucking stupid.'

'So what tipped the balance, Phoebe? I'm right in thinking that you came to a decision to get out?'

'One trip to Meadowhall, I had to drive the ambulance to this abandoned factory yard and leave it for an hour, which left me walking about a mile back to civilisation. I'd parked up and left the

445

keys on top of the front nearside wheel as usual, but after a few minutes it started to rain. So I doubled back to get my brolly and when I got there they had the luggage compartment open and they were unloading the boxes. But it wasn't drugs they were collecting, it was guns. I wouldn't have known except one guy took one out of a crate and started waving it around pretending he was going to use it.

'I must have gasped or something because they all looked round. I ducked out of sight, but I couldn't say for certain if they saw me or not. I knew one of the guys, so if he did see me, he could have recognised me. I got away as quickly as I could and no-one came after me, so I hoped – still hope – that they didn't see me. But it shook me up, brought me to my senses.'

'So what did you do?'

'I just played it straight on the day. Went back after an hour, retrieved the keys. No-one was around so I assumed they thought everything had gone to plan. I drove to Meadowhall to wait for the customers. And nothing's happened since, so perhaps they didn't suspect anything.'

'Did you tell anyone about what you saw?'

Phoebe's eyes filled up again. 'Yes. I told Curtis. We'd become good friends, he gave me a lift quite often and we talked a lot. And I wonder now whether telling him is what got him killed. I don't know how it would, but I can't stop thinking about it.' She began to cry, elbows on her knees, holding her head in her hands.

Jo reached across, squeezing her hand and waiting until she recovered 'When was this, Phoebe, when you talked to Curtis about it?'

'Not long ago. End of November, beginning of December.'

'And what did Curtis say?'

'He said he knew they were moving guns, and Class A drugs as well, and he'd had enough and was planning to leave. I said I couldn't carry on knowing what was happening. He said I should come up with a real strong reason that they would believe, not just sort of hand my notice in with no explanation. So I decided I would try to get back in uni. It would work out well with the timing, I'd just pick up the second term of the same course having completed the first one a year ago.

'He said that might work okay but he didn't know whether they'd let him leave, which really scared me, him saying that. He also said if anything did happen to him, he'd left something in his vehicle that the police would find that would bring them down on Easy Rider like a ton of bricks.'

Jo nodded. 'He certainly did. So let's talk about what happened on the twenty-second of December.'

'Oh, I staged it all. I'd planned it a week in advance. The row with my parents followed by the row with Benny. None of them deserved that, but I thought they'd think that was why I'd done a runner, because I was fed up with them all. I went up onto the moor; it was a bit of a shock meeting a neighbour of ours out with his dog, but I set off as if I was heading for my parents' place. Then I used one of my old theatrical wigs as a disguise, stuffed cotton wool in my mouth and cheeks, put on a pair of glasses. It was quite like old times. Don't ask me why I scattered all that stuff around on the moor, because I haven't a clue. Not thinking straight at that moment.'

'You were thinking straight enough with the disguise and getting off the bus and the tram.'

'Yes, but that was part of the plan.' She shook her head and sighed. 'All this was just to give me time to think. I meant to get in touch with Benny and my parents, but I thought if they knew where I was, then our man in the cop shop would be able to find out from them. Anyway, I went to stay with a friend in Sheffield. A guy from the course. I'd spoken to him in advance, told him I'd split with my partner and needed to get away for Christmas. He said I could stay with him. But don't ask me to give you his name, because I don't want him getting into trouble. He has nothing to do with the drugs. Okay?'

Jo smiled. 'I bet he thought Father Christmas had been especially kind.'

'Not really. I'm definitely not his type. I have one very important appendage missing.' They both laughed. 'But with all the publicity and appeals about me, he got really nervous about "sheltering a fugitive" as he put it, so I got in touch with Des Saunders and moved in with him and his two friends.'

'Is that who you were with when you were away those times for a couple of days?'

'No, sometimes we did a run without any customers although very rarely, and always through Rob. That was mostly Blackpool; there's a lot of demand there for what we have – drugs, anyway; not sure about guns. And it meant staying away one or two nights, which was fine because we didn't have people to take home.'

'It was a big risk going back to Des if he was part of the organisation.'

'I didn't know whether he was or not, because, as I said, he'd moved away from Manchester. But it turned out he still is, though he's not driving for them now, and I think he would have liked to help but his mates insisted he got in touch with… whoever, over here. And then I saw on the news about Curtis being murdered and that did it for me. I sneaked off early in the morning and went in to the police station in Sheffield to hand myself in. I should have done that right at the beginning, but I'd been so thick, I didn't think you lot would believe I hadn't known what I'd got in to.'

'Just one thing, Phoebe, you travelled pretty light for someone going away indefinitely. I usually take two cases with me on a long weekend. You must let me know your secret.'

Phoebe gave a little laugh. 'It helps when you have nearly two grand in cash in your purse, and good old Primark right on the doorstep – in Meadowhall. Their stuff is brilliant for what they charge for it.'

'Which begs the question, or questions, where did the two grand come from and how big a purse do you need to carry it around as cash? We know you haven't drawn anything out of your account since well before you went missing, or even checked your balance. In fact, you might be interested to know that a payment has been made into the account – from Easy Rider on the second of January.'

Phoebe flushed a little and looked down at her hands.

'The extra for moving the goods was paid each month in cash, on top of the wage – or salary, as Josh insists on calling it, although we were only psid for the days we actually worked. And as for the size of the purse, a lot of it was in fifties. Not easy to spend. Most of the cahiers in the shops had never seen one before. Kept having to consult the store managers.'

'And how much was this monthly supplement?'

'I'd rather not …'

'You'll have to tell us, Phoebe. We can't draw a line under this without all the facts.'

Phoebe took a deep breath. 'Two and a half grand. Bit more than a student loan, but I wish I'd stuck with that.'

'We did wonder how you'd managed to fill your locker with all that top of the range stuff. The contents of my wardrobe add up to around half of that pair of Jimmy Choo's.'

'Well, I've decided to hand it all over to a charity auction. That's if I get the chance.' She sighed and spread her arms. 'Now you know it all.'

'Not quite, but let me ask, have you told anyone else any of this?'

'Benny and Mum and Dad know some of it but, only you know the whole story.'

'The whole story except for what happened on the Snake, although I think we've pieced that together. However, I'd like to hear it from you, but shall we have a top-up first? My round.' Jo picked up the now empty mugs and replenished them before setting them down again on the table. 'Right, go on.'

'Well, the inspector, Kenny, got in touch with Bury police…'

'That was me,' Jo said.

'Right, and a few hours later these two turned up, a man and a woman, and we set off over the Snake. I could hardly believe it to be honest but I was pretty much out of it and must have thought they knew what they were doing. The weather got so bad we couldn't go any further and we stopped at the Snake Inn. They both went inside, the guy first and then the woman joined him, and another car turned up, an Audi A5, with two other policemen in it. They actually phoned me from their vehicle and said the first two were fake and dangerous, so could I disable the car and get into theirs. Which I did, but we'd only been going a few minutes when I realised they'd phoned me on my burner, and only people in the organisation had that number.

'So I pretended I was going to be sick, they stopped the car and I bailed out down the side of the valley. God knows how I got to the bottom without killing myself, and the poor bastard who chased me down didn't. I assume he broke his neck judging from the angle his head was at.'

'You're right about that, and you were right about the second pair of officers. They were the fakes. And then...?'

'I followed the river upstream for a while and eventually got back up to the road. But I'd lost my phone and the pass was closed both ways, so I didn't know what to do. Then I found this field barn, I think that's what they call them, a sort of animal shelter, and made a bed out of hay and a load of sheep shit – just because it was still warm...' she gave a little laugh '... which got me through the first night. I remember next day I saw the first two cops again. They were walking along the road towards Glossop. I think they'd been following a snowplough, because there was one stopped on the road with their car alongside it. I can remember soon after that stealing some food from the snowplough, but after that hardly anything except I think I heard or saw a helicopter at some point, but I might have dreamed it. Next thing I remember was waking up in the ambulance which brought me here. I don't even recall Mum and Dad visiting me in the hospital in Ashton although they tell me I was talking to them there.'

Jo sighed and leaned back in her chair. 'Wow,' she said. 'What a story. I think we should take a break, don't you?'

Phoebe leaned forward. 'Any chance I could see Andy now?'

*

'I thought you might have left us on our own. I'm sure that's what she wanted.'

'That's why I didn't,' Jo said. 'Not sure of her motives. This one-to-one with me is enough of a risk without me encouraging our main witness to seduce an investigating officer. Anyway, I figured you'd have used up most of your best lines with the doc.'

'She's okay when she relaxes and stops being in charge of something. We had a good chat.'

They were heading back to the station after leaving the hospital at just after twelve o'clock. Arrangements were in place to return Phoebe, secretly, to her parents' home in Hawkshaw pending an official interview timed for the following day, Sunday.

'She wasn't too pleased about not going back to Benny's, was she?' Jo said. 'I'm not sure she bought the rationale that she had to be under Bury Police jurisdiction on the basis that we were handling the case. It sounded a bit thin even to me when I was telling her.'

'Hardly surprising. Not much opportunity for a good reunion shag at Ma and Pa's, even though they're inviting Benny round to stay. Separate beds do you reckon?'

'Separate bedrooms, I shouldn't be surprised.'

Jo was serious for a moment. 'And you'll be pleased to know I've arranged for surveillance overnight. Hawkshaw will be the securest place on the planet for the next few days at least.'

They drove in silence for a while.

'So what next, I wonder, when we get back,' Jo said. 'DC Malik again?

'Or, if we get half an hour or so, I can perhaps furnish you with the answers I promised you to some of those questions. Perhaps all of them.'

★

'The first one – the single digit "1" – was just a knee-jerk reaction to the wanker moment. Pure anger and petulance, looking back. A sort of "right, that's one", you know like "three strikes and you're out". So the next time anything like that happened, I'd probably have texted "2". But then we got the report of Phoebe going missing, last seen near the very spot where I knew Ellen Strange was found murdered, and it just triggered a thought, linked, I suppose, to my hang-up about local knowledge.

They were seated in one of the ground floor interview rooms, away from the CID team, each nursing the obligatory carton of coffee.

'I see,' Jo said. 'What I can't see though, is why you should immediately think of Ellen Strange.'

'I can't really answer that, except that she's always been a person of interest to me.'

'Really? A sort of *very* cold case, do you mean?'

'My father worked in R & D for a multinational food company based in Chicago. The company had an office and factory in Manchester and he came over on an expat assignment. There he met my mum, who was a research assistant in the same department and who lived in Holcombe Brook. He moved in with her and they married and went over to Chicago at the end of his assignment. My mum was already expecting me by that time. Apparently, my dad had fallen in love with the place and thirteen years later when he was offered the R & D Director's position on a permanent basis, they moved back over here and bought a house in Summerseat. Dad, like a lot of Americans, loved the idea of local history and family roots and such, and he became obsessed with the legend of Ellen Strange.'

'I'd love to hear the end of this story, but…'

'Bear with me. Ellen Strange's husband was called John Broadley, so her married name was Ellen Broadley, but the locals who erected the cairn in her memory had known her all her life and to them she was still Ellen Strange. What fired my dad's imagination was the fact that my mum's maiden name is Broadley and her family have always lived in and around Ramsbottom. He set out to trace her ancestry to try and establish if she was a descendant of John Broadley, and perhaps even Ellen Strange if they'd had any children together. I don't think Mum shared his enthusiasm for linking her to a murderer, and he never got back that far in his search, although he did trace her ancestors as far as the 1820s. But short of building a time machine he couldn't get any further.'

'Actually, putting impatience and cynicism on one side, that is a fascinating story. But it doesn't explain why you started pissing me about with those digits.'

'As I said, I can't really answer that, but it struck me as a good way of introducing you to some local history. I couldn't use the actual grid reference, because I'd already sent you the first digit "1" so I just switched it round, trusting to your skill as a detective to work it out. Which you did.'

'To what end, for God's sake?'

Andy sighed and shook his head, looking down at his hands.

'God knows, Jo. I guess it will be okay to call you that when I'm a civilian. It's all to do with nonconsequentialism.'

'Driven by actions with no consideration for consequences,' Jo said.

Andy looked up, wide-eyed in surprise and a little bit of the anger returned, quickly subsiding. 'You *have* done your homework.'

'Get to the last digit and the boots. You haven't explained those.'

'Someone had left the boots in a sealed bag outside the MCV. It occurred to me they would make a fitting finale.'

'So where did you keep the boots?'

Andy shook his head. 'In a fridge in the garage, would you believe? Had to take everything out – shelves and all – to get them in. I only intended to keep them a few days until the end of the search, then put them under the stones. But I didn't get round to sending the last digit and sort of abandoned the idea. Then I thought, what the hell, we've come this far… and the rest you know. God knows why, but it's too late now.'

'If it's any consolation, your show of indignation that night on the moor was absolutely brilliant. It completely ruled you out in my mind as the likely perp.'

'Well, it's *no* consolation, but thanks anyway.'

They sat in silence for a long time.

'The other question that you, yourself, were hoping to find an answer to,' Jo said, 'was why you put your life at risk last night to save mine. That's a million times more important to me than the digits and the boots.'

Andy took a long time to reply. 'I went into your office to leave you a Post-it note. The note said, "You talk to Phoebe alone." I wasn't planning to come in until after you'd have left. Still angry, I guess, at being thrown out of her room.'

'But I did explain that…'

Andy held up his hand to stop her. 'Then I saw the message under the grid reference. It made sense right away, because for me the month and date were the right way round. And I knew you'd work it out. It was easier than the grid reference. I figured someone was trying to get you out there, and if it hadn't been for my original message, that wouldn't have made any sense, and you'd have been safe at home with man mountain. So if it's easier for you to reconcile my actions with my previous behaviour, put it down as being driven by guilt rather than chivalry. That might be more accurate, anyway.'

'Well, whatever it was, I…'

'Oh, yes. The other reason was that I very rarely get the opportunity to dress up in my cowboy gear.'

★

Before Jo had managed to fully absorb Andy's account of his actions and motives, they were summoned to the Detective Superintendent's office, where Jo brought him up to date with her meeting with Phoebe.

'That seems to have gone well,' Mal said. 'And we've had a bit of a development here. DC Malik has asked for an off-the-record meeting before he arranges for his solicitor to attend. Just with you, Jo. He asked to see me about half an hour ago with the request. My guess is that he wants to do some sort of deal, although I'm not sure what he can realistically expect.'

Jo and Andy exchanged a glance.

'To be honest, sir,' Jo said, 'I wouldn't be happy agreeing to that. A one-to-one with Phoebe was one thing, given what she had been through, and her delicate condition. Malik has been complicit in a kidnapping and possibly a murder and attempted murder. I'm not even sure about off-the-record, but I would definitely need DS Mills in with me.'

Mal looked from one to the other with a little smile. 'Well, I never thought I'd see the day... I agree it should be with the two of you, but if it's off the record, then I don't see any harm. If he says something that he might deny *on* the record, then we haven't lost anything, *and* it gives us something to aim at.'

'Did he say anything other than ask for the meeting?' Andy asked.

'Well, he did actually. He said he didn't send the earlier texts to DI Carter, but he knows who did. I thought that was a bit of trivia given all the other stuff he's been accused of. Perhaps you can draw him on that.' He spread his hands. 'You two are already halfway through your second day without sleep. Shall we arrange this for tomorrow?'

'I'd like to go with it now, sir, if Andy can stay awake a while longer. I feel we should move this along quickly. And with that thought in mind, I suggest we set up surveillance on Reeves' and Challinor's houses, and the depot. By now, they will almost certainly be aware that Chadwick and Malik are out of circulation. They may even be planning a trip to the airport themselves. If so, we may already be too late.'

★

Jo was finding it difficult to read DC Malik as they faced him over the table in the same interview room. He seemed outwardly relaxed and in control, but it was hard to believe that was what he was feeling inside.

'We're listening,' Jo said, the first words spoken in the room since they had arrived and taken their seats, nearly two minutes ago.

'I'm here to listen, too,' Mo said, his voice strong and confident. 'You have a lot of circumstantial evidence against me, enough to end my career. But I'm thinking perhaps ending my career isn't your prime objective, and in exchange for my helping you achieve *that*, I wondered what you might do for me in return.'

There was a long silence before Jo responded.

'Are you aware what happened early this morning, DC Malik?'

'Yes, I was forcibly prevented from catching a flight to…'

'Try five hours earlier than that,' Andy interrupted, 'and please don't play fucking games.'

'That was around midnight and I was asleep.'

'So the shock at seeing DI Carter enter the interview room was just an act, was it? Because you looked like you'd just seen a ghost.'

'I was surprised to discover the Detective Inspector worked nights, if that's what you mean.'

Andy sprang to his feet and leaned a long way over the table. Mo leaned back slightly in his chair.

'Don't get fucking clever with me, Malik,' Andy said.

Mo didn't flinch, he looked at Jo. 'This is why I wanted to speak to you alone, ma'am. So we could have a *civilised* chat.'

'*Civilised?*' Andy spat the word into Mo's face. 'I'll tell you what's civilised, *ex*-Detective Constable Mohammed Malik. Civilised is *not* betraying your colleagues, *not* kidnapping people, *not* murdering people.'

He sat down again, his eyes burning into Mo's. Mo remained silent.

'I assume, from your earlier comment, DC Malik,' Jo said, 'that you are offering to extend your recent record of betrayal to include your associates at Easy Rider, in exchange for some degree of leniency. Am I right?' Mo didn't reply. 'Not sure? Then why are we here? DS Mills and I have been without sleep now for over thirty hours, during which time there has been an attempt on both our lives. So I'm not prepared to sit here looking at that fucking smug expression unless you are going to tell us something.'

That same expression remained for a few more seconds, then dissolved into one of potential cooperation, if not submission.

'I don't know what I can realistically expect,' he said, his voice not much above a whisper. '"A tiger by the tail," someone said recently or was it "he who rides the tiger"? It started with a few favours. I had a reliable informant who fed me consistently accurate info on all sorts of stuff, mainly drug-related. His input was one of the reasons for the success of GMP's Revoke Scheme against organised crime gangs in Bury the year before last. In return I provided him with tit-bits that kept him and a few others out of trouble. Low level stuff...'

'Low level?' Jo asked.

'*Really* low level. Stuff like crackdowns on fly-tipping, petty thieving from cars and sheds – you know, areas in Bury that the police would be targeting. Given the massive upside, it made sense. We were getting more than we were giving. Then the stakes got higher and higher and I was sucked in. I guess the tipping point came when GMP Central mounted a massive operation based on a tip-off they'd got about an arms delivery in the Six Towns area. It was really hush-hush and the official story was a minor drugs raid. I got wind of the *official* line and flagged it with my grass, and he got to the big boys in time for them to abort. Made him a hero with them and put me permanently on the hook. From then, I seemed to be dealing directly with the big boys.'

'You're telling us that you're just a victim of circumstances,' Jo said. 'So when we check your and your wife's bank statements, which we will be doing very soon, we won't find any evidence of monetary gain. No payments for services rendered.'

'You'll find large amounts of money going in and out of my wife's account. You'll discover that the payments *out* were to accounts held in Pakistan, where it was sent to help her extended family, who are living in near poverty. Or who *were* living like that. Now they have food every day, shoes on their feet...'

'Stop, stop,' Andy cried, 'you're breaking my heart. You took money for betraying a trust and for complicity in kidnapping and murder. What you did with the money is fucking irrelevant, even if you'd given it all to Children in Need.'

'Which is what I did in effect,' Mo said. '*Our* children in need. I'm explaining how it happened, not asking for forgiveness, and you're the last person in the world I'd expect to understand, or even *try* to understand. A creeping decision, "just a bit more won't matter," that sort of thing, when no harm seemed to be done; or at least the balance of harm and benefit seemed to weigh heavily on our side.'

They remained silent for a long time.

'Going back to what you can realistically expect,' Jo said, 'I don't believe we can offer much in return for what you tell us. The leaking of information is one thing, but it's gone way past that, hasn't it? DS Mills said you were complicit in Phoebe's kidnapping. The definition of complicit is "involved in some way." You actually *planned* her abduction, didn't you? You were the main man. And it took a lot of planning, as did the Knox murder and the attempt on your boss's life last night. You were so keen to prevent me talking to Phoebe you decided to remove us both.'

'You flatter me, ma'am. I don't get to make decisions like that, and if it means anything, I'm glad Phoebe survived, and that you did, too.'

'Well, it means *nothing*,' Andy said. 'You're only glad because you've been rumbled. Makes the crime less if nobody has died, or if less people have died. And Phoebe *was* meant to die, wasn't she?'

Mo seemed to have run out of fight and words. He stared down at his hands, twisting together on his lap.

'One thing I don't understand,' Jo said, 'is why you sent me the clues. First the location of the moorstone and then…'

Mo's head came up. 'I didn't send the first texts,' he said. 'No way.'

'It must have been you who sent me the one yesterday.'

'I'm telling you, it wasn't me who sent you the co-ordinates.' His anger had returned. 'It was him…' he nodded at Andy '…it had to be him.'

'You're suggesting two different people from my own team sent me cryptic messages via burner phones. Is that what you're asking us to believe?'

'I told you, I don't have a burner phone…'

'Oh, I think you do, DC Malik. I think everyone associated with Easy Rider has one, and that usually means one thing, doesn't it? I received the first digit of the co-ordinates on the morning of the twenty-fourth of December, around six hours *before* Phoebe was reported missing. It had to have been sent by someone who already knew about her disappearance. Someone with sources of information outside the police. The only person it could have been was you.'

'Well, I'm telling you categorically it was not me who sent the original messages. And how would anyone know where Phoebe had gone?'

'Not *where* she'd gone, just that she'd done a runner. It's clear, in retrospect, that when DS Mills and I first interviewed Josh Reeves, he knew something about what had happened to her. At least knew no harm had come to her.'

Mo remained silent. Jo leaned forward.

'Here's something for us all to think about. If you really mean it about being pleased Phoebe is okay, you can help her. We'll be charging her, along with others, very soon, for the trafficking of illegal drugs, and probably arms. She says she believed she was not breaking any laws, and when she realised she was, she was informed that it was too late, she's in it whether she likes it or not. If what you've told us about your own circumstances is true, then I'm sure you can identify with that.

'I'm not sure what will happen to her; whether she gets a long or short custodial sentence, or a suspended sentence, but what I do know is, when we descend in numbers on Easy Rider very soon, people will link it to Phoebe being already in custody. They will assume she has blown their cover, which will make her a target for as long as she lives, which might not be very long. You can help avoid that, if you fully co-operate by giving us everything we need to shut down that operation and those groups linked to it. We could leak the news that it was you and not Phoebe who gave them up. That would make you a target, of course. A bent cop is bad enough, but a bent cop who shops his associates is about as low as they go. And you'll be doing time, DC Malik, and that makes you very vulnerable indeed.

'I don't know yet what we can give you in return, that's for us to think about while you consider your part of the deal, but there just might be something. Alternatively, you can call your lawyer and take your chance against all our *circumstantial* evidence. Do you understand?'

Mo nodded.

'I think we're finished here,' Jo said, and she and Andy got to their feet. Andy knocked on the door and it was opened by a uniformed officer. As they left, Mo called after them.

'I didn't send those messages.'

★

The imposing figure of Sergeant Geoff Brazendale was waiting for them when they returned to the operations room. He was seated at Eva's workstation, she being the only other occupant of the area, where they were sharing a coffee and dipping into a packet of Doritos. Jo looked across at Mo's desk with a sense of sadness, but also anger, recalling the friendly banter they had engaged in when she first arrived and now knowing the hypocrisy behind it.

'Hi, Geoff, what have you got for us?'

'Morning, ma'am, Andy. We've set up surveillance on all three properties, but there seems to be no-one home at any of them. Not only that, but the only vehicle we found was the Freelander in Melbury Avenue. Both cars at the addresses on Dell Road and Turks Road have gone.'

'Have we checked the airport car parks, airlines, flights…?'

'DC Knapp is on to that now, but even if they drove there, or anywhere, separately, I'm not sure how they could take four cars with them.'

Dylis called across from her desk, pointing to her PC screen.

'Challinor and Reeves were booked on the thirteen-forty KLM flight from Manchester to Amsterdam, take-off was delayed by thirty minutes due to a fire in one of the car parks with the smoke blowing across the runway. It's now due to land at Schiphol at sixteen-thirty, which is fifteen-thirty our time.'

They all instinctively turned to the digital wall clock, which told them it was 14.50.

'We need to make some calls,' Jo said.

★

'So, what do you think, sir? Do we have any wiggle room with respect to leniency?'

They were back in Mal Jones's office where he had informed them he had listened in to the interview, though not observed it through the one-way glass.

'We'll have to consult with the judiciary, but I can't see them agreeing to it just to protect another player in the same organisation. And any agreement between the prosecution and the defence isn't binding on the court. Only the judge can decide the sentence. I don't know what we could offer him in return. A new identity in an establishment a long way from Manchester, perhaps, with a different set of crimes to take inside with him. But it's unlikely to be a reduced sentence. Phoebe's best chance for the future is if we successfully bring this to a conclusion with the evidence we've collected rather than what she tells us.

'Anyway, you two have had a busy couple of days. I suggest you take tomorrow off and we'll do the formal bit with Phoebe on Monday. Oh, but before you leave, what did you make of his insistence that he didn't send the earlier texts?'

Jo and Andy exchanged glances.

'I don't know why he's insisting on that, sir,' Jo said. 'It's absolutely clear to me that he must have sent them. He's the only one who could have known Phoebe had gone missing before it was reported to us. And, as you know, I got the first digit in advance of that. *And* from a burner.'

Mal frowned. 'Interesting though that he vehemently denies sending you the ones that were just a prank and more or less admits he did send the one that should have led to your death.' He looked from one to the other and shook his head. 'Off you go, then.'

They walked to the car park in silence, stopping together briefly before getting into their separate cars. Andy held out his hand, which Jo was quick to take.

'Thank you,' he said.

Jo smiled. 'I think that's my line, Doc.'

She watched Andy drive off and reached for her phone to call

Seb. Before she had a chance it trilled with an incoming call. Jo looked in surprise at the screen.

'Sir?'

'I've been meaning to ask you, but couldn't just now. How did Seb react when you told him about your spy mission? You were a bit concerned he wouldn't approve.'

'Well, I'm ashamed to say I haven't told him yet, sir. I've not seen him in person for nearly four weeks and I've kept telling myself it needs to be face-to-face. But the reality is, I bottled it.'

Mal laughed. 'Well, it's worked out well, then, hasn't it?'

'How do you mean, sir?'

'I mean, you don't have to tell him, or anyone else. You found the bad apple during the course of investigating the case. It turned up without you digging for it. So, you can stop agonising, Detective Inspector. You have no news to impart.'

If only that were true, she thought.

★

It was 5.35 p.m. when Jo finally got home. Seb banned her from talking about the case until the fleece of the sheepskin rug had been well and truly flattened. Afterwards, they had laid naked, in each other's arms in front of the roaring fire, with the rug pulled round them, until it had got too hot and they had unfurled it.

'This is just perfect,' Jo said. 'I was beginning to think the bloody rug was cursed.'

Seb laughed and raised himself on one elbow. 'I've got some news for you, young lady.'

'*Young* lady?' Jo looked around the room as if wondering who he was talking to, making him laugh again. 'Go on.'

'You've got me for a week. Got five days off for good behaviour.'

'Really?' Jo's eyes opened wide.

'Well, no, not really. I'm on a four-day course but it's on-line and I've been given the green light to work from home. And for the next week, this is home. So, it's really just the one day for good behaviour.'

'Oh, Seb, that's brilliant. How did you manage to swing that?'

'By working hard and late, and weekends. The woman you

spoke to was not an official at the club, it was the new DI, Ruth Jameson, who's just started and is covering for you. I think you met her a couple of times before you came up here. She was on the late shift and I was at the station getting ahead with a report I was working on so I could get the time off. I couldn't really call you because I was tied up all day with other people.'

'So there was no lost phone?'

'No, I was out of the room in the toilet when you called and I'd left the phone on my desk. DI Jameson answered it.'

'And the booze-up?'

'No again, I was in the station, working late. Sorry about the pack of lies, but I wanted to surprise you.'

'Surprise me! You had me worried out of my mind, you bloody great fool! I didn't realise you were such a talented liar. I'll never believe another word you say.'

She pulled him down again pressing herself hard against him.

'Steady, now. I'm going to have to pace myself.'

When they pulled apart there were tears in her eyes, then just the slightest sob.

'Oh, Seb,' she said, again, but in a very different voice. 'I've got some news for you as well.'

Seb's eyes opened wide in surprise. 'Hey, what's wrong?' He wiped a tear away from her eye. Raising himself up on one elbow again, he kissed her on the forehead. 'You can tell me, I'm a policeman.'

Jo choked out a laugh through her tears. Seb got to his feet and pulled her up beside him. They sat together, still naked, on the sofa. Seb pulled the rug over them up to their waists and wrapped his arms around her.

'I've done a really bad thing,' Jo said.

'I don't believe you,' he said.

'What...?'

'I don't believe you could do anything bad. So tell me, prove that I'm right.'

Jo swallowed hard, composing herself. When she spoke it was with a calm, measured voice. 'You know we've always said this was going to be a challenge, you in one place and me... well, not knowing where I'd be. And we accepted that would limit us in what sort of a marriage we could have.'

'Look, Jo, if this is about having a family…'

'That's *exactly* what it's about.'

'And I've told you a million – no, a million and a half – times that it's…'

'Seb, I'm pregnant.'

There were several seconds of absolute silence.

'*What?* How?' Seb unwrapped his arms and turned towards her, wide-eyed.

'Towards the end of last year,' Jo said, 'when I'd been at Leicester for over twelve months, and there was talk of making the transfer permanent, I took a unilateral decision. Knowing how much you wanted a family, deep down…' she placed her hand on his mouth to prevent him interrupting '… I came off the pill. I figured if we sat down and talked about it you'd convince me or we'd convince each other that it wouldn't be practical. So I thought, just go for it. Then I got the posting to Bury and went straight back on it, but it was too late. I'd missed a couple of periods, but that's happened before. So, I did a test earlier this week. I didn't know how to tell you…'

Seb's eyes had remained wide, and his smile eventually caught up with them. He grabbed his wife and squeezed her to him, rocking backwards and forwards.

'Jo, that's brilliant. Magic. I can't believe it. What a clever, *clever* girl.' Jo pulled away and looked into her husband's eyes, which were full of tears. 'I'm going to be a dad.' His voice was just above a whisper, as though he was sharing a big secret.

'You're not mad with me?' Her own eyes were tearing up.

'Really? I mean it's going to change everything.'

'You bet it is! I can't wait.'

Jo laughed through her tears. 'Well, you'll have to. I've got seven months still to go. Sal is going to beat me to it.'

'Magic!' he said again. 'I'll be able to watch Sky Sports with Jonno while our kids are playing together outside.'

★

The two men shuffled along in the non-EU queue at Schiphol Airport, each with their cabin-size luggage cases and clutching their passports.

'So what have you got lined up for me tonight in Europe's sex capital?' the shorter of the two men said. 'If we can't get laid here, we can't get laid anywhere.'

'Lots of time for that,' the other man said, with a grin. 'We need to get settled in first. They'll be waiting for us at the apartment.' He frowned. 'You're sure about the cars, aren't you? They'll be safe for now?'

'Yes, except for the Fiesta.' He gave a little laugh. 'Hey, that was something, wasn't it? Flight delayed because of a car on fire in the car park. People should be more careful. Let's see if the clever bastards can find any blood or fingerprints in that. And don't worry about the cars, Des will arrange to get them from the lock-ups and take them over to Sheffield. Then, when everything's quietened down, they'll get the new plates and bring them over through Hull to Zeebrugge.'

'And in the meantime, we can take up cycling. Everybody has a push-bike in Amsterdam.'

They laughed, and stepped forward to the window, the short man pushing his passport through the small gap at the bottom to the smiling woman behind the glass. She checked the details, comparing the photo with the man in front of her. She nodded to the second man.

'Are you two together?'

'Yes.' The second man slipped the passport to her, and she repeated the checks before reaching under the counter.

'Are you here on holiday or on business?' she asked, the smile still in place.

'A bit of both...'

It was at that point that both men noticed the reflections in the glass window. They turned to face four men and one woman, all five armed and wearing the black combat gear and mid-blue berets of the Royal Marechaussee, the national police force of the Kingdom of the Netherlands.

'Mr Reeves, Mr Challinor, would you come with us, please,' the woman said, in perfect English.

AUTHOR'S NOTE

If you're thinking of having a night out in Helmshore – or just a couple of pints, maybe – don't arrange to meet at the White Horse. It doesn't exist – not any more. The pub, on the corner of Holcombe Road and Alden Road, closed in 2013 and became an Italian restaurant, the Anacapri, which itself finally closed in 2019. On the site today are two prestigious semi-detached houses. The modern properties have been tastefully constructed in sandstone brick, in keeping with the original building. The development is an attractive one, but you won't get a pint, a pizza or a glass of Sauvingnon Blanc there. It only survives in the context of this story.

Similarly, don't bother searching for the Lancashire Gate in the centre of Bury. You won't find that either, although there is a pub where this one is located in the story.

ACKNOWLEDGEMENTS

Words of thanks are due to those who have contributed, in various ways, to the completion of my fifth novel.

To Inspector Kevin Wright of the Bury Division of Greater Manchester Police for giving up his time on more than one occasion to provide me with advice on police procedures and practices, along with a tour of the main Bury Police Station. I could not have written the book without Kevin's input. Also, thanks to Alan Isherwood, of GMP Bolton Division, who has made my life easier with his advice on specific elements of police work which feature in the story. Alan has been a key source of information for all my books.

I am indebted to Tom Jackson, manager at Vodaphone in Bury, who answered my questions on the intricacies of mobile phones. His major contribution was delivered without the slightest trace of a snigger in spite of the obvious depth of my ignorance of the subject.

Special thanks to John Simpson, librarian at Accrington library and local historian, for sharing with me his in-depth research into the dark deed which took place on Holcombe Moor in the distant past, which is a central feature of this story.

To my publisher, Troubador, for their support and advice during the production of this book and my four previous novels. Their expertise and friendly service have made the experience such an enjoyable one. Special thanks, as always, to my editor Gary Smailes of Bubblecow, whose detailed critiques and excellent guidance have helped me so much over my years as a writer. His constantly stepping outside his formal role to offer advice and wise counsel has been invaluable.

To Carol, my wife for fifty-four years (and my illustrator for the last ten), for her excellent cover design. It is challenging enough for artists to get their own ideas onto canvas, but representing someone else's requires a lot of patience and commitment. Carol will confirm!

Finally, thanks to all the people whose generous appraisal of my books and ongoing encouragement have motivated me to write this latest novel.

Author Photo by Carol Knaggs

MICHAEL KNAGGS was born in Hull in 1944. He moved to Thurso, Caithness in 1966, where he was employed as an Experimental Officer at the Dounreay Atomic Energy Power Station for two years, before attaining a degree in chemistry at the University of Salford. From 1970 up to his retirement in 2005, he worked for the Kellogg Company, the global breakfast cereal manufacturer, latterly as Human Resources Director with responsibility for pay and benefits policy across the company's European organisation.

Michael lives In Prestwich, Manchester, with his wife, Carol. Their passion is hill-walking, and over the past 12 years they have completed many of the long-distance national trails, including the West Highland Way, twice, and the 180-mile Offah's Dyke Path. They have two children and two grand-children.

The Moorstone is his fifth novel. His previous four comprise the *Hotel St Kilda* series of books, which contain themes of crime, politics and the military, with family drama at their heart. *The Moorstone* is Michael's first stand-alone crime thriller.

This book is printed on paper from sustainable sources managed under the Forest Stewardship Council (FSC) scheme.

It has been printed in the UK to reduce transportation miles and their impact upon the environment.

For every new title that Troubador publishes, we plant a tree to offset CO_2, partnering with the More Trees scheme.

MORE TREES
LET'S PLANT A BILLION TREES

For more about how Troubador offsets its environmental impact, see www.troubador.co.uk/sustainability-and-community